Advanced

"... a moving novel, crackling with sexual volatility and emotional intelligence. An engrossing emotional drama, both shocking and thoughtful." —***Kirkus Reviews***

"... an uplifting story of realistic struggle, a desperate drive for connection, and ultimately Christian redemption." —***BookLife Reviews***

Denise-Marie Martin's debut novel is beautifully written, and I could not put the book down. It's told from the point of view of an adopted child who grows up with many questions. As an adult, when she reaches out to find her birth parents, the story takes an unexpected and disturbing turn. The characters are so real that I felt I was in the story with them. The writing is beautiful, rich in imagery, and the story is compelling. I highly recommend this incredible book!

—***Ellen Gable***, award-winning author of ten novels,
including *Where Angels Pass*

"I love you, Lizzie, just like all my other grandkids. I make no difference between you and them," Granny said. Secrets just had a way of pushing their way out of Granny's mouth. That 'difference' lay silent and undisturbed between us like a sleeping dog with an uncertain pedigree." ... Until Lizzie Schmidt realizes what she's long thought to be true, that she isn't a member of the family she's been told is her own, and begins her search to find out who she really is in both body and soul. Lizzie's heartrending and very human desire to belong and be loved leads her down a laborious, sometimes staggering, road to self-discovery, forgiveness, and the mercy of God. A wonderful book!

—***Kaye Park Hinckley***, award-winning author of *Absence*,
Shooting at Heaven's Gate, and many others

Tangled Violets:

A Novel of Redemption

Denise-Marie Martin

Misericordia Publishing

Cover design by Hannah Linder Creations

Cover images licensed from Shutterstock.com. Internal images purchased from Digital Work Designs and Old Art Printables on Etsy.

ISBN: 978-1-7352388-4-5 (print)
ISBN: 978-1-7352388-5-2 (digital)

For Aimee

> Your greatest ministry will likely come from your deepest pain.
>
> —Rick Warren

Beauté sans grâce est une violette sans odeur.

~ Proverb

Contents

Your accumulated offenses do not surpass the multitude of God's mercies. Your wounds do not surpass the great Physician's skill.

- St. Cyril of Jerusalem (313-386 AD)

Part One: 1959, 1988 - 1990

I was ready to be sought out by those who
did not ask, to be found by those
who did not seek me. (Is 65:1)

Lizzie

I DON'T KNOW HOW I knew, but I did. Maybe Momma and Daddy just smelled wrong, which wasn't the same as stinking. Although, my parents, Marie and Fred Schmidt, did their fair share of stinking, too. They thought deodorant was unnecessary as long as a person bathed once a week. Any more than that was a waste of water and hard-earned money. But this was different and unsettled me, much like listening to a piece of music played on an out-of-tune piano.

My earliest memory is that of Momma; my sister, Jeannie; and me crowded into our pink bathtub on Saturday nights. As Momma poured bubble bath under the gushing water, the fragrance of blue carnation filled the bathroom air. That heavenly fragrance only partially alleviated my discomfort at three naked bodies packed together like sardines in the tub.

Those dreaded baths are how I learned about the twins. A long, puffy scar ran from below Momma's large, pendulous breasts down to her girl parts. An angry keloid was the forever testimony to the retained placenta and resulting infection that almost claimed Momma's life. That was eighteen years before I was born and twenty years before Jeannie.

Momma and Daddy lived with Granny and Grampa Schmidt back then. Granny delivered the stillborn twins. Momma baptized them in the hopes they'd bypass Limbo. Momma still cried about losing those baby boys. Kenneth and Andrew, she'd named them.

Aside from the communal baths, Saturday was my favorite day of the week. The half-dozen other kids that Momma babysat weren't underfoot, bickering, polluting the air with their smelly diapers, taking naps on my bed, or messing up my perfectly organized bedroom.

While Jeannie watched Saturday morning cartoons, I sat on the floor in my bedroom closet under a canopy of dress shirts. The freshly ironed shirts belonged to the doctors, lawyers, and dentists whose wives paid Momma to do their laundry in our small town.

Tucked away in quiet bliss, I'd select a random volume from one of the two boxes of Collier's encyclopedias packed with alphabetized knowledge ready for my eager consumption. My brain was a hungry sponge, absorbing fragments of things I didn't fully understand but effortlessly retained.

My second favorite day of the week was Sunday, despite the downside of attending Mass with Momma and Jeannie. My sister and Mass didn't mix. Jeannie rolled around on the pew, kicking her feet, throwing a conniption fit until Momma took her outside.

While I hoped Jeannie was getting a well-deserved paddling, I entertained myself by picking out the prettiest moms in the pews. I fantasized that Mrs. McCullough, with her blonde beehive updo, or Mrs. O'Leary, an olive-skinned dark-haired beauty, was my mother instead of Marie Schmidt. I figured those mothers smelled as sweet as they were beautiful and far less like the sweat of hard work and sour of unhappiness that tainted Momma.

1959

DADDY GULPED DOWN THE fried egg sandwich Momma made him for lunch and changed out of his sawdust-covered work clothes. The four of us piled into our 1956 Ford Country Sedan station wagon, a four-door pink and white behemoth on wheels. Granny and Grampa's house was as close to a vacation as we got.

We snaked our way along Highway 12 en route to Clarkston, near the Washington-Idaho border, passing through teensy towns like Touchet, Waitsburg, and Dayton. I judged these towns by the dingy restrooms of their gas stations: empty toilet paper holders, pink powdered soap all over the sink that nobody bothered to clean up, and enough stink to haunt my nostrils for miles down the road.

A half-hour into our nearly three-hour trip, the odor of rotten eggs announced our proximity to the pulp mill at Wallula Gap. My gag reflex was in full swing by the time I saw the tall concrete tower spewing its white cloud of nastiness skyward. My queasy stomach twisted and wretched like a cat struggling to get rid of a hairball.

"Lizzie's gonna throw up on me!" Jeannie shouted as she drew away in horror.

Daddy blew a lungful of cigarette smoke out the car window over his dark-tanned arm and turned toward Momma. "Why the hell do we have to go through this every damn time we make this trip?" And then to me, "Lizzie, stop the damn hysterics!"

Daddy had little patience with my extraordinary olfactory giftedness. Why couldn't I be like Jeannie? She could tolerate unpleasant smells. Heck, she could eat pickled pig's feet and Limburger cheese while sitting on Daddy's lap in a cloud of cigarette smoke.

Poor Momma. She tried to calm me as she handed me an empty brown paper bag. "Here, Lizzie, put this over your mouth."

Five minutes later, the dreadful odors were gone and Momma threw the bag and its disgusting contents out the car window.

As quickly as Daddy got all fired up, he could simmer right down with some help. "Marie, pass me the bottle."

Momma retrieved a pint bottle of Old Crow whiskey from a brown paper bag under her car seat, holding it between her legs while she unscrewed the lid. Daddy steered the car down the road with one hand on the wheel, the other hand outstretched towards Momma in anticipation.

Using the rear-view and side-view mirrors, Daddy ensured there were no cars nearby and took a couple of swigs from the bottle. Once Momma got the bottle back, she took a slug, too.

"Can I have a sip, Momma?" I asked.

"Me too," Jeannie parroted.

"Just a sip. Sit down on the floor, and I'll hand it back to you," Momma said.

Jeannie and I promptly moved from the opposite corners of the backseat and settled into each of two perfectly fitting floor-area cubbies created by the car's driveshaft. Momma handed me the bottle first.

The sip of whiskey burned like fire going down my throat. I liked the smell of it—fruity, flowery, and clean. But mostly, I appreciated that "Old Crow" tamed Daddy's roar.

The boring scenery and the rhythm of the tires beating on the road soon rocked Jeannie to sleep. Reading was a sure recipe for getting car sick, so instead, I counted the telephone poles that swooshed by, keeping track of each group of twenty-five with tics on my Magic Slate.

One group of 25, two groups of 25, three groups of 25, ... nine groups of 25 ...

The sound of our station wagon groaning its way up the steep gravel driveway shared by my grandparents and their next-door neighbor, Cecil, roused me from my slumber. I opened my eyes to discover my Magic Slate on the car floor and an expansive backyard planted with apple, crabapple, peach, cherry, quince, and black walnut trees.

"Kids, wake up. We're here." Momma's voice drew Jeannie back into consciousness, but my adrenaline was already kicking. I turned my face toward Cecil's side of the tree grove. A perfect spring day showcased the fruit trees wearing delicate, buzzing hats of white, pink, and purple blossoms.

My eyes locked onto a tiny treehouse, the size of a small doghouse, secured to the branches of the tree where Cecil tied his pet monkey in nice weather. The rope and collar hung empty. No monkey today.

The monkey's tree may as well have been in Granny and Grampa's backyard as no fence separated the properties. There was no physical barrier to keep Jeannie, the monkey, and me apart except the formidable threat of Daddy's temper.

"Make sure the kids stay away from that damn monkey." Daddy threw Momma a threatening glance along with his words. His arms stretched toward the robin-egg blue sky as he exited the car. He tossed his cigarette to the ground, grinding it into the gravel with the heel of his shoe.

"You can't trust a male monkey. That damn monkey put Cecil's wife into the hospital. It ought to be against the law to keep a dangerous animal like that!"

The back door that opened into the kitchen stood wide open. Daddy called out, "Mom, we're here!" as he walked empty-handed towards the boxy, white clapboard house.

When first constructed, my grandparents' house had four rooms, all of similar size: a kitchen, a dining room, a living room, and a bedroom where Daddy and his three sisters were born. Daddy had added indoor plumbing and a bathroom, which jutted off the kitchen, sometime after I was born in 1953.

Jeannie bolted from the car, grabbing Daddy's hand. Momma and I followed behind, bringing our small suitcase, a couple of extra pillows, coloring books and crayons, and my library books.

Granny wiped her hands on her apron, dotted with pink and white cabbage roses, hanging loosely over her housedress. The slight breeze carried the aroma of dinner already in preparation. Daddy's embrace nearly swallowed up his squatty, rotund momma.

When I entered the kitchen, Granny engulfed me in a bear hug. I stiffened in her arms but willed my arms to wrap around her.

"Look how big yer getting, Lizzie. We need to get some meat on them bones." She cast a critical glance at Momma, who stood behind me. "Don't ya feed the child?"

It wasn't Momma's fault that I looked like a piece of spaghetti. God just made me that way.

Granny's snow-white hair was twisted into spit curls, held in place with crisscrossed, black bobby pins. The top of her head resembled a spherical tic-tac-toe board, every space occupied with Os and Xs.

After a count of five, I escaped Granny's wrinkly arms into the bathroom, closed the door, and locked it. The bathroom wasn't really my favorite room. But it was the one room where, for just a few minutes, I could be alone and escape the demands of the noisy, touchy-feely world.

I studied the wringer washing machine and the adjacent laundry table from my porcelain throne. The aroma of Granny's potato bread swirled under the bathroom door, mingling with the pungent odors of menthol rub and the earthy smell of Grampa's pipe tobacco.

Granny cooked on a black cast-iron wood stove, vented through the kitchen ceiling and the roof to the outside. It had a big oven for baking and heavy round plates on the top surface formed the burners. When Granny lifted the plates with a detachable handle, I could see the wood fire that burned underneath. That old stove heated the house in winter and tortured the occupants in the summer if they wanted a hot meal.

I sat on the back stoop, hoping for some sign of Cecil's monkey, until Granny hollered at me to come in for supper. She laid out a spread of fried chicken, hot chard, mashed potatoes, white gravy, fresh peaches, and potato bread. Granny didn't have regular milk, but she gave me watered-down evaporated milk.

Daddy, Momma, and Granny talked and laughed throughout dinner while Grampa focused on eating. He didn't have teeth or dentures but "chewed" by using the area between his lower lip and gum to smash his food. I marveled at the volume of Grampa's food "pouch," which resembled the bubble a male frog makes when calling out to a prospective female. Simultaneously repulsed and fascinated, I struggled not to stare.

After eating, Momma got all fancied up in a dress, low heels, and lipstick. She smelled of carnations when she kissed me goodbye on her way out the door with Daddy. I never asked where they went on their Saturday night dates in Clarkston, and she didn't offer.

They'd return well after I fell asleep. As always, the following morning, I would awaken with Momma and Jeannie nestled in a double bed under a bearskin blanket in the dirt-walled basement cellar of Granny and Grampa's house.

Once Momma and Daddy left, I busied myself with my crayons and coloring book at the dinner table while Jeannie watched TV with Grampa in the living room. Granny soon joined me with her quilt pieces, scissors, needle, and thread.

"What kind of quilt do ya want, Lizzie?" Granny made each grandkid a quilt.

"One with sailboats, cuz I wanna see the world." Even then, I'd wanted more than what my world held.

"Can you get down your 'doctor' book, Granny?"

"Lizzie, ... again?"

She never refused me. According to Momma, Granny had been the one to name me Elizabeth Ann. And besides, I was the one grandkid who lived for the yarns she spun around her life growing up near the Nez Perce Indian reservation. She was a natural storyteller, and I couldn't hear enough about a world I'd never seen.

Granny pushed her sewing off to the side with her needle docked mid-stitch. She rolled her bright, still-feisty, black-brown eyes and tweaked my nose. Her protruding tummy jiggled with captive laughter as she pushed away from the table.

She returned from the bedroom clutching the "doctor" book with both hands. The book had been passed down from her grandmother to her mother and now to her.

Within its cracked brown leather cover, split binding, and yellowed pages, diseases of the human body and mind and their prescribed treatments had been cataloged. It was twice as thick and even heavier than the family Bible that collected dust on the upper shelf of my parents' bedroom closet back home.

A postmarked envelope marked the section on palmistry from our last foray into the secrets of doctoring. Granny pushed her glasses back up on her nose and traced her finger over the words and pictures.

My hands itched with anticipation. That old book smelled like the passage of time. How many eyes had studied its tattered pages? How many fingers traced the words on each page?

"Hold yer hands up under the light so I can see 'em better, Lizzie."

I lifted the palms of my hands towards the yellow glow emanating from the milk-glass lamp hanging overhead as Granny scooted her chair closer to me. She angled one hand underneath mine and lightly rubbed my left palm with her other hand. Veins protruded from the top of her hand, meandering through a forest of brown age spots.

"Now yer left palm holds the traits that yer born with, Lizzie." Granny followed the lifeline on my palm with her index finger.

"That's different than yer right palm. The right's a mix of what yer born with and ..." Granny pondered a bit, "... the particular circumstances of yer life.

"It's like this. In a card game, each player gets dealt a startin' hand. Ya don't choose them cards; chance does. That's like yer inborn nature or what's written into yer left-hand palm.

"After you get that first hand of cards, ya decide how yer gonna play 'em. Luck and skill come into play. How other people play their hands impacts yer choices, too. That's all rolled up into the reading of this here right palm."

Granny tapped my right hand.

As Granny spoke, I imagined a small, weightless ball balanced in my right palm, reflecting my face, the faces of my family, our house, my cat, our car, Cecil's monkey, and everything I'd seen of life. It was all there looking back at me. As I held open my left palm, I visualized only my reflection.

"Lizzie," Granny called me back to attention. "Ya understand?"

I nodded.

Granny launched into her prognostication about my long life, stable personality, and dependability in times of crisis.

Then came the part I loved best. "When you were born, Lizzie, two different lives were possible. Fate handed you this one."

Such was my grandmother's analysis of the discrepancy between the lifelines of my two palms. The lifeline on my left began with two branches and merged into one. This feature was absent from the single continuous lifeline of my right palm.

Granny spoke with such authority as if only she could divine certain secrets. She didn't elaborate on my dual "almost" destinies, nor did I probe her for details. Ever.

Granny licked her finger and turned to the next page in the doctoring book. "Read this here." She tapped her finger on the page.

I read aloud, "The heart line starts between the index finger and the middle finger and ends below the little finger."

"Here's your heart line. Some folks call it your love line. But they're the same." Her fingers felt soft and feather-like as she traced out my heart line, first on one palm, then on the other.

My heart lines were a big fat mess. Creased, fleshy tributaries branched out above and below my heartlines. I could make no sense of it.

Granny consulted her doctoring book again. She scratched her head as if pondering what to tell me.

"Well, you're headed for a complicated love life, Lizzie." Granny sat quietly with pursed lips for a bit after she delivered the bad news.

"Can we do the bumps on my head next, Granny?"

I was ready to go onto the phrenology section in the doctoring book. "Phrenology" was a word that I could spell but had no idea how to say since Granny never pronounced it.

"That's harder, Lizzie. Yer head's still a growin'."

"I know, but we can see if it changed since last time," I pleaded.

"I'm all tuckered out tonight. Let's save that for your next visit."

Granny resumed her hand basting. I watched as parallelogram-shaped pieces of fabric formed perfect eight-pointed stars, a cacophony of color and print.

"I love you, Lizzie, just like all my other grandkids. I make no difference between you and them," Granny said. Secrets just had a way of pushing their way out of Granny's mouth.

That "difference" lay silent and undisturbed between us like a sleeping dog with an uncertain pedigree.

The Letter

JANUARY 1988

THE BRIGHT NOONDAY SUN did little to soften the biting cold wind that blew through my coat. My hair flew in my face, briefly blinding me, as I hurried to my car. The parking lot remained deserted, no change since my arrival at the break of dawn. I headed home after donating yet another Saturday morning to the lab.

Extra hours were my drug of choice, a temporary salve to calm a gnawing sense of inadequacy that haunted my waking hours and pushed its clammy fingers into my dreams.

I checked and rechecked every calculation, every line of computer code, and sentence summarizing my research findings as if my life depended on it. In a way, it did. Climbing the professional ladder to personal self-worth allowed no mistakes.

On the drive home, I reviewed my five years at the National Laboratory. I'd doubled my salary in the first 24 months of my employment and had received two promotions. One of only a few women in a senior research management role, I now managed a cadre of other scientists. Yet, nothing was enough to remove the stigma of being Elizabeth Ann Schmidt.

I sailed up the driveway a half-hour late, hit the brakes, and turned off my black BMW. My husband expected me home from the lab by noon on Saturdays, and rightfully so. Joe deserved the same freedom to attend to his research in the afternoon that he allowed me in the morning. I dashed into the family room through the garage entry doorway to assume my childcare shift.

Head down with pen in hand, Joe sat at the table in one corner of the spacious family room, absorbed by the assembly language code he crafted. His thinning, unkempt hair bore the oily sheen that evidenced a lack of morning shower.

"Sorry I'm late. Time got away from me," I said.

"Did you get your paper done?" The corners of his blue eyes crinkled, his smile hidden beneath his overgrown, dark mustache.

"Don't I wish! Clearance has to have it by Monday. Any later and there's no chance to make the conference submission deadline." National Laboratories, although not academia, had their own version of "publish or perish."

I scanned the room for Abby and Noah. "Where are the kids? Don't tell me they've already gone down for naps."

I'd planned on a productive hour and a half while Abby and Noah napped.

"Afraid so. Noah fell asleep around 11:30. Abby's been down for about thirty minutes."

Finding the last few hours to polish my paper before my ex-husband Leo dropped off my three older kids would be tough now.

Joe placed his engineering pad, populated with zeros and ones, into his briefcase, and he was off. No exchange of goodbye kisses, no hugs, no further small talk. That's how it was between Joe and me, and it suited me just fine. I'd never been one for big displays of affection, publicly or privately.

Not physically demanding, Joe seemed satisfied with our predictable once-a-week lovemaking and foot rubs. My feet and his hands. Joe was crazy about me, and I knew it. That had been the point of marrying him five years ago come June.

After Leo Trembley, I had needed to feel loved.

I married Joe Keller one month after my divorce from Leo was finalized. Abby was born thirty-eight weeks later, and Noah trailed a year after.

Less than ten minutes later, I heard a car door slam shut outside and heavy footfalls echoed up the garage steps leading into the family room. My mother, Marie, was making her weekly visit. She knew our Saturday work routine and was often "just in the neighborhood" once Joe left for the Lab.

Mom was my bulwark in the storm, my cheerleader, the constant in my life, and my model for sacrificial, unconditional love. Nothing gave me pleasure like watching a huge smile dance across her face or hearing her laugh with abandon. Yet, my heart dropped with the cadence of each step.

Is a Saturday afternoon, just the kids and me, without Mom, possible? I thought.

My mother had the kids all to herself Monday through Friday. Due to my work schedule, I spent so little time with my kids, and I guarded what time remained zealously.

My mother walked into Joe's house whenever she pleased. No knock, no phone call. Ever. I was used to it, but Mom's lack of boundaries drove Joe crazy.

"Does Marie even know how to knock? She barges in unannounced and uninvited whenever she pleases!" Joe often complained. But at seventy-four years old, there was no retraining (or restraining) Mom. Any boundaries that I erected to placate Joe would only hurt my mother's feelings.

Mom's long, thin fingers loosened the knot in her sheer lavender headscarf as she entered the family room. She set her purse down on the couch and removed her gray overcoat.

"I won't stay long, Lizzie." Mom's voice carried a twinge of apology despite her smile.

Guilt wrested a win over my resentment as I settled into good-daughter mode. The truth was that without Mom's help, the fabric of my life would completely fray. Something that Joe failed to appreciate.

Before Mom could get a word in edgewise, I whispered, "Abby and Noah are asleep."

So much for working on my paper now, I thought on my way to close the kids' bedroom doors.

When I rejoined Mom, she was already attacking the mountain of clean laundry that covered the long counter of the wet bar in the family room. Given free reign, she'd transform the whole pile of clothes into neat stacks and be glad to do it. The woman was a saint.

Mom and I had a symbiotic relationship. We both gave, and we both got. The chores I performed for her, like vacuuming her house, mowing her lawn, or running errands, weren't emotionally taxing. Those things were simply time-management challenges. But being Mom's entire social life and financial security, that's what sucked me dry.

"Look at you, Mom. What's the occasion?" My mother had on her Sunday-best clothes and had applied lipstick to her thin lips, the extent of her makeup regime. Her purple polyester pantsuit stretched tightly over her apple-shaped torso.

"I spent the morning at the beauty parlor. Can't you tell?" Mom tentatively fingered her tight, short curls. She turned her head left and right to give me the full view.

"Yes, it's lovely. Date tonight?" I quipped. Of course, I knew better.

"Heavens, no! Why would I want to take care of another man, waiting on him hand and foot? No, t-h-a-n-k you!"

That pretty much described Mom's life with Dad. She had spent a decade as his caregiver while tasked as the primary wage earner.

Within a year of Dad's death, seven years ago, Mom had moved back to the god-forsaken place in southeastern Washington state where I'd grown up and still hadn't managed to escape. I shared no DNA with those who thought the sagebrush and sand of the mid-Columbia plateau were beautiful.

"Mom, don't fold the laundry. Just relax."

"You work all week. Let me help you. I don't mind."

"You work all week, too, taking care of my kids. That's harder than what I do!"

"Oh, that's not work, Lizzie. Besides, what else would I do?"

I'd often wished I could siphon off my mother's predilection for childcare and fill my tank with 100-proof of whatever it was that fueled her. Naturally, I loved my children, but I preferred a career to staying home and raising kids.

My knack for mathematics, coupled with my parents' meager finances, had been my golden ticket to post-high-school scholarships and grants. The resulting degrees had been my springboard to a secure and comfortable lifestyle and a sense of pride absent from my youth.

"Noah and Abby could sleep for an hour more. Forget the clothes. Come on, sit down. How often can we have a simple conversation without the kids interrupting?"

I walked into the kitchen. "I haven't had lunch yet. Want a sandwich?"

Mom abandoned the pile of laundry and walked over to the open counter that divided the family room from the kitchen.

While I searched the refrigerator for lunch options, Mom plopped down on one of the swiveling barstools. Ugh, peanut butter and jelly, I couldn't do it.

"I'm not hungry. But I'll take a beer if you have one," Mom said.

I grabbed a can of beer out of the refrigerator from Joe's stash and poured myself a glass of wine. I pulled out a stool and joined my mother at the counter.

Mom fished a single tissue from the bulging stash stored in the front pocket of her tunic-style blouse. Using the tissue, she blotted the yellow drainage from her prosthetic eye, noticeably more prominent and a darker hazel than her natural eye.

As a child, I'd noticed that Mom's eyes didn't track one another and that her left eyelid didn't completely close when she blinked or slept. Better prosthetic eyes were available nowadays, but any discussion of an upgrade required that I acknowledge the existence of her false eye. And that was impossible. She was far too sensitive and self-conscious.

I proposed a toast. "Here's to long kid naps and lazy Saturdays."

Mom touched her beer can to my wine glass and took several long gulps. "Aah, good stuff," she said, wiping her mouth with the back of her hand.

Floral notes of Estee Lauder's White Linen perfume, a strategic gift from me, competed with the miasma that ebbed and flowed as Mom inhaled and exhaled. A lifetime of chronic, untreated sinus and ear infections had rotted my mother's mastoid bone. Mom had little sense of smell, while mine was extraordinary and could easily win an olfactory Olympics.

"Oh, before I forget ..." Mom removed a small, rectangular postal notice from her other pocket. "Leo dropped this off when he picked the kids up last night."

I'd bought Mom a house once my divorce from Leo had been finalized, and that's where she watched the kids while Leo, Joe, and I worked.

"Registered Mail Delivery Attempt Notice" was printed across the top of the yellow form that Mom handed me. I scanned the information that the postman had filled in: Elizabeth Schmidt Trembley and Leo's home address.

"Someone still thinks I'm married to Leo." I doubted anything sent by registered mail would augur good news but diluted my worry with wine.

"Must be something important," Mom offered.

"I guess. I'll find out Monday. The post office closes early on Saturdays."

"How about another beer?" Mom asked.

I retrieved another beer for Mom and poured myself a bit more wine, already feeling the relaxing effects of the wine on my empty stomach.

"Maybe I am the long-lost heiress of a fortune, and someone is trying to contact me." I pulled a ridiculous face to match my ludicrous comment and sat back down.

Suddenly Mom's face went from rosy to ashen. I realized she'd taken my playful words as a backhanded reference to my adoption as an infant.

But honestly, was it so wrong to want answers? I hungered for substantial, meaty information about my biological origins. Yet Mom only fed me the same sparse, unsatisfying morsel: "You're Black Irish," as if those few words formed my complete story.

Fate had placed me into a family where I'd been a square peg forced into a round hole. Maybe if I'd fit in better, I wouldn't have obsessed so over my biological family. But it sure didn't help any that my adoptive sister and I were so different.

Physically Jeannie and I looked nothing alike. My sister could easily pass for a real Schmidt with her darker skin tone, blondish-brown hair, and chocolate brown eyes. She was short and sprouted womanly curves well before her teen years.

And me? I resembled an elongated, inverted exclamation point with porcelain skin, dark marine blue eyes, and black hair. But our differences were most evident in the classroom. In school, I excelled and found the only identity I cherished, whereas Jeannie struggled and eventually dropped out of high school.

Eventually, I realized that asking questions about my birth family made Mom feel unloved. Marie Schmidt was as fragile as a China doll. Caverns of rejection and loss had been carved into her soul at a tender age and still tormented her.

She had been five when her mother died. Her step-father dumped Mom and her three older full-siblings at an orphanage in Idaho. His two biological kids, Mom's younger half-siblings, were spared a life at the orphanage with the help of his family.

"Well, maybe it's true," Mom whispered dolefully. With slumped shoulders, she released a heavy sigh.

"What's true?"

"Maybe you do have an inheritance coming."

"What are you talking about, Mom?" Nobody had any money on Mom's or Dad's side of the family.

"We never should have done it. I shouldn't have listened to Auntie Sister." Mom raided the tissue wad from her pocket again and dabbed at both eyes.

Auntie Sister was Mom's oldest sister. She'd left the orphanage years before Mom to become a religious sister. Since she was both a nun and an aunt, we called her "Auntie Sister."

"I knew it was wrong for us to tear up that letter. You've always wanted to know ..." Mom's words trailed off.

"What letter did you tear up?" Confused, I pressed in, hoping for a few threads to pull.

"After you gave birth to Noah, your biological aunt wrote you a sweet letter telling you that she loved you and had prayed for you your entire life. Auntie Sister brought that letter with her when she came to stay with me that summer. She felt it best to say nothing about the letter to you, so we destroyed it. I let her talk me into it. I know the letter would have meant so much to you. I'm so sorry, Lizzie."

My face stung as if my mother had slapped me. In some ways, she had. Just from the inside out.

Mom blew her cover in that instant. She knew a whole lot more about me than simply "Black Irish." I would not back down this time; my need to know came first.

"What's the name of my aunt who wrote the letter?" *Surely, I have a right to that much information!*

Silence, followed by more silence. Her lower jaw moved back and forth as if grinding grain. "A-A-li-ce."

"My biological mother's sister is named Alice. Right?" I repeated the name, savoring it, verifying that I'd heard my mother correctly.

Mom nodded.

"What's the connection between Auntie Sister and Alice?" I asked with laser focus.

"Alice and Auntie Sister became good friends when they taught in the same elementary school. Alice told Auntie Sister that her unmarried, younger sister had become pregnant. She planned to give her baby up for adoption but only to a Catholic family. Auntie Sister contacted me about adopting you. Auntie Sister had remained in contact with Alice over the years."

Mom threw her head back and drained the last of her second beer. "Alice and Auntie Sister may have been responsible for Fred and me adopting you, Lizzie, but it was just like I was pregnant with you. I counted off the days on the calendar for six months awaiting your birth."

"But if Alice thought you gave me her letter, she'd have assumed I didn't want any contact with her ... that's beyond sad." My voice cracked. "Did you write down Alice's address before you destroyed the letter?"

"No." Mom avoided looking at me.

I wiped my face dry with the sleeve of my sweatshirt. "It's okay, Mom. What's done is done. We can't change the past." I felt sorry for Mom and wanted to comfort her. But it wasn't okay; I felt crushed and betrayed.

I waited for my voice to steady. "But why did the registered notice move you to tell me about Alice's letter after all this time?"

"It's what you said about the 'long, lost heir.' Alice's father, your biological grandfather, was a successful businessman in the Los Angeles area. He had two daughters, Alice and your biological mother. Alice never married or had children. Your birth mother died, but not before she turned right around and got pregnant again! I don't know why she didn't let me have the boy. She should have let me have the boy, too."

A sense of entitlement, resentment, and outright disdain for my biological mother spilled out of Marie as she spoke of the male child denied her. Did she think that adopting me gave her first right of refusal for my half- or full-brother?

"Maybe someone is trying to contact you about your grandfather's estate. I don't know. But destroying that letter has bothered me for almost three years now."

"I believe you, Mom. I'll survive. It's not the end of the world." Making Mom feel worse than she already did wouldn't help me dislodge the last bit of information that I now knew she was withholding.

"What was my birth mother's name?" I grasped Mom's hand, a visceral attempt to squeeze out her name. "If she's dead, what difference does it make if I know her name? Please." My heart pounded like a ticking time bomb.

Mom's splayed fingers kneaded the countertop as if dough. I had to get her talking again to advance my footing in this emotional tug-of-war.

"Was my adoption through an adoption agency?" I asked calmly, belying the storm that whipped inside me.

"No, it was a private adoption."

"Mom... she's dead. What can it possibly hurt if I know my birth mother's name?" I implored, clinging to the slippery edge of Mom's dark cavern and hoping not to fall inside.

Mom shifted her weight on the barstool and turned towards me. Her "good" eye narrowed as she glowered at me. Then the heavens parted and from the lips of Marie Schmidt rained down the two words that would change my life forever.

"Liddy Maher."

The sound of my birth mother's name unleased an exhilaration within me as if a window were opened, blowing the fresh air into my face. But Mom's next words cut short my joy.

"You hate me, don't you, Lizzie? Admit it."

I sat there stunned. As always, her judgment pronounced me guilty, and any defense on my part was futile.

Mom let herself out, leaving me alone with her accusation. My head became a boiling stew of emotions, spinning out of control until it hit my stomach.

Racing to the nearest bathroom, I watched my breakfast float on top of a mixture of wine and coffee in the toilet bowl. I knelt on the bathroom floor, rocking back and forth. I wrapped my arms tightly around myself to force my sobs to silence.

Losing my grip, I fell into my mother's cavernous grief, swirling downward into my childhood memories. I saw my eight-year-old self, hurting my mother all over again.

1961

AS I LEANED UP against the car, the lingering brightness of the late September air warmed my face. Indian summer, my parents called that time of year, when the leaves began to wear their autumn colors, but before the days shortened. The sun wouldn't set for at least another hour. Hungry, I wanted to get home and wished that Sr. John Frances and Mom would stop talking.

Momma had finished preparing, cooking, and cleaning up after the evening meal as she did each weekday at the convent. The religious sisters who taught at the school Jeannie and I attended lived there. Momma traded her excellent cooking for our tuition.

My ears perked up when I heard my name. "Lizzie favors you, Marie, especially through the cheekbones." Sister smiled and nodded toward me.

"I think so, too!" Momma felt her cheekbone and stole a furtive glance at me.

"See you tomorrow, Sister." Momma waved goodbye and then got into the car. Sister waved goodbye and went back inside the convent as Momma started up the car. Offended and mad as a hornet, I climbed into the front seat and slammed the car door, registering my displeasure.

Momma drove through the school's parking lot, which doubled as four-square and basketball courts, and entered the church's adjacent parking lot. I could no longer hold my tongue and unleashed the full force of my nasty temper.

"Why didn't you tell Sister that I was adopted? Why do you always pretend I'm your real daughter? I can't look like you!"

Momma stopped the car in the middle of the church parking lot. Her face grew tight, cold, and judging.

"You hate me, don't you, Lizzie?"

Desperate to escape the evidence of injury I'd inflicted, I ran out of the car as fast as my legs would carry me. I entered the unlocked church and waited in the narthex until I heard the car drive off.

Low-angled sunlight still passed through the large rectangular stained-glass windows that lined the back of the church. Tiny dust particles danced on rainbow shards of light. I followed the rays to a pew up front, a few rows back from the communion rail.

Soundlessly, I lowered the kneeler, not to pray but to crawl beneath the long wooden bench of the pew. I lay on the floor, hiding, sobbing quietly, trapped in a morass of guilt and resentment.

A trace of incense, earthy and woodsy, hung delicately in the air. The blanketing silence nestled next to me like a sleeping cat, an island of calm, dousing my internal firestorm and releasing me from its clutches.

After I crawled out, I stood in front of the life-sized statue of Mother Mary in the alcove tucked just beyond the communion rail. She looked down upon me from her pedestal. Ten rows of twelve votive candles angled up in front of her on a black metal stand. The soft, flickering candlelight seemed to animate her beautiful face into a smile. I made the Sign of the Cross and uttered my prayer aloud to the Blessed Virgin Mary, "Please, let Momma know that I don't hate her. Thank you. Amen."

Sealing my request with a Hail Mary, I left the Church and walked the three blocks home as the sun dipped to kiss the horizon. I didn't want Momma to worry, nor did I want to miss dinner.

Lunch

THE REMAINDER OF THE letter-bombshell weekend appeared like any other, on the surface anyway. Leo dropped off the three older kids Saturday evening just before supper. As usual, they were tired and hungry and crabby. There were meals to cook, dishes to wash, laundry to wash and fold, Mass to attend Sunday morning, squabbles to break up between kids, homework to inspect, and mental gymnastics to ready myself for another work week. But under the surface, seeds of a new kind of selfishness began to germinate.

I teeter-tottered between betrayal-tinged hurt and repressed-smoldering anger. It didn't take a rocket scientist to understand why my mother had destroyed the letter and then hid her actions for three years. Mom was insecure. Not just about my affections but everybody else's too. After Dad's death, she'd lamented always playing second fiddle to his youngest sister, Pearl. My mother was a black hole sucking in love and attention without satiation. I realized that, to some degree, I shared those same traits.

By Monday morning, I wanted off the emotional pendulum. The pressure of a deadline turned my focus back to work. I delivered my research paper to the lab's clearance office late afternoon. The lawyers and technical staff assured me they could finish their review and accommodate the conference submission deadline.

I called Joe to let him know. Soon afterward, he picked me up outside my office building and drove us to the post office, racing to arrive before closing.

Joe pulled up in front of the post office and shifted the car into park. "It's unlikely that letter has anything to do with your birth family. You know that, right?"

"My brain knows that, but still ..." My hope in some birth-family-related correspondence had grown exponentially in the last fifty-two hours.

I grabbed the claim slip out of my purse and pulled a manilla folder from the briefcase that sat at my feet.

"Why the folder?" Joe asked.

"Don't laugh ... but I brought my divorce decree from Leo."

"Okay ... and?" Joe raised his eyebrows in question.

I held up the lab-issued picture ID hanging around my neck. "My ID says Schmidt, not Trembley." I'd gone back to my maiden name after my divorce from Leo. "Plus, my driver's license has a different address. Yours, not Leo's. Just a little extra insurance if the post office hassles me because my name and address don't match the notice."

"You're a basket case, Liz. Good luck." Joe smiled as he squeezed my arm.

"No argument there," I said and exited the car.

Ten minutes later, I rejoined Joe. "I hit the jackpot," I said sarcastically, waving the contents of the registered letter at Joe.

"Lucky me. The National Science Foundation randomly selected me from the pool of women who earned graduate degrees in mathematics between 1970 and 1985. And my prize? I get to fill out a survey. The whole registered letter business was to preserve the integrity of their sample. From the questions, it seems like they want to know if I'm underemployed."

"Sorry, Liz, I know you're disappointed."

I nodded. Disappointment seemed like an understatement. I felt like a doused campfire. But the survey had kindled my quest for what I desired most: truth, identity, and wholeness. A search that would soon erupt into a forest fire.

That evening, I sat on the bed in Joe's master bedroom, examining my birth certificate closely with a magnifying glass and trying to make out the attending physician's signature. Why had I never tried to get my original, unaltered birth certificate before? Although I now knew my deceased birth mother's maiden name, perhaps the unaltered version could lead me to my birth aunt. Somehow. I needed to tell Alice Maher that her letter never made it into my hands.

I decided to call the Department of Vital Statistics in Sacramento the next day. That meant driving home midday since long-distance personal phone calls were not allowed at the lab. But I had to try.

Sixteen hours later I unlocked Joe's front door, set my purse down on the counter, and dialed Sacramento.

"Hello. How may I help you?" said the woman who answered.

"Hi. I'm calling about my birth certificate. What is the process to gain access to my original birth certificate?"

"Were you adopted?"

"Yes, sorry. I should have said that to begin with."

"Well, it all depends on when you were adopted and why you want access to your original birth certificate."

"I was born in 1953."

"Because you were born after 1935, you'll need a Superior Court order to release your unaltered records. Typically, that happens only in life-or-death medical situations."

"Curiosity is certainly not a life-or-death situation, though it feels like it sometimes." I tried to make light of the bad news with a nervous laugh. "Why the 1935 date?" I asked.

"Because on September 1, 1935, the California legislature passed the Vital Statistics Registration Act. Chapter 608 sealed adoption birth records absent a court order."

I jotted the information down in my notebook as she spoke.

"Is there anything else I can help you with?" she asked.

"Do you know why they passed that law in 1935?" I couldn't help wondering.

"To protect children from the stigma of adoption and prejudices of having 'bad blood.' Those were different times back then. The law also protected the mothers who gave their children up for adoption by guaranteeing their privacy."

"That makes sense. Thank you for your time."

"Sorry I couldn't be of more help. Have a nice day," she said and hung up. Click.

Her words, "bad blood," dredged up an unpleasant memory that I'd packed away for almost thirty years.

It had been a hot summer evening when the whole neighborhood gang was outside playing and choosing up sides for a game of Red Rover. My cousin, Joey Schmidt, was visiting from Clarkston. If second-graders can have crushes, I had one on freckled-faced, brown-haired Joey. I never forgot the tizzy fit he threw when we ended up on the same team.

"Lizzie's got bad blood," Joey had said, his face pinched up and ugly-like.

Both horrified and ashamed, I had looked myself over. No blood anywhere. Whatever "bad blood" meant, it wasn't good. The shame of Joey's barb clung to me like a stubborn case of ringworm, amplifying the detachment that I felt, even then, from the Schmidt clan.

I STRUGGLED TO CONCENTRATE at work. Thoughts of Liddy and Alice Maher camped out in my brain, taking up prime neuronal real estate. My eyes searched for a diversion other than the computer screen and fixed upon the empty Limoges bud vase sitting on my desk.

My fingers abandoned the keyboard to trace the purple violets and heart-shaped green leaves artistically painted upon the delicate porcelain. My love for Limoges porcelain was an adult offshoot of my childhood fascination with all things French.

I looked over at the framed poster of Mary Cassatt's "Children Playing on the Beach" hanging on the wall adjacent to my desk. I'd tried to make my office less institutional without screaming, "Caution, woman on board!" I relaxed into the soft burnished golds and marine blues of Cassatt's idyllic ocean scene of two young children, perhaps sisters, playing on a sandy beach.

Below Cassatt's soothing image, I had positioned my children's most recent school pictures atop the metal bookcase. Leah's eighth-grade picture captured her smirk, Jonah's first-grade picture revealed his missing-a-tooth grin, and Hannah's tentative smile displayed the bashfulness of a kindergartener. A snapshot of Abby and Noah, back when they were both in diapers, completed the collection. I made a mental note to bring in a more recent photo of my two youngest.

I searched for the commonalities amongst the smiling faces. I saw their father's features primarily, yet I was the constant across all five faces. Mystery traits popped up here and there: Leah's widow's peak; Hannah's dimples and chin cleft; Abby's lazy eye; Noah's hyperactivity and extreme allergies. I knew I'd given Jonah his gifts with math, but where did I get mine? And what about my crazy, keen sense of smell. Was I part bloodhound?

It irked me that people took their blood connections to family for granted. What a gift to look into someone's face and see a reflection of oneself—an umbilical cord through history—literally etched in one's DNA. A connection to the past yet anchored in the present. I may not be the perfect mother, but I could give my children knowledge of their biological mother.

My sister, Jeannie, could have cared less about her biological roots. Yet I dreamt of a family that looked familiar. That smelled familiar. That shared my passions and even my shortcomings. A look of wordless recognition that whispered, "I know you, crafted as we are, from the same flesh. Parts of the same whole."

Had I desired so many children for a selfish reflection of myself in that new individual, flesh of my flesh? Were my fantasies of biological family idealized? Probably. A hole within my being craved to be filled.

I removed the phone book from my desk drawer and turned to the yellow pages under "Adoption." I scanned for local agencies and found three. One agency stood out, "New Hope Adoption Agency." I needed some hope. An adoption agency might know something that could help me.

I wavered in my determination to call. It felt weird and scary to share my story with a stranger. But drowning in a sea of desire to find Aunt Alice, I wasn't above grasping at straws.

"Hello, New Hope Adoption. Amy speaking."

"Hi, Amy. My name is Elizabeth Schmidt. Do you have a few minutes to answer an adoption-related question?"

"Sure. How can I help you?"

"I was adopted in 1953. My adoptive mother recently shared some information about my birth family. My birth mother is dead, but her sister, my birth aunt, tried to contact me through a letter I never received. I know the names of my birth mother and her sister. Are you aware of anything that could help me connect with my birth aunt?"

"The only thing I know about is the Soundex International Registry. It pairs up adoptees with birth mothers if both parties register."

I took notes as Amy spoke. "Do you know of anyone who has used this registry?"

"Not really. I work at the front end matching children, usually infants, with prospective parents. The registry's headquarters is located in Nevada somewhere. They started up in 1975, about the time everything changed from closed to open adoptions."

I did the relevant math in my head. "My birth mother would've died way before 1975."

"Come to think of it, you might be interested in an article that appeared in *People* magazine recently. It was about a doctor who had been adopted as an infant and found her birth parents. Once she had a child of her own, she became curious about her biological parents. Hers had been a closed adoption. The article traced her journey to find her birth parents using the information provided by her adoptive parents and the services of a private investigator."

"Wow, I'd love to read that!"

"The birth mother lives right here in the Tri-Cities. They gave her name in the article. I made a copy of the article. Let me pull it out. Hang on."

I heard the rolling sound of a metal file drawer, followed by paper-shuffling sounds.

"Here it is. The birth mother's name is Ellen Balondis."

"I'm dying to read that article. Can I swing by to make a copy?"

"No need. Just give me your mailing address, and I'll send you a copy."

"Perfect!"

I gave Amy Joe's home address and thanked her.

After hanging up the phone, I paged through the phone book. There was only one "Balondis" listing, an "Andres Balondis."

I taped a "Do Not Disturb" sign outside my office door and shut it tightly. After pacing back and forth a few times, I dialed the number. I took a deep breath as the number for the Andres Balondis residence rang.

"Hello." A mature-sounding woman answered the phone.

"Is this Ellen?"

"Yes, who's this?"

"My name is Elizabeth Schmidt. I heard about the *People* magazine article that featured your birth daughter's search."

"Look, I'm pretty tired of getting phone calls about that article." The irritation in Ellen's voice was unmistakable.

"I bet you are. But, please, may I have just five minutes of your time? I'm adopted, too." Without waiting for Ellen's reply, I launched into a different version of my story than I had shared with Amy at the adoption center. I told Ellen that I had wanted nothing more than to know my biological mother my whole life.

When I told Ellen about my adoptive mother and Auntie Sister tearing up the letter, my voice broke. "I know my birth mother is dead, but I want to find my aunt who wrote the letter to me."

"How do you know your birth mother is dead?"

"My adoptive mother told me. She died not long after I was born."

I paused to catch my breath. Were my five minutes expended? Was she still on the line?

"Where do you live?" Ellen asked.

"In Kennewick."

"Meet me at Shari's on Columbia Center Drive this Saturday at noon for lunch."

"Thank you, Ellen. I will be there."

Click. That was it. She didn't even say goodbye.

JOE WENT INTO WORK early Saturday morning. Too addled for any intellectual pursuits, I stayed home with Abby and Noah. The kids' need for constant attention helped keep my focus off lunch with Ellen. I changed my clothes several times and ate every piece of dark chocolate in the house while watching the slow turn of the clock.

Once Joe returned home, I began the short drive to Shari's Restaurant and arrived a bit before noon. How would I recognize Ellen? I hadn't yet received the *People* magazine article in the mail from Amy at the New Hope Adoption Center. And she didn't know what I looked like either.

A tired-looking waitress with mousy brown hair bobby pinned into a chignon led me to a table. I scanned the customers for a woman sitting alone in her late fifties or early sixties. The back counter in front of the cooking station was populated entirely by men. A teenage couple sat several tables over who appeared more into each other than their food. No Ellen.

I kept a steady gaze at the door, praying that Ellen would show. Finally, a petite middle-aged woman entered the restaurant. She held what appeared to be a rolled-up magazine in one hand, the other hand clutching a purse. That had to be Ellen.

I waved my hand to get her attention. She nodded as she walked to the table where I sat. Her layered blond hair fell in loose curls to the shoulders of her silver parka.

"Elizabeth?" I recognized her voice immediately.

"Yes. Hello, Ellen. Thank you for meeting up with me." She smelled like cigarette smoke mixed with Calvin Klein's Eternity perfume.

Ellen remained a beautiful woman with a heart-shaped face and bright cornflower blue eyes. She removed her jacket and sat down opposite me, acknowledging my smile with a slight, neutral nod.

The Formica-topped tables nearby were empty. I hoped that they would remain vacant so we could talk freely. Ellen placed the magazine onto the table between us. The November 14, 1987 issue of *People* unrolled towards me.

After ordering our sandwiches and coffee, Ellen said, "You probably wonder why I suggested we meet for lunch."

"I did, especially when it sounded like I was just one of many people pestering you about the article. But whatever the reason, I'm very grateful."

"I was adopted as an infant, just like you. My whole life, I had a gaping hole in my heart that I couldn't plug. God knows I tried with five different husbands."

An uneasiness settled in me when Ellen spoke of her five marriages. I thought about my three by age thirty.

"It can be hard for adoptees ever to feel loved, Elizabeth. There's never enough."

Ellen was preaching to the choir. The proverbial black hole! "Then you do understand!"

"Yes, and I recognized the pain in your voice when you called me. I suppose that is why I'm sitting here right now. How old are you, Elizabeth?"

"Thirty-five."

"On the phone, you told me your adoptive mother said your birth mother was dead; I doubt that's true. She's probably younger than me," Ellen insisted, looking me straight in the eye.

My mother, Marie, didn't lie, but I left her comment unchallenged because I wanted to hear what she had to say.

Without any encouragement, Ellen launched into her story. She had worked as a secretary for the medical school at the University of Washington in her early twenties. One of the faculty members, a doctor named Jack, had invited her to a private party. She was thrilled and flattered to attend as his date.

"I'd only had one drink. Jack must have put something in my drink because it knocked me out."

Ellen assured me that she was no stranger to parties or drinking and could hold a couple of drinks without passing out.

"When I came to, Jack and I were in a back bedroom. I was dizzy and confused, so I left him on the bed while I dressed clumsily and called a cab to take me home."

Ellen paused her story when the waitress brought our sandwiches and refilled her coffee cup.

"I really didn't know how to handle the situation. Jack avoided me after that, and I did my best to forget the horrible incident. I had no boyfriend at the time and wasn't dating anyone else. I'd had a serious boyfriend before and wasn't a virgin, so I just told myself to get over it." Ellen paused and took a sip of her black coffee.

"Without my job, I had no means of support. I'd be damned before letting Jack take that from me, too. That was easier said than done. I missed my period that month and began having bouts of morning sickness. A doctor's appointment confirmed that I was indeed pregnant."

She took a bite of her sandwich before continuing. My BLT sat untouched.

"I went to Jack's office to tell him that I was pregnant. He asked what that had to do with him. He denied having sex with me at the party, stating unequivocally that my baby's father was not him. I never thought about abortion; they weren't legal back then anyway. But I could never abort my baby, no matter how conceived."

I could relate to what Ellen said. The conditions surrounding my conception were a total mystery.

"My adoptive parents didn't understand why I'd want to keep my baby if

I was date raped. They thought I was lying, although they never came right out and said so. They didn't have to. It was evident from their lack of support and embarrassment over my pregnancy.

"I was truly on my own. I ended up living in a home for unwed mothers in Seattle. It killed me when I gave my baby girl up for adoption. I had no other option."

"Ellen, I haven't read the article in *People* yet, but someone who has said that the daughter you put up for adoption found you. How did that happen?"

"Sharon, my daughter, hired a private investigator to help her search. When I gave birth to my daughter, I listed Jack's full name as her father. I used his office at the medical school as his home address. I refused to write "father unknown" on the birth record as the adoption agency had advised me."

Ellen paged through the magazine until she found the article featuring the story of her birth daughter's search. She pointed to an image of a woman running behind while pushing a toddler in an expensive jogging stroller.

"This is Sharon. The article gives plenty of details about the private investigator and her agency. I should think you could start by contacting the private investigator that Sharon used.

"This article includes nothing about my feelings or how the process has been for me." Ellen turned the page. She pointed to a picture of an older man with Sharon. "That's Jack.

"Sharon had a great life in the Boston area, went to the best schools, and became a medical doctor. She was very close to her adoptive parents. The private investigator found Jack first and then me. Since I'd given birth to Sharon, I'd had five different last names. That had to complicate finding me.

"I got a letter asking if I wished to be in contact with Sharon. At that point, it was like a dream come true. My daughter had come looking for me.

"When Sharon contacted her father, I assume through a letter as well, but I don't know, Jack said we'd had consensual sex. I told Sharon the unfortunate truth, which she refuses to accept." Ellen pressed her clenched fist to her quivering lips.

"Perhaps because Jack's a successful doctor, now with a prestigious position at the Mayo Clinic, Sharon prefers his story to mine. The irony is that Jack married but never had any children other than Sharon, who he wouldn't acknowledge when I was pregnant with her. Now he's rewarded for his callousness with a daughter, son-in-law, and a beautiful grandson.

"Sharon wants little to do with me. Maybe she thinks I am a liar. I'm not. She's happy to interact with my four children, though." Ellen pointed to another picture. "Here are three of my kids at the first-meeting 'reunion' with Sharon."

Ellen pulled a paper napkin from the holder on the table and wiped her eyes.

"I don't know what to say, how hard and unfair this all seems. I am so sorry, Ellen." I grabbed a napkin, too.

"It turned out well enough for my children and Jack. Sharon was an only child and is happy to have siblings. I try to be happy for them all." Ellen shrugged her shoulders. "Maybe things will change down the road, and Sharon will have a place for me in her life."

"You must understand that searching for your birth family is not a game. I don't believe for one minute that your birth mother is dead. People sculpt lies into the truths that they want to believe. If you aren't prepared to have a relationship with your birth mother, don't go hunting for your birth aunt."

I understood where Ellen was coming from now. I couldn't soften Ellen's sorrow, but I assured her that I desired a close, long-term relationship with my birth aunt and my birth mother, too, if only that were possible.

"You never know what you'll find with this searching business. It can stir up a whole lot of pain. I'll leave the magazine with you; you can read the details."

Ellen finished eating her sandwich, and I ate half of mine. There wasn't much else to say. Ellen never asked anything about my life. That was just as well, as her story had drained me emotionally.

After we said our goodbyes, I walked out to my car. I almost felt relieved that Liddy Maher was dead. There was no chance that I could rekindle the kind of pain in Liddy that Sharon had inflicted on Ellen's unhealed wounds.

I sat in the restaurant's parking lot with the car's engine running, and the heater cranked on. I read the whole article. Twice.

There was no mention of the circumstances surrounding Ellen placing Sharon up for adoption, only that she and Jack were not married. The article emphasized why Ellen's daughter wanted to find her birth parents. Notably, there was no picture of Ellen.

According to the article, Sharon had hired Kait Klosen, a private investigator whose company, Klose Investigations, was located in San Francisco.

Ellen's story of giving up Sharon as a baby, Sharon's snub of Ellen, and Sharon's subsequent bonding with Jack and Ellen's children seemed so unfair and heartbreaking. I set the magazine down and, with tear-blurred vision, pulled out of the parking lot.

My thoughts were full of gratitude to Ellen for sharing her story, but also—and this surprised me—to Charlie Davis, my first husband and Leah's biological father.

Nineteen, sexually inexperienced, and hormonally ripe, I had met Charlie Davis the summer between my sophomore and junior year of college. A Vietnam veteran, Charlie was a tall blonde with inviting, brown, puppy-dog eyes. Easy-going, relaxed, flexible, affectionate, and uninhibited, he was everything I wasn't. A committed, serious relationship for me equated to an open, causal relationship for Charlie.

But Charlie did marry me when I became pregnant with Leah. Absent a strong work ethic, emotional stability, an ounce of ambition, or marital fidelity, Charlie had taken responsibility for the human life growing inside me. The enormity of that gift hit me like a ton of bricks after my conversation with Ellen.

I marveled at how much the world had changed for unwed mothers since Ellen had become pregnant with Sharon. Women had begun to keep babies born out of wedlock by the time Leah was born.

Abortion had become legal four months before I conceived Leah. And to Charlie Davis's immense credit, he never once mentioned abortion, nor did it cross my mind. I had loved my baby, just as Ellen had loved Sharon.

Following Ellen's suggestion, I would hire a private investigator to help me find Alice Maher. I aimed my scope at Kait Klosen and adjusted the crosshairs.

Weekend

FEBRUARY 1988

TWO HOURS AFTER MY lunch with Ellen Balondis, I'd secured the phone number for Klose Investigations. I dialed the number twice over the next hour. Each time the dreaded answering machine had greeted me. Without leaving a message, I'd hung up. As I counted the unanswered rings on my third try, I fumbled through my last-minute decision to leave a message.

"Hi, my name is Elizabeth Schmidt. I'm trying to locate my aunt, who lives in California. Well, maybe she does. Actually, I'm not sure where she lives ... or if she's still alive. Please return my call on weekdays after 6 p.m. Pacific time or after noon on weekends."

A beep cut me off just as I left the last digit of my contact phone number. "Good grief," I said aloud, irritated at the prospect of calling Klose Investigations back for the fourth time.

Startled, Abby and Noah turned to me with worried eyes, holding their crayons in midair.

"Ignore Momma. It's okay. I'm just talking to myself." I forced a smile.

The kids returned to their artistic endeavors while I called back for the fourth time, leaving only my name and Joe's home phone number.

Regardless of the cost of hiring a private investigator, my horns were down, and I was charging ahead.

As sunset approached, the ubiquitous Mid-Columbia wind had whipped the air into an invisible swarm of icy stingers. By 5:45 p.m., I had prepared dinner, and all I lacked were the last three hungry mouths. Once Leo dropped off the older kids on Saturday evenings, food needed to materialize lickety-split. They were usually famished.

The ride from Leo's house to Joe's place was just long enough for Jonah or Hannah to conk out. Unenforced bedtimes on Friday nights combined with reduced winter daylight hours extracted their toll on the kids.

I sat between Abby and Noah on the couch in the living room, reading a book aloud while awaiting the joint custody handoff circus. Peering out the large picture window as I turned each page, I watched for the headlights of Leo's van.

When Sam-I-Am decided that he really did like green eggs and ham after all, Leo's minivan entered the cul-de-sac. It stopped in front of Joe's house, smack-dab in the middle of the street, with the engine running.

Leo refused to escort the kids to the front door or even pull up into Joe's driveway. Such niceties would require that Leo set foot on Joe's property, which wouldn't happen in my lifetime. The two men detested one other.

Predictably, Leo avoided looking towards Joe's house. Jonah was first out of the van minus his coat, indifferent to the cold air. He headed straight for the smooth river rocks to the side of the driveway. Leah was next out of the minivan with her backpack slung over one shoulder and Jonah and Hannah's striped clothes bag half-dangling over her other shoulder. She carried her coat and Jonah's, too.

The war between Charlie Davis's gene pool and mine fueled Leah's inner furnace. And if that fire needed kindling, she knew how to orchestrate Leo and me against one another like a master conductor. There'd be sparks tonight as I'd refused Leah's request to spend the night at a girlfriend's house.

Leo had adopted Leah, at my urging, when she was five. He was the father that populated her childhood memories. However, it killed me to give Leo joint custody when we divorced. But to do otherwise seemed unfair to both Leah and Leo. Fatherhood consisted of more than sperm donation, the only part Charley Davis had mastered.

Leo exited the van to lift a drowsy Hannah out of the backseat. Without a single step forward, she wailed from the base of the driveway where Leo had set her down. At least she had her coat on, I thought.

I charged out the front door up from the couch, scooped Hannah up into my arms, and kissed her wet cheek. "That's a brutal way to wake up. Isn't it, little girl?"

Why did Leo have to make everything so hard? Had he never heard that divorce could be civilized?

Repositioning Hannah in my arms, I steered Jonah towards the house and away from the rocks bordering the driveway. Jonah, my mini-David, reluctantly dropped his smooth stone weapons. He would hold off his slaying of giants for another day. But the real giant got back into his minivan, made a U-turn, and headed back home or to tonight's female recreation or both.

As irritated as I was at Leo, his handsome face and the way he moved his muscular body still elicited the same hypnotic effect on me as it had the first time that we'd met. I had Karl Blinker and Washington State University to thank for introducing us. My divorce from Charlie had been final for six months when I moved to Pullman with Leah that summer to start graduate school.

I'd taught two undergraduate math classes as part of my teaching assistantship. A massive bouquet of red roses was delivered to the math department office bearing my name during my first semester. The enclosed card read, "Beautiful, like you. Enjoy." There was no signature.

I wasn't dating anyone. Taking care of three-year-old Leah, studying for my classes, and teaching classes left no time for anything else. The mystery flowers generated plenty of undesired attention among the other grad students and faculty. My embarrassment only increased when a large box of chocolates appeared the following week. Again, no signature, just a cryptic note, "Sweet as you." I left bonbons in the office for the faculty and staff to enjoy.

Not long after the chocolates arrived, a student in one of the undergrad classes I taught began scribbling notes in the margins of his homework assignments. Karl was about ten years older than me and much older than the typical college freshman. He wrote things like "Our destinies are intertwined" and "My electrons are dancing." I didn't know if his odd notes were directed to me or just random thoughts. Either way, it creeped me out.

Karl began waiting for me outside the classroom so he could walk me back to my office. His attentions were nerve-wracking, but I didn't know how to stop them without hurting his feelings. One day after class, Karl handed me a wrapped gift, obviously a book.

"For me? Why?" I asked him.

"Just because you are a great teacher. I think you'll like it."

I should have said, "I can't accept this." My flustered brain managed only a "Thank you." Once back to my office, I unwrapped a vintage 1930 hardcover of *Candide* by Voltaire.

Shortly after that, somehow Karl got my home phone number. He asked me out on a date. I declined and said that I was seeing someone else. I wasn't.

Then the notes on his homework took a more negative twist, like "You should not have done that!"

That's how I ended up at the campus counseling center. I'd scheduled a meeting with a clinical psychologist just like my math professor-friend had suggested. I had scheduled an hour meeting with a random clinical psychologist, Dr. Leo Trembley. I'd never seen a therapist or talked to a clinical psychologist before, and, honestly, I felt embarrassed and somewhat ashamed to be there, as if I'd done something wrong.

Leo, as Dr. Trembley insisted that I call him, earned his doctorate from the University of Chicago the same year I had received my undergraduate degree. I read his credentials from the framed diploma hanging on his office wall.

The man was handsome in a Dr. Zhivago kind of way. His killer smile elicited trust, a fast heart rate, and heavy perspiration. For me, it was love at first sight and smell. He'd grown up in Quebec, which had imparted a sexy French accent. He had a sweet clean scent like honey and lavender.

I brought Leo up to speed on the mystery gifts and how the comments on Karl's homework had grown darker after I refused his request for a date.

"Do you think he's dangerous?" I asked Leo as he handed me the cup of tea brewed for us. His hand brushed mine as I took the cup from him. There was no wedding ring on his beautiful hands.

"Probably not. But he's certainly an odd duck. Don't accept any more gifts from him." He handed me back the copies I'd made of Karl's homework with the odd notes in the margins. "Hang on to these," he instructed.

"If the tenor of the notes on his homework increases or gets outright threatening, I need you to contact the Pullman police immediately. Not the campus police. Tell them the same things that you told me. Make copies of any other notes on his homework. Don't be afraid to reach out to me again if you get worried."

"Okay." I had the feeling that I'd caused this situation with Karl. But I couldn't figure out what I'd done for the life of me.

"Do you feel less anxious?" Leo seemed genuinely concerned.

"I do." Calmer, yes, but wholly mesmerized by Leo, I'd lost track of time. My hour was likely up, plus I needed to pick Leah up from daycare.

I stood up to leave. "Thank you for seeing me."

"Wait. Not so fast. Would you like to get together socially?" Leo asked. There was that melt-me smile again.

"Do you get together socially with all your clients?" I asked incredulously.

Leo laughed. "I never get together with any of my clients socially. It's forbidden. You are not my client, Elizabeth. We are colleagues."

"So, it's ... okay?" I needed reassurance from him and permission from myself.

"Very okay. And highly desired." His dark eyes sparkled and held me hostage. Only then had I realized that Leo had just asked me out on a date.

"It could take me a while to find a babysitter. I have a three-year-old daughter, Leah."

"Bring Leah along. I love kids."

And just like that, he stole a piece of my heart, that bit still within his grasp.

SOMETHING AWAKENED ME IN the middle of the night. I sat up in bed and attempted to orient myself. Nestled to my right, Joe remained soundly asleep in his king-sized bed. The LCD digital clock flipped from 2:59 to 3:00 a.m.

Bits of moonlight slipped through the slats of the vertical blinds that hung in the long, narrow windows of Joe's bedroom. The house was tranquil. Noah wasn't ratting through the kitchen drawers as he sometimes did in the middle of the night.

I canvased the bedroom to get my bearings. The tall chest of drawers stood in the recessed area between my closet and Joe's. On top of the bureau sat the jewelry box that Joe had given me for my birthday, still opened with my pearls draping over the side of the box as I had left them for weeks. Besides the pearls and the heart pendant that Joe had given me for my birthday, everything I owned was inexpensive costume jewelry.

A flicker of movement grabbed my attention in the corner of the room. Near the unattractive metal desk and chair that Joe had salvaged from the lab surplus sale, an amorphous shadow coalesced into the shape of a person. Simultaneously transfixed and frozen, the person walked toward me.

I panicked, assuming that a robber was in the room. My mind raced as adrenaline pumped through my veins. My jewelry was not worth the trouble of breaking in. In a weak pretense of self-protection, I grabbed the receiver off the princess phone from the end table next to me.

Once past the bureau, only steps from the end of the bed, now in sharp focus, stood a man of medium build, perhaps in his late twenties. Slightly wavy brown hair hung almost to his shoulders. His red plaid shirt was opened at the neck, exposing a gold-colored, round medallion or medal.

An electric sense of fright ran through me. I tried to scream, but my voice wouldn't work. Whether I had awakened from a dream or had fainted and was coming to, I found myself lying crosswise on top of my husband with the phone receiver in my hand.

Poor Joe, jounced awake by the fall of human timber. "What's wrong?" he sputtered.

"There was a man in our room, over there ... by the dresser." Sitting up, I pointed to where he'd been with the telephone receiver. "He was walking towards me."

Now Joe was wide awake. He sat up in bed and turned on the light on his side table.

"No one is in the room but us." Joe put his arm around me and placed his other hand over my wildly beating heart. Then he noticed the phone receiver in my left hand. "Were you going to phone someone?"

"Maybe I was going to hit him with it. I don't know. It seemed so real. Sorry I woke you up," I said while placing the receiver back on the phone. I struggled to integrate the fleeting presence of a strange man with his now conspicuous absence from the room.

"It's okay. I'll go right back to sleep," Joe reassured. He eased us both back into a lying position. Within minutes Joe was softly snoring. I lusted for his sleep gene.

I'd had my share of nightmares since childhood. But tonight, I'd inadvertently pulled Joe into one.

Morning finally arrived, relieving me from the frustration of trying to fall back asleep. Getting everyone fed and the younger kids dressed for Mass competed with the memory of last night's visitor. The man's face seemed familiar, but I couldn't place it. Perhaps my brain wove some memory fragment into a disturbing dream.

I led Abby and Noah to the bathroom to remove the sticky, greasy remnants of their French toast and bacon breakfast while I shouted orders at the older kids like a drill sergeant.

"Leah, make your bed and get dressed. Don't make us late for Mass!"

"Did you brush your teeth, Jonah?"

"Hannah, if you want me to fix your hair, get a move on it."

Once all five kids were in acceptable form, I had eight minutes left to get myself ready for Mass. I found Joe pacing in our bedroom, still in his pajamas.

"Joe, are you coming or not?"

My impatient question released him from whatever thought held him captive.

"Oh, yes. Getting ready now!" Joe said.

Joe went to Mass as a favor to me, not because his twelve years of Catholic education had instilled a great love for the Catholic faith. He was agnostic. Why I went to Mass was more complicated. I'd bought into bits and pieces of what the good sisters had drilled into me during my nine years of Catholic school, including the importance of raising a child in the Catholic faith.

I wanted my kids to have a wholesomeness and legitimacy that I'd always felt was beyond my reach. The Catholic culture was part of the equation that equaled good things for my kids. After the debacle of my marriage to Charlie Davis, I'd applied for a declaration of nullity from the Church. That was before Leo Trembley was part of my life.

My annulment had allowed Leo and I to marry in the Catholic Church. Nevertheless, I wasn't a wife Leo's family could accept. As a previously married woman with a child, I was tainted, their disdain becoming a source of conflict between us.

After Leo and I divorced, I'd vowed never to file for an annulment with Leo. But two years later, Leo did, and now my second marriage had been annulled. When I filled out the paperwork, I emphasized that I had married

Leo Trembley for life. There had been no invalidating elements from my side of the aisle when we exchanged our wedding vows.

All seven of us filed into Mass. We took up temporary residence on seven plastic chairs back up against the wall in the last row. Here bleating kids, squirming like angleworms, would cause less of a disturbance. Joe and Leah bookended our family pod. Hannah and Jonah sat between Leah and me. Joe and I corralled Abby and Noah between us.

Leah's buttressing presence was a great help to me. But she disliked being so much older than her other four siblings and having to help out. She had loved her seven years as an only child. Already five inches taller than me, Leah could easily pass as half-a-dozen years older due to her curvy figure and disarmingly beautiful face—all of which generated a whole host of other problems. She was no wiser or emotionally mature than her fifteen years.

Once settled in place, Leah grabbed my arm while pointing at Joe's feet. "Mom, look!" she mouthed, wide-eyed. Her body shook from suppressed laughter.

Joe's plaid pajama bottoms hung outside his navy-blue dress slacks by an inch onto the top of his shoes, one black penny loafer and one brown slip-on.

Leah's animation pivoted Hannah's and Jonah's attention to Joe. They giggled aloud as they spied Joe's fashion faux pas. Joe donned his disciplinarian's face and brought his index finger to his puckered lips to shush the kids. He had no idea that he was the object of the children's laughter.

I reached over and gently touched his arm. Once his eyes met mine, I pointed out his eclectic ensemble. I moved over next to him and whispered, "Joe, it's fine. No one will notice your shoes. Just fold your pajamas up into your pants."

A flush crept across Joe's narrow face. He leaned over to fold the hem of his pajama bottoms up and under his slacks. His hands shook as they often did when he was excited or embarrassed. Joe was overly sensitive about those kinds of goofs. Today was my fault as I hadn't made the time to check Joe over before we left for Mass.

The congregation stood as the priest processed down the aisle flanked by two altar boys. With perfect timing, the acoustic guitars and voices of the folk choir drowned out the remaining commotion emanating from the white plastic chairs pressed against the wall at the back of the church.

Joe picked up a wiggling Noah so that he could see. I gathered Abby into my arms. I whispered to Jonah and Hannah, "Behave, and we'll go for ice cream after Mass. No more laughing." I mouthed to Leah, "Enough," and gave her my best evil eye.

During Mass, Aunt Alice and her connection to Auntie Sister occupied my thoughts. Although Auntie Sister was still alive, she had developed dementia. Her mental decline had begun with a vengeance after a severe hip fracture two years ago. She now lived in a retirement facility operated by the Sisters of St. Joseph of Carondelet in Los Angeles. By the middle of the homily, I'd hatched a plan.

"Yes!" I exclaimed aloud as if passionately affirming the pastor's sermon. Joe, the kids, and half of the row seated in front of my family looked at me curiously. Leah eyed me quizzically with one raised eyebrow.

Auntie Sister and Alice Maher had remained in close contact over the years. In Auntie Sister's personal effects, she had to have an address book just collecting dust. The "M" section contained the key to my search. Executing my plan would take equal parts luck and audacity.

JOE'S HOUSE WAS DELICIOUSLY quiet. I turned away from the visual pollution of the family room and dialed the phone number for the Carondelet Retirement Facility.

A woman picked up on the first ring. I explained that my aunt was being cared for at the facility and had dementia.

"Can you connect me to the administrator?" I asked.

"Let me see if see Sister Mary Margaret is available. Who may I say is calling?"

"Elizabeth Schmidt, the niece of Sister Marie Theresa Swan."

After a couple of minutes, a cheerful, business-like female voice came on the line.

"Good afternoon, Elizabeth. This is Sister Mary Margaret. How may I help you?"

"Thank you for taking my call, Sister. I'm calling regarding my aunt, Sister

Marie Theresa." I jotted the name Sister Mary Margaret in my notebook.

"Of course. While I have you on the line, let's make sure your aunt's next of kin data sheet is current."

Mom was Auntie Sister's only living sibling. I was delighted to learn that I was the alternate contact for my mother. That would make my request easier.

"I don't recall meeting you, Elizabeth. Have you visited Sister Marie Theresa previously at our facility?"

"No, Sister. The last time I saw my aunt was two years ago before she broke her hip. How is she doing?"

"Her hip healed well enough, but her mental decline has accelerated. She doesn't care much about eating these days. However, most of the time, your aunt still has a pleasant disposition, which is a blessing."

"It's such an awful disease. My aunt had a sharp mind; it's hard to imagine her with dementia. I don't want to take too much of your time, but I have another reason for calling. Sister Marie Theresa taught with a woman named Alice Maher for several years. They kept up with each other for more than three decades. I'm sure Alice would want to know about my aunt's condition. Unfortunately, I don't have Alice's contact info. My aunt always kept an address book. Could someone there retrieve the last address for Alice Maher in Sister Marie Theresa's address book?"

I left my request bare-boned without the savory flesh that motivated my scavenger hunt. Any additional details ran the risk of muddying the waters of cooperation should Sister Mary Margaret have any desire to help me.

"Let me see what I can do, Elizabeth."

Sister Mary Margaret suggested calling her back in a week if I did not hear from her first.

As long as I was home, I phoned Klose Investigations again. Buoyed by the giant step forward on the address book, I left another short message for the answering machine:

"Hi, Kait. Elizabeth Schmidt here. Just checking back in. I look forward to hearing from you soon." Click.

JOE AND I HAD just finished a dinner of chicken-broccoli pasta with lemon butter sauce when the phone rang.

Noah and Abby were trying to outdo one another by eating "trees," Noah's name for broccoli. The mature palates of those two tykes amazed me. Since Leo had the older children every Wednesday night, they were likely eating a cold cereal and ice cream dinner. I'd never win a parent popularity contest against Leo.

When I picked up the ringing phone, it was Kait Klosen. I could not have arranged a more perfect night: no homework to oversee, only two baths to give, and no teenage drama.

"This is Kait Klosen returning your calls," said a commanding alto voice.

"Thank you so much for calling me back. I've made a pest of myself, leaving you multiple messages. Take it as a compliment," I said.

Kait chuckled. "So, you are trying to find your aunt?"

"Yes, but she is my birth aunt, and I've never actually met her. However, she knows all about me and wrote me several years ago. I never received that letter because my adoptive mother destroyed it."

"Sounds like an intriguing story."

"I read the *People* magazine article from last fall about you helping a doctor named Sharon find her birth parents."

Kait laughed, "That article has spawned some interesting jobs."

"I bet it has. My situation is different than Sharon's in the article. My birth mother is dead. I'm simply trying to contact the birth aunt who wrote me the letter. She lived in California at one time. I don't have an address for her, and I only have her maiden name."

"Before we get too far, you should know how I charge for my time—fifty dollars per hour. For any leg work, you'd be paying for my travel time, airfare, and car rentals. It can get pretty spendy."

"Could you see how far five-hundred dollars takes you towards finding my birth aunt? When you get close to spending that amount, we can decide if continuing makes sense. How does that sound?"

"Sounds reasonable. I've got a whole lot on my plate at the moment. But I'd like to help you out. I'm adopted like you, although I've never had the faintest interest in finding my birth parents. I was adopted as an infant and had a fairy tale childhood."

"I'm envious, Kait. Ever since I can remember, I've wanted to know my birth story and why my mother gave me up for adoption. When I heard about the letter Mom destroyed, I was ... devastated." I swallowed the lump in my throat.

"Alice Maher was my birth aunt's maiden name. I don't know if she ever married, but she did live in Southern California for a part of her life. She taught at a Catholic school with Sister Marie Theresa Swan for several years. Perhaps in Oxnard, perhaps in Anaheim. I'm unsure about all the places Sister Marie Theresa taught. It never seemed to matter when I was growing up. It was just Southern California.

"Alice and my adoptive aunt, Sister Marie Theresa Swan, had maintained contact for decades. Sister Marie Theresa now has dementia and can't help me with my search."

I said nothing about the scavenger hunt for Auntie Sister's address book, but I did share my birth mother's name and a range for Alice's age based on my guess for Liddy's age.

"Can you do anything with just a first and last name and that my aunt lived and worked in California at one time?"

"Using your aunt's maiden name, I can search public records for real estate transactions, death and marriage records, lawsuits, and civil judgments in California. There is no guarantee that anything will show up, especially if Alice never owned property."

"I know there's no guarantee of anything. But I have to try," I said.

"And, Elizabeth, rest assured I get all messages on my answering machine," she chuckled again. "In my line of work, you're not likely to catch me in the office. I'll update you on my progress in about two weeks."

We said our goodbyes. I circled the last Wednesday in February in red ink on the calendar thumbtacked to the wall by the phone.

Serendipity

NEARLY A WEEK HAD passed since Sister Margaret Mary had offered to look for Auntie Sister's address book. Though I understood that the fire of impatience burning within me didn't constitute an emergency for anyone else, it still didn't lessen the intensity of my impatience.

I willed myself to patiently wait for Sister Margaret Mary to call amidst a familiar sense of unsettledness. Did I think that my life would change should Aunt Alice be found? I found myself wishing my life was somehow more exciting. More interesting. More something. More anything.

What was my problem? My thoughts, unfortunately, wandered to Leo. There had been no shortfall of excitement when I'd been with Leo. To squelch any pang of affection, I enlisted my usual defenses. I told myself that Leo was a jerk and that he had never really loved me. I stoked whatever unpleasantness I could towards him.

Like a dog shaking off water after a swim in a murky pond, I abandoned thoughts of Leo. I shut down my computer, straightened my desk, and gathered up my things. Joe would be in the parking lot, ready to head home. I relaxed into the anticipated ease of an evening with only the two youngest children and Joe.

As I headed out the door, my office phone rang. In case Joe was running late, I decided to answer. To my delight, it was Sister Margaret Mary with an update on Auntie Sister's address book. I sat back down at my desk, suddenly in no hurry to leave.

"Well, I have good and bad news," Sister said. "I was able to find an address book among Sister Marie Theresa's things. It's quite old, and some sections had fallen out from the stitched binding. I found all the missing sections in the box except for the one chunk, which unfortunately included the M section."

Worst luck. I could hardly believe my ears.

"There are two other small boxes that I haven't had time to go through yet. Just lifting the lids for a quick look, one box contains loose photographs and photo albums, and another has craft items: yarn, knitting needles, crochet hooks, and the like."

"I appreciate what you've done so far, Sister. Could I pay someone there to go through the other two boxes of items?"

"No need to pay anyone. The next time I'm in that wing, I will take another look. Give me another week."

After we hung up, I sat at my desk, stunned. How bizarre that Auntie Sister's address book was missing the very section that I needed!

KAIT KLOSEN SURPRISED ME by answering her office phone at eight o'clock Thursday night. Sister Margaret Mary had called me earlier that day with the fantastic news that she'd found the missing section of Auntie Sister's address book. It was at the very bottom of the small box containing the photographs. I gave Kait the San Diego address for Alice Maher that Sister Margaret Mary had provided and she brought me up to speed on her research.

She'd found no trace of Alice Maher in any of the public records for the state of California. Alice Maher didn't show up on any property transactions or legal proceedings. But she didn't show up in any death records for the last ten years either, and I took that as good news.

Once Kait had a physical address, she could do two things that I couldn't. She could look up who owned the property and find any phone numbers associated with the physical address. She promised to get back to me when she had something significant.

A week later, I won the birth-aunt lottery.

"Elizabeth, I think I've found Alice Maher." I heard the excitement in Kait's voice.

"You're kidding me. Fantastic! How?"

"I flew to San Diego for another job. I had a two-hour break, so on a whim, I decided to drive to the address you gave me last week for your aunt. I knocked on the door, and a middle-aged woman answered the door.

"I said that I was looking for Alice Maher for her niece and that this was the only address we had. I learned that the house had been used as a temporary residence for single women discerning vocations to the religious life in the 40s and 50s. The house is now a permanent rental residence for single Catholic women.

"Alice Maher had lived there at some point. I'm not sure when but it doesn't matter. The important thing is that Alice has remained in contact with another woman who still lives there. That woman received a Christmas card last December from Alice. I have the return address from the envelope of that card."

"Oh my gosh. That's amazing."

"With that address, I could link it to the phone number for an Alice Maher and an apartment in Arcadia, California. I've not called that number. I'll leave that to you, Elizabeth."

"That's fantastic!" Amazed by the fortunate stroke of serendipity, I reflected on how the pieces of my search had fallen in place.

I wrote Alice's information in my notebook as Kait relayed it. Kait said to let her know if I needed anything else. Otherwise, she would send me an invoice for around two hundred dollars.

Once we got off the phone, I found Arcadia's location on a map of California. Arcadia was in Los Angeles County in the San Gabriel Valley. Pomona, my birthplace, was about twenty miles southeast of Acadia. The city, county, and state of birth are never changed, even in the altered birth certificate of an adoptee. I felt confident that I had my aunt Alice's contact information.

As the freezing mid-February wind blew bits of frozen rain against my kitchen window, the warmth of hope spread through my body. It had taken less than four weeks to find Alice Maher. I would soon have answers.

TO KEEP NOAH AND Abby out of the bedroom, I closed the door and locked it behind me. I sat on the side of the bed, placed my open notebook on the end table, and dialed Alice's phone number. "Breathe, remember to breathe," I told myself as the phone rang.

"Hello?" a soft, slightly shaky female voice greeted me.

"Hello. Is this Alice Maher?"

"Yes, it is."

"This is Elizabeth Ann Schmidt. I am trying to reach Alice Maher, the sister of Liddy Maher. Liddy Maher is my birth mother."

"Oh, Elizabeth, how wonderful to hear your voice after all these years! Yes, I am your aunt Alice."

My muscles relaxed, and my eyes closed. I fell back into the softness of the bed while clasping the receiver to my ear, reveling in the moment. The warmth of my aunt's voice was palpable. Her words nourished the child within me, starved for connection.

"You can't imagine what it means to me to hear your voice, Aunt Alice. Is this an okay time to talk with you? If not, um, I can call back on a different evening or this weekend, if you prefer."

"This is just fine. I am retired now, so my days are much easier. I volunteer part-time at Holy Angels School, supervising the children during their lunch-time recess. Somedays, I help out with remedial reading after recess. How is your aunt, Sister Marie Theresa? I've lost contact with her. Is she still alive?"

"I haven't seen her in a while since she can't come to visit anymore. She has Alzheimer's disease now. She broke her hip several years back, and after that, her mental faculties rapidly deteriorated."

"Oh, I am so sorry to hear that. I will pray for her."

"Alice, do you remember the letter you wrote me about three years ago?"

"Yes, I gave it to Sister Marie Theresa to hand-deliver to you."

"Right, but I never received that letter. My mother, Marie, only recently told me about your letter. Sister Marie Theresa and Mom decided that it was best not to share your letter with me." I said, wanting to minimize the impact of Auntie Sister's and Mom's actions. "I'd have been delighted to receive your letter. Since I found out about the letter, I've been trying to find you."

"Oh, Elizabeth, don't worry one little bit about that letter. I left it up to Sister Marie Theresa and your mother's discretion whether they gave it to you. Sister Marie Theresa had contacted me asking about cancer in our family several months before I wrote that letter. In that letter, I reassured you of my continued prayers. Are you okay, Elizabeth?"

"Yes, I'm ... fine."

I couldn't make sense of Aunt Alice's question until I remembered my health scare when three months pregnant with my youngest child. A meager medical history had surfaced overnight as I had awaited biopsy results for what turned out to be a benign growth in my neck.

My relief had eclipsed my curiosity, and I'd never pressed Mom for her information source. I now realized it must have been Aunt Alice by way of Auntie Sister. Things started making sense; that was why Alice had written the letter.

"You named him Noah, right?" I was astonished that Alice knew his name.

"Yes, he's just turned three."

"You have five children, now. Yes?"

"I do, five, three girls and two boys with a fourteen-year age spread among them." I hoped that Auntie Sister hadn't kept Alice up to date on my multiple marriages.

"Your aunt, Sister Marie Theresa, and I taught in the same school when Liddy became pregnant, which is how you came to be adopted by the Schmidt family. Liddy wanted to make sure that a good Catholic family adopted you. Over the years, Sister Marie Theresa and I remained in touch, she showed me pictures of you, and I heard about all your accomplishments.

"Liddy had just turned twenty when she had you. Liddy and your father didn't marry, so Liddy gave you up for adoption. I remember meeting your father. He was tall, very handsome, and had such a distinctive voice. And your mother, Liddy, was and is still a beautiful woman."

"Wait, you mean my mother, Liddy, is still alive?" Flabbergasted, I struggled to integrate the raw joy of my birth mother's resurrection from the dead with the virtual sainthoods of my mother and Auntie Sister. Either Mom had lied to me, or Auntie Sister had lied to my mother.

"My dear Elizabeth, Liddy is very much alive. She lives in the greater San Diego area with her husband. Liddy had two other children after you: Lily, who is about four years younger than you, and Martin, two years after Lily. Sadly, Martin died about two years ago in a head-on collision with a drunk driver. His death just devastated Liddy. She still struggles with it."

I couldn't move beyond Liddy being alive to ask about my half-sister or deceased half-brother. "Honestly, I had no idea that Liddy was still alive when I called you. For some reason, my mother Marie thought she was dead." With a gush of emotion, I blurted out, "Can you put me in contact with Liddy?"

"Um, er, oh my goodness. I'm not sure. I'll have to pray about it." She sounded utterly flummoxed by my request. "Liddy knows nothing of my interactions with Sister Marie Theresa over the years. I promised Sister that I would never share any information about you with Liddy."

There it was, Auntie Sister had been the gatekeeper. And now, she was locked away in a solitary world of dementia for which no key existed. A thirty-five-year promise locked the door between my birth mother and me.

I waited for Alice to speak to no avail and, finally, interjected, "Would it be okay if I called or wrote to you in the future, Aunt Alice?"

"I gave no promise regarding our communications, so that would be lovely. But I must pray regarding your contact with Liddy. Given her continued grief over Martin's death, contact with you could be healing for her. I must pray for a sign. You'll have to be patient with me."

I heard myself say, "I understand your predicament, and yes, I'll be patient," but inside, I was screaming, *Can't Liddy decide for herself?*

Cordially, I ended the phone call before my frustration registered in my voice. I had no input into the rules for this game of hide-and-seek.

"Thank you so much for talking to me tonight. You have given me so much hope. We'll speak again soon."

"Goodbye, and God bless you, Elizabeth."

"You, too, Aunt Alice. Take care."

When I walked into the kitchen, Joe had his back to me, loading the dinner dishes into the dishwasher. He turned at the sound of my footsteps to ask, "So, how'd it go?" When he turned towards me, he saw my red face. "Oh no, did it go badly?"

"Not bad, just shocking and ... frustrating. Liddy Maher's not dead!" My voice faltered at the weight of this new development. "She's fifty-five years old and lives near San Diego. Ellen Balondis was right when she insisted that my birth mother was probably still alive. And remember what Mom said about that brother, born shortly after me, the one she'd insisted should have been her adopted son? Well, he never existed. At some point, Liddy married and had another daughter and then a son."

"I'm not surprised that Marie lied to you," Joe said critically.

Always defending Mom, I barked at Joe, "Don't be so hard on her, Joe. Auntie Sister seems to be the gatekeeper, and I suspect Mom only knew what Auntie Sister told her. And get this: Auntie Sister told Alice all kinds of things about me my whole life."

"So, did Alice give you Liddy's contact information?"

"No, that's the frustrating part. Alice has to get a sign from God to ask Liddy if she wants contact with me. Alice made some promise to Auntie Sister to never share any information with Liddy about me."

"Did you tell Alice that Auntie Sister had Alzheimer's?"

"Yes, but that's not the issue. It's a God thing. Like a vow or something."

"This is nuts. Alice should let Liddy decide if she wants to be in contact with you."

"I know. If only Alice were comfortable doing that. She must be super religious."

"You could try to find Liddy like you did Alice."

"Right, except that I don't know Liddy's married name. In Liddy's generation, women didn't keep their maiden names. All I know is some Liddy lives in the greater San Diego area. Alice is no dummy. During our conversation, Alice revealed nothing to help me find my birth mother."

"What happens now? Do you wait for God to send Alice a miracle?" Joe said sarcastically while raising an eyebrow.

"Yes and no. I'll write Alice every single solitary week until God sends his divine sign. My request will be foremost in her thoughts."

Once Abby and Noah were bathed and had fallen asleep in their beds, I sat at the kitchen counter, rifling through my box of cards and stationery. I sought the perfect instrument to carry my first written words to Aunt Alice. I settled on a notecard printed with a colored lithograph of purple violets by a Dutch artist circa 1800.

Tuesday, Feb 16, 1988

Dear Aunt Alice,

Thank you again for your warm and welcoming conversation with me tonight. It is hard to express what it meant for me to hear your voice.

Calling you was an easy decision for me, given that I believed my birth mother, Liddy, was dead. I do not mean to cause hardship or trouble for you or Liddy.

Please know, however, that the greatest desire of my heart is to know Liddy. I have never been able to shake the hunger to know her. I pray that God will give you the peace and guidance you seek.

Your niece,

Elizabeth Schmidt

I placed another weekly correspondence in the mail for Aunt Alice on March 14th. "And off you go, number four," I groaned. It took me forever to write each note. I tried to make my perfectly boring life sound exciting as if that would convince Alice to reach out to Liddy. I said little about Mom, except she was a great blessing to have nearby.

Beyond those topics, I asked Alice questions about her family of origin, whether she and Liddy had other siblings, where they had grown up, and about her parents. Each letter ended in the same way, hoping that she would have peace and put me in contact with Liddy.

I never received any written reply. I hadn't called Alice back since the first time we spoke. My weekly letters seemed sufficient goading.

ON WEDNESDAY, MARCH 16TH, the phone rang just as I got dinner on the table. I wiped my hands on my apron before answering. After my initial hello, I planned to tell the caller that we were sitting down to dinner and to please call back in a half-hour.

"Hello, Elizabeth. This is Aunt Alice."

"How wonderful to hear from you. Hang on. I want to take the call in another room."

I walked over to Joe with my hand over the receiver. He was busy seating Abby and Noah in their booster seats for dinner.

"It's Alice. I want to take the call in the bedroom. Will you hang up once

I pick up? Just eat without me. I'm not sure how long this call will take."

I hurried down the hallway with my trusty notebook and into the bedroom.

"What a nice surprise, Aunt Alice!" I heard the click as Joe hung up. "How are you?"

"I'm just fine. I've enjoyed hearing from you and about my great-nieces and great-nephews in your letters. I'm sorry that I haven't answered any of them. But if you have time, I can answer some of your questions tonight."

"Yes, I have time. Do you want me to call you back, so you don't have to pay for this call? I don't want you to feel rushed."

"No, no, it's fine. Don't worry. I owe you several letters worth of answers to your questions." And so, she began the story of the three Maher sisters. As she spoke, I jotted down the details in my notebook, balancing the receiver between my ear and shoulder and scribbling as fast as possible.

"The three of us were born to Irish Catholic parents in White Plains, New York. I'm two years older than Maura, who is two years older than Liddy. By the time Liddy was born, our mother was already sick, and when Liddy was two, the doctors admitted Momma to a mental hospital. At twenty-eight years old, she was diagnosed with premature dementia. Later, the doctors refined her diagnosis to schizophrenia. I'm the only one who has memories of Momma.

"The three of us were farmed out to live with two of Momma's older sisters for the next six years. Maura and I lived with Aunt Bridget, and Liddy lived with Aunt Genevieve. Daddy moved to California when he finally gave up on Momma ever getting better.

"When I was twelve, we all rode the train cross-country to California and moved in with Daddy in La Jolla. It was the first time we'd all lived under the same roof since Momma had been committed. Liddy was still living with Daddy in La Jolla when she became pregnant with you."

As Alice paused, I snuck in a question, "What were your parents' names?"

"Momma's name was Rose Conception. She was an O'Brian before she married your grandfather, Ciaran Patrick Maher. Outside of County Tipperary, where Daddy's people are from, there aren't many men named Ciaran. Everyone called Daddy Pat."

I wanted to know more about my grandmother's illness. "Did Rose ever get well and rejoin the family?"

"No, she never left the mental hospital, although she was moved into a regular nursing home once her breast cancer became terminal. Momma died at age seventy-nine, less than four years ago. Daddy died of a heart attack at age fifty-three, too young, and twenty-seven years before Momma."

The idea of my grandmother, Rose, spending almost fifty years in a mental institution was horrific. It was sad that both Liddy and my adoptive mother, Marie, were bereft of their mothers.

"Maura, Liddy, and I flew back to attend Momma's funeral. They had a beautiful requiem Mass for her. I remember lying down in my hotel room after the funeral and praying a Rosary for the repose of Momma's soul and being inundated by the scent of violets. I knew then that Momma was with the Lord and that Mother Mary had sent me a message. Did you know St. Bernard called the Blessed Mother the Violet of Humility?"

"You know much more about those things than I do, Aunt Alice. But it's a lovely story."

Aunt Alice was making me feel a bit uncomfortable with her brand of "over-brewed" Catholicism. I gently tried to steer the conversations to Liddy and me.

"Have you thought any more about letting Liddy know that I've found you?"

"Yes, and that's the main reason I called tonight."

My chest tightened at her words.

"As you know, I have good reasons for not putting you in contact with Liddy, but other reasons make it seem like a wonderful thing. I asked God for a sign, and I believe that He has sent me one. Martin may be interceding for you and Liddy to be reunited."

"Martin, my half-brother. Really? What happened?"

"Well, it is a couple of things that I have no earthly explanation for and that, when taken together, are convincing evidence of his direct intervention."

"Can you share what happened? I'm all ears. My husband has the kids under control. I've got all night."

"It won't take that long," she said. "On each side of my kitchen sink, I have some hanging shelves where I've placed statues of Jesus, Mary, and Joseph, and St. Thérèse of Lisieux. My middle name is Thérèse, so I have a great devotion to the Little Flower.

"I have a picture of Martin up there with my statues to remind me to pray daily for the repose of your brother's soul. The snapshot isn't in a frame; I have it propped up against the back of the shelf.

"A few days after we first spoke, I found Martin's photo laying face up on the counter adjacent to the sink just below the shelving. I thought that the picture had fluttered off the shelf from my walking by.

"But the same thing happened several more times over the last few weeks. Oddly, the photo always landed face-up. The weather hasn't been warm enough for me to open the kitchen window, so it's not as if a gust of wind blew it down. Martin's been dead for two years now, and I've had Martin's picture in the same place since before he died. This snapshot showing up on the counter has never happened before, even when I've had the window open during warm weather."

I thought that a snapshot landing face-up on the counter was awfully weak evidence for spiritual intervention. But if it helped move Alice forward to connect Liddy and me, I was happy to concur with her analysis.

"Well, I guess that must have seemed unusual, always landing face-up," I said, sounding as convinced as possible.

"But that is not all. Then the most unusual thing happened on Monday at the school where I volunteer. While watching the children at lunch recess, a small boy walked up to me with an armful of long-stemmed pink roses. The Little Flower said she'd let a shower of roses fall to earth once she got to heaven. I'm very devoted to the Little Flower, you know."

"Yes, you mentioned that before." I rolled my eyes and shook my head. How many diversions would Alice take before she arrived at her point?

"Anyway, I recognize most of the children at the school because I've been helping out since the beginning of the school year. But I'd never seen this little one before. I said, 'Oh, what lovely roses!' He held out the roses towards me, saying, 'These are for you.' I couldn't believe it! No one had ever given me a gorgeous bouquet of roses. I've never had a beau or dated, you know. And there wasn't a single thorn on them."

Aunt Alice, you're killing me here! Was she going to connect me with Liddy or not?

"Then I said to the boy, 'I've not seen you before. What's your name?' He answered, 'Martin.' Just then, another volunteer, who also monitors the playground, called out for me. She wanted to know if I needed a ride home; she sometimes gives me rides because I don't have a car. I looked away from Martin in her direction, waved with my free arm, and answered, 'Yes.' When I turned back to little Martin, he was gone. But not the roses; they were still in my arm. I have them in a vase at home now. Unlike the roses you get at the florist shop, these roses smell so sweet."

"What do you mean, he was gone?"

"I couldn't see hide nor hair of him. He had vanished. When my friend drove me home, she inquired about my gorgeous roses. I told her about the little boy named Martin and asked her if she'd ever seen him before. She said she never saw anyone with me, only the roses, when she had called out to me."

"What did Martin look like?" I asked.

"Everything happened so quickly. I can't remember much except that Martin was young, maybe six or seven years old. A beautiful little boy. His eyes had a brightness about them, and his face had a kind of perfect balance. I don't remember much more than that; I was rather captivated by the roses."

I didn't know how Aunt Alice's story could get more bizarre. But it had caused the hair on the back of my neck to stand at attention. I wondered if she was mentally stable.

"So, I prayed all the more ardently to know if the flowers from little Martin meant I was free from my promise to Sister Marie Theresa and that I could let Liddy know about you.

"When I woke up Tuesday morning, I felt a lightness in my heart, a peaceful release from my previous ambivalence. That's when I knew the Lord had released me from my promise to Sister Marie Theresa.

"I called Liddy last night to tell her that you had contacted me. I asked her if she would like to be in contact with you. She didn't hesitate for a second and replied, 'Absolutely. Yes!'"

When Alice said that Liddy would be expecting my call at 7 p.m. tomorrow, I thought my heart would explode from joy into a million pieces.

I wrote my birth mother's phone number in my notebook and circled it with a heart. The blue lines of the paper blurred into one another as tears coursed down my cheeks.

Finally, my yearning to know, see, and smell my birth mother could be satisfied. Liddy's "Absolutely. Yes!" reverberated within an empty recess in my heart that only she could fill. I loved her already.

Shamrocks

MARCH 1988

LYING IN BED FOR a few extra minutes, I listened to the sound of running water from Joe's morning shower. After last night's conversation with Alice, the resultant gush of adrenalin had kept me awake until the wee hours of the morning. But tired or not, today promised to be an unforgettable St. Patrick's Day; I would hear my birth mother's voice for the first time.

It was fitting that the missing pieces of my search came together on this particular day. Mom had been right about one thing. I was indeed Irish. I'd long celebrated March 17th with something akin to religious fervor. The breath of my mother's words, "You're Irish, Black Irish," had been the wind catching my sails and pointing me to St. Patrick's Day since my childhood.

Once showered and dressed for the workday, I double-checked the setting on the crockpot loaded with fixings for tonight's special meal: corned beef brisket, cabbage, onions, carrots, and potatoes. I pulled the shamrock-shaped sugar cookies and the Irish soda bread out of the freezer to thaw for dinner. Baked on the previous Sunday, my planning-things-to-a-gnat's-eyelash would work double-time in my favor tonight.

Joe and I left the house with Abby and Noah still in their jammies fifteen minutes later than usual. That allowed Leo time to drop off the three older kids and depart before we arrived.

When we walked into Mom's house, Jonah and Hannah had already dressed for school. They sat at the counter, finishing up their bowls of cereal and orange juice. Leah sat in the adjacent family room, parked in front of Mom's television, which filled the air with mindless chatter of morning talk show hosts.

Setting Abby and Noah's clothes bag down, I retrieved the three shamrocks that I'd made last night from the front pocket. I fastened a shiny, green-foil shamrock on Jonah's red and white striped t-shirt and onto the collar of Hannah's blue dress. In my best Irish brogue, I recited this year's silly ditty:

Don't be pinchin' yer little friends,
If they not be wearin' the green.
We'll both get sent to the principal's office,
For being unkind and mean.

Jonah looked straight at me and, with a mischievous grin, announced, "I'm gonna pinch somebody not wearing green, so you have to go to the principal's office."

Hannah wrapped her arms protectively around my legs and said to Jonah, "Don't you dare send Momma to the principal's office."

I squatted down to return Hannah's hug properly and said, "I think Jonah is just teasing Momma." Although, with Jonah's quirky sense of humor, I never quite knew what was percolating in his precocious little brain.

I handed Leah her shamrock, knowing she'd outgrown such homespun traditions. When she rolled her eyes, I pretended not to notice. At least she didn't ruin the moment for Hannah and Jonah, who still felt special wearing their little shamrocks when their classmates weren't lucky enough to wear them.

"Come straight home after track practice, Leah," I said. "We have a big dinner tonight."

"Not corned beef and cabbage again?" she whined.

"Yes, your favorite," I said, missing the sweetness of the pre-puberty Leah and winking at her.

The kids knew nothing of my searching over the last several months, first for their great-aunt, Alice, or my subsequent efforts to connect with their birth grandmother, Liddy. Leah was certainly old enough to keep a secret, and I planned to tell her at some point. I just wasn't sure when. Jonah or Hannah would inadvertently tell Grandma Marie about their "new" Grandma Liddy in their naivete. Time would have to iron out the details.

Joe wasn't keen on my new expanded family. He classified my new relatives as "complications that you don't need, Liz," which I translated to complications that he, Joe, didn't want. Nevertheless, I was bursting at the seams to share my thrilling news with someone. And the person I most wanted to share my happiness with was my mother, Marie. My joy doubled when I shared the good news with Mom. But in this case, she was the last person I could tell about Liddy.

I'd probably never know whether Mom honestly thought my birth mother was dead. But I was pretty sure she wasn't ready to hear that I'd found Liddy. Alive.

By 6:45 p.m., the seven of us had finished our St. Patrick's Day dinner, and I'd loaded the dishes into the dishwasher. Leah was in her room, supposedly doing her homework. Joe sat on the couch with the other kids preparing to watch a movie, a treat on a school night. The phone rang as I loaded the "Princess Bride" into the VCR.

Wasn't I the one that was supposed to call Liddy? Aunt Alice must have got it wrong. I ran to the master bedroom to close the door.

"Hello. Liddy ...?"

"Hi, Lizzie. It's me, Jeannie. Who's Liddy?"

Holy crap! What horrible timing my sister had!

"... er, my birth mother. Tonight, I'm going to speak to her for the first time. At seven, which is why I can't talk now."

"What? How come you never told me you found your birth mom?"

"It's way too complicated to explain in the next few minutes. I just got her phone number last night. Can we talk tomorrow? Is everything okay?"

"Things could be better, that's for sure. Trav and I are between jobs. Rent is due, and with Dex and Mia, and, well, money is tight."

Jeannie's life was either feast or famine, mostly famine. She was the lead singer in the same band as her husband, Travis. Jeannie was a natural entertainer and had the musical gifts, looks, and moves to sizzle when on stage. As much as I shunned the limelight, she glittered like gold under the lights.

Six-year-old Dex was the spitting image of Jeannie's first husband. Mia, Travis's child, was just one year old, a little blonde dumpling who shared Jeannie's giant chocolate eyes. The last time I'd seen Jeannie was at her wedding to Travis six months back.

"I promise I'll call you back tomorrow night. Got to go now; it's almost seven. Wish me luck."

"I can't wait to hear about it! Don't forget! Call me tomorrow. I really need to talk to you. I love you, Lizzie."

"Love you, too. Bye."

Would I always be my sister's keeper? Could I ever hear from my sister without the fear of having to bail her out of some financial pickle?

I looked at the clock on my bedside table. It was almost time. My heart raced as I gulped down the half glass of water on my bedside table remaining from last night. A few minutes later, I dialed Liddy's phone number.

"Hello?" A woman's voice answered on the first ring.

"Liddy?"

"Yes. Elizabeth?"

"Yes, it's me." Every fiber of my being danced in jubilation.

"My husband, Andy, is on the phone line downstairs. Is that okay with you? Just for the first part of our call."

"Of course, whatever makes you most comfortable. I'm just happy you're willing to talk with me!"

"Willing to talk with you? It is like a dream come true for me, Elizabeth."

Although I'd never imagined the sound of my birth mother's voice, I felt drawn to Liddy's lyrical, clear voice. She would sing alto, like me, or possibly second soprano. I delighted in the timbre of it.

"It's a wonderful thing that you have done, finding your mother. Liddy and I are delighted to welcome you to the family," a male voice interjected.

"When I found Alice, I didn't consider whether I'd be an intrusion in your life. My mother, Marie, told me that you were dead. I mean, I'm thrilled you're not dead! But I imagine giving up a child for adoption and then having her suddenly show up as an adult ... that could be very disruptive for some families."

"Don't worry, Andy already knew about you, and my daughter, Lily, has known since she was a teenager. Martin ... my son," Liddy's voice cracked, "He never knew unless Lily told him. Martin would have been twenty-eight if he was still alive.

"Alice shared little with me except that you wanted to be in contact. I don't even know how you found her. She didn't go into all that when she called me Tuesday night. Or if she did, I don't remember. I was so excited. I didn't sleep much last night. Forgive me if I rattle on or don't make sense."

"That makes two of us," I said, reflecting on how my mother, Marie, had always called me a high-strung racehorse. Perhaps that came from Liddy.

"You had the best of prenatal care. Once I found out that I was pregnant with you, I quit smoking until your birth. I lived with the doctor that delivered you, Chuck Fester, and his wife, Norma. I helped them out with childcare and—"

"—Liddy, I'm going to hang up, so you and Elizabeth can talk privately," Andy interrupted.

Once Andy was off the phone, Liddy paused for a few moments and then continued in a soft voice.

"I didn't want to say this when Andy was on the phone; he gets so upset when I talk about your father. I didn't want to give you up for adoption. But when your father called off our wedding two weeks beforehand, I was already pregnant. I'd no other choice but to go away to have you and put you up for adoption.

"Back then, children conceived out of wedlock were shunned if their unmarried mothers kept them. As a young girl, I walked past a house where a little girl, born out of wedlock, had lived with her mother. My father told me never to speak to that little girl as if she were a leper. I couldn't bear people treating my child like that. My father made it clear that keeping you was not an option once your father called off the wedding.

"Once I delivered you, the nurses swept you away before I could see you or hold you. Norma, the woman I lived with, worked as a nurse in the nursery. She snuck you into my room briefly before they discharged me. I just couldn't give you up without looking at you. You peered right into my eyes. I'll never forget that moment. You were such a beautiful baby."

Tears streamed down my cheeks as Liddy spoke. I remembered looking into the eyes of Leah and Jonah and Hannah and Abby and Noah shortly after each was born, that rush of love still palpable as if I was in the moment. I couldn't fathom giving a child up for adoption.

"So, you didn't live in Pomona? My birth certificate says that I was born in Pomona General Hospital."

"You were born there because that's where Dr. Fester and his family lived.

But I've lived in the San Diego area since I was eight years old except for when I was pregnant with you."

"I've never heard the name Liddy before. Is that an Irish nickname for Lydia?"

Liddy laughed softly, "No, my Aunt Genevieve nicknamed me Liddy when I lived with her after Momma got sick. It's a nickname that just stuck. My first name is Elizabeth, just like yours. I was so pleased when Alice told me that your adoptive parents had given you my first name. My middle name is Rose, like my mother's first name."

Mom had told me that Granny Schmidt had named me. Now I wondered if my first name was a loving tribute from my mother, Marie, to Liddy and had nothing to do with Granny.

"I've never gone by the name Elizabeth. My friends call me Liz, and my mother ... my adoptive mother, Marie, still calls me Lizzie."

"Shall I call you Liz, then and leave Lizzie as the special name that your mother, Marie, uses?"

"Liz would be perfect. My Dad called me Liz sometimes; he's been dead for seven years. I'm desperate to know what you look like, Liddy. Can you send me some pictures? I'm very visual."

"But of course. I have to have pictures of you. I'm very visual, too. You had such a head of black hair when you were born. Is it still dark?"

"Yes, most people say my hair is black, but there's almost a reddish cast in the sun. What color is your hair?"

"My natural color was a light auburn. In the summers when I was young, I swam in the La Jolla Cove and sunbathed every moment possible, then my hair lightened to a strawberry blond. Since I started going grey, I've kept my hair a frosted blonde. It's your father who had the dark hair."

I wanted to ask questions about my birth father. Still, my first conversation with Liddy wasn't the right time, especially knowing, as I did now, that my birth father had called off the wedding.

"Did Alice tell you that I've been married three times?" I laid all my nasty cards out on the table. She had to know the worst of me upfront, warts and all.

"No, Alice didn't share your marital history, but you come by your multiple marriages naturally." Liddy laughed deeply. "Andy is my fifth husband, and Lily is on her third. And, Andy, well, I am his sixth wife. Please don't get caught up in the shame of past mistakes. We all make them, myself included."

Liddy's words were surprising, a little bit shocking, but at the same time comforting. She wasn't going to reject me for my many marriages.

"Alice did tell me that you have five children, my only grandchildren! I expected that my only grandchildren would be my step-grands through Andy. Lily is not interested in ever having children, and Martin," she paused, "died before he fathered any children."

"Well, now you have five grandchildren: three girls and two boys. Leah's fifteen, Jonah's seven, Hannah's six, Abby's four, and Noah's three. Leah, Abby, and Noah all just had their birthdays last month."

"Liz, I must say this before we go any further." I gripped the phone's receiver tighter at her words. "I've two big fears about us being in contact, and I need you to reassure me that I needn't worry about either.

"I was afraid that I would encounter an angry woman embittered that her mother gave her away and that once you contacted me and satisfied your curiosity, you'd have nothing more to do with me. If I let you into my heart, please, you must promise to stay in my life."

As Liddy's exposed her vulnerability, all pretense of strength dissolved in me. I wanted to crash through space and time into this woman's arms. "Let me assure you, my heart's greatest desire is to know and love you, Liddy. I harbor no bitterness towards you, only gratitude that you chose life for me."

"Well then, dear daughter, let's make plans for you to come down here to visit me. I want to meet my grandchildren, but you are my top priority. When can you come to stay with me for a few days?"

"I'll need to make arrangements to take some time off from work and check with Joe's work travel schedule but maybe within the next month. I'll see what I can arrange."

"In the meantime, Liz, let's write to one another. I work part-time at a small custom jewelry store. Business is slow most of the time, and I've plenty of time to write you. I can't stand to have idle time."

"That sounds wonderful. I will try to write, but my life is pretty hectic with work and family. Don't be disappointed if you don't get as many letters back."

"I do understand and don't feel under any pressure."

Before we hung up, Liddy asked about what my job entailed since her husband, Andy, was an engineer, and he would pump her for details about my work.

"I don't know how I could do everything without my mother, Marie, watching the kids," I said. I felt the need to bring Marie into the conversation. I wondered how Liddy felt hearing me call another woman "mother." While Liddy was my birth mother, only Marie Schmidt could be my Mom.

We exchanged mailing addresses during the remainder of the call and agreed to talk by phone every other week.

The whole conversation had lasted a half-hour but had left me shaking and spent. After five natural deliveries, I could only compare this to the transition stage of childbirth.

So ready to push but not allowed to do so ... "Blow, blow, blow. Don't push yet," the attendant medical staff had ordered. When I could hold back no longer, I remember the simultaneous burning pain and relief at pushing forth a new life. With audible sobs, I expelled my throw-away child and the afterbirth of self-hatred. My birth mother wanted me.

THREE DAYS LATER, I still hadn't slept. I drove myself to the Immediate Care Clinic and now sat on the examination table covered in white paper, crinkling at my slightest move. The room smelled of disinfectant. I told the medical technician, who readied my chart for the doctor, that I hadn't slept for three days and couldn't work, think, or eat. I lied and told her that there had been a death in the family. There had been a kind of death, just a symbolic one.

The doctor walked into the examination room. Strands of grey hair laced his mousy brown hair, most prominent at his temples. I was too exhausted to care if he thought I was nuts. Maybe I was.

"Has this ever happened before, where you went days without sleeping?" he asked.

"Never. If I'm terribly worried about something, I might have a night here or there where I can't sleep. But nothing like this. I feel like I'm going to go crazy if I don't get some sleep."

"Did something trigger this?"

"Yes," I shrieked and began blubbering out of control. The doctor handed me some tissues.

"My birth mother was supposed to be dead. But she wasn't. And ever since I spoke to her three days ago," I gasped between my shallow breaths, "I haven't been able to sleep. Can you give me something that will knock me out?"

"I can see that that could be upsetting," he said. "Have you ever taken any kind of sleeping pills before?" He felt my neck for swollen glands and looked down my throat.

"No, never," I said when he withdrew the wooden tongue depressor from my mouth.

"Any heart conditions?" he asked as he listened to my heart and lungs.

"No."

"Any bipolar in your birth family that you know of."

"No, but my maternal grandmother had schizophrenia." Even in my run-down state, I realized that was the first time I'd ever had any medical history to give. "May I have another tissue?"

"Do you use recreational drugs?"

"No, never."

"Well, I don't have a problem prescribing a week's worth of sleeping pills. If your insomnia worsens, or these pills don't work, you should see your regular doctor."

Relieved, I left the clinic with a prescription in hand. On Sunday night, blissful sleep arrived thanks to the sleeping pills. Monday morning, I went to work and felt almost like myself again. I told the kids and my mother, Marie, that I was over the flu. Everything settled back to the new normal.

A WARM SPELL USHERED in an early spring that year. The air danced with warmth and the promise of a new season. Lawns turned from yellow to green, and deciduous trees pushed forth their fuzzy buds in rebirth. The last daffodils had nodded off to sleep until next year, their spent glory now subsumed by tulips stretching their colorful chalices heavenward. I made the drive to Joe's house under a canopy of cerulean blue punctuated with puffy, white clouds.

The mail usually came by 10 a.m., and I'd allowed an hour-and-a-half cushion. Liddy's photos had to arrive today, supplying the brushstrokes to the canvas of my birth mother's face that remained empty and featureless. My eagerness had outweighed the efficiency of waiting the additional six hours until after work to check for mail.

Less than a week ago, I'd first heard Liddy's voice, so different in timbre and intonation from Aunt Alice's. Like the sweet warbling of a meadowlark echoing off the sagebrush-covered hills behind Joe's house, Liddy's voice beckoned me as I turned into the cul-de-sac.

Joe's mailbox sat in the middle between four other mailboxes, mounted in a row on a creosote-treated timber plank. I pulled down the hatch of the black metal mailbox and quickly removed a 6x9 inch clasped envelope addressed to me in beautiful cursive handwriting. A sticker with the image of an angel holding a wreath of flowers was in the upper left-hand corner of the envelope with Liddy and Andy's return address.

Turning the envelope over, I tore through the tape to have at the contents. I brought the inside of the envelope to my nose and inhaled, detecting a faint floral scent. I emptied the contents onto my lap. On top was a card bearing an image of Mother Goose wearing a straw bonnet tied with a blue ribbon and orange polka dots. Two young children, dressed from a time past, were nestled under her wings. I savored the vintage illustration and recognized it as one of Jessie Wilcox Smith's. It seemed that I shared my mother's nostalgic taste and love of art.

As I opened the card, three snapshots fell out onto my lap. As much as I wanted to read Liddy's words, I reached for the photos.

The color snapshot on top of the pile was that of a smiling woman. The writing on the back of the picture read "Liddy—age 45." I was mesmerized by the delicate, perfect beauty of my birth mother.

The resemblance between us was undeniable, but unlike me, Liddy was shockingly beautiful. She'd swept her wavy frosted-blonde hair back in a loose updo away from her heart-shaped face. Between her prominent high cheekbones sparkled almond-shaped glacier-blue eyes. She had a broad, inviting smile with petal-shaped teeth.

Liddy had given me her cheekbones and almond-shaped eyes. But my square jawline, dark marine blue eyes, and raven hair must have come from my birth father.

The second black and white image showed a much younger Liddy in a waist-length fitted sweater and slacks. She had pulled her legs up beneath her as she leaned to one side, sitting in a tufted Louis XV-style chair. Her chin rested in one hand, her elbow resting on the chair's narrow wooden arm. Her short, wavy hair was brushed back from a pensive-looking, or perhaps sad, face. An unsmiling expression accentuated a cupid's bow upper lip and full lower lip.

I flipped the picture over. "Liddy—age 20, shortly after I had you" was inscribed on the back.

The last picture was a recent snapshot of Liddy sitting next to a young woman on a rose-colored couch in front of a lavishly decorated Christmas tree. The back read, "Liddy and Lily, Christmas 1987 at home in La Mesa." Liddy's hair fell in loose curls framing her face in a layered shoulder-length style. My mother was still captivating.

And there was my half-sister. Though lovely in her own right, Lily looked little like her mother, except for her wide Hollywood-starlet smile. My half-sister had a dark tan or simply a darker complexion than Liddy's porcelain skin which amplified Lily's dazzling white teeth. If Liddy was like a rose with layers and layers of delicate beauty, Lily reminded me of a tiger lily, slightly exotic with her dark looks and flamboyant orange outfit.

I put the photos back into the envelope while checking in the rear-view mirror that no one was behind me, trying to get their mail. My attention shifted to the note Liddy had written.

March 18, the morning after

Dearest Daughter,

I'm in such a state of excitement and joy. I will write more at length, but today I am working. Pictures always flatter me; naturally, I have sent good ones.

I cannot wait to see your picture and you. It is like being a child on Christmas morning. Lily will come down after you have been here for a day.

You have accomplished so much that I am awed. I thought I had learned resignation to life's sorrows, and now you have opened the door to new life and new hope and joy.

I am trying so hard to contain myself and not fly apart. I want to shout from the rooftops and cry out how good is God for what you have done in finding me.

Liz, I can't be disappointed in anything about you.

Yours in faith and love,

I don't know how to sign my name ... Liddy

Meeting

April 1988

I parked my car in the first row of long-term parking at the Tri-Cities airport. Joe had grudgingly conceded that there was no point waking up Abby and Noah so that he could drive me to the airport. "I drive myself to the airport whenever I take a business trip. I'm fully capable of doing this!" I'd protested. But the truth was, I didn't want to share this Friday morning with anyone. The next three-and-a-half days were all mine, and they began the second I left the house.

Getting early to the airport hadn't helped me change my seat assignment on the sold-out flight. I remained stuck with my bulkhead window seat. So much for quick, unimpeded access to the minuscule restroom if my nervous gut acted up.

I'd sorted out all the details for my trip to San Diego two weeks ago, telling Mom, the kids, and Leo that it was a business trip. No one questioned that it extended over a weekend. Occasionally, a conference did that. A necessary lie to preserve Mom from hurt, I told myself. I'd return on the first flight home Monday morning and head directly into work from the airport. I'd see Abby and Noah Monday night and the older kids Tuesday night.

Thirty days after my first conversation with Liddy, I climbed the airstairs and stood on the metal platform, awaiting my turn to board a direct flight to San Diego. Making my way past the privileged first-classers, I arrived at what remained of my bulkhead seat. The remnant lay between the window and an elderly woman, whose fullness occupied her seat and a substantial portion of mine. Her back spilled over the retracted armrest normally partitioning the seats.

With a smile and a doggedly positive attitude, I greeted her. "Excuse me. I have the window seat next to you."

She acknowledged me with a slight nod and a smile. A white rim encircled her cloudy gray irises, and her tight snowy-white curls reminded me of Mom's favored hairstyle. She was probably older than Mom by ten years.

Before stowing my red leather shoulder bag in the overhead compartment, I removed my copy of Pilcher's *The Shell Seekers* and tossed it onto what remained of my assigned seat. I looked forward to a few hours of pleasure reading during the flight. Something about dysfunctional families made me feel sane and elicited a sense of comfort like the warmth of an old bathrobe on a chilly morning.

My seatmate failed to move either her legs or feet. I climbed over her with a herculean step while balancing myself with one hand on the overhead compartment and the other on the carpeted wall defining the bulkhead space.

She smiled at me sweetly while I scootched in. My seatmate's vintage perfume, "White Shoulders," wafted a floral symphony in our shared space. The pleasant scent more than compensated for the invasion of my personal space. I made a mental note to ask Liddy about her sense of smell and prepared myself for the three-hour nonstop flight.

During the airplane safety lesson, sweat began to roll down my temple. My usual nerves about flying, worry that Liddy might not like me, and the donated body heat of my neighbor amped up my heart rate. I opened the air vent above, removed my blazer, and placed it over the book in my lap.

I had labored over what to wear for our first meeting and finally settled on my favorite Liz Claiborne ensemble: a loose-fitting red linen jacket; a tucked-in, button-down shirt; roomy blue and white checked slacks; and a wide, waist-clinching, red leather belt. Each item had been strategically chosen to camouflage my thin physique and hide my small bustline. From the multiple pictures Liddy had sent, it was apparent that Liddy had a movie star figure, which Lily, my half-sister, had inherited.

Once airborne, I pulled out Liddy's last letter that I'd stashed in my book. I studied how she wrote my name and address on the envelope. Her penmanship looked just like the Palmer cursive method charts pinned in the narrow band of corkboard above the chalkboards in grade school. A slight lean to the right and open, free-flowing curves. The stamp on the envelope was a pink tea rose, unfurled, with the word "LOVE" underneath. She'd sealed the envelope with a sticker of a Victorian-looking angel.

Liddy had tucked the letter inside a notecard bearing an image of a mother cat, with eyes closed and cuddling her little kitten, both tabbies. She'd written only a few words inside the card, "I can't wait to see you. Love, Mother." I reread the letter, written on paper torn from a yellow legal pad.

Thursday, April 9, 1988

Dearest Daughter,

What a joy it is to be able to call you "dearest daughter," a gift that I never imagined possible. Should my letters ever touch too sensitive a cord, please let me know, and I will go slower. I have a great hunger to know you and to be known by you.

Know that I am not trying to replace Marie's special place in your life as "Mom." I am forever indebted to Marie and Fred Schmidt for caring for and loving you all these many years that I could not. You are now a mother of five, yes, five children, my only grandchildren. There is no impediment to my showering you with all the love that I've kept locked in my heart all these years except for my possible missteps.

I dream that someday you will call me "Mother," as I now call you "Daughter." I count the days between now and when you will come to visit me so that I can feel you in my arms.

Don't worry that you don't have time to write as often as I do. I'm in a different season in my life. I only work part-time, three days a week on Tuesday and Wednesday afternoons, at a custom jewelry shop in El Cajon, not far from where I live.

Tuesdays and Wednesdays are exceedingly boring, long days as business is often slow. The owner, Larry, pays minimum wage to have me mind the counters so he can concentrate on his creations.

I also work all day at an antique store on Thursdays specializing in higher-end antique jewelry, porcelain, and clothing near my home.

Love,

Mother

This was my favorite letter from Liddy. My heart surged to overflowing as I reread the first paragraph for the umpteenth time, savoring her words like chunks of dark chocolate melting in my greedy mouth. I folded up the note and placed it back inside the card and envelope and into my book.

After reclining my seat, I continued reading where I'd last left off in Pilcher's novel and sipping the ginger ale that the flight attendant brought me. My world was good and only going to get better.

THE FLIGHT ATTENDANT AWAKENED me. "Pull your seat into an upright position and stow your tray table in the side pocket," she said as she reached for the plastic cup still half-full of ginger ale. After rubbing the sleep from my eyes, I picked my novel up from the floor near my feet. Shortly after that, I heard the thud of the landing gear.

The flight attendant returned to ask me to please remain seated until everyone else had deplaned as they would need to get a special wheelchair for the older woman who sat next to me. The burn of tears stung my eyes. I'd waited for this moment my entire life, and now I was forced to wait even longer. I literally would be the last person off this plane.

What if Liddy thought that I had missed the plane? The woman turned her sagging face and cloudy eyes towards me just as tears began rolling down my cheeks. She reached for my hand with her gnarled hand and patted it gently.

How could I possibly be upset with this kind soul? I tried to explain away my tears. "I am meeting my birth mother for the first time in my life when I step off this plane."

"Almost. Almost. Almost." She spoke in a soft voice with a peculiar intonation, like a stroke victim who had lost the ability to express herself fully. But she had understood; I saw it in her eyes as a single tear slid down her cheek. I took a deep breath and reminded myself to slow down. I was exactly where I was supposed to be at this particular time.

Once all the other passengers had deplaned, two airline employees arrived with a special wheelchair whose wheeled legs fit in the aisle.

"Ma'am, we're going to lift you into this wheelchair to help you deplane. Ready? Here we go." The men grunted as they hoisted the woman into the wheelchair.

She turned her head and looked at me one last time. "Almost. Almost. Almost," were her departing comments. She was right. My search was almost over.

I immediately grabbed my shoulder bag out of the overhead compartment. My stomach was turning summersaults.

My heart pounded loudly in my ears and hammered my chest as I walked down the gangway. Crazy, anxious thoughts peppered my excitement. What if she thinks I'm ugly or too skinny?

An intoxicating scent of the peonies drew me forward. A woman stood at the end of a roped-off area that guided the deplaning passengers into the terminal, holding a giant bouquet of pink and white double peonies and blue Dutch irises. It had to be Liddy!

My first thought was, *How could I, Elizabeth Ann Schmidt, have such a beautiful mother?* My second thought was, *This woman does not look fifty-five!*

My last half dozen steps broke into an all-out run towards my birth mother as she set the bouquet on a nearby chair. Thirty-five years in coming, we wrapped our arms around one other in a tender, tight embrace. Anais Anais floated a fragrant cloud of celebration around us as we had both worn the same perfume. But underneath the layers of fragrance and flowers was a primal scent that I recognized as "mother."

No one else remained in the gated area when we released each other. We were utterly alone, as if time had whisked everyone else away.

Liddy pulled my hair back to examine my ears. "Attached earlobes, just like me." Then she pulled her hair back and rotated her gold earrings up to reveal her earlobes. I had never even thought about earlobes before, attached or detached. I had no idea whether my children had attached or detached earlobes. I would have to look once I returned home.

"At long last, you are here!"

"Yes! Finally! And the last one off the plane."

She held me at arm's length, examining me head to toe. As she studied me, I memorized her every feature.

Her layered, shoulder-length hair hung in loose frosted curls framing a heart-shaped face, defined by prominent cheekbones and a still youthful, feminine jawline. She wore soft red lipstick and accentuated her glacier-blue eyes with blue-grey eyeliner and dark mascara. She had applied liquid cover-up and blush, not to hide but to accentuate her light complexion.

Liddy was short. Even in her white, two-inch strappy heels, I stood several inches above her in my flats. She had none of my long-arm or long-leg lankiness and was as perfectly proportioned as the swimsuit model she had been in her younger days. She wore a sleeveless cotton eyelet blouse tucked into her floral print skirt, cinched by a wide navy-blue belt.

She cupped my face in her trembling hands, "This is what my daughter was supposed to look like!" I felt more beautiful at that moment than I had ever felt in my entire life.

"I hope you're hungry. Your cousin, Margot, Maura's daughter, is meeting us for lunch at the La Valencia Hotel in downtown La Jolla. The hotel has gorgeous views of the bluffs and the cove. The lobby area will be a wonderful place for pictures."

While we waited for my single checked bag, I took Liddy's leave to use the restroom. I studied my facial features in the mirror as I washed my hands, hunting for hints of Liddy. They were there, unmistakably so, but not so polished. Liddy was an artist with makeup, her face the canvas. I wore mascara, period. Marie had never worn makeup other than the rare mauve lipstick, Instant Mocha by Avon. But the shape of our faces was almost identical, except my jawline was more squared. In contrast to my birth mother's thin, light brown eyebrows, mine remained full and black.

We collected my suitcase from the baggage claim and exited the parking lot outside Terminal 2. As we drove past the waving palm trees on North Harbor Drive and the majestic clipper ship, Star of India, moored in North San Diego Bay, I fell under the spell of this city. I understood why Liddy had never left the area.

On the drive to La Jolla, Liddy explained that her husband, Andy, had initially insisted that he take the day off from work to accompany her to pick me up at the airport. "Andy can be stubborn when he gets his mind set on something. I told him that I didn't plan to share the moment of our meeting with anyone but you. Thank God, he relented."

Liddy outlined the schedule for my short visit. After our lunch with

Margot, we'd swing by San Diego State to say hello to my aunt Maura. My half-sister, Lily, would drive down from Los Angeles on Saturday afternoon and spend the night. The four of us, Liddy, Andy, Lily, and I, would go out to dinner Saturday evening. Lily would head back home on Sunday morning. Liddy and I would go to Sunday evening Mass. We'd have a quiet dinner at home on Sunday, our last night together. Then Liddy would drop me off at the airport Monday morning.

"I know it is a lot to squeeze in, but Margot, Maura, Lily, and Andy are all excited to meet you, too," Liddy said as she pulled into a parking space on Prospect Street in downtown La Jolla.

We walked past high-end jewelry stores, art galleries, and elegant restaurants on our way to the landmark hotel. Constructed in the 1920s, the La Valencia still bore its signature bright pink stucco exterior. Margot was waiting for us in the large lobby, which also served as a waiting area for the restaurant.

"I am so happy to meet you, Liz, and just thrilled for you and Auntie!" Margot's light blue eyes sparkled as her freckled arms enveloped me in a warm, welcoming hug. Naturally curly, yellow-blonde hair fell below her shoulders, framing an oval face with delicate features and a slightly upturned nose. She reminded me of a sunflower in her yellow sundress, which draped over her lean build of medium height.

As Margot and Liddy chatted and laughed, I inhaled the grandeur of my surroundings. In warm shades of russet and brown, a towering wood ceiling spanned the entire lobby. Rows of black inlaid octagons marched in tandem between massive, exposed beams. Inscribed in the center of every four neighboring octagons was a five-petaled flower. The geometric-floral motif imparted a definite Moorish atmosphere. Black metal chandeliers were hung from the ceiling, each holding ten wax candles.

At the end of the rectangular lobby, floor-to-ceiling windows showcased the La Jolla Cove's rocky coastline with palm trees waving gently in the breeze. Side doors opened onto an outside courtyard with tile floors in bold blue, orange, and yellow floral designs. Jungle-worthy planters boasted exotic, colorful floral arrangements strategically placed to add an air of intimacy around the tables and chairs.

Being surrounded by so much beauty, I never wanted it to end. When I'd begged for beautiful things as a child, ignorant of the cost and our family's limited finances, Mom had chided, "You'd think you were born with a silver spoon in your mouth!" I now banished all guilt, knowing I'd been born to drink in beautiful people, places, and things. And I was thirsty. Very, very thirsty.

Liddy announced, "Let's take pictures before we eat and our lipstick gets all smudged with lunch. You girls aren't too hungry, are you?"

Lipstick? I never wore lipstick. There was nothing to smudge.

I hated having my picture taken, but I did want to document this special day of my life with my new family.

"I'm not the least bit photogenic," I warned.

"Don't worry. I'll tear up any horrible pictures. I don't keep any unflattering pictures. There'll be no ugly pictures of me around when I'm dead!"

Margot, a drama major at San Diego State where her parents taught, had incredible patience throughout the photo session. She adored having her picture taken as much as Liddy. Liddy charmed a random person to take photos of the three of us. Margot took pictures of Liddy and me, I took pictures of Margo and Liddy, and Liddy took pictures of Margot and me. It was exhausting, but I knew I'd be glad later.

After the better part of an hour, my cheeks were hurting from forced smiles and posed pictures. Liddy promised she would send me copies of the best shots.

Our conversation during lunch began with Margot's love life for Liddy's edification. As soon as the topic of discussion moved away from Margot, she lost interest. Perhaps she was accustomed to being the center of attention as an only child. At any rate, she displayed no curiosity about Liddy's newly acquired passel of grandchildren.

Liddy checked the time on her wristwatch. "It's quarter to three! I told Maura we'd be at her office at three."

"Gosh, I need to get back to work," Margot announced.

I hadn't finished eating my cobb salad, so I quickly stuffed the part of a boiled egg into my mouth. I grabbed a sourdough roll with me as we headed back to the Liddy's car.

Margot seemed such a young "twenty-two." I couldn't help but compare my life at twenty-two with Margot's comfortable, carefree life, still living at home in Del Mar on her parent's dime. I felt the familiar bite of envy for those who'd grown up with the comforts and security of money. But I was equally envious of her effusive, uninhibited ways. If only those traits were part of the fabric of my personality, but I was cut from a more reserved, introverted cloth.

WE RODE THE ELEVATOR to Aunt Maura's office on the fourth floor of the Mathematics, Computer Science, and Statistics building. Late by twenty minutes, Liddy fairly ran out of the elevator as I followed closely behind. I scanned the names on the office doors, looking for "Dr. Maura Campbell."

Liddy leaned into an open door halfway down the long hallway as I caught up. "We're here!" Liddy said.

A smiling woman wearing black "half-eye" glasses swiveled around in her office chair, turning away from her computer monitor to face us.

"And so, you are! Liz, how wonderful to meet you!" Maura rose from her chair to hug me.

As Liddy was elegant, Maura was "au naturelle." She wore no perfume or makeup. She shared Liddy's high cheekbones, which imparted subtle grace to her countenance. Her light brown hair was laced with strands of grey and hung in a blunt-cut pageboy angled to her chin.

Maura wore a simple blue denim skirt that hit below her knees, a short-sleeved lighter blue denim shirt that rested mid-hip, and flats. Maura's mannerisms were relaxed compared to Liddy's high energy. But then she was meeting a niece that she had always known about, not meeting a daughter for the first time.

"Please sit down. My office is as good a place as any to chat. Liddy, pull the door closed."

Maura's left arm was swollen. Liddy had warned me about Maura's lymphedema, a lingering side-effect from her mastectomy five years ago.

"Oh, my! Such a resemblance between you and Liz," Maura said to Liddy. "Honestly, she favors you far more than Lily."

"That is what I thought, too. I was amazed when Liz stepped off the plane." Liddy reached over to squeeze my hand.

Maura and Liddy continued to analyze my appearance as if I wasn't present. I found it entertaining, given that I'd spent my entire life performing this same analytic dissection of people's appearance. Privately, of course, because it seemed uncharitable to notice such details, especially when it came to Mom.

As they chatted, I observed Maura's dangling gemstone earrings, southwestern design, in blues, purple, and pink. Liddy would tell me later that Maura attended gemstone shows in Arizona and had custom jewelry made. It was her one extravagance.

"We had a nice lunch with Margot. She is charming," I said to Maura, diverting the conversation away from my physical appearance.

"Margot was so excited to meet you. That was all she talked about last night. Well, that and the new boyfriend." Maura massaged her swollen left upper arm as she spoke.

"Oh yes, we heard plenty about him," Liddy added as she applied a fresh coat of lipstick to her lips.

"Liz, Liddy told me that you have five children and work full-time as a senior research scientist. That must keep you busy."

"It does, but Mom ... my adoptive mother, Marie, makes it all work. After Dad died some years back, she moved back to the Tri-Cities. After that, working full-time with five kids became infinitely easier."

"That's in Washington State, right?" I nodded to Maura's question as she continued. "I've always heard Washington is such a beautiful state, so green. But I've never been there."

"The green part is the west side of the state. I live on the opposite side, which I think is the ugliest part of the state. There's a radioactive dump nearby, too, and it is anything but green."

Maura sat back in her chair, raised her eyebrows, and laughed, "Well, guess I won't be going there any time soon."

"How long have you worked here, Maura?" I wanted to know all about my aunt's work as a mathematician.

"Forever, it seems, but it's only been about ten years. I was thirty-eight when I had Margot. I worked as an architect first, and then after I had Margot, I went back to school to complete a doctorate in mathematics.

"I had my oldest daughter, Leah, when I was a junior in college while working part-time graveyard shift. I can't imagine trying to work on a doctorate with a baby." I thought back to the nightmare of finishing my undergraduate degree when Leah was a baby and the challenge of graduate school with a preschooler.

"Well, it wasn't as bad as it sounds, my husband had a good income, and we could afford to hire someone to come into the house to care for Margot while I attended classes and did my homework on campus. I teach mostly undergraduate statistics classes and publish a paper here and there on applied statistics. My last paper looked at enrollment trends for women at this university in math, statistics, and computer science."

When Maura asked about my job, I grew anxious as I explained my work at the lab. Why did I always feel that I had to prove myself? What was the source of my angst? Maura was as sweet as she could be.

Liddy smiled as Maura and I shared our common research interests. I knew Liddy had never been to college, and the few times she worked as a bookkeeper were during the brief periods between her marriages. She was only working now to earn enough credit to qualify on her own for Social Security benefits.

"Liddy may not have told you that she graduated at the top of her class," Maura offered as she nodded towards a smiling Liddy. "Our father thought it a waste of time to send a woman to college. But by the time your mother graduated from high school, she was far more interested in modeling, men, and a good time anyway."

"Wow, I had no idea," I said, turning to Liddy.

"Liddy has always focused more on her appearance than scholarly endeavors," Maura said, adding a smile to her slight reproach.

LIDDY BACKED HER LINCOLN Continental into the steep driveway on Mt. Helix. She had lived with Andy in this home since their marriage five years ago. But Andy had lived in this house with his other five wives, one after the other.

"We'll have about an hour alone before Andy gets home from work. He will be interested to hear about your job. Expect many questions." Liddy was much less relaxed as she spoke of Andy's return.

We walked a winding path from the car through the manicured backyard, passing rectangular grassy areas enclosed by low rock walls, stepping stones, flowering trees, and a profusion of roses that led to the front door of the rosy-tan stucco tri-level house.

"You wouldn't believe what a mess this yard was when I married Andy. I nearly killed myself getting it in shape. My hands will never be the same. Andy and I nearly killed each other trying to work together. He is not the easiest man to get along with. Let's hope he is in a good mood tonight."

Liddy unlocked the front door, and I followed her inside. The living room had a vaulted ceiling with a single exposed wooden beam down the center and a floor-to-ceiling antique brick fireplace with a raised hearth. Oil and acrylic paintings filled every space on the white walls, all Liddy's artwork.

Her paintings, both large and small, oozed with character. Her brush strokes brought to life the wrinkled face of an old crone in a straw hat, a nude woman whose long flowing chestnut hair hid her face as she reclined on an orange couch, a child's face framed in dark hair and wearing a yellow bonnet (which I fantasized was me). She also painted still life flowers, fruits, and scenery.

The house she shared with Andy was modest and dated, but Liddy had transformed the space into a vibrant piece of art that echoed beauty and resonated with her creativeness. Her talents extended beyond the canvas to landscaping and interior design. My mother was a multi-talented artist.

Two burgundy Rococo-style chairs sat off to the side of the informal entryway. I rolled my suitcase over the polished brownish-red pavers towards a large, gilded antique-looking French mirror hanging over a console table.

I stopped to examine the eclectic collection of frames that showcased Liddy's and Andy's family pictures atop the table. Lily was easy to recognize. I saw the single photograph I'd sent Liddy of myself now added to the collection. Then I saw HIM.

He was standing in a picture with Lily. The same red plaid shirt, the gold medal around his neck, the shoulder-length wavy brown hair, and the handsome face smiling into the camera. My hands trembled as I picked up the framed picture. I studied the image intently while willing my hand to remain steady.

There was no mistake.

Goosebumps ran up my arms, and the hair on the back of my neck stood on end.

"Who's that with Lily?" I asked, turning to Liddy and modulating my alarm.

"That's my son, Martin. Sadly, that's the best picture I have of him. The photo was taken the year he was killed in a head-on collision."

The Walk

I AWAKENED WITH THE La Mesa sun streaming into my eyes through the sheer curtains hanging in Liddy's guest room. I'd slept, but not soundly. The newness of everything had unsettled me, and the haunting photo of Martin had played through my restless mind during the night.

I'd said nothing to Liddy about the shocking resemblance between my deceased brother, Martin, and the young man I had imagined in Joe's bedroom two months ago. Perhaps the similarities resulted from some déjà vu-like brain glitch or my overactive imagination tricking me. Regardless, sharing such an eerie coincidence required a deep trust that needed time to build.

Listening for sounds of activity downstairs, I lay in bed, running my hands over the bedspread of creme-colored moiré silk. Gathered folds of fabric fanned out at the bottom corners under enormous bows in pale rose tones that matched the frilly shams and throw pillows. Liddy had an impeccable sense of color and décor. I loved what she loved and luxuriated in the peace I derived from being near her and her things.

Sitting up in bed, I studied my reflection in the mirror above the dresser, tracing with my fingers the evidence of her motherhood chiseled into my face. Liddy had arranged the flowers she'd given me at the airport in a transferware pitcher and set them off to one side on the dresser, their fragrance still heady and sumptuous.

Liddy's tender oil rendering of a Madonna and child hung near the doorway, another reminder that I was finally with my mother. I located her signature in the lower right-hand corner. Her signatures bore the letter "L," followed by her married name at the last brushstroke. I'd counted three different surnames so far but was surprised that none bore "Anderson," her current surname.

Instead of the jeans and t-shirt that I'd throw on at home, I dressed in white cotton slacks and a short-sleeve turquoise linen shirt, standard work attire. I tarried upstairs in the guest room until I heard Andy and Liddy arguing about something. Once the bickering stopped, I made my way down the staircase.

Liddy sat in the living room, wearing a floor-length, robin egg's blue robe in what I now knew to be her favorite chair, a tufted European design in navy velveteen with a single flower carved at the top of the surrounding wood frame. She'd gathered her hair into a loose top knot, and loose tendrils framed her face. She smoked a cigarette and sipped her morning coffee.

"Good morning, Liz. Did you sleep well?"

"Yes," I lied, then nodded at the cigarette in her hand. "You smoke," I said, sitting down nearby. "I knew you or Andy were smokers the instant I'd walked into the house yesterday. I'd hoped that it was Andy. My dad died of emphysema yet continued to smoke even when hooked up to oxygen. He never stopped smoking until he dropped dead. His heart, in the end."

"I never smoked once I was pregnant with you, but it helps me cope with ... life."

"What do you mean?" I watched gray curls of smoke rise from the end of her cigarette.

"Andy's bipolar, and smoking helps me cope. But beyond that, smoking dulls my sense of smell. Andy's hygiene went south once we were married. I've got a heightened sense of smell, and the world can be a pretty stinky place."

"You passed that on to me." I laughed, feeling affirmed that my hypersensitivity was a gift, not a vice.

"I try not to smoke when other people are around." She extinguished her cigarette in the cloisonné ashtray that sat on the end table between us.

"Would you like some breakfast, or do you need to wake up with some coffee first?"

"I've been up for a while. Breakfast sounds great."

I followed Liddy into the dining room, which shared an L-shaped space with the living room. Over the polished walnut dining table hung a chandelier. Its flame-shaped, incandescent bulbs rested in bronze-verdigris roses, and teardrop-shaped crystals dangled below, reflecting the morning sunlight. A French shell armoire stood against the wall with beveled mirror inlays. Sliding glass doors opened up onto a second-story deck overlooking Liddy's gardens.

In the middle of the dining table sat a low glass bowl that floated a fully opened rose, emitting a strong damask fragrance.

"From your garden?" I asked.

"Yes, Mister Lincoln, my favorite," Liddy said.

I remembered planting a Mister Lincoln rose bush with Mom at Joe's house. It had been a wedding gift from her. Mister Lincoln had been Mom's favorite rose, too.

Liddy pulled out a chair from the table where a gift lay wrapped in shiny white paper and tied with a purple ribbon.

"For you, a small gift to commemorate our first visit together," she said, bubbling with excitement.

"Should I open it now?"

"Yes, I refuse to feed you breakfast until you do." There was her playful smile again.

"Okay. Then open it, I must!"

I settled into the comfy chair covered in fabric with alternating gold, cream, and burgundy stripes. While Liddy watched from the chair directly across, I untied the ribbon with a single pull, tore off the wrapping paper, and lifted the lid from the box. After removing the surrounding tissue paper, I held a painted plate. Smaller than a dinner plate but larger than a salad plate, this was not a dish to eat upon but rather the "food" to feast one's eyes upon.

In various shades of purple and green, three symmetric clusters of violets with heart-shaped leaves reached from the plate's edge inward to kiss a central violet. A half-inch band of gold shimmered around the circumference, and the heart-shaped leaves bore veins of gold.

"Oh, Liddy, I love it. I adore violets. How did you know?" I instinctively clutched the plate to my chest.

"I didn't know, but I love anything Art Nouveau, which is the style of painting on the plate. My sister, Alice, claims that our mother loved violets and carried a bouquet of violets when she married Daddy."

Liddy instructed me to turn the plate over and explained the marks on the back. "The porcelain plate, called a blank, was made in one of the Limoges' factories in France between 1884 and 1900. The maple leaf is a trademark that Pickard artists used after the turn of the century. It's not worth a lot, but I thought it was lovely. When I saw it at the shop, I knew it should belong to you." She walked around the table and hugged me from behind.

"It is worth a fortune to me. Thank you so much." I held onto her arms with my hands.

"Can I come up and join you for breakfast now?" Andy's voice boomed from the family room, one level below, and into the dining room.

Liddy leaned in towards me and whispered, "I asked Andy to let me have some privacy when I gave you your gift. These are special moments for me. I don't want to share them with anyone but you."

"Yes, we're all done, Andy. You may join us now," she shouted to Andy and then whispered to me, "Andy is hard of hearing, but he refuses to wear his hearing aids at home."

The moment he entered the room, I felt the shift in the air like the decrease in barometric pressure preceding a storm. Gone was the doting mother, and in her place was a woman who guarded each word out of her mouth.

LIDDY AND I WATCHED for Lily's arrival on the deck outside the dining room overlooking the backyard. Here we had a bird's eye view of the steep driveway up to the house, which formed an offshoot from the circuitous street winding up the Mt. Helix residential area. A gentle breeze stirred the white clematis, purple wisteria, and pink climbing roses that framed the view from our second-story perch.

The drive from San Dimas to La Mesa was supposed to take less than two hours. "But on I-5, one never knows," Liddy said. "Lily planned to leave at noon, so I expect her anytime."

I was curious to meet Lily but somewhat apprehensive. It had been my birth parents I'd hungered to know. I'd given no thought over the years to birth siblings.

Lily had a big personality, according to Liddy. A flamboyant persona emerged from Lily's clowning around in her many photos placed around the house. She appeared to love the camera as much as the camera loved her.

Sitting in white-painted wicker chairs, Liddy and I shared intimate reflections from the thirty-five years we'd lived apart. "My biggest worry was that you would be an angry young woman because I gave you up for adoption. I am so relieved that you are, well, ... just how you are." Liddy smiled softly and reached for my hand. I didn't pull away as I often did when people touched or brushed against me. I craved her touch.

"Did you ever try to find me?" I had wanted to ask Liddy this question since our first conversation.

"No, and I never worried about you because I knew you would have a life without any financial worries and would be well taken care of, much better than a life with an unwed mother.

"After the lawyer drew up the adoption papers, I walked them from the lawyer's office to his secretary's office through a short hallway. I had just enough time to take a quick peek into the folder. It was a private, closed adoption, so I wasn't supposed to know anything.

"I remember seeing that your adoptive parents lived in Washington state and that your father was a general contractor. That was all I could take in during the few seconds I had. I visualized you growing up in a big house wearing cashmere sweaters."

I forced a smile. "Well, things weren't quite like that. But if they'd been as you imagined, perhaps I'd not have had such a longing in my heart and feeling of incompleteness that led to my finding you."

Just then, a taupe-colored compact car drove pulled into the steep driveway. A petite woman with waist-length, medium brown hair and oversized sunglasses stepped out of the vehicle.

"Lily, we're up here!" Liddy jumped up, waving enthusiastically.

"I'm coming!" Lily waved both arms dramatically as she made her way across the stone pavers in the backyard to the wooden stairs leading up to the deck. She removed her sunglass as she climbed the two flights of stairs.

From the neck down, Lily was a clone of Liddy but with deeply tanned skin that I surmised was more olive than ivory even with her deep tan.

"Hi, Mom." She gave Liddy a quick, perfunctory hug and stopped directly in front of me, "You have my mother's face!" Lily's large brown eyes searched my face. Her mouth, painted with fire-engine red lipstick, formed a straight line. "That's not fair. I always wanted to look like Mom," she said with a pout.

Without knowing Lily, I couldn't tell if she was teasing or not, but she didn't seem pleased.

"Well ... you have her body," I demurred. "Surely that counts, doesn't it?"

Although stunning in a Southern Mediterranean way, Lily looked nothing like her mother from the neck up except for those perfect lips. She'd not inherited Liddy's high cheekbones either. No one would guess they were mother and daughter unless they studied them from the neck down.

LILY INSISTED THAT THE two of us walk to the top of Mt. Helix during the hottest part of the afternoon. "Oh, please, Liz, walk with me. It's a breathtaking view from the top, and there's a cross and an amphitheater, too. You'll love it."

She seemed to know that Liddy wouldn't walk with us as she had stopped making the trek to the top some time ago when her knees started bothering her. Sometimes Andy accompanied her; otherwise, Lily hiked Mt. Helix alone. I had no interest in sweating or exercising, but I agreed. It would be an opportunity to learn more about my new half-sister better.

Liddy loaned me a pair of shorts, a tank top, and sunglasses for the trek, and she snapped pictures of Lily and me on the first part of the trail. My white legs and arms formed a blinding contrast to Lily's burnished copper limbs.

Ten minutes in, the conversation progressed from casual and comfortable to something entirely different. I now understood why Lily wanted to be alone with me, and it wasn't for sisterly bonding.

"You mustn't idolize our mother. You've no idea what it was like growing up with that woman," she said bitterly.

She proceeded to tell me about her three different step-fathers, not counting Liddy's boyfriends in between husbands nor Liddy's affairs during her marriages.

I couldn't believe that Lily thought this was the appropriate time to dump all her Liddy-trash on me. I'd been with Liddy just over 24 hours and with Lily less than four hours.

I wanted to shout back at her that at least she always had her real mother and always had a relationship with her real father and that she hadn't grown up poor or felt rejected by her adoptive relatives. But people like Lily had no idea what a blood connection was worth. Few people did.

With restraint, I responded, "I'm sorry, Lily, that would be hard. But nobody has the perfect mom."

Each soap opera-like story led to another, and Lily became increasingly agitated. Would this never end? I struggled to keep up with her quickened pace as the climb was getting steep, and the conversation weighed on me like a backpack full of boulders. I ran out of breath, just keeping up with her while swallowing my words.

"All those marriages! My brother, Martin, couldn't stand it; he left home as soon as possible."

All those marriages? Was she serious? Here was the pot calling the kettle black. Lily was thirty-two and on her third marriage. I didn't want Lily to think I was minimizing her emotional pain, but this conversation needed to end.

"Mom had no clue how to be a mother. Her mother was committed to an insane asylum when she was just a baby."

So cut Liddy some slack, I wanted to add. Instead, I levied a softer retort. "It's hard to be a good mother even under perfect circumstances, which yours weren't. My oldest daughter, Leah, could reel off a long list of my shortcomings. And I have been married three times, two times too many to be a perfect mother."

Being a mother was the most challenging and humbling job on the planet and a job for which Lily had no experience but plenty of judgment.

Lily stopped in her tracks and turned to me, "You have no idea!" Lily spewed her words as her body stiffened. Her eyes flashed with rage.

"I'm sure I don't, Lily, but my relationship with Liddy is based on the present, not on her past sins and failures as a mother. I can't handle the litany of all her failures right now. For heaven's sake, I only met her for the first time yesterday."

"You should be glad you were adopted!" Lily shouted hysterically and pushed me away. Hard.

Stunned and off-balance, I fell into the weeds to the side of the dusty path, using my hands to break the impact of my fall.

Lily turned and ran back in the direction from which we'd come. Still in shock, I remained in the dirt, my heart pounding. I made no effort to catch up with her and was clueless about how to salvage the mess.

Other than agreeing with Lily that her life must've been intolerable and that our mother was a monster—which I refused to do and didn't believe—there seemed little I could do to tame the beast that my presence had unleashed in Lily.

Is this what Liddy meant when she said Lily had a big personality? A better warning would have been: "Beware of Lily, she's easily upset, and conversations can become an emotional train wreck in no time flat."

I pulled my knees up to my chest, wrapped my arms around my legs, and tucked my head. Angst knotted in my gut, paralyzing me. Had it been too soon for Lily and me to meet? Did she resent me for laying some claim to her mother?

When I arrived back at Liddy's house, Lily had shut herself into the smaller spare bedroom upstairs, where she was to spend the night.

"Are you okay, Liz?" Liddy asked. "Lily said nothing. She just stormed upstairs, clearly upset."

"She melted down on the walk." I felt like saying, *Lily is your angry daughter, not me*, but I didn't.

"I wish Lily had stayed home on your first visit, but she insisted on coming. She can get so ... agitated. She didn't hit you, did she?"

I avoided Liddy's question altogether. "I'll go upstairs and try to talk with her," I said.

Nothing in me wanted to spend more time alone with the human volcano named Lily. But, neither did I want to field questions from Liddy about what had worked Lily up into such a lather.

As I reluctantly climbed the stairs of doom, Liddy's question replayed in my mind: she didn't hit you, did she? Was this a regular occurrence for Lily? As the mother of five, I had seen my share of temper tantrums. When I reached the top floor, I put on my "mom" hat and knocked on the bedroom door.

"Lily, it's me, Liz. May I come in?"

Silence. Then the creak of mattress springs, the sound of footsteps, and Lily opened the door. Her eyes avoided mine. She returned to the twin bed, where she sat on the pillows cross-legged. Black streams of eyeliner and mascara ran down her face.

There was no chair in the small room, so I had to join Lily on the bed or sit on the floor. I chose the foot of the bed, with my back resting against the wall. I had no idea how to begin a conversation that I didn't want to have. So, I sat quietly, hoping that Lily would start. Or, in the best case, we could keep wordless company and, magically, the whole episode could be swept under the rug as if it'd never happened.

My eyes traveled the room, seeking distraction. Two dolls sat next to one another atop the oak armoire on the wall opposite the bed, one blonde and the other brunette. Long, loose ringlets and wispy bangs emerged from frilly, feathered hats that matched the dolls' elaborate dresses. Lifelike glass eyes, one set blue and the other brown, were framed by painted eyelashes. I imagined the dolls to be Lily and me and wondered if she would ever desire or even accept a sister.

When I could bear the silence no longer, I asked, "Are you okay?"

"I suppose. Are you?"

"Feeling confused and a bit scared. Are you sorry that I found Liddy?"

"No. But I'm not going to lie; this is a messy family. I'm sure my mother hasn't told you everything."

Whoa, our mother, Lily! Was this about Lily learning to share the mother that she so resented?

"Probably not. But every family is messed up—just in different ways."

"Did she tell you that Martin was diagnosed with schizophrenia when he was eighteen?" She sniffed, "Half the time, he thought he was Jesus Christ. There were long periods when we had no idea where he was or what he was doing. It was so awful."

"No. I didn't know about Martin's mental illness. Both Liddy and Alice told me about their mother's schizophrenia." I had studiously avoided asking Liddy anything much about Martin, but Alice hadn't mentioned Martin's schizophrenia either.

"Alice... Don't get me started. She's half off her rocker, too. She suffers from scruples, which is why she was rejected from the convent that she tried to enter in her twenties."

Okay, here we go, I thought. Lily had more dirt to dish. I had hoped that she had fully lanced the boil of her misery, but I was wrong; she'd just hit her stride.

"Did Mom tell you that I pulled out all my eyelashes and most of my eyebrows when I was little? I was diagnosed with multiple personality disorder. It drove her crazy when I referred to myself as "we." The good Lily didn't allow herself to be hurt or get angry; the bad Lily let it all hang out. I've been seeing a therapist for years. I still am."

Over the next hour, Lily blamed her mother for Martin's and her mental illnesses. Given Rose's schizophrenia, it seemed grossly unfair. Eventually, as I probed, Lily revealed that an aunt on her father's side had been diagnosed with schizophrenia before taking her own life.

Martin and Lily had a genetic predisposition towards mental illness on both sides. I kept those thoughts to myself as Lily wasn't ready to let go of her resentment towards her mother. Perhaps, blaming gave her relief. I understood how that blame game worked and had Leo to thank for that lesson.

We came down the stairs together after Lily had offloaded her burdens onto my shoulders. I felt traumatized, but maybe the last hour had done some good. Lily was civil to Liddy and far more relaxed around me. I better understood how my showing up in her life further jumbled her complex feelings towards our mother.

"Would you girls like a glass of chardonnay before dinner?" Liddy offered. She asked no questions, dodging the shrapnel from the emotional detonation of the last two hours.

"YES. P-l-e-a-s-e. Make mine a double," Lily said.

Liddy looked at me. "Liz?"

"Sure. Why not. But half as much as Lily."

After handing us our wine, Liddy refilled her giant glass with diet cola.

"You don't drink wine?" I asked her.

"I don't drink anymore, period. I never made my best decisions when I drank. Now I avoid it altogether." She looked around to ensure that Andy was out of range. "Besides, Andy drinks enough for the two of us, and I am more likely to lose my temper with him if I drink. Much easier to keep my emotions in check this way."

As I drained my glass of chardonnay, the rough edges between Lily and me seemed to smooth out.

"We will be going out for dinner soon. You girls should get dressed. Lily, you might want to wash your face and reapply your make-up," Liddy directed with a quick smile and slight nod.

Andy, Liddy, Lily, and I went to the Marine Room in La Jolla for dinner. Tall waves crashed against a wall of glass windows on the view side of the restaurant. By Lily's third glass of wine and Andy's second highball, the two began to tangle over their differing versions of stories that each wanted to tell, and the other felt the need to correct.

Once we returned to the house, Andy went down to the family room, nursing a glass of Bombay Sapphire on the rocks with the TV as his companion, leaving Liddy, Lily, and me to talk.

Liddy, Lily, and I talked in the living room. Lily took a drink from the glass of wine she'd poured herself when we got back to the house.

"Mom and I expected you to be overweight when we learned you'd had five kids. But you're thinner than Mom or me. What gives?"

"I've always been thin. Too thin for my liking. I have to be pregnant to have any curves." I quickly added, "I always wanted to have a large family, but not with so many different husbands."

Lily was almost thirty-two, and I wondered if she heard the ticking of her biological clock.

"You have no interest in having any children, Lily?" I asked, even though Liddy had told me as much. I now suspected that Lily's disdain for motherhood was motivated by her conflicted feelings towards Liddy.

"I have NO interest in being a mother. I got pregnant before I married my second husband and had an abortion." Lily glared at Liddy as she said this.

"Lily, I asked you not to talk about that," Liddy said.

"Oh, come on, Mom. You had an abortion after you had Liz before you married Dad. Don't you think Liz should know that about you?"

Liddy looked crushed. Would Lily stop at nothing in her efforts to turn me against Liddy? But it wasn't going to work.

"I couldn't give up another baby for adoption. It almost killed me to give you up." Liddy looked at me with pleading eyes. "Please understand."

I felt Liddy's pain. "It's not my place to judge anyone. We all have to make peace with our choices. But as an adopted woman, abortion would never be an option for me. If you had chosen abortion, I wouldn't be sitting here." I reached for my mother's hand. "I owe you my life."

Marie had been wrong about Liddy giving a baby boy up for adoption after she had me. There had been only a nameless child who'd never seen the light of day. Liddy had gone to Mexico for her abortion.

ON MONDAY MORNING, LIDDY drove me back to the airport. I was relieved that this trip had been short. It had been an incredible gift but emotionally exhausting for me, as I'd assumed it had been for Liddy. Lily and Andy were pretty prickly characters, but I would miss Liddy.

"If you and my birth father had married, did you ever think about what name you might have given me?"

"I would have named you Rose. In some ways, I guess I did. I prayed for you as my Rose."

Her words warmed my soul. I had wished that Liddy had registered with the Soundex Registry or had come looking for me. But after this trip, I realized that there'd been no room in her life for me until now. Somehow, Martin's death had opened up space for me in Liddy's life.

I'd been fearful to ask Liddy the name of my birth father. Perhaps an irrational fear, but I had to ask before saying goodbye.

I baited my hook and cast my line into virgin waters. "What was my father's name?"

"I've been waiting for that question." Before answering, she took a long drag off her cigarette and exhaled out the cracked car window. "Ned. Ned Blue."

I pulled the line and wiggled the bait. "Was Ned a nickname or his full name?"

"I'm not sure," she said as she signaled to take the exit for the airport.

The fish remained elusive and only toyed with the bait. "Was Ned's last name spelled like the color blue or like the wind that blew or something else?"

"I'm sorry, I don't know. I've done my best to forget him."

Before I visited San Diego, Liddy told me that my birth father was a couple of years older than she was and had been stationed at Coronado when they'd met and dated. Her description matched Aunt Alice's: tall, dark, and handsome.

I tried again, letting out a bit more line, "Do you remember anything else, like where he was from?"

"Maybe the Chicago area. His parents came out to visit him once when we were dating. Chicago sort of rings a bell."

I reeled in the line and packed up my pole and bait. I'd got what I wanted. Answers.

Preparation

MAY 1989

I FELL IN LOVE with my birth mother at the age of thirty-five. As an infant must learn to detach from its mother, I was discovering the pleasures of attachment. "Liddy this ..., Liddy that ...," I'd croon to Joe. As a daughter, claimed and loved by my birth mother, I'd found another identity beyond that of Marie and Fred Schmidt's adopted daughter.

Liddy's acceptance of me begat a new dimension of self-love. Like all new relationships, this one came without a rocky past to sort through. The same addictive endorphins bathed my brain as when I'd first fallen deeply in love with Leo. My passion for Liddy was different, but it was every bit as pleasurable, with the bonus that it was unlikely to crush my soul as Leo had accomplished.

Liddy became my best friend, and we shared many things. Although I had little discretionary time to read, she decided to expand my literary horizons. She recommended books for me to read that she would re-read simultaneously. We would then discuss it over the phone. She chose books like Isabel Allende's *House of the Spirits*, Gabriel Garcia Marquez's *In the Time of Cholera*, and Fitzgerald's *Zelda*. Rather than disappoint her, I found time to read when I had none.

Finding my birth mother was akin to a spiritual experience, and my obsession with "all things Liddy" continued to grow. Based on the frequency of his sighs and eyerolls, Joe grew to resent my birth mother as much as he disliked my adoptive mother.

My mother, Marie, still had no idea that Liddy Maher was fully alive and part of my life. I'd flown down to visit my Liddy several more times over the thirteen months since my first trip to San Diego, the last time two weeks prior. But she had yet to fly up to Washington to meet her five grandchildren, which she desperately desired. My kids still knew nothing about their new grandmother. Because for them to know ran the risk of Mom knowing, and I still couldn't bring myself to tell her.

THE PICTURE ON THE card from Liddy was idyllic. Two women, one older and one younger, and a child walked along a beach wearing oversized floppy straw hats. The older woman carried an open umbrella, shielding herself and the younger woman from the sun. The child played in the tidewaters. The artist had rendered the scene in pastel hues of blues, pinks, and yellows. I turned it over and read the credit, "Roger La Manna, 1988, *By the Sea*," and then inhaled Liddy's words:

May 17, 1989

Dear Liz –

Just a quick note. Isn't this picture just a perfect dream life? There we are: you, me, and Lily at the seashore, and the day is neither too hot nor too cold. No one has to cook, wash, or iron. We live on manna, and dragonflies have irradiant wings and light on every flower.

I hadn't spoken with Chet, the doctor that delivered you, for many years. I picked up the phone, called information for Pomona, and reached him so easily. He is 71 now. The conversation progressed just as if it were yesterday that we had last spoken.

He said, "About two days ago, I sat here wondering about that baby girl (you) that I delivered and what had happened to her." Remember, I lived with this doctor and his wife in exchange for helping out with daycare for their four adopted children.

I'm not sure if I told you that he had wanted to adopt you, but the Schmidts had already secured the legal rights. During that phone chat, he confessed that he hadn't called your adoptive parents until the sixth day after you were born, hoping they couldn't get there in time to pick you up. He knew they had to "claim" you within a week of your birth.

I am sending Chet your picture. He was so happy for us and will be coming to La Jolla soon to visit an old friend, and we will meet up. He told me about his four adopted children. All have had problems. None have achieved anything like you professionally. Perhaps he gave them too much. They even had a second home in Palm Springs. I guess you were given the parents who would help you make the most of yourself. God really does not make any mistakes.

At Mass Sunday evening, a friend I teach CCD with said, "I saw you with your daughter at Mass last weekend. That was your daughter, wasn't it?" She thought you were Lily, although she's never seen Lily but has heard me talk about her.

I told her about us, and she was overwhelmed. I just happened to have your children's pictures with me. Is this feeling that I have a preview of paradise?

Love,

Mommie Liddy

After reading that letter, I decided to tell Mom about Liddy. I had delayed for over fourteen months. It wasn't fair to Liddy to deprive her of interacting with her grandchildren, and I'd never kept any big secrets from Mom before. It just felt wrong.

I POKED MY HEAD into Leah's bedroom. She sat at her desk, staring at her geometry and history textbooks. Both remained closed. At least, she'd turned on her study lamp.

"Busy?" I asked, knowing the opposite to be true.

"Yeah. Can't you tell?" She held up a piece of paper with "Leah Trembley" and "Geometry" written in the upper right-hand corner, and, instead of proofs, she had drawn hearts and flowers all around the top and down the left-side margin.

I didn't know whether to laugh or cry. Leah had been "studying" in her room for the last forty-five minutes. Besides her geometry homework, she had a history test tomorrow. Charley Davis's genetic material had silenced any inborn love of school or mathematics that she might have inherited from me.

"Could you help me with something in my room for a minute?" I asked.

"Sure. I need a break from studying." A wry grin spread across Leah's face.

"I can see that," I said, shaking my head in defeat, unable to suppress a smile.

Joe and the four younger kids were glued to the TV, watching their favorite Sunday evening TV show, *Life Goes On*, oblivious to us passing through the family room. I locked the door behind us as we entered the master bedroom.

"Come sit down next to me on the bed. I want to talk to you about something." I patted the bed next to where I sat.

"Am I in trouble or something?" Leah made a long face.

"No, I have some news to share." I smiled, banishing any thoughts of her incomplete homework.

"M-o-m, you're not pregnant again, are you?" she moaned, elongating my name with adolescent drama.

"No, Leah, you'll love what I have to say. But, first, you must promise not to tell the other kids or Grandma Marie. Especially Grandma Marie." I took her hand and met her curious eyes, "Promise me."

"O-k-a-y, if it's that b-i-g of a deal."

"Yep, bigger than a big deal,"

I pulled out the bottom drawer of my nightstand and removed the photo album my coworkers had given me after my first trip to San Diego to meet Liddy. Within the oval frame mounted on the album's front cover, I'd inserted a photograph of Liddy and me in a rapturous embrace.

"Who are you hugging?" Leah's face buzzed with interest and energy.

"That's your grandma, Liddy, my birth mother."

"W-h-a-t? She is so p-r-e-t-t-y. You both look so happy." Leah's blue eyes pooled.

"Over the last thirteen months, three of my work conferences weren't conferences at all. They were trips to San Diego to spend time with my birth mother."

"But why can't Grandma Marie know?" She tilted her head.

"It's complicated. Grandma Marie thinks that Liddy is dead, that she died not long after I was born. But I plan to tell her very soon."

Leah knew that Marie and Fred Schmidt had adopted me as an infant, but we'd never discussed anything beyond the fact of my adoption.

"This is so cool. Can I go visit her when school gets out?"

"There'll be time for that, Leah, and Liddy very much wants to have you visit. You kids are her only grandchildren. But I need to sort out telling Grandma Marie first."

"We could say that I'm going to visit Charley Davis. You could take me to the airport, and nobody has to know but you and Grandma Liddy."

Thanks to a new wife, Charley had shown up again in Leah's life. Leah now spent one week a year with them each summer in Montana.

"I'm not comfortable with that plan, Leah. I need to tell Grandma Marie because Grandma Liddy plans to come up here this summer."

"Far out. I want her to come now!"

"Me, too. But first, I must tell Grandma Marie about Grandma Liddy. And until I do, you can't say anything to the other kids or even Leo."

"Can I call Grandma Liddy?"

"It's too late to call tonight, but you can call her next weekend. Or maybe Tuesday or Thursday night if you get your homework done early enough."

"This is so cool."

Leah lay sprawled out on Joe's king-sized bed, supporting her chin with one hand while turning the pages in the photo album with her other. Together we viewed her new crop of relatives. I fielded questions about Liddy, Lily, Martin, Margot, Alice, Maura, and Andy as each new face showed up.

"By the way, your new grandma is a fabulous pen pal. She'd love for you to write her. I have a whole stack of letters from her," I said as I stood up.

"When you're done with the album, please put it back in the drawer where I got it. And by the way, Liddy is a nickname. My birth mother's first name is Elizabeth, just like mine."

"Awesome," she said, entirely captivated by the faces in the photo album.

"Ten more minutes. Then back to your room and your homework." I shut the door behind me.

JOE HAD ALREADY LEFT for work when Mom made her way into the family room. She headed towards Abby and Noah, who sat in their booster chairs, finishing their peanut butter and jelly sandwiches.

Mom's gait was stiff from her arthritis. Her grey hair laid flat against her head, clearly untouched by comb or brush, such a contrast to Liddy. With an age difference close to twenty years, Liddy continued to shine, vibrant and healthy, while Mom struggled under the burden of her seventy-four years.

"Grandma is here for her kiss," Mom said as she planted a wet kiss on their gooey lips. "Yum, Yum," she said, licking the telltale peanut butter off her lips.

I busied myself in the kitchen, hiding from the damp kiss with my name on it. Kissing on the cheek, I could manage. But Mom insisted on lip kissing. As a small child, I'd wipe the wetness onto my arm whenever Mom kissed me. "You always wipe off my kisses," she had complained. Now I either hid from them or preempted them with a peck on the check.

"Want a cold beer, Mom?" I pulled a can of Miller-Lite from the fridge and waved it at her from the kitchen. I'd bought a six-pack last night specifically for her visit today.

"You bet." She seemed a little out of breath, which was odd. She hadn't walked far. It was just a few steps from the driveway through the garage and into the family room. Mom pulled up a seat at the table.

I handed Mom the can of beer. There was no backing down; Liddy had already purchased her round-trip plane ticket.

"Mom, I need to talk to you about something." I sat down at the opposite end of the table.

Marie diverted her attention from the kids back to me and flipped the tab on her beer can.

"A year ago last January, you told me that my birth mother had died not long after she gave birth to a second child. Well, it turns out that Liddy Maher isn't dead. I was able to contact her sister, Alice, and through Alice, Liddy herself. This summer, she'd like to come for a visit to meet everybody."

I made no mention of my three trips to San Diego, the volumes of correspondence and many phone calls, or how long ago I'd found Liddy. Mom's face showed little if any reaction to my life-shattering news. We could be talking about the price of tea in China.

"The kids don't know anything about Liddy yet. I wanted to let you know first." Yes, that was a white lie. Leah knew but didn't count.

"When does she want to come?" Mom asked after taking a long swig of beer.

"She'll need to arrange to get time off from work. But I'm guessing it will be sometime this summer." Okay, that was another fib. Liddy planned to come in July, the week of the fourth.

That was all there was to it. I'd created a neurotic mountain of a molehill. Mom and I folded laundry together until Abby and Noah went down for their nap. And that was the last of it, and Mom headed home after another hour.

That Saturday evening, Leah spent the night with her best girlfriend. I'd given the four youngest kids early baths in preparation for family movie night. We had all settled in to watch the movie, *Honey, I Shrunk the Kids*, that Joe had rented at Blockbusters on his way back home from the lab.

Hannah and Jonah sat in their kiddie rockers in front of the television set in the family room. Abby and Noah sat between Joe and me sat on the couch. I'd made a giant bowl of popcorn, and everyone was digging into their bowl of salty, buttery goodness.

The ringing phone disrupted the movie. I licked my fingers on the way into the kitchen to answer it, instructing Joe not to pause the VCR.

"Hello," I said.

"You hate me, don't you?" It was Mom.

Over the last several hours, she had stewed in the juices of her perceived rejection with my Liddy's-not-dead news and could hold it in no longer. My stomach lurched, and I began to shake.

"No, I don't hate you, Mom." I tried to sound firm and calm.

"You've always hated me!" Again, she hurled the charge and verdict of my guilt.

I pictured Mom's face, her flashing eyes, her mouth set hard. I pulled on the phone cord and ferried the receiver around the corner and into the formal living room, hoping that Joe and the kids wouldn't hear me.

"Mom, you can't talk to me like that anymore. I'm thirty-six years old. I'm not a child."

"You hate—"

"Stop. Please stop. No more," I screamed into the phone and then dropped it as I slid down the wall and crumpled to the floor.

Joe appeared and grabbed the phone off the floor. He knew who it was. Only my mother could bring me to the brink of madness.

"What's going on here?" he demanded into the receiver.

Once Mom heard Joe's voice, she hung up.

Joe fell to his knees, trying to soothe me. His mouth was moving, but a rhythmic pounding drowned out his words. The air grew thick, and it was hard to breathe. I broke out in a sweat, although I was freezing. I rocked back and forth to the beat in my ears, moaning, "What have I done, what have I done?" But I knew what I'd done. I'd crushed my mother in my selfishness.

My meltdown must have frightened the children terribly, but there was no room for them where I found myself. The dark spiral sucking me downward barely had room for me, so crowded it was with hopelessness and shame and fear and failure.

In the time it took to drive between her house and Joe's, Mom charged into the family room through the garage door entrance and hurried towards the rocking ball of flesh on the floor.

Joe shot up from my side, spreading his arms to restrain my mother as she tried to push her way toward me.

"See what you've done!" he shouted, pointing at me. "Get out of here. You're not welcome in this house."

Mom's presence and Joe's harsh words catapulted me out of my hysteria.

"No, Joe, don't talk that way to Mom. Let her in," I shouted at Joe while springing to my feet and watching their exchange in horror.

Abby was crying, and Hannah pulled at Joe's leg, ordering him to leave Grandma alone. Noah stood on the couch, yelling for Mommy, while Jonah had spilled his bowl of popcorn all over the floor as he stood transfixed by the unfolding chaos.

Joe pushed Mom out of the family room and into the utility room, shouting, "Go," repeatedly.

I heard Mom shout, "I'm sorry, Lizzie. I'm sorry ...," and then Joe pushed her into the garage and locked her out. I ran to the master bedroom, locking the door behind me.

Joe still didn't understand about Mom. The rules were different for her, and allowances had to be made. An abandoned child wailed silently from within my mother's hurt. She didn't mean it; she never meant it.

I was still curled up in the fetal position on the bed after Joe put the kids down and came to bed that night.

"Are the kids okay?" I asked.

"They're fine. Kids are miraculously resilient."

"What did you tell them?"

"I explained that you had two mommies. That Grandma Marie was your adoptive mother, but that another woman, named Liddy, had carried you in her tummy. I said that you had found Liddy and that she was coming to visit them soon. Grandma Marie was still adjusting to the news. I told them everything would be fine, and they shouldn't worry." Joe made it sound so simple.

Joe said the children hadn't asked any further questions and went back to watching the movie. I apologized for my absence and thanked him profusely for talking to the kids afterward.

"One more thing," he said. "I promised them you would talk to them about their new grandma, Liddy, and show them pictures of her tomorrow."

"Yes, that's a good idea." And with that, I rolled over and pretended to fall asleep.

I knew how things would play out come Monday morning. Joe and I would drop the kids off at 7:30 am, and Mom would act as if nothing had happened. And I would never bring it up again. It was the rhythm of my life with Mom.

JULY 1989

I OPENED JOE'S FRONT door and hollered, "We're here, kids." Five excited bodies rushed the entryway, with Leah leading the pack. Liddy looked like a movie star in her tortoise-shell sunglasses as she walked through the door.

Spicy and floral notes of Ann Klein II perfume announced Grandma Liddy's grand arrival in her form-fitting sapphire blue dress. Extra folds of its clingy fabric were gathered over one hip by a rhinestone buckle. Her high heels perfectly matched the same jewel-toned blue.

The girls were immediately enchanted. Leah registered her approval of her glamourous Grandma Liddy with mouth agape while Hannah and Abby hovered underfoot like honeybees drawn to nectar. Leah ushered back the buzzing "bees" as we made our way through the entryway with the luggage.

Jonah watched the procession from the safety of the living room, less impressed with the pageantry but still not wanting to miss anything. Noah stood next to him, swishing a twisted end of his blanket back and forth under his nose.

I pulled Liddy's suitcase inside and made introductions.

"What's in there?" Hannah pointed to the small turquoise makeup case in Liddy's hand.

"That's my face." Liddy's laugh reminded me of tinkling bells.

Hannah looked from Liddy's face to her makeup case and back to her grandmother's face, a canvas with hints of colors and shadows that made the most of Liddy's attractive features.

Liddy smothered each of her five grandchildren in a bear hug before making her way into Jonah's room. During Liddy's five-day visit, Jonah would bunk in Noah's room on the three nights he was with me.

Two days later, Liddy, Abby, Noah, and I stood outside Mom's front door. I'd prearranged the day and time for Mom and Liddy to meet.

Liddy dressed casually in a fitted cotton skirt, covered in a profusion of red, purple, and yellow flowers, and a sleeveless princess-seamed blouse that buttoned in the back. She wore white sandals with a small stacked heel.

I knocked on the front door, opened it slightly, and hollered in, "Mom, we're here. Should we come in?"

"Yes, of course!" We joined Mom in the family room as she clicked off her televised soap opera using the remote control. She rose from her recliner with a grunt and oof. Mom wore her best polyester pantsuit and had curled her hair for this special occasion.

Liddy clasped each of my mother's hands in her own. She gazed into Mom's eyes intently for a few moments before she spoke as if the moment was sacred or she was praying.

"I am so pleased to meet you, Marie. I never imagined in my wildest dreams that I'd have the privilege to thank you in person for adopting Liz and forming her into the wonderful person that she is."

"Thank you for giving me Lizzie." Mom paused, seemingly overcome by emotion. "I am happy to meet you, too."

Liddy nodded slightly and parted her red lips in a wide smile. Mom smiled back warmly. A surge of love wound through me as I watched my two mothers, one bestowed by nature and the other earned through the hard work of nurture. The two women were as different as night and day but united by the glue of my existence.

"Here, I brought this for you." Liddy retrieved a small package wrapped in gold foil with a purple bow from her purse.

"Oh, you shouldn't have!"

"But I wanted to! Open it up," Liddy prodded gleefully.

Marie sat down in her recliner to open her gift, revealing a cameo broach. I doubted Marie would ever wear the cameo, but how could someone like Liddy imagine the simple appetites of someone like Marie Schmidt. Mom thanked Liddy graciously and set the cameo and the wrapping on the nearby end table.

I turned the television back on and found the channel with *Mister Rogers' Neighborhood* to keep the kids occupied. After giving them a bowl of vanilla wafers, I joined Liddy on the couch as she and Mom engaged in small talk.

How was Liddy's flight from San Diego? Had Mom ever been to San Diego? Had Liddy ever been to Washington State before? How long would Liddy stay? Nothing earth-shattering until Liddy brought up my name.

"I was so moved when I found out that you had named our daughter Elizabeth." She paused before continuing, "My name is Elizabeth, too, but you knew that from the adoption papers."

"Yes. That's why I chose the name Elizabeth," Mom said, the words sliding from her mouth like butter off a hot plate.

I froze. My attention riveted to Mom. Had she forgotten that Granny Schmidt had named me Elizabeth? That was the story Mom had always told me. This discrepancy was a big deal to me, especially since Mom had told me Liddy Maher was dead. Without the temerity to confront Mom about the conflicting stories, I told myself that both accounts could be true. No child—even at age thirty-six—wants to believe that their parent is capable of lying.

❀❀❀

THE EVENING BEFORE LIDDY was due to fly back home, she called me into Jonah's bedroom, where she'd been sleeping. "I have something special for you," she said as she removed a rectangular box from the bottom of her suitcase.

The last thing I expected to unwrap was a floor-length, heavily beaded vintage gown.

"You have to try it on for me," Liddy said.

I held up the sea-foam green satin gown with its sweetheart neckline. Form-fitted to the mid-thigh, the dress then fanned out gently with triangular organza inserts of the same soft green, falling elegantly like tulip petals to the floor. It was beautiful, museum-worthy, and reminded me of something that Zelda Fitzgerald might have worn to a ball in the 1920s with a sequined headband and feather.

A sinking feeling enveloped me as we carried the gown to Joe's bedroom, where floor-length mirrors covered the closet doors. I'd never wear such a gown in public, besides Joe and my non-existent social life presented no occasion to parade about in it.

With Liddy's help, I began the shimmying process of pulling the slinky garment down over my raised arms, shoulders, and torso, squeezing myself into it. Liddy zipped up the back from the derrière to the neckline and fastened the tiny buttons down the back of the waist-length, fitted organza over-jacket.

I looked at my reflection in the mirror. The gown was a masterpiece but uncomfortably tight by design, and the long sleeves of the over-jacket were too short. My style was understated, while this gown shouted from the rooftops, look at me.

"You look ravishing," Liddy said. "Turn around and model for me."

I complied half-heartedly.

"Liz, when you walk into a room wearing this gown, every man present will want you!" Liddy proclaimed proudly.

"But my fantasy is to walk into a room and be invisible to every man present," I said.

I saw the disappointment in Liddy's eyes and fought to contain the sting in my eyes. Did my birth mother truly know me, or had she fabricated a daughter that was a reflection of herself?

"I do wish you understood how lovely you are." Liddy's perfect red lips formed a pout. "When I saw this gown at the shop, I knew you would look gorgeous in it with your ivory skin, black hair, and dark blue eyes. I swapped a month's pay for this gown at work."

"That was so thoughtful of you, but I just can't accept this expensive gown. The sleeves are too short, see." I held my arms out for her inspection. "I'd ... I'll never have any occasion to wear it. But it is a fabulous gown and a wonderful gift."

"Veronica told me that I could return the gown if it didn't fit, but I think it fits you perfectly ... but if you won't wear it ..."

"I'm truly sorry, but it's just not me."

"It's okay. I wanted to see you in it, and now, well, I have."

My birth mother had graduated at the top of her class, yet she had made her way in life by being beautiful and desired by men. Many men, by her own admission. She wanted that for me, too, as if I were an addendum to her self-image. But that role didn't fit me any better than the vintage gown that she now folded up and placed back into the box.

I hadn't wanted to disappoint my birth mother and had sincerely attempted to be the "Gumby" of her wishes. But at that moment, I realized I was more like Marie than Liddy. Applying a suitcase full of makeup to perfect my facial features or wearing sexy clothes to draw attention to myself was simply not who I was. Any attempt to reconfigure me as such was destined to fail. Although the beautiful world of Liddy attracted me, I lived in the unadorned and practical world of Marie.

Time would unravel the thread connecting those two opposing worlds, but that would take the deft hands of a man I had yet to find.

Breakthrough

SEPTEMBER 1990

MOM'S HEALTH WAS FAILING. Her spells of labored breathing increased in frequency, leaving her fatigued and light-headed. The three-bedroom house that I'd bought for her became too much, as was babysitting the kids. I hired a nanny to watch the kids at Joe's place and moved Mom into a one-bedroom apartment.

Although the apartment was nice enough, Mom was listless and spent most days in bed. It was hard to disentangle her medical problems from her depression. I blamed myself for her profound loss of purpose when I'd yanked the babysitting role out from under her, but it wasn't safe for the kids.

Antidepressants helped Mom articulate that she wanted a place of her own. It didn't matter how small. It just needed to be hers, not mine and not a rental, but all hers.

I found a two-bedroom manufactured home that she adored. She sat outside in the wooden swing hanging from the awning that shaded the front patio from the harsh summer sun. Her mental health improved with the new place and continued medication, and her physical health seemed better.

Mom's "dollhouse," as she called it, had ruffled Priscilla curtains in the main living areas and a garden window installed above the kitchen sink. I mowed her lawn, tended to the petunias I'd planted surrounding her front patio, and performed house cleaning tasks for her. We had the best relationship ever. Any insecurities that Mom had with Liddy had long since evaporated.

So much had happened in the two years since I'd found Liddy, and I couldn't imagine life without her. My letters had waned, replaced by weekly phone calls, yet Liddy remained the faithful pen pal.

My relationship with Lily remained in the bud stage. She wasn't much interested in having a sister and had zero interest in being an auntie. But we'd found our safe zone. We talked about work, capitalizing on our identities as career women, and she stopped recounting the sins of Liddy according to the gospel of Lily.

I hadn't completely given up on searching for my birth father, but finding him seemed impossible. All I had to go on was the pronunciation of his last name, not even the spelling, and I had no idea what his actual first name was. Ned might be his given name, but Ned was also a nickname for Benedict, Edward, Edmund, Edgar, or Edwin. His surname could be Blue, Bleu, Bleau, Bleue, Blew. And if Liddy has misremembered, possibly Blues, Blewis, or Blewes.

Kait Klosen said it was too costly to search all candidate combinations of the first and last names I had amassed. Mathematically, millions of combinations existed among the myriad of possibilities. Plus, we had no idea where my biological father was living.

I spent many weekends at the local public library, paging through the available phone directories for the greater Chicago, San Diego, and Los Angeles areas, checking all the different possible spellings of surnames. Lines of small black type blurred into one another, yet I found no surname spellings linked to a potential first name variant.

There had to be a way to leverage my birth father's military service to whittle down the possibilities. He'd been in the Navy when Liddy met him at Coronado's officer's club. There had to be a way to access records for commissioned officers between 1949 and 1952. But how?

I decided to call the most extensive library in the world, the Library of Congress in Washington, D.C. I hoped someone there could tell me how to access military records for the Navy.

Serenaded by a sea of clicks, I imagined my call bouncing between every department at the Library of Congress like a ping-pong ball. Finally, a male voice rewarded my patience with a crisp hello.

"Hello, my name is Elizabeth Schmidt. I am trying to reach the head of the military records."

"Speaking. How may I help you?"

"I'm going to be upfront with you. I'm adopted and trying to find information about my birth father. He was a pilot and a commissioned officer in the Navy. I need to verify the correct spelling of his first and last name. He would have received his first commission before the end of 1952. Do you know how I would go about finding that information?"

The mention of adoption would either put off the man or enlist his sympathies, but I knew no other way to explain my informational void.

"You don't know how to spell his first or last name?"

"No, but I do know that he went by Ned and that his last name sounds like the color blue. There are multiple possibilities, millions actually. But if I knew where records were kept, perhaps I could fly there and look through them."

"Did someone tell you to ask for me to help you with this search?"

"No. I kept getting transferred and ended up with you."

"I asked because my wife and I adopted a baby girl recently, and when she is old enough, we plan on sharing the information that we have about her biological parents."

Sharing our common ground of adoption, I filled him in on the high-level details of my search story. He listened and asked questions demonstrating what I interpreted as genuine interest.

"I can't answer your question directly, but I know who can: Richard S. Johnson. He published the book *How to Locate Anyone Who Is or Has Been in the Military*."

The librarian then told me where he thought Mr. Johnson lived. "I bet if you got his book or contacted him, he would help you."

I thanked him, and we said our goodbyes.

After one call to directory assistance, I had a phone number for "a" Richard Johnson and hoped it was the author. On the second ring, a deep masculine voice picked up.

"Good evening. My name is Elizabeth Schmidt. I am trying to reach the Richard S. Johnson who wrote a book about finding anyone who served in the military."

"Speaking."

"Excellent! I got your name from the head military librarian at the Library of Congress. He thought you could tell me where to find the records of commissioned naval officers between 1948 through 1952 inclusive."

"Piece of cake."

"Really?"

"Those records are kept at the Air Force Academy Library in Colorado Springs, Colorado."

"The person I am looking for was in the Navy, not the Air Force."

"The records for the Navy are there as well. You'd need to have access to the base to view the records at the library, or you could try to get someone there to help you."

After a bit more back and forth, I provided him with more details about why I was searching. I thanked him, and we hung up. Mr. Johnson said that the first commission of my birth father was likely a Lieutenant Junior Grade, given that Liddy said he'd had some college.

I was inching closer to finding out my birth father's name. One more call to directory assistance, and I had the phone number for the reference library at the Air Force Academy in Colorado Springs, Colorado.

"Cadet McGuire speaking, Reference Section."

"Hello, Cadet McGuire. My name is Elizabeth Schmidt. Might you have five minutes to help me with a research issue?"

"We are close to closing soon, but I can try to help you if it is quick."

"Does the Air Force Academy Library contain the reference books for the US Navy, giving the complete list of commissioned officers between and including the years 1949 and 1952?"

"Yes, ma'am, it does."

"I'm looking for information about a man who likely received the rank of Lieutenant Junior Grade sometime during those dates. There are a couple of problems, though. I don't know if his last name is spelled like the color blue or like the wind blew or one of several alternative French spellings. He went by Ned, but that could be a nickname rather than his given name." I reeled off the list of possibilities for first and last names. "But since the last name is fairly uncommon, that should narrow the possibilities down considerably."

I then proceeded to tell Cadet McGuire how I'd approach the problem and ended by saying that I'd be happy to pay him for his time.

"I know you can't search tonight ... but maybe some night if you aren't terribly busy?"

"Tell me your name again, please, ma'am. I need to take some notes to search." Cadet McGuire was very polite.

I went through everything again for him, the dates, all possible spellings of my birth father's first and last name, and probable rank. The information as I knew it. He didn't ask who "Ned Blue" was, and I didn't offer.

He worked the next three nights and suggested that I call him back about the same time, shortly before closing, on the third night.

"It shouldn't take too long to dig through the information if your data are even close to correct. I know exactly where the physical records are housed."

And with that, we said goodbye. I felt like a cliff swallow heading into Capistrano after a long, arduous flight home.

Cadet McGuire answered when I called at the appointed hour three days later. He had found a Benoît Simon Bleau, commissioned Lieutenant Junior Grade in 1951, with a birthdate of October 26, 1929. He was the only man with a surname pronounced like the color blue and the targeted officer grade within my time window of interest.

"The first name threw me initially," Cadet McGuire said. "But after digging around, I discovered that Benoît is French for Benedict. And you did say that Ned was a nickname of Benedict."

I could barely breathe. This man had to be my birth father; I felt it in my bones. But beyond the name, October 26 was my birthday, too! It felt like a sign from the heavens.

Cadet McGuire refused my offer to pay him for his time. I thanked him profusely and told him that Benoît Simon Bleau might be my birth father. He said he'd suspected something like that.

I added the information provided by Cadet McGuire to my notebook, the repository of all my notes since I began searching for Aunt Alice. I paged back to Kait Klosen's contact information. With the confidence of a marathon runner on her last quarter-mile, I dialed Kait's number and left a message on her answer machine.

"Kait, Elizabeth Schmidt here. You helped me find my aunt, Alice Maher. I think I've found the information to locate my birth father." I spelled out the information Cadet McGuire had provided along with the birthdate he'd provided. "Would you please run this name through your databases? My contact information has not changed in the year and a half since we last talked. Thanks a zillion!"

I had sent Kait a snapshot of Liddy and me sitting together shortly after our first meeting. In that envelope, I'd included other data like Liddy's full name and birthday and my birthday just in case Kait ever needed that information.

"I FOUND HIM, ELIZABETH, and he wants to talk to you. I have given him all your contact information: your work and home phone numbers and home address," Kate said.

"Oh my gosh, so fast! He's really open to connecting?" I jumped up from my desk and closed my office door.

"He sure is. I just got off the phone with him."

"How did you find him?" I asked, pacing, still in shock by Kait's news.

"I found his name on a real estate transaction for some acreage near Lake Tahoe, on the California side, from a couple of years back. The address on that deal was still current."

"What did you say to him?"

"I asked him if he was the Ned Bleau who knew Liddy Maher in 1952 and early 1953 while stationed in Coronado. That Liddy had given birth to a daughter, which she gave up for adoption, and that you, the daughter, had hired me to locate him. I explained that you'd instructed me to keep his information confidential unless he was open to some level of communication.

"He became quite emotional." Kait paused, clearing her throat, while I grabbed a tissue. "I gave him your contact information. He wants me to call him right back, to let him know if he can call you now."

"Heck, yes. Thank you so much, Kait! I'll let you know how it goes. I'm hanging up now."

Excitement sizzled through my veins. Forcing myself to sit back down, I stared at my phone until it rang five minutes later.

"Hello. Elizabeth Schmidt speaking."

"Elizabeth, this is Ned Bleau. Kait Klosen said you were expecting my call."

Aunt Alice had said Ned's voice was unique, now I understood why. My father's voice was silky-smooth yet the epitome of masculinity.

"Yes, thank you for calling so quickly." I swallowed the lump in my throat.

"When Kait said 'Liddy Maher,' I just knew that this had to do with you. Of course, I knew Liddy was pregnant when I sailed for Korea. But I never knew what happened, if the baby made it or whether she had a boy or girl. We didn't stay in touch. I went back to where Liddy had lived in La Jolla with her father after returning to Coronado, but only once, and they no longer lived there. Honestly, I didn't talk to the neighbors or try to find her beyond that."

"So that you know, I'm not trying to make you feel guilty or get anything from you. Nor am I resentful. Liddy worried about that when I found her."

"That never crossed my mind. I have to tell you that I've always loved the name E-li-za-beth." He pronounced each of the four syllables, stretching out the sound of my name.

"My friends call me Liz." I laughed nervously. "But Elizabeth does sound prettier than Liz." *Especially when you say it,* I thought.

"When Kait called, I felt like the last brick of my life's foundation fell into place. The whole episode abandoning a pregnant Liddy has been an unsettling chapter in my life. I feel as if I can finally have ... closure." He cleared his throat.

"I know Kait gave you my contact information, but she didn't share your personal information. Where do you live?"

"I've lived in Honolulu for the last twenty years. I stayed here when I retired from the Navy."

"Did you ever marry and have children?"

"Yes, several years after you were born, I married Gwen, a Korean war widow, with a little girl, and then we had three daughters of our own. So, you have three half-sisters."

I felt a tinge of something. Jealously? He had abandoned a pregnant Liddy at the altar and married shortly after that, only to raise some other man's daughter as his own. I changed the subject quickly.

"What do you look like? I've been told that I have Liddy's face, but I don't share her coloring or body type."

"I have dark hair and green eyes. I was six foot two and on the thinner side in my prime. At fifty-nine, I've lost an inch or so in height and gained more than that around the middle."

"I got your dark hair, and I bet my two boys have your green eyes because one dad has brown eyes and the other blue. Like me, my girls all have blue eyes but lighter like Liddy's."

"Goodness, you have five children. I thought four was a lot."

"I'd wager those four girls were more work than my three girls plus two boys, at least based on life with my oldest teenage daughter. Is your wife still alive?"

"Yes, and ... yes." He clarified. "Gwen and I divorced at the end of my military career. I married Karen six years ago."

"Can you send me some photographs of you now and when you were younger? I can do the same, including some of the kids, too. Would it be okay if I call you sometime after I get the pictures you send?"

"Yes, of course. I'll send the pictures Fed-Ex, so you get them in two days."

"If you send two-day, do you mind sending them to my work address? I might die if I had to wait until after work to see them."

With a delighted laugh, Ned agreed. After exchanging addresses and phone numbers, we hung up. My head was spinning. I knew I was the luckiest woman in the world. I called Joe to share the good news and floated through the rest of my workday.

NED SURPRISED ME BY overnighting the photos from Honolulu. I ran back to my office with the Fed-Ex mailer and carefully removed the contents, organizing them across my desk like chocolates to be savored one by one.

An 8x10 professional photo in sepia tones shocked me to my core. I had a striking resemblance to the young pilot standing next to the plane. My angular features and something uniquely "me" stared back at me in the man's handsome face. I knew he would recognize his younger self in the photographs of me that I'd put in the mail this morning. As beautiful as Liddy was, this man was every bit as gorgeous. Perhaps more so if that were possible.

He wore military flight gear: a leather flight jacket, an unbuttoned inflatable life vest, a leather cap with large sound-muffling earflaps and dangling chin strap, and cargo pants. Goggles rested on top of his head like sunglasses, and something like a leather bag hung over his left shoulder at his hip, perhaps a parachute. One of his beige leather-gloved hands rested on the side of the open cockpit. "1952" was written on the back of the photograph in pencil.

I picked up a more recent picture, a professional color headshot. Perhaps for work, whatever his job was. I'd forgotten to ask yesterday. His hair was still black, with distinguished bits of gray at his temples. Here I could study his eyes, dark green with hints of gold. He had retained his disarming good looks evident from the pilot picture. The notation on the back read "about five years ago."

There were several other black and white photos. One marked "1945" showed Ned, as a teenager, lying in front of a Christmas tree in pajamas and a bathrobe. In another, dated "Sep 1954," Ned wore white naval officer garb and held a blonde female child, perhaps two years old. Below the date were the words "Wedding to Gwen, me holding Vicki" penciled on the back in barely legible printing.

There was a snapshot of Ned standing alongside four girls. The back of the color snapshot read "1969 Honolulu – Vicki (16), Joni (13), Sandi (12), Terri (10), and Ned (40)." I studied all the faces. I saw some resemblance between Joni and myself. She alone, among her sisters, had Ned's ebony hair. I did the math; Joni was two years younger than me and two years older than Lily. Ned had wasted no time in marrying after he left Liddy.

I suspected that the last photo was current, although it was undated. Ned lay on the floor next to a chocolate Labrador retriever. There was no picture of his current wife.

Finally, I unfolded the accompanying letter, which Ned had typed:

Tuesday night

Dear Liz –

We spoke earlier in the day, and I wanted to get these pictures off to you as soon as possible. As I said on the phone, I feel like the last piece of my life's foundation has been fit into place. I very much look forward to getting to know you and am grateful that you found me.

You may keep all the pictures, but I would like to have the one by the plane back as that is my only copy. I was a pilot in the Navy and landed on aircraft carriers. That picture was taken the same year that I met your mother, Liddy, before I shipped off to the Korean War, which ended before we even docked port.

I stayed in the Navy until my early forties, when I retired. I tried various professions but ended up in real estate, which I do now part-time, and that ended up being my forte.

I didn't have a recent picture of all the girls together. The one I included is old, but at least you can see them all. As I mentioned on the phone, Gwen was a widow when I married her, so Vicki is my stepdaughter. Joni, Sandi, and Terri are your half-sisters. Sandi and Terri live in Hawaii; Vicki and Joni live in California. Their mother, Gwen, and I divorced in my forties. I remarried several years ago to Karen, the woman who owns the dog.

Please feel free to call anytime. We have a lot to catch up on.

Love,

Ned

As I folded up Ned's note and placed the photos back in the Fed-Ex mailer, I reflected on the last two years and nine months since I first began searching for Aunt Alice. Adoption had touched many of those who'd helped me find my birth parents.

Amy, who worked at the New Hope Adoption Agency, had given me the name of Ellen Balondis from a *People* magazine article. Ellen Balondis had been adopted and had given up a child for adoption. Ellen had encouraged me to contact the private investigator, Kait Klosen, who had been adopted as an infant. The head librarian at the Library of Congress, an adoptive father, had told me about Mr. Johnson, which led me to Cadet McGuire at the Air Force Academy.

MOM WAS STILL IN the hospital the day that I received the pictures from Ned.

Her spells of struggling to breathe had returned. As I walked down the corridor, the aroma of institutional hospital food hung unappetizingly in the air. I lightly rapped on the open door of her room.

"Hi, Mom. Do you feel like company?"

"Yes, come on in."

As I walked to the side of her bed, she removed the cover over a plate containing some over-cooked broccoli, a couple of thin slices of turkey, and mashed potatoes covered with yellow gravy, hardly touched. "I'm done. Are you hungry?" she asked.

"I'll pass, Mom. Any updates from the doctor?"

"I get to go home tomorrow." She added brightly. "They're putting me on blood thinners. That is supposed to help me breathe better."

I'd thought Mom might be having a heart attack when I'd brought her to the hospital two nights ago. But her labs showed no evidence of cardiac stress. The doctor thought blood clots from her legs were causing her shortness of breath. Mom's diagnosis and continuing health issues confirmed that I had made the right choice to hire an in-home nanny for the kids, although it had been hard for Mom to relinquish that role.

"Call me at work when they're almost ready to discharge you. I can get here in twenty minutes to take you home. I want to hear your discharge instructions."

"Jeannie called me this morning," Mom said, pleased.

"I don't suppose Jeannie said anything about coming down from Spokane to see you, did she?" I tried to sound upbeat and not resentful.

Fortunately, when I'd called to let Jeannie know Mom was in the hospital, she had been performing with her band at a nightclub in Spokane and not on the road. Otherwise, I would have had no idea how to reach her.

"No. But you know how she is, Lizzie, living paycheck to paycheck ..."

Jeannie always had an excuse to avoid spending time with Mom. And Mom always made excuses for Jeannie's absence.

I rolled Mom's tray table off to the side and handed her the picture of Ned in his flight gear standing by the plane.

"Who does this picture remind you of, Mom?"

"Turn the overhead light on for me, Lizzie, so that I can see better."

Mom stared at the image through her bifocals. Slowly the corners of her mouth turned upwards into an unmistakable smile.

"Lizzie, this man looks just like you. Who is it?"

"My birth father, Ned Bleau. I talked with him yesterday for the first time and got these pictures in the mail from him today. He lives in Hawaii."

I didn't go into all the details of what it took to find him, and Mom didn't ask.

Mom flipped through the rest of the pictures. "You favor him so much, Lizzie, much more than Liddy," she said smugly. "Especially your coloring, even more so than his other daughters," she said when she came to the photo of Ned standing with his other daughters. "He could never deny you, that's for sure."

She read the note that Ned had included with the pictures. How different this all was from sharing the news about Liddy. I'd never once let Mom read any of my correspondence from Liddy, who by now had sent a dresser drawer full of letters and cards.

"Well, I'll never have to worry about you. He'll always take care of you, Lizzie," Mom said like she was privy to a crystal ball and peering into my future.

Part Two: 1990 - 2001

In those days there was no king in Israel;
all the people did what was right
in their own eyes. (Jgs 17:6)

Seattle

OCTOBER 1990

MY MORNING FLIGHT LANDED a couple of hours before Ned's flight was due to arrive at the Seattle-Tacoma airport. He had arranged for us to meet in person less than a month after our first phone conversation. As I watched his plane taxi to the gate, I ran to the restroom to check my appearance one last time.

I looked myself over in the mirror, displeased with my reflection. Why hadn't I worn one of my new outfits? My friend had insisted we go shopping, saying, "You need something special to wear when you meet your father for the first time." Instead, I'd packed both new outfits and had donned my old standbys: blue jeans, a favorite purple sweater, and my black lace-up granny boots. Comfort clothes that maintained my invisibility.

And why had I let Leah talk me into chopping off my hair? My new Wynona-Ryder look had left me with one or two inches all over. I had yet to master the tousled look. I fingered the stiff strands, wondering if gel might have been better than hairspray. Now I wished I'd kept my hair long, feeling naked without the cover of my long hair to hide behind.

I raced back to the gate and recognized Ned the instant he deplaned. There was much that the photographs hadn't captured: his fluid movements and the power of his smile or slight nod on strangers as he passed. His cowboy boots made him look taller than I'd imagined, and the fit of his jeans and the hang of his brown bomber jacket coupled with a full head of dark hair belied a man who'd just turned sixty. He could easily pass for fifty, maybe less.

Stepping forward from the clump of eager people awaiting their loved ones, I waved tentatively at Ned. He recognized me and waved back enthusiastically. We hurried toward one another with big smiles. I stood there in silence as if his handsome face, perfectly-formed white teeth, thick dark eyebrows, and green eyes had paralyzed me.

Stupidly I said, "I'm Liz," as if he needed confirmation of my identity and then extended my hand in greeting.

"And so you are," he said, sandwiching my hand between his two in a touch that felt as intimate as embracing.

"I need to run back to the gate to ask the agent a quick question about my return flight before he leaves. Don't go anywhere. I'll be right back," he said.

Starstruck, I watched him walk away. My breathing quickened, kicked into high gear by an incredulous pride that the hunk moving toward the counter was my birth father.

As Ned stood in line only steps away, awaiting assistance, he turned around to look back at me. His eyes slowly traveled the distance from my head down to my toes. It was an odd feeling and one that I've never forgotten. Although not particularly paternal, his gaze signaled approval, which I had been longing for.

Since I'd already retrieved my suitcase from baggage claim and Ned had carried on his bag, we walked directly to the car rental counter one floor below. I asked how his five-hour flight had been from Honolulu, and he inquired about my one-hour flight.

"Thank you again for paying for my airfare to Seattle, the hotel room tonight, and the car rental," I said. Ned's generosity had made it hard for Joe to object to the trip. I'd been hesitant to accept his generosity, especially since I'd paid for all my trips to visit Liddy, but he'd insisted, minimizing the cost.

"My pleasure. Thanks for giving up your weekend to meet me."

His eyes were so green that I found it hard not to stare. As we clipped along, I followed his eyes, which settled on every pretty woman who walked toward us: first lingering on her breasts, then up to her face, then back to me and our conversation.

"Enjoying the scenery in Washington so far?" I said, half peeved and half in jest. Not that Ned was the only man ever mesmerized by the bouncing bosom of a random passing female, but I surprised myself by calling him on it.

"Yes, I am," he replied sheepishly. "Hey, I'd like some real lunch. Can you recommend a place for us to eat?"

"Let's head to Pike's Place Market. There are lots of great places on the waterfront."

"Sounds perfect. I'll be the driver, and you can be the navigator," he said as we loaded our bags into the rental car's trunk a short time later.

Ned thought the drive north from SeaTac into Seattle was lovely. His closest comparison was an area around Lake Tahoe where he had purchased some property.

"The infamous real estate transaction that Kait Klosen used to connect us?" I said.

"That's right. I'd hoped that my wife, Karen, and I could build a house and retire there for at least half of the year."

"Hoped? Does that mean it isn't going to happen?"

"Very doubtful. Karen never had kids; her two dogs are her kids. She won't leave them to travel anywhere with me. The last trip we took together was four years ago. Most trips I take alone."

"Well, not this one." I smiled at Ned as he turned towards me. "Hopefully, you won't be sorry!"

"Sorry? I'm already thrilled."

As he drove down the freeway, I studied Ned's profile. His aquiline nose had to be French or Roman.

"I've never met anyone named Benoît before or with the surname Bleau. Very French sounding."

"My grandfather was named Benoît. Few people know my first name; Ned is much simpler. My mother grew up in a rural part of Louisiana, southwest of New Orleans. French was her first language. When she'd get together with her sisters, they'd speak French. I couldn't understand a word of their conversations. Mom didn't learn English until grammar school.

"Do you speak French?"

"No, Mom felt that speaking French caused people to look down on her, so she never spoke it to my brother or me. Mom, your grandmother Pauline, is eighty-eight years old. My brother, Henri, moved her into a retirement community after Dad died. I'm not sure Mom has ever forgiven my brother for that."

"How long ago did your father die?"

"About four years ago. He'd have called you 'Sugar' in his New Orleans accent. I can still see him with a cigar hanging out the side of his mouth, whether lit or not, with his two giant dimples and deep cleft in his chin."

"You got your dad's cleft in your chin. So did my middle daughter, Hannah. His dimples, too. It's fantastic to learn where these mystery traits come from."

After finding parking, I led Ned to Ivar's Restaurant on Pier 54 along the waterfront in downtown Seattle. I'd never been inside Ivar's, although I'd eaten outside at their fish bar a couple of times when living in Seattle as a college student.

Once inside, we walked past a long, polished bar and entered a cozy, pub-like room overlooking Elliott Bay. Pictures covered the dark wooden wall. I pointed out the Space Needle and explained that it had been built for the World's Fair in Seattle when I was in third grade.

Ned ordered their best bottle of chardonnay after perusing the wine list and querying the server. When the waiter returned to pour a sample for Ned, he held it up to the light, swirled the glass, smelled the wine, and took a sip.

"Perfect, like a sip of cool water," he said.

When the server returned, I ordered fish and chips, as did Ned on my recommendation. Before handing the menu back to the waiter, I must have mindlessly smelled the menu.

"Did you just smell the menu?" Ned asked.

I burst out laughing, "Probably. It's weird, I know. I have an intense sense of smell."

"That's so funny. Your grandfather, Henri Senior, was the same way. It drove your grandmother crazy. He was a cigar salesman and said his nose never failed to pick out a winner."

"I wish I could have met your father."

"Were you close to your adoptive parents, Liz?"

I chose my words carefully. "I felt very loved by Mom and Dad. My sister, Jeannie, was closer to Dad, and she would say that I was closer to Mom."

"But what would you say, Liz?" As he searched my eyes for details, I felt like a candle melting under the flame of his gaze.

"Jeannie's probably right. As a child, I felt like Mom's protector. Even back then, she seemed so," I paused, "fragile. Things haven't changed much."

I talked about Mom's childhood and my life growing up in the Schmidt household.

"Dad had a bad temper, but he had a soft heart. Just a little rough around the edges. He died when I was twenty-eight. A year later, Mom moved in with Leo, my husband at the time, and me. Now Mom lives less than ten minutes from Joe and me. She tells people that I'm her angel, but I'm sure angels help without feeling sorry for themselves, which I confess, I sometimes do."

"Don't be too hard on yourself, Liz. We aren't perfect, and neither were our parents. People do the best they can. It can take a long time to work out the kinks in the relationship with our parents. My Dad couldn't show any affection toward me until he had a stroke a couple of years before he died.

"I was in the Navy while my daughters were growing up, so we moved around a lot. Plus, I was gone for months at a time when actively flying. I feel closer to my girls now than when they were growing up. By the way, I haven't told any of them about you yet; I was waiting until we met. You probably had a much more stable life with Marie and Fred than I'd have given you."

"Stable, yes, that's one way to describe it," I said. "We didn't have a fancy life, but I always had a home, clean clothes, and good food. Once Dad got sick, we lived on Social Security disability and what Mom made from her ironing, babysitting, and odd jobs.

"I wanted a different life for myself than I had growing up. Dad always said, 'A man can always dig ditches, but a woman needs an education to take care of herself.' I took his advice, which wasn't hard since I loved school, unlike my sister, Jeannie. And I was fortunate to get scholarships, grants, and teaching assistantships to help pay for my education.

"Things got tricky when I became pregnant and got married at nineteen. I lost all my financial aid except my scholarship once I married. I worked graveyard shift the whole time I was pregnant while still going to school full-time. Not fun, but it all worked out." I smiled, "We do what we have to do."

"I graduated from USC in international law when Gwen was pregnant with our last daughter. I remember how crazy that was with three little girls and one on the way. Are you and your sister close?" Ned asked.

"As close as we can be, given that we are complete opposites. She's a singer in a rock band. But what about your family? What was growing up like for you, Ned?"

"My one sibling, Henri, was six years older than me and set the bar pretty high. Henri was everything I wasn't and the apple of my father's eye. During WWII, he spent fifteen months in a German POW camp. Don't get me wrong, Henri is the best brother in the world, but living in his shadow, I felt like a disappointment to my father.

"I was the risk-taker and the one always getting in trouble. Little things, really, but they impacted my relationship with Dad. But Mom thought I was the cat's pajamas no matter what I did."

"Gosh, look at the time. We need to finish eating, or we'll miss our appointment," I interjected. I'd told Ned about our appointment at the portrait studio downtown on the ride from the airport to lunch but hadn't thought of it once since.

Twenty minutes later, we walked into Olan Mills Studio. The photographer positioned us in several different ways. For the last pose, I was close enough to inhale Ned's leather and spicy scent. The photographer had me stand behind Ned, seated on an adjustable stool. He draped my stiff arms around Ned's shoulders and pulled me in close to him. He brought our heads together gently, tilting mine slightly.

As Ned relaxed into my arms, I felt a connection, an unearned intimacy, from our biological bond. My birth father thoroughly delighted me, and I loved being with him.

After the photo session ended, we walked back to the waterfront area, wandering through curious little shops while talking nonstop. As the sun began to dip towards the horizon, we got back into the car, and Ned drove to the hotel.

We checked into our rooms at the Westin Hotel downtown. I changed into one of my new outfits, a black and white belted gaucho dress and black heels. Ned met me downstairs, looking dapper in dress slacks and a jacket and tie.

He drove us back to Pike Place Market for dinner at Maximilien Restaurant, which had been recommended to him earlier that day when he'd asked where the best French cuisine was in Seattle.

Once past the main entrance, we turned left beyond the fish market and entered the restaurant's main floor. Our table overlooked Elliot Bay with a giant Ferris wheel brightly lit in the foreground. I forced myself to taste the appetizers Ned ordered, escargots à la Bourguignonne. One was enough for my uninitiated palate. Although the buttery, garlicky sauce was yummy, I couldn't get past the idea of eating snails. I left the rest for Ned.

I ordered a seared sockeye salmon with a creamy tarragon sauce. Ned ordered confit de canard, a bottle of Veuve Cliquot champagne, and a glass of Oregon Pinot Noir for later when they served his entrée.

Dinner proved excellent, and Ned seemed not to mind the exorbitant price. Food and wine were a high priority for my birth father. Although stuffed to the gills, I made room for crème brûlée, my highest priority, which the chef had creatively flavored with strained lavender flowers.

As I scrapped the last bit of my favorite dessert from the porcelain ramekin, Ned removed a small box from the inside vest pocket of his jacket. The turquoise blue box was stamped Tiffany & Co and tied with a narrow white ribbon.

"Should I open it now?" My eyes moved from the box to his sparkling eyes.

"Yes, please. I must know if you like it."

I untied the bow and lifted the lid, savoring the moment, cementing it into my memory. The extravagance of its contents shocked me: a one-inch gold pendant bearing three rows of small diamonds set within its stylized heart shape. Even in the low overhead lighting, the diamonds sparkled like fire against a backdrop of midnight blue velvet.

"It's gorgeous." I pried it loose from the ties that secured the pendant and chain to the box. Ned stood and moved to my side of the table. Taking the necklace from my hand, he gently fastened it around my neck.

"To commemorate our first meeting," he whispered, seemingly mirroring the emotion that filled my heart to bursting.

IT WAS A LONG three months before I would see Ned again. I felt like a lovesick puppy. That was how I described my funk to Joe.

"You acted and spoke the same way after finding Liddy," Joe said.

"I suppose, but gosh, this feels more intense. What's the matter with me? I feel like a teenager with a bad crush on my birth father," I shook my head in disbelief.

During those months, my relationship with Ned flourished with letters and phone calls, providing a welcome respite from the demands of work, kids, and my mother, Marie.

Mom hadn't improved sufficiently on blood thinners, so her local doctor scheduled her for a cutting-edge procedure at the University of Washington Hospital. A mesh filtering device would be inserted in her leg, trapping blood clots before reaching her lungs.

Jeannie, who'd recently moved to Seattle with her husband and two kids, met Mom at the airport the day before her procedure. There were no complications, and everything went as expected. Mom would stay with Jeannie for a few days afterward until the doctor cleared her to fly home.

I had a work-related conference in Portland, Oregon, while Mom was grounded in Seattle. Ned suggested that we meet up for the weekend in San Francisco after my Wednesday through Friday meetings.

I felt guilty being gone from the kids for another two days after already being gone for three, but not guilty enough to deprive myself of Ned's company. Besides, all I'd ever seen of San Francisco was the inside of the airport. And so, I flew from Portland to San Francisco Friday evening after my last presentation.

Ned had already spent several days in the Bay Area when he met me at the airport. He had rented a suite at a lodge in Tiburon north of San Francisco across the Golden Gate bridge.

He said there was a slight mix-up on the suite and that instead of two bedrooms off a shared kitchen and living room, there was only one bedroom, but the sofa in the living room converted to a pullout bed.

"Will the sofa bed work for you, Liz?"

"I can make it work." All I cared about was spending time with Ned again.

During breakfast Saturday morning, Ned told me something that Liddy had never shared.

"When I broke off the wedding with Liddy, I had a plan for you, Liz."

Ned's eyes were soft and warm as he spoke. He reached for my hands across the table.

"My brother, Henri, and his wife wanted to adopt you. Henri had proposed this idea as they'd never been able to have children. So, it wasn't as if I was totally abandoning you. But Liddy would have nothing to do with the idea.

"I've told Henri about you finding me. He's thrilled for us and wants to meet you, and so does your grandmother, Pauline."

While I could understand Liddy's feelings, a part of me grieved for the life I might have had with my birth uncle, Henri, a well-educated, world-traveled chemist.

After breakfast, we strolled along Fisherman's Wharf past a flotilla of docked sailboats, sidewalk vendors, and sunbathing sea lions. Pungent fishy smells mixed precariously with the aroma of tempting food as we moved from pier to pier. The sun had burned off the remnant of the morning fog. Across the bay, we had a clear view of softly undulating hills punctuated by buildings of varying heights, shimmering white in the sunlight. Even Alcatraz Island, long deserted, looked peaceful off in the distance.

Only four months ago, I'd found Ned. Yet we shared our hearts with a delicate vulnerability comparable to a lifetime. Ned told me that he and his first wife had conceived a child before marrying. He had driven her across the border and into Mexico to have an abortion.

I didn't judge Ned harshly for his actions, as I hadn't judged Liddy for a similar choice. Still, I grieved the lost lives of two half-siblings, amazed and grateful that I'd not met the same fate.

Ned stopped at an outdoor merchant selling fancy leather goods near Pier 39 and perused the ladies' jackets hanging on the racks. He held up a black leather jacket that reminded me of a feminine, more sophisticated version of the brown leather bomber jacket that he wore.

"Lambskin," the saleswoman said. "You'd pay twice as much for this in a shop in the Marina District." She showed Ned the price tag.

"You have to try it on," he insisted, holding the jacket up to me.

"I don't need a leather coat." While I'd never owned a leather coat, I couldn't imagine wearing anything with that kind of a price tag.

"Who said anything about needing one," Ned said, slipping it off the hanger. "Let me see how it looks on you," he said, holding the coat open for arms.

The saleswoman, sensing my reluctance, took over. She zipped the jacket up, tied the belt at my hipline, and ran her arms across my shoulders. "A perfect fit. It's made for her," she said, smelling a sale.

Ned walked over and pulled the collar up. "You look smashing, Liz." He turned to the saleslady and said, "We'll take it."

We lunched on clam chowder and sourdough bread at midday while gazing out onto the steely-blue bay from our outside table. Wooden planter boxes, teeming with English primroses in blue, pink, yellow, and white, enfolded us in garden-like coziness. I felt like Cinderella, but instead of a fairy godmother, I had a fairy birth father and wore a black leather jacket instead of an evening gown.

After lunch, Ned drove us back to the lodge so he could watch a football game. We sat together on the couch in front of the TV. Football wasn't my thing, but I was content watching him watch the game and simply being near him.

We used the small coffee table as an ottoman for our stockinged feet. "I see now where I got my super narrow, long feet," I said, remembering the sixth-grade boy calling my feet banana boats. Having inherited those "banana boats" from Ned had made them infinitely more acceptable.

Ned shared how empty his marriage to Karen had become. They now slept in separate rooms, and he paid her rent every month. Ned was a die-hard romantic, and I empathized with his loss. The depth of his sadness drew me near him emotionally, wishing to comfort him.

As if by some inexplicable, outside force, we turned towards each other. Our lips touched lightly and then locked passionately. My hunger for a physical connection with him superseded my sense of reason. Ned's response was strong, deep, and longing.

I had never once imagined or thought of kissing my birth father. But when our lips made contact, I became a pile of mindless metal filings pulled inexorably towards the poles of his powerful magnetism.

"You okay, Liz?" Ned asked as he touched my face gently, his eyes moist.

"Yeah, I think so." Part of me wanted to run away from—no, flat out deny—what had just happened. But the other part of me wanted never to extricate myself from the delicious disaster of our kiss.

Moments later, I stood up quickly as if the couch were on fire. I touched my face where his hand had stroked me tenderly. "What time is it?" I asked, struggling to downregulate my wild emotions.

Ned looked at his watch. "It's four-thirty. Why?"

"St. Hillary's Church is about five minutes from here, ten at the most if I get lost. It starts at five."

I'd checked out the Mass schedule earlier that day. Ned removed the car keys from his pocket and held them out.

"I promise to be careful," I said. And taking the keys, I left for Mass, running for the car. I needed time to think and process what had just happened.

Kneeling in the last pew at St. Hillary Church, my thoughts ricocheted back to Ned, the couch, the kiss, the unbridled forbidden desire. My brain was stuck in replay mode. I remember nothing about that Mass except that my entire being, the core of who I was, felt engaged in a battle I felt helpless to fight.

I'd fly home the following morning, back to my old life. The one that I thought was as good as it got before Ned had changed everything. I didn't know what to expect when I got back to the hotel. But to my surprise and relief, there was no awkwardness between us. Everything seemed back to normal. Had I imagined the whole thing?

The Carnelian Room was on the 52nd floor of the Bank of America Building. Ned had eaten there by himself several times before but always alone. It was his favorite restaurant in San Francisco.

He had requested a special table for two when he made the reservations a week ago. Golden chargers lay atop a white starched tablecloth, and three different sizes of wine glasses awaited us. Floor-to-ceiling windows framed an expansive view of the city outlined in glittering lights.

After studying the wine list, Ned ordered a three-hundred-fifty dollar bottle of Bordeaux.

"This place is off-the-charts spendy," I said, scanning the menu.

"It's worth every penny, given that I get to be with you, Liz. I know you haven't experienced this kind of extravagance. It's a gift for me to be the first one to share fine things with you."

Ned ordered a rack of lamb, medium-rare, encouraging me to do the same and not to worry about the price. But I never ate lamb, the rank aftertaste of mutton dinners as a child had scarred my palette permanently. Despite Ned's advice that the wine could overpower my entree's mild flavor, I ordered sole meunière.

"Our being together has made me realize that I need so much more. I've just been settling with Karen. You have brought such happiness to my life."

We split a Caesar salad after watching it prepared tableside. After we finished the salad, two waiters brought out our entrees covered in cloches. They lifted the silver domes in unison after placing them in front of us.

"Bon appétit," Ned said.

I forced myself to eat, although my stomach twisted and turned each time my mind revisited the afternoon's kiss.

Again, two waiters served our dessert, Grand Marnier soufflés. Ned gently opened the top of my souffle with a flick of his spoon and poured in a warm, sweet vanilla-orange sauce. He handed me my dessert with his beautiful hands and prepared his own.

The candlelight flickered across Ned's face as he tasted his souffle, closing his eyes in epicurean ecstasy.

"I had no idea that to find the perfect woman, I had to create her myself." He reached across the table to touch my hand as he spoke.

If I'd fallen off a cliff earlier in the day, Ned's words now severed my safety line; I could no more rappel myself back up that cliff than fly to the moon. I felt terrified, but not of Ned as I trusted him with my life. I was frightened of myself.

THE MORNING DRIVE BACK to the airport was painful for both of us, and we hardly spoke. The line we had crossed by our kiss hung heavy in the air. The impossibility of our relationship was apparent, but my heart refused to accept logic or be confined by social mores. Once we passed security, I kissed Ned goodbye on the cheek, and we went our separate ways.

I felt the wetness of my tears before I realized that I was crying. My life no longer made any sense. How could I live without the one person I finally felt I belonged with? But how could I belong to the one person I shouldn't be with?

My stomach turned as I pondered the impossibility of the situation. But like it or not, I had to acknowledge that I would never be the same again.

Goodbye

ONCE AIRBORNE SUNDAY MORNING, I rehashed my last thirty-six hours with Ned. When we'd parted in San Francisco, my heart had been ripped out and replaced with a sinkhole of conflicted feelings. I longed for something that I couldn't have and shouldn't want.

Glancing out the window at clouds floating beneath me, I recalled the last time I'd felt so confused—the last years of my marriage to Leo Trembley. At the time, I had no idea how shaky our marriage was nor how ripe I was for Joe Keller's picking. The mess I'd made of my life should have warned me that I was capable of great foolishness when chasing after love.

SUMMER 1980

LEO AND I HAD plenty to celebrate the weekend we drove to Seattle for a mini-holiday. I had successfully defended my thesis the week before, we were one week away from moving into our brand-new home, and we were celebrating our second wedding anniversary. I'd arranged for six-year-old Leah to spend the weekend with friends, leaving us footloose and child-free.

I was surprised but not upset when Leo suggested that I spend the afternoon with a college roommate while he went to Longacres to watch the horse races with an old friend. I didn't enjoy horse racing and was happy to oblige. Nothing could nip the bud of my joy; my life was perfect.

Leo was four hours late in picking me up. By the time he returned, it was almost 10 p.m. Inexplicably antisocial, Leo rang the bell and returned to the car without coming inside or waiting for anyone to open the door. Although relieved that he was okay, I was hotter than an agitated yellow jacket, hurt, confused, and embarrassed that my extended visit had required my friend to cancel her evening plans.

"Where have you been? I've been panicked. Why didn't you call the house?" My words fired off like a machine gun.

Leo's eyes stayed glued to the roadway as he puffed away on his cigarette.

"I'm in love with another woman. I'm divorcing you." Leo spoke firmly, absent any emotion. "My mind's set, and you can't talk me out of it." He never looked at me.

Leo's words knocked the wind right out of me. To say I was stunned and crushed would be an understatement. I'd spent the better part of the day telling my friend how happy I was married to Leo and how deeply I loved him.

Resolute in his decision, Leo refused to answer my questions, no matter how I begged, cried, or screamed. This heartless Leo was a stranger to me. After a sleepless night of hysterical sobbing, I drove home at daybreak, leaving Leo behind in Seattle at the hotel.

A week later, Leo returned home with a warped version of reconciliation. He would stay with me if I met his conditions. There'd be no questions about the other woman, no explanation for his about-face regarding the divorce, and no probing into where he'd been.

I'd have done anything to keep him, so I agreed to his impossible terms and never mentioned the whole nightmarish episode to Leo or anyone else. The unpleasant affair scabbed over but festered beneath the surface.

With a vengeance, I took on the task of wiping clean and reformatting the hard drive of my marriage to Leo and considered my efforts 100% successful. Within two years, we were a family of five with Jonah and then Hannah's birth. Jonah and Hannah bound Leo to me as intended, but less so me to Leo, as Joe Keller would help me discover.

MAY 1984

JOE KELLER WAS MY project manager, and it was impossible to avoid him. He began showing up in my office to chat as if he had something on his mind but never came forth with it. After a month of these occasional visits, he asked me out for lunch. A business lunch, I presumed, which was not uncommon.

"Would you prefer to go to a restaurant or my house for lunch?" Joe asked once we got in his car. He had purchased a new house recently. Perhaps he wanted to show it off, I thought. I knew from secretarial chatter that Joe lived with his girlfriend, an engineer who worked at a different company.

"I'd prefer to go to a restaurant."

"Let's go to my house," he countered.

Although going to Joe's house made me uncomfortable, I gave no outward indication. I wanted to be treated like one of the guys. As the only woman in the technical working group, I was reluctant to draw any attention to my gender. Yet my discomfort stemmed from just that: Joe was a man, and I was a woman.

When we got to his house, there was nothing to eat for lunch. All he had in the refrigerator were several bottles of beer. I managed one swallow. The only way I could drink beer was to douse it with tomato juice. Once he finished his liquid lunch and I ran out of conversation, Joe gave me a tour of his house.

At the end of a long hallway, Joe entered the master bedroom. I stood outside the doorway but peered inside. The king-sized bed was in jumbles from the night before, sheets and comforter gathered into a rumpled central pile.

"Would you like to make love?" Joe asked as if that were a typical business lunch activity.

Without answering, I walked away and returned to the family room and sat at the small table where we had previously had "lunch." I covered my face with my hands in panic and wished myself invisible.

Joe rejoined me at the table. "I'm sorry," he said, "I thought you wanted to make love as much as I did." What had I done to encourage this man? I had no idea how to rewind the last hour and salvage our working relationship.

Uncovering my face, I replied, "I'm in love with my husband. I'm so sorry I gave you that impression." I felt like crying. But I didn't want to cause trouble at work or, even worse, lose my job.

Just as I'd pushed down my misgivings about going to his house for lunch, I hid my shock and fear under a false take-it-in-stride bravado. "You're an attractive man, Joe, but casual sex is not in my repertoire."

When I told Leo what had happened that evening, he'd said, "He just wants in your pants." Part of me wanted Leo to say, "Quit. We'll make do," while another part of me feared just that. I'd worked so hard to get where I was professionally.

I couldn't avoid Joe at work, but I avoided walking down corridors where he might be. I worked nearly every Saturday morning, but Joe often worked Saturdays, too.

Several weeks after the "home tour," Joe walked into my office one Saturday. He sat in the chair adjacent to my desk without invitation. "Would you let me take you out for lunch to apologize? I promise we'll go to a restaurant." He smiled, and I felt sorry for him. I imagined that he felt as uncomfortable around me as I was around him.

Thus became the pattern of our Saturday lunches. I lost my discomfort around Joe. Despite his technical brilliance, Joe had great difficulty reading people's emotions and poor social skills.

With no warning, on the fourth Saturday impromptu lunch, Joe professed his undying love for me. He was utterly convinced that we were meant to be together. His ways were awkward and nerdy, but I knew his ardor was sincere.

He had kicked out his live-in girlfriend, who had been using him for free rent, and proposed marriage with a ring. Never mind that I was married to someone else and that Joe had never even kissed me. Yet somehow, Joe's love felt sacred and pure and undefiled.

Months later, I filed for a divorce. Leo finally confessed that his father had forced him to return to me four years ago, saying, "There has never been a divorce in the Trembley family and no son of mine will be the first."

Leo's best argument for my staying with him was that he had abandoned the woman he loved to stay with me. Therefore, I should be able to turn my back on whatever feelings I had for Joe. That was only fair.

But fair had nothing to do with anything. I was Joe's first choice, whereas I was Leo's booby prize. Besides, I knew Leo would be fine without me. I wasn't so sure about Joe.

Leo never imagined that I would leave him, and I could hardly believe it myself. And so, in the end, I was the one to abandon my marriage to Leo. I traded my worship at Leo's altar for Joe's adulation at mine.

One year, one month, and three days after my first day at the lab, Leo and I were divorced. The following month I married Joe. Mom had lived with Leo and me for three years by the time I'd married Joe.

"I hadn't been here a week before I knew you two didn't have a real marriage," Mom had said when I told her I filed for divorce. The Catholic Church must have agreed with her because Leo petitioned and received a decree of nullity for our marriage two years after Joe and I married.

AFTER PUTTING THE YOUNGER kids to bed, I drove over to Mom's place the night I got back from my weekend with Ned in the Bay Area. Although it was late for me, my mother was a night owl, and I knew she'd still be up. Mom had flown back from Seattle the previous day. Joe had picked her up at the airport, with Abby and Noah in tow, while I was still with Ned in San Francisco.

I watched her through the three rectangular windows in her front door for a few moments and then knocked to get her attention. Mom sat with her feet up in her recliner, laughing along with a television show, the TV remote in one hand and a Miller Lite in the other.

She saw me, motioned me in, and hollered through the closed door, "Door is open."

"How do you feel, Mom?" I sat down on the couch next to the recliner as she turned the volume down on her program.

"Better than I've felt in a long time. Those doctors must know what they are doing."

"Well, they're supposed to be the best."

"Are you feeling good enough to drive yet? I wanted to make sure you have enough food in the house."

"Heavens, yes. I drove the car to the store yesterday after Joe dropped me off. I got everything I needed. I even went to Mass this morning. How about that?"

"That's great, Mom. Glad to hear it. Here, these are for you."

Mom took the brown paper bag containing the two decks of cards I'd purchased at the San Francisco airport. The backside of one deck had a picture of the Golden Gate Bridge and the other an image of Fisherman's Wharf. It wasn't much, but Mom enjoyed playing solitaire.

"Thank you, Lizzie. How was your time with your father?"

I described the sights, my new leather jacket, and the fancy dinner at the Carnelian Room. Having never been to San Francisco, Mom took a vicarious pleasure from hearing about everything.

"I'm so happy you've found your father. Now you can be at peace." Mom drifted off in thought for a few moments before she spoke again.

"I've never told you this before, Lizzie," Mom downed the last of her beer, "and I doubt you remember. You were so young. Just shy of your fourth birthday, if I rightly remember.

"I was ironing in the utility room and didn't know you were sitting on the stairs, watching me from behind. Then I heard your quavery little voice, 'Momma, who am I?' I answered, 'You're Lizzie Ann Schmidt. That's who you are.' But you said, 'No, Momma, tell me who I am,' I didn't know what to say. You see, Lizzie, we hadn't told you that you were adopted yet."

Mom looked at me and nodded, "You always wanted to know. Now you do.

"As much as you always wanted to know, Jeannie never seemed to care one hoot."

"Do you know anything about Jeannie's birth parents?" I was curious even if my sister wasn't. Jeannie had expressed some mild interest to me privately after I'd told her about finding Liddy and even more so when I told her about finding Ned.

"I don't know much," Mom said. "Aunt Hazel was a nurse in the delivery room when Jeannie was born. She called me saying that a baby girl was available for adoption but that I had to make up my mind in a hurry. I expected some pushback from Fred, but he was all for it. When I got up that morning, I had no idea that I would have another baby girl by bedtime."

Jeannie and I had heard that story of Mom's half-sister delivering Jeannie. There wasn't much new there.

"Do you know the names of Jeannie's birth parents?" I wondered if Mom knew anything else.

"Only that her father's last name was Savoca."

That was an unusual last name; I'd never heard it before. The next time I spoke with Jeannie, I'd pass on her birth father's last name. But who knew when that would be? Jeannie was unpredictable; we lived in different orbits.

TODAY WAS MOM'S BIRTHDAY. She and Leo shared the same birthday, January 24th. Mom was happy to delay her party for one day until my night when all the kids would be together at Joe's house. I could hardly ask Leo to switch nights with me when it was his birthday, too. I planned to pick up Mom's cake at the bakery on my way home from work, and we'd celebrate tomorrow evening.

When the phone rang, I picked up.

"I ... I ... can't ... can't ... breathe ... help." It was Mom.

"Mom, I'm calling an ambulance and heading right over."

I hung up and called 911. Flustered and panicked, I grabbed the car keys, ran out the front door, and raced to Mom's place. I ran up the steps and turned the handle to enter. She'd locked the front door. Mom never locked her door. Why tonight? Through the windows in the front door, I saw Mom in her recliner, struggling to breathe with one hand on her chest.

My hands shook as I searched through the keyring to find the right key to unlock Mom's door. "No," I screamed. I had grabbed Joe's keys, not mine. Both sets for the BMW looked identical, but only mine had the key to Mom's house. I pounded on the door, tears streaming down my face.

"I don't have the house key. Can you let me in?" I cried out frantically.

Mom sat in the recliner as I continued pounding and begging her to try to get up and let me in. What would happen when the ambulance arrived, and they couldn't get in?

"God have mercy," I shouted as the ambulance rounded the corner. I tried to get Mom's attention one last time. "Mom, the ambulance is here, but I don't have the key. Can you unlock the door?"

Somehow, my mother got up, walked the three steps to the front door, unlocked it, and fell back into her chair. I flung the door open as the emergency workers appeared at the door.

Mom's breathing was ragged and labored. "Wa-wa-ter ... wa-," she said with great effort.

I looked from Mom to the paramedics. One of the men had put a blood pressure cuff around her arm, and the other held a stethoscope to her chest.

"Can I get her water?"

"No, not yet," said the younger man, working the cuff firmly.

"Wa ... wa." Mom begged again.

But the other man said, "Wet a washcloth, hold it to her lips, and let her suck on it."

I ran to the bathroom and wet a washcloth. As I held the wet cloth to Mom's blue lips, a third man appeared with a gurney.

Her body jerked as the two paramedics strained to lift Mom out of her recliner onto the gurney. She released a soft shriek, followed by a jerk, and then she went limp.

The two paramedics got in the back of the ambulance with Mom, while the third closed the back doors and drove off with his siren howling. I followed them to the ambulance entrance of the hospital, where three and a half months earlier, I'd first told Mom about Ned.

The back doors of the ambulance flew open once it stopped. They rushed Mom, strapped to the gurney, out of the ambulance and onto the pavement with a hard bounce. The sheet over her torso slipped halfway off, revealing one bare breast and a limp arm, both swinging loosely over the side of the gurney.

It had been two weeks since Mom had returned from having a stent put in at the hospital in Seattle. She had been so upbeat and happy.

I parked my car and waited in the sitting area outside the emergency room. I'd never seen anyone die, but I feared my mother was already dead. A life force had seemed to exit her body, shrieking and jerking in protest, as the attendants had loaded her onto the gurney.

A doctor walked out of the double doors. After checking with the receptionist, he walked toward me grimly. I stood up as he approached, knowing what he came to tell me.

"I'm Dr. Blake."

"I'm Elizabeth, her daughter."

"I'm sorry. We worked for twenty minutes to resuscitate your mother to no avail. She was dead on arrival."

I choked out a feeble "Thank you," trying to deny the loss that grabbed at my throat. I sat back down on the black vinyl couch.

He sat down next to me. "Are you okay?"

I nodded, trying to distance myself from his news and the disorientation I felt. "She had a mesh filter inserted into her leg two weeks ago to keep blood clots reaching her lungs. She was doing so well. Why did she die?"

"I suspect she died from a pulmonary embolism or a heart attack. Only an autopsy can determine the exact cause of death."

"I want an autopsy." It shouldn't have mattered what killed Mom, but I had to know. Maybe if I'd left the house with my keys instead of Joe's, and she hadn't needed to let me in. Perhaps then she might have lived. I'd been responsible for Mom's care; had I failed her at the very end?

"There is some additional paperwork for an autopsy. You'll want to sign before you leave," the doctor said as he touched my elbow.

"Thank you." I watched the doctor walk back through the swinging doors.

As the doctor disappeared, I imagined Death with brutal finality trailing behind and turning back to glance at me with callous eyes and a triumphant smile. Beyond those doors in some room lay my mother's lifeless body growing cold.

The doctor had confirmed what I'd already known in my heart and seen with my eyes. But hearing his words, "dead on arrival," sent a tsunami of destabilizing grief over me. The opportunity to speak unspoken words or apologize for carelessly uttered words was gone. Mom's book had closed; her final chapter finished. A frighting emptiness and sense of loss pervaded my soul as her life snapped shut.

I called Liddy the day after Mom died.

"Do you want me to fly up for Marie's funeral?" she had asked.

"It means a great deal to me that you offer, but I think not. This is the last time Marie Schmidt gets to be my mother. I don't want to subtract from that," I had said.

Ned hadn't offered to come when I'd called him later that day. He'd never met my mother, as had Liddy. Besides, my emotions had been too much on edge to throw Ned's presence into the mix.

I paged through Mom's address book and contacted anyone still living with whom she had maintained contact or that I'd ever recollected meeting. But the list was small. Many on Dad's side were dead, hadn't kept in touch, or couldn't come. Melanie, the daughter of Dad's youngest and favorite sister, was the one Schmidt-side relative I thought would come. Coeur d'Alene wasn't all that far away. But her husband was in the hospital and not doing well.

Since Auntie Sister had died the previous year, Mom had outlived all her siblings. Aunt Hazel's adult children, Penny and Jimmy, were the only relatives to contact on Mom's side. Mom had babysat Penny and Jimmy while her sister had worked as a nurse at the hospital in Pasco. Both of them said they would come.

Lastly, I let Trixie Dixon, our next-door neighbor from our old Pasco neighborhood, know about Mom. She said that she would be there.

Within twenty-four hours, an autopsy confirmed that the cause of Mom's sudden death had been a pulmonary embolism. Neither the blood thinners nor the mesh insert had worked.

Grateful for the busyness that kept Mom's death at a distance, I handled the details with the mortuary and funeral Mass. I wrote her obituary and eulogy and made arrangements for Mom's body to be transported to and buried in the Catholic cemetery in Spokane next to Dad.

Jeannie would drive over the night before the funeral while her husband, Travis, would stay home with her two children. My sister and I would meet up at the Rosary prayer vigil.

MOM'S BODY LAY SERENELY in a pearl-white casket at the Rosary vigil prayer service. Purple, scarlet, and white African violets were arranged in a massive tiered display at the two front corners of her coffin. A double spray of white and lavender roses, joined in the center as a double fan by a purple ribbon with "Mom" in gold letters, lay on the closed lower half of the casket.

Mom was dressed in a lilac pantsuit, one of several that I'd found in her closet, unworn and still with price tags attached. As per my request, Mom smelled of White Linen perfume and had Avon Instant Mocha applied to her lips, which I'd taken to the mortuary. The mortician had closed both eyelids completely, thankfully. Mom looked rested and well-loved.

Liddy had sent a lovely flower arrangement of white irises, peach roses, and bells of Ireland, which sat on a table to the right of the casket. Ned had sent the all-white standing spray of carnations, spider mums, snapdragons, and asters.

Jeannie rushed into the funeral parlor, reeking of cigarette smoke, as I announced that the Rosary would begin. I had the kids scoot over so she could sit next to me. Besides my family of seven and Jeannie, only three others were present: Leo and Aunt Hazel's daughter, Penny, and her husband with his fire-engine red hair.

No priest came to lead the Rosary, so Penny and I alternated leading the decades. Jeannie said she wasn't sure she knew how to pray the Rosary anymore, so she didn't want any part in leading anything. The last time I'd said a Rosary was at Dad's funeral, and the time before that was in ninth grade.

PENNY'S AND JIMMY'S FAMILIES came over for the post-funeral luncheon at Joe's house. Leo, his sister, and his mother had attended the funeral Mass but predictably had passed on my invitation to stop by for lunch afterward. Trixie Dixon from the old neighborhood also stopped by to help eat the ridiculous amounts of food that I'd set out: Kentucky fried chicken, potatoes and gravy, baked beans, coleslaw, rolls, and Mom's birthday cake, now three days old.

I had picked up Mom's birthday cake one day late, explaining that my mother had died on her birthday. The woman at the bakery had offered her condolences and then had refused payment for the cake.

When I opened the box to put the cake on the table, I felt a flicker of joy for the first time in days. To the original message, "Happy Birthday, Mom," written in pink icing, the woman had added "In Heaven" in blue icing.

January 24th had acquired a double significance: the date Mom had arrived in this world and the date she bid it goodbye. In time, it would obtain a third.

Chapter 13

Birthdays

"IT WON'T TAKE LONG. No more than an hour. Just take a quick look, Jeannie. Let me know which of Mom's things you want and which I can donate to charity." My sister finally agreed, even though she had said she needed to head back to Seattle immediately after Mom's funeral luncheon.

It was a task I dreaded but couldn't accomplish without my sister's cooperation. And who knew when the wind would blow Jeannie back this way again? Like anything Mom-related, the logistics defaulted to me.

Jeannie followed close behind my BMW in her old beater of a car. As I watched her through my rearview mirror, I wondered if Mom's death might begin a new chapter in our relationship. Perhaps it was time to bury my resentment for what I considered my sister's emotional abandonment of our mother. After all, Jeannie had taken good care of Mom during her time in Seattle while I had been in San Francisco drinking expensive wine with Ned.

We parked out on the street as Mom's nearly new Buick Special occupied the cement pad next to her house.

"Mom wanted you to have her car," I said as we walked past it and up the steps to the front door.

"Man, I can sure use a dependable car," Jeannie said. "Thanks, Mom!"

I unlocked the front door and switched on the lights for the front room. The image of Mom sitting in her chair, struggling to breathe with the paramedics working on her, played fresh in my mind.

Everything remained as Mom had left it. A deck of cards lay on the dining room table in an unfinished game of solitaire. A coffee cup sat by the sink, half-full, Mom's last cup. The garbage under the kitchen sink smelled. I made a mental note to take it out when I left.

"Take a look around. Decide what you and Travis can use. You're welcome to it all. I can't use any of it."

While Jeannie wandered around, I added some water to the potted plants in the garden window. I looked inside the refrigerator for perishable items that couldn't be ignored for a couple of weeks.

I offered Jeannie one of Mom's beers and poured myself a glass of cranberry juice when she rejoined me in the kitchen. She looked through Mom's kitchen cupboards.

"I'm happy to take all of Mom's furniture, her washer and dryer, and kitchen items if you really can't use anything, Lizzie."

"It's all yours. I plan to sell Mom's place. Do you mind if I keep the furniture until it sells?"

"No problem. Keep everything as long as you need it. I need to make arrangements with Travis to pick everything up anyway. We'll have to rent a truck. I'm not sure how long that will take," she said, surveying the living room, dining room, and kitchen.

"Do you have time to see if there are any personal items in Mom's bedroom that you might want?"

Jeannie followed me into Mom's bedroom, beer in hand, still dressed in black over-the-knee platform boots and a short black dress from the funeral.

"Remember this, Jeannie?" I held up a round ceramic container with raised roses and leaves, painted in pinks and greens. "You made it for Mom." I opened the lid, and inside was a smattering of loose change. "Do you want to keep this?"

"Nah, it would just get lost or broken."

"Then I want it."

"It's yours," Jeannie said, walking over and giving me a one-armed shoulder hug. The one thing I envied about Jeannie was her ability to show affection effortlessly. I leaned into her hug stiffly.

I opened Mom's dresser drawers, one by one, and rummaged through the contents to see if they contained anything other than underwear or socks or the usual things. I first felt and then saw the lacquered black box, painted in a Japanese motif.

"I've never seen this before. Have you?" I held the box up towards my sister.

"I don't remember it. Anything in it?"

I shook the box gently as if a Christmas present. "Sounds like something."

Moving back to the bed, I sat next to Jeannie and opened the box. "I've never seen this before." I handed her a gold heart-shaped locket with a silver cross on the front.

Jeannie opened the age-tarnished locket. Mom had placed tiny pictures of Dad and her on each side. "Look at Mom and Dad. They're so young. Dad looks so handsome, and Mom is so skinny."

"Jeannie, don't you want this sweet locket?"

"Yes, but I'm afraid I'll lose it. Why don't you keep it for me?"

"Okay. When you're ready for it, you'll know exactly where it is."

But it was the two jewelry pieces remaining inside the black enamel box that I coveted: a tarnished silver and marcasite choker with dainty violet-like flowers and a hollow-hinged, gold bangle bracelet.

"Remember this?" I said, removing the antique choker and setting the open box between us as I handed the necklace to Jeannie. I found this snooping through Mom's things as a kid. I loved this necklace."

"Then you should keep it. You like old-fashioned stuff. It's not my style."

"Do you recognize this piece?" I handed Jeannie the bangle bracelet. "Mom told me that the bracelet and choker had belonged to her mother."

Jeannie opened the clasp to slip the bracelet over her wrist without answering my question. She rotated the bracelet to study the engraved design. "What letter is this supposed to be?" She squinted her eyes. "Maybe a P?"

"Hard to say, it could be. I'm ashamed to admit this, but I don't even know Mom's mother's first name."

"Me neither. There is so much about Mom that's a mystery. She kept everything about her childhood bottled up inside."

She removed the bracelet and handed it back. "You can have this. I'd just pawn it."

"No way. It's too lovely; I'll take it." I knew the vintage pieces would be lovely with proper restoration.

"When we were little, Mom kept the choker and bracelet and our birth certificates in a shoebox up in her closet." I recalled the pleasure those jewelry pieces had given me as a child, admiring them on my small neck and wrist, listening for Mom's footsteps down the hallway should I be discovered.

"What's this?" Using her confetti-glittered fingernails, Jeannie worked free a piece of paper folded tightly and wedged snuggly into the base of the lacquered box.

"Look, another copy of my birth certificate," she said.

"Can I see it?" It listed Marie and Fred Schmidt as her parents, our family doctor as the attending physician, and Pasco as her place of birth. But something was amiss. "Hey, isn't your birthday October 23rd?"

"Yeah, why?"

"This birth certificate lists your birthday as the 21st."

"What? Let me see that." She grabbed the document from my hands. "You're right. It does say the 21st. That's weird."

I couldn't understand why Mom would have saved a birth certificate with a typo? Why not just toss the erroneous certificate? It made no sense.

"Mom told me something about your adoption not long before she died if you're interested in knowing," I offered.

"After this, maybe I am. All Mom ever told me was that Aunt Hazel had delivered me when she worked in maternity at Lourdes."

"Yeah, that's all I ever heard, too, until Mom told me your birth father's last name."

"Really? What was it?" Now Jeannie was all ears.

"Savoca. It sounds Italian to me."

"Write it down for me. Okay?" Jeannie couldn't spell worth beans. I found a pen and paper on Mom's nightstand. "Do you mind if I keep this birth certificate long enough to make a copy? I'll mail you back the original."

"Fine, but why?"

"I'm not exactly sure."

As a data analyst, I knew that the odd data point sometimes contained another story. The more interesting one. This birth certificate was such an outlier, and it didn't quite fit my sister's birth story.

THE NEXT TIME I saw Ned was Easter that year. Our long-distance relationship had remained intense, fostered along by weekly phone chats and letters. Both of my parents were pen pals extraordinaire. Ned's correspondence lacked the literary beauty of Liddy's and was limited to a half page, but I lived for his letters. He composed his short missives at work between selling multi-million-dollar homes, whose exorbitant price tags didn't even include the dirt on which they were built.

Shortly after our time at Tiberon, Ned and Karen abandoned their year-long efforts at marriage counseling and, amicably, filed for divorce. According to Ned, Karen had never wanted to marry, preferring to cohabitate. Their marriage had been his idea. He moved out and into a two-bedroom waterfront townhouse in Hawaii Kai.

On Good Friday, he flew to Eastern Washington and met his new grandchildren for the first time. As much as Liddy loved being called Grandma, Ned hated being called Grandpa. The kids were to call him "Ned," just as his other eight grandchildren did.

My kids were utterly charmed by him, especially Hannah and Abby. They insisted on sitting at his side whenever possible. Jonah wanted to know all about his airplane and asked him to give him flying lessons when he was older. Joe was cordial and proper.

Ned insisted on staying in a hotel, and Jonah was quite happy to retain his bedroom. I was pleased with the arrangement as it afforded me a bit of time alone with Ned as I ferried him to and from his hotel during his three-day stay.

On Easter Monday, Ned and I took a fifty-minute flight from the Tri-Cities airport to SeaTac. After landing, we took a taxi to Pier 69 in downtown Seattle, boarded the Victoria Clipper, and embarked for Victoria, British Columbia. We spent the next several hours gliding upon the Salish Sea, heading to the southern end of Vancouver Island.

Our plans included spending the day at Butchart Gardens, a six-minute walk from the ferry terminal, and overnighting at the Empress Hotel. We'd part ways the evening of the following day. I'd be back at home Tuesday night and back to work on Wednesday morning.

Butchart Gardens did not disappoint with fifty-five acres of mind-boggling flora. A profusion of rose bushes exploded into intricate geometric designs. Stone pathways led from one part of the garden to the next, beneath arched trellises draped in velvety, fragrant climbing roses.

We strolled hand-in-hand, serenaded by the gurgling sound of fountains, not as father and daughter, for no one knew us, simply as two people enchanted by the beauty around us and each other's company.

Retracing our steps back towards the harbor, we lingered at the circular fountain in front of the legislative building, whose stately grey-stoned stories stretched out beneath thirty-three copper domes weathered to a brilliant turquoise.

Later that afternoon, we checked into the Empress Hotel, which overlooked the Inner Bay with its many sailboats moored in the shimmering, blue waters. We took afternoon tea at the Empress and snacked on miniature pastries and scones with clotted creme.

The ambiance of the tea room transported us back into a different century with beige Ionic columns, high coffered ceilings, gilded chandeliers, and polished wood floors with contrasting Athenian-inlay designs. Grand by any reckoning, the Empress rendered my memories of the La Valencia lobby in La Jolla plain by comparison. My birth father was rewriting my memories and sensual appetites.

That evening, our desire for connection and intimacy found its expression in a form that could never be explained or justified to anyone else. We acted according to what was right in our own eyes. But crossing this line only intensified my hunger to be with my Ned, installing a constant pain in my soul.

When we said goodbye in Seattle the following day, Ned said, "Be nice to Joe." I knew what he meant. I was to compartmentalize my feelings for Ned (and our actions) while continuing with Joe as if nothing had happened between Ned and me. But serial monogamy had been my calling card since age nineteen, not polyandry.

MY MOTHER, MARIE, HAD never drafted a will, and at age thirty-seven, I had never once thought about wills until Mom died. Over the six months of probate, Jeannie and I kept in close contact during this period. She was anxious for everything to be settled and to receive the cash payouts that might be forthcoming from Mom's tiny estate.

Mom's home had sold almost immediately for what she had paid plus a tad more. The "dollhouse" effect had paid dividends. In a rented U-Haul truck, Jeannie's husband, Travis, and his two brothers made the four-hour trip from Seattle to retrieve Mom's furniture, her washer and dryer, and everything else that Jeannie had wanted.

I signed the title of Mom's car over to my sister and gave the mauve Buick Special with its off-white Landau top one last look as Jeannie's brother-in-law drove it off. Mom had loved that car. I thought back to the day she had purchased it, hesitant to spend so much money on a vehicle. "Life is short. Go for it," I had prodded, encouraging her to splurge for what she considered a luxury automobile. I just didn't know how short her life would be after buying her dream car.

I kept the locket, bangle bracelet with the mysterious engraved initial, marcasite choker, ceramic rose-bud dish Jeannie had made, Mom's teacup collection, and the African violets I'd given her. Everything else worth saving went to Goodwill or St. Vincent de Paul or the dump.

After the close of probate, I flew down to spend a weekend with Liddy to celebrate her fifty-eighth birthday. She peppered me with questions about Ned. It was evident that Ned Bleau still had a hold on her heart, which I understood. He had a vice-hold on mine.

My relationship with Ned introduced a wrench into the smooth workings of my relationship with Liddy. I hadn't shared any pictures of Ned with Liddy, although I had described him as still incredibly handsome after my first meeting with him in Seattle the previous year. I hadn't planned to tell Liddy that Ned had divorced his wife and had moved out, but she pried it out of me with her direct questions.

Liddy informed me that she had scheduled a facelift. The plastic surgeon wouldn't touch her face until she had quit smoking for three months. As a result, she had recently stopped smoking cold turkey and was jumpy. I suspected that her desire to see Ned was behind her facelift decision. And that smelled of trouble. I had no interest in competing for my birth father's affections with my birth mother, and I feared that was where things were heading.

Two days later, Liddy pulled into the passenger drop-off zone for Terminal 2 at the San Diego airport. She shifted her Lincoln into park and came round to the back of the car to hug me goodbye.

"How come you never mentioned that Ned's brother, Henri, had wanted to adopt me?" I said, pulling my roller bag out of the trunk. I had wanted to ask Liddy that question ever since Ned had told me eight months ago in Tiberon. My life would have been so different.

"I never thought you'd find your father. You had so little to go on," she said, pulling out a cigarette from her purse.

"I thought you were quitting—"

"I won't light it," she said, cutting me off. "Why would I let your father's family have you when he made it impossible for your own mother to keep you?" Resentment bristled in Liddy's eyes.

Liddy's words, "Your own mother," hung stiffly between us. After Mom had died, Liddy always referred to herself as my mother and Ned as my father. She had asked me to call her "Mother." "It would mean a great deal to me," she had said, though not in a demanding way. I struggled to comply.

I could write "Dear Mother" in cards and letters, but that was as far as I could go. Liddy was not "Mom" any more than Ned was "Dad." Although I possessed a consuming inborn love—almost a genetic affinity—for my birth parents, a seemingly impassable mental divide separated Liddy and Ned from any parental association. Marie and Fred Schmidt were Mom and Dad, and Liddy and Ned were not.

I SAT AT THE counter, writing out my grocery list for Thanksgiving dinner. Our dining room table sat eight, but it would just be the seven of us this year. Mom's chair would remain empty. As I finished up my list, the phone rang.

"Lizzie, you won't believe what I'm going to tell you. You better sit down." My sister sounded breathless. "I just got off the phone with my birth mother."

"Birth mother? You're kidding me! How did that happen?"

Nearly ten months had passed since I'd told Jeannie the surname of her birth father. I'd heard nothing about any search. And now she had found her birth mother? I could barely believe my ears and felt a new respect for my sister. I had seriously underestimated her pluck.

"I'll tell you, but she told me who my father was. And it wasn't a guy named Savoca like Mom told you. It was Dad."

"What do you mean it was Dad? Dad, like in Fred Schmidt? No way."

"I know. Unbelievable, isn't it?"

"I don't ... You'll have to convince me." A disquieting wave of alarm washed over me.

"Two weeks ago, on a whim, I looked in the Seattle phone book for the last name Savoca and found one listing for a Lester Savoca. When I called the number, a man answered. I introduced myself and said that I was searching for my birth father, whose last name was Savoca.

"He wasn't defensive or insulted when I told him when and where I'd been born. He laughed, saying that if he was my father, it was news to him. He said his only daughter was born a couple of years before me and that she'd had cerebral palsy, and his only son was born several years after me.

"Then he told me his ex-wife, Maisie, had a sister who lived in Pasco. Maisie had lived with her during a rough patch in their marriage, sometime between the birth of their daughter and son. He gave me Maisie's number before we hung up if I wanted to call her, saying, 'Maybe Maisie's your aunt.'

"Today, I finally called Maisie, saying that I was trying to find information about my birth parents. I told her I had called Lester Savoca, and he had suggested that she might be my aunt.

"I relayed my birth details and that I'd heard Lester Savoca was my birth father. Then she said, 'You were born on October 21st, not the 23rd, and I ought to know because I was there. I'm not your aunt; I'm your mother.'"

Goosebumps rose up on my arm. "Had you told her about the birth certificate we found at Mom's with the 21st?"

"No, absolutely not. Then she told me that Lester Savoca wasn't my father. That a man named Fred Schmidt, from Pasco, was."

"Wait. Did you tell her that Fred Schmidt was your adoptive father?"

"No. I was too shocked. Part of me wants it to be true, but part of me doesn't. You know how close I was to Dad." Jeannie's voice broke and she took several deep breaths before continuing.

"But there's more. Maisie said she signed papers to send me to a foundling home in Spokane after the head nurse in the delivery room told her I was born with cerebral palsy, just like her first daughter. Maisie said there was no way she could handle two kids with cerebral palsy."

"You probably already thought about this, Jeannie, but you know who the head maternity nurse was when you were born. Right?"

"Yeah, Mom's sister, Hazel."

"Do you think Maisie could've made up that part about the nurse saying you had cerebral palsy?"

"Maybe, but why would she do that?"

"I don't know. Maybe so you wouldn't be upset with her for giving you up for adoption? Liddy thought I might be angry with her when I first found her."

"But how would Maisie know Dad's name? Plus, the date she says I was born matches that on the birth certificate that Mom had hidden. And if Maisie said she signed papers to send me to a foundling home, how did I end up with Mom and Dad with a new birthday? And how did I magically get cured of cerebral palsy?"

"All great questions. But I swear Mom thought Savoca was your father's last name. I doubt that Mom knew anything about Fred Schmidt being your real dad if any of this is true." Nothing in me wanted to believe a word of what Jeannie had just told me.

"Maisie gave me my brother Mark's contact information. He lives nearby, in Tacoma, with his wife and daughter. I'm going to call him as soon as we hang up."

After we said our goodbyes, I sat back down at the counter, holding my head in my hands. I felt dazed like a fly ball had conked me on the head from left field. Was there anyone still living who could verify or refute Maisie's crazy story about Dad?

It boiled down to three weak possibilities: Penny, Hazel's daughter, our first cousin on Mom's side; Melanie, a first cousin on Dad's side; and Trixie Dixon, our next-door neighbor from the old Pasco neighborhood.

Aunt Hazel had died a couple of years after Dad, but her daughter Penny still lived in Tri-Cities. Maybe Hazel had said something to Penny beyond what Mom had told Jeannie and me.

If there had been any truth to Maisie's story, Dad might have said something to his favorite sister, Pearl. Although she had predeceased Dad, we'd lived across the street from Pearl and her family for eighteen years. Her daughter, Melanie, lived only a couple of hours away. Maybe Melanie knew something to help disentangle Jeannie's paternity.

Mom and Dad lived next door to Trixie Dixon the whole time they lived in Pasco. Although Mom was pretty tight-lipped, Trixie was as close to a best friend as Mom had. If Mom knew anything about this, maybe she had confided in Trixie.

I called Jeannie back and shared my thoughts. "After you've had time to process all this, let me know if you want me to contact Penny and Trixie. They're both local, so I can easily visit them to pick their brains. You're closer to Melanie, so you might have better luck getting information out of her. But I'm happy to go with you to meet up with her. Just give me the go-ahead, and I am so on it."

"Okay. I'll let you know. But right now, I'm worn out from all this ... and other things." Exhaustion rang through Jeannie's voice.

I didn't even want to know what those other things were, so I didn't ask. My circuits were already overloaded.

When I hung up the phone, I began to weep. I tried to tell myself that Jeannie's paternity was her deal. But my heart said otherwise; it was Mom's and my business, too.

I didn't want to call Jeannie's birth mother an outright liar, but I refused to believe her story without some form of independent corroboration. It wasn't fair to Dad or Mom.

Ultimatum

MAY 1992

BY THE SECOND MOTHER'S Day after her death, I had airbrushed Mom's memory through the lens of love and loss, rubbing out any imperfections. Mom had been the shelter beneath which I'd crawled when life felt too brutal. I missed the protective armor of her unconditional love. And in her absence, I gorged on the lavish affection offered by my birth parents.

I sent Liddy a white wicker basket filled with rare Myakka Trail African violets for Mother's Day. Even if she didn't have the patience or perfect location to cater to their finicky nature, the stunning purple violets would be lovely for a good while. Liddy was delighted, especially with the short note that I'd directed the florist to include, "Dear Mother – Enjoy your day. With love and gratitude, Liz."

I sent a second Mother's Day gift to my new grandmother, Pauline Bleau. My correspondence with Ned's mother began shortly after Mom's death. Our notes, though relatively brief, had created a promising, budding relationship between us.

When I wrote that I'd been raised Catholic, Pauline shared that she had been raised Catholic but had continued her faith journey in the Methodist Church after marrying Henri, a staunch Protestant. Nevertheless, she had baptized both of her sons in the Catholic Church as infants. I wondered if Ned was aware of this.

The week after I sent Pauline the card and a jar of body cream, smelling of violets and roses, I received a letter bearing a canceled stamp from El Toro, California, and the shaky penmanship that I now recognized as my grandmother's.

May 11, 1992

Dearest Elizabeth,

You and I have not met yet, but it won't be too long before God brings us together. You have your father's genes. You do everything so well and with such good taste. Darling Elizabeth, I thank our Heavenly Father for you, a precious love so late in my life.

I am trying to rest as much as possible to overcome all my ailments before July 4th, that great day when we shall meet, God willing.

Thank you again for the beautiful card and lovely gift that I know I will enjoy and help soothe my dry skin. I love the smell of violets and roses.

God bless you, and I hope you had a very Happy Mother's Day.

Lovingly,

Grandma Pauline

As I folded the letter and placed it back inside the envelope, time seemed to be running out to meet my grandmother face-to-face. She'd been fighting leukemia for a while. At age 89 and with her latest setback, our July visit seemed in jeopardy. A familiar feeling of loss-tinged urgency spurred me to action. I had to hear her voice before it was too late. After a quick call to Ned, I had my grandmother's phone number.

"Hello?" an elderly female voice spoke softly.

"Pauline?"

"Yes, this is Pauline. May I help you, dear?"

"Grandmother...It's me, Elizabeth Schmidt, Ned's birth daughter."

"Oh, how wonderful to hear your voice."

"It's great to hear your voice, too. Ned told me that you are feeling poorly. I'm so sorry."

"That is just par for the course, I'm afraid. At my age, I'm on borrowed time. Elizabeth, I want to thank you for the great happiness you have brought to Ned's life." Pauline's sickness had not robbed her of the joy that resonated through her words.

"He has done the same for me." While true, Ned had also brought a conflagration of conflicting emotions into my life.

"I must apologize to you. I'm afraid I did my best to discourage Ned from marrying your mother. And, as it turned out, he had a miserable marriage to his first wife. I very much regret my meddling. I hope you can forgive me."

Pauline disclosed her prominent role in proposing that Liddy permit Ned's brother, Henri, and his wife to adopt me. As Pauline faced her mortality, she fearlessly unearthed the uncomfortable truths buried beneath her regrets. My grandmother's apology witnessed humility and honesty, virtues that I admired but had not achieved. I still preferred to blame others for my mistakes.

"Things have a way of turning out the way they were supposed to," I said. "My adoptive parents were good people, salt of the earth folks, as Ned calls them. They taught me many things for which I am grateful. And look, here we are, all together anyway."

That was my last conversation with Pauline Bleau. Three weeks shy of our July visit, she died in her hospital room, alone.

NED PLEADED WITH ME to attend my grandmother's funeral, although begging was hardly necessary. When I deplaned at John Wayne Airport in Orange County, he was waiting for me. We embraced in frantic greeting as he sobbed like a child in my arms.

"Thank you so much for coming. I don't know how I could do this without you. I've missed you so much," he said.

I'd never seen my birth father so distraught.

We walked through the small airport to the baggage claim nearby, and he pulled me back into his arms and held me tightly. I sank deeply into his embrace, wishing never to leave those arms.

"I know you wanted to meet Mom, and she was looking forward to meeting you," he said as he wiped his eyes.

"It's sad that it turned out this way. Thank goodness I was able to speak with her in May."

Ned's profound grief over the loss of his mother afforded me a glimpse into his emotional neediness. He had hungrily lapped up Pauline's adulation and attention, which he had not received from his first or second wife.

And what had I given Ned? Adulation and attention, plus unconditional love and ready-made bonding, packaged together in a woman twenty-four years his junior. Perhaps he needed me as much as I needed him.

Our first stop was to have lunch with Henri Bleau, the man who could have been my adoptive father had fate arranged things differently.

Uncle Henri stood, waving to get our attention as we entered Marie Calendar's Restaurant. The brothers embraced with obvious affection as I studied their interaction.

Henri stood several inches shorter than my birth father. He embodied composure while Ned's passionate nature spilled over in salty rivulets. Henri's thick, black hair had no flecks of gray as his six-years-younger brother. They shared the same razor-thin, aquiline nose.

As the two men released one another, Henri turned to me. His full lips parted in a wide smile mirrored in his friendly blue eyes. After a warm, welcoming hug, Henri continued to hold my hand.

"I'm so pleased to meet you, Liz. You have made Ned so happy. All he seems to do is sing your praises."

"Finding Ned has been a great gift for me. Please accept my condolences on Pauline's passing."

"Mom had a long, good life. She is in a better place now. Please, let's sit down." Henri gestured towards the table. I sat next to Ned, directly opposite my uncle.

My uncle studied my face like a scientist, silently for a few moments.

"Liz has Mom's eyes, the same navy blue. Don't you think?" Henri looked at his brother for confirmation.

"I never noticed. But Liz has beautiful eyes." Ned squeezed my hand under the table and turned towards me as he spoke.

"Mom gave us all her black hair, but Liz has Mom's deep set eyes, color, shape ... everything. It's uncanny, almost like I'm looking into Mom's eyes."

Henri turned his gaze back to me, "Ned probably told you that we adopted a baby boy, Kip, ten years after you were born. We thought we couldn't have children. Then when Kip was four years old, we got pregnant with Nelly. You'll meet Kip and Nelly at the cemetery tomorrow."

NED AND I JOINED the other family members assembled at El Toro Memorial Park for my grandmother's graveside service. Pauline was to be buried next to her husband of sixty-three years. Henri's wife, a short blonde marshmallow of a woman, greeted me affably, as did my cousins, Kip and Nelly.

Nelly, recently divorced by a husband who didn't want to be married anymore, was a slim, attractive, dark-haired woman with the warm brown eyes of her mother. Kip was morbidly obese yet moved with grace. From Ned, I knew that Kip was a successful lawyer. He had graduated at the top of his class at UC Berkeley in Economics and then summa cum laude subsequently from UCLA's law school.

Only the six of us had gathered to pay our final respects. My half-sisters, Joni, Terri, and Sandi, and Ned's step-daughter, Vicki, did not attend Pauline's burial service. For some reason, their absence saddened me.

There had been no funeral at a church or chapel, which felt odd given that Pauline had a deep, abiding Christian faith and had been raised Catholic. Henri had made this decision without consulting Ned, but I doubt Ned would have objected.

Surely my grandmother deserved more than this ten-minute goodbye. Soon, the groundskeepers would lower her coffin into a deep, greedy hole, adding back the fill dirt now hidden beneath a large green swath of artificial grass as if to protect those present from the reality of their mortality. Words pronounced by the priest on Ash Wednesdays decades ago, "To dust you are and to dust you shall return," rang through my mind.

The few of us standing at Pauline's gravesite would continue on as before, the tiny blip of my grandmother's life overshadowed by tomorrow's busyness. There had to be more to life than death. But that more required a faith that I didn't have.

A heavy sadness settled upon me. For whom or what did I mourn? Was it Pauline, Ned, my mother Marie, myself, or the finality and emptiness of death itself?

Lost in reverie, I felt a tug at my elbow. Kip invited me to walk away from the others. He wanted to chat privately. I welcomed the diversion, discreetly wiping my face, embarrassed by tears that seemed out of place since I barely knew Pauline.

"My father told me about you soon after you found Ned. I have looked forward to meeting you," Kip said.

We exchanged the high-level summaries of professional selves, and then Kip switched to more personal observations.

"Sometimes, I think Dad has never lived, unlike Uncle Ned. The fact that you exist is testimony to that."

"I'm not sure why you say that. From what Ned has told me, Henri has had a pretty exciting life living in different parts of the world working for different chemical companies."

"We had everything a person could want, for sure. But my parents got married so young, and then Dad was shipped off immediately at nineteen to fight in World War II. He never really got to live for himself."

Having married the first time at nineteen, I knew more about what Kip was getting at than I let on. But Henri seemed very content to me. I wondered if Kip was projecting some personal unsettledness upon his adoptive father.

"Kip, I know that you were adopted, too. Haven't you ever wanted to know anything about your biological parents?"

"No, not really."

"Well, that is a gift right there. Many things have to click between a person and their adoptive family for an adoptee not to wonder. I always wanted to know who my biological parents were and why I had been up for adoption. Now I know."

After the brief graveside service, the small party disbanded. Henri, Ned, and I rode together to Pauline's apartment in the senior living center, where she had rented a suite on the independent living floor. Not bad for eighty-nine years old, I mused.

"Let me know if you want any of Mom's things," Henri said as the elevator door opened onto the third floor.

Henri unlocked the door, and we entered the minuscule apartment. I remembered when I had faced the same daunting task, sifting through the physical remnants of Mom's life. I didn't envy my uncle. I realized the bulk of the effort would fall to him, not Ned, just as everything had fallen to me, not Jeannie, when Mom had died.

"Anything you don't want, I'll donate to Goodwill," Henri said as he walked into the kitchenette. Ned wandered into the bedroom and called my name.

Ned stood in front of a petite secretary desk with spindled legs as I entered the bedroom. He folded back the roll top, revealing an array of differently-sized cubbyholes. Pauline had filled them with stamps, empty envelopes, and letters.

"I used to hide under this desk when I was a little boy," Ned's voice choked with emotion, and he sucked in air to avoid losing it.

"You should take the desk," I said. "I bet the legs unscrew. It would be easy to ship."

"I hate to think this desk and all its memories will go to Goodwill, but I have no place for it in my townhouse. Why don't you take it, Liz? I'll pay to ship it to you."

"Really? I do love it, and the chair, too." I ran my fingers over the engraved rose in the top rung of the chair back. The needlepoint seat covering was a burst of flowers in reds, blues, and purples, all my favorite colors. "If you're sure you don't mind, I'd love them. Thank you."

"They are yours," Ned said, kissing me on the cheek.

I pulled out a stack of envelopes that my grandmother had stashed in a cubbyhole and tied together with a purple ribbon. "Look. Here are the letters I sent to Pauline. I want to take these home with me."

Three sepia pictures hung on the wall above the desk: headshots of Henri Senior and Pauline when they were young, Ned thought before they had married, and the third of my grandparents, in their sixties, dressed as a cowboy and as a saloon girl.

While looking through my grandmother's closet, I discovered a 1950s-style waist-length, fitted black cashmere sweater with tiny pearl buttons down the front. It was a perfect fit. I carried home the ribbon-tied bundle of letters and cards I'd written to Pauline and wore her sweater on the plane ride home that night.

A LARGE ENVELOPE MARKED "Photographs – Do Not Bend" awaited me upon my arrival home from Pauline's "funeral." I removed an enclosed note and two identical 8x10 inch photographs of Liddy. Setting the note down without reading it, I held one picture in each hand in a stereophonic trance of horror and captivation.

The words "Glamour Shots" were stamped in gold in the lower left-hand corner of the photo. Her bare shoulders and ample cleavage emerged from a wrap of red cellophane. Large red, teardrop-shaped earrings dangled from her ears. Her blonde-highlighted locks looked wind-blown and loose, and her makeup was flawless, clearly applied by an expert.

She looked beautiful, seductive, and more youthful than her fifty-eight years. There was no evidence of swelling or bruising from her facelift, which she hadn't needed, in my opinion, but had managed to transport her appearance to a younger version of herself.

The results were undeniable: my birth mother could now pass for my voluptuous big sister. The head-and-shoulder shot of Liddy was undeniably gorgeous and overtly sexy and provocative. Before reading her note, I knew what she wanted me to do.

Wednesday, June 8, 1992

Dearest Daughter—

I am so happy with the pictures I took after my facelift. I have healed up well and am delighted with the results. So is Andy. I have enclosed two copies of my favorite shot.

Keep one, but I'd like you to send the other one to your father. I know Ned has separated from his wife, and he has been on my mind quite a bit lately ...

I laid Liddy's note down on the counter mid-sentence and couldn't finish reading it. I had been right. The facelift was about getting Ned back once I'd told her that he and Karen were divorcing. But Liddy didn't know how I felt about Ned, and she would never suspect. It was beyond the pale of possible. I picked up the letter to finish reading it once my hands stopped shaking.

... and I would very much like to arrange a meeting with

Ned. I need closure.

Call me when you can. I only work Saturday morning and will be home Sunday after Mass if you want to talk.

I love you,

Mother

I called Liddy immediately and, after some minor chit-chat, dispensed the meat of the call.

"I got the pictures you sent. I'm sending the picture back you wanted me to send to Ned. You'll have to send him the picture yourself if you want him to have it."

I didn't tell her that I would hide the copy that she'd sent me and that I would never show it to anyone.

"You aren't comfortable sending it?"

"No, I'm not. Please, leave me out of your interactions with Ned."

I detested the resentment and jealously that had stirred up in me. Besotted with Ned, I wasn't about to tell her that we competed for the same man's affections and, most importantly, that Ned was in love with me.

"I'll give you his mailing address at his townhouse."

"Hang on. I need to get a pen and paper and check where Andy is. He loves the picture, but he wouldn't be too happy about me sending a copy to your father," Liddy whispered.

"Is it a good idea, Liddy, if it would upset Andy?" I knew it was a bad idea all the way around!

"I need closure. Andy wouldn't understand, and he doesn't have to know."

THEIR LUNCH DATE SHOULD have been long over, yet I'd received no debriefing call from Ned. I battled the sense of dread that spilled over me in jealous waves. Liddy had said nothing about meeting with Ned in our two conversations since Ned had finalized his travel plans. He'd landed in San Diego yesterday. Tomorrow, he would fly into Sacramento to visit Vicki and Joni, his two oldest daughters, and then check on his property near Lake Tahoe before heading back to Honolulu.

The nagging worry of what the word closure meant to Liddy had left me in a foul and irritable mood all day. I sat around the table with Joe and the kids, joylessly eating the dinner meal I didn't remember preparing. My nerves frayed more with each passing moment.

The kids could do nothing right. I managed to spread my unhappiness around the dinner table like butter on burnt toast as I groused at the kids during dinner.

When the phone rang, Joe got up to answer it. "Liz, Ned's on the phone." Joe held the phone out to me.

My heart lurched in my chest. "I'll take it in the bedroom. Please hang up when I pick up."

"Got it, Joe. You can hang up now. Thanks." I waited for the sound of the click.

"Joe has hung up. You can speak freely." I felt myself trembling.

"Liz, sorry to dump on you, but I just needed to talk to you."

"I didn't expect you to be with Liddy all day. Did something happen?"

"Well, yes, but not how you mean ... exactly."

"That makes no sense. I don't understand."

"Let me explain. We met for lunch at the hotel Liddy selected. It turns out that she'd rented a room in that hotel so that we could talk in private. After our lunch and several glasses of wine, she asked me to come up to the room to finish our conversation. But I wasn't prepared for what she had wanted to happen in that room."

"Why did you go up to her room with her?"

"It was a mistake, but I just didn't want to hurt her."

"But she came on to me. Strong. She started kissing me, and pulled up her sweater and grabbed my hand—"

"Stop! I can't hear this. I'm hanging up," I said, filled with anger and hurt at Ned's betrayal.

"Don't hang up. I need to finish. Hear me out. I pushed back and told Liddy that I couldn't be with her like she wanted and was leaving.

"She said, 'You're running out on me again.' Then I said, 'If you must look at it that way, then I guess I am.' It was a mistake. I should never have gone up to the hotel room."

"Come on. Given the picture Liddy had sent to you, can you honestly tell me that you're surprised? I need to go. The kids are all here, and we're in the middle of dinner. We can talk later after you are back home in Honolulu."

I slammed the receiver down onto the phone. My emotions convulsed like a tree whipped about in hurricane winds. It made little sense for me to be upset with Liddy. I could understand her feelings toward Ned. After all, I shared them. Ned had let things go too far by going up to Liddy's hotel room. Why did she need a hotel room? And what was Ned thinking? That they were going to play pinochle.

The absurdity of the situation was not lost on me. The two people getting hot and heavy in that hotel room were the very ones who had created me through an act of sexual intercourse.

I didn't want to live like this anymore. Thoughts of Ned consumed my every spare moment. When would I see him next? How could we create a life together? I lived for the rush of our time together and died in the excruciating pain of his absence. Our trips, each letter, and every phone call only intensified my need for him. It was never enough. There was no right or wrong. Only my need to be with him.

I let the cold water run in the master bathroom sink and looked at myself in the mirror. A pathetic-looking woman stared back at me. The cold water washed away my tears but not the red splotches covering my face and neck. I walked back to the dining room and resumed my place at the table.

"What's wrong, Mom?" Hannah's face showed genuine concern. "Is Grampa Ned okay?"

"He's just dandy," I said, wiping my nose on a table napkin.

Joe met my eyes and raised one eyebrow. My husband deserved more than I could give.

After everyone else in the house was soundly asleep that night, I stepped outside in my nightgown and slippers onto the back deck. The relentless heat of the late August day had dissipated into a pleasing coolness that pressed against my face. A bright full moon stared back at me with two brooding eyes, a round nose, and a downturned mouth. Waiting a few days for my emotions to settle down was impossible. Enough was enough.

Coming back into the house, I composed my letter to Ned while sitting at the kitchen counter. My letter would be waiting for him when he arrived back in Honolulu. I would not speak to him until he had read it.

July 21, 1992

Dear Ned—

As much as I hated to hear the details of your rendezvous with Liddy, it was helpful in one way. I realize that I can't keep going like this, living with Joe as his wife while feeling as I do about you. But regardless of my feelings, it's not fair to Joe. I can't be physically intimate with him feeling as I do about you. I'm not put together that way. Maybe you are, but I am not. We must decide what the future holds for us, if anything.

Moving to Hawaii is impossible, as you have suggested. I won't leave my children nor separate them from their fathers. So unless we can create a life together that includes my kids, which probably means right here in the armpit of Washington State, our situation is hopeless, and it cannot continue.

Yet when I try to imagine a life without you, I can't bear it. I am drowning, taking in water. The waves are too high for me, and there is no lifeboat in sight.

I love you but ...

Liz.

Decision

AUGUST 1992

MY BIRTH FATHER AND I had spent the last three days "island hopping." The mid-air views from the co-pilot seat, first to Kauai, then to the Big Island, and now to Maui, had been breathtaking. The Elizabeth Schmidt who'd never flown in an airplane until hired by the lab was a distant memory. I hardly recognized that woman.

"Kahului Tower, Piper Seneca Two Zero Zero Tango, ten miles northwest, request landing." Ned radioed the air traffic controller from the pilot seat of his twin-engine aircraft as we approached the commuter airport in Maui. "Roger that," he replied into his headset. My heart overflowed with pride and admiration as I watched my birth father flip switches and gizmos on our final approach to the tiny airport.

Ned's landing was smooth as glass. I exhaled and relaxed my clenched muscles as Ned taxied to a stop.

The ostensible reason for this trip was to meet my two half-sisters who lived in Maui. While I did want to meet my half-sisters, that was my secondary focus. After Ned had received my ultimatum letter, he had decided to relocate to the Tri-Cities so that we could be together.

By now, Joe knew that my heart belonged to Ned Bleau, a fact I didn't deny and had fully disclosed. But like my infatuation with Liddy, Joe still expected the flame of Ned-obsession to extinguish, and when it did, he would be waiting for me with open arms. Joe Keller was far too patient for his own good.

A slim, young woman, wearing a form-fitting black dress with a plunging neckline, stood just outside the chain-link fence surrounding the hanger.

"That would be your half-sister, Terri," Ned motioned to the woman, waving her arms excitedly. Terri was dark-tanned, with sun-kissed highlights in her long chestnut brown hair.

I exited the plane and stood off the side, enjoying the gentle breeze that blew through my now shoulder-length hair.

By the time Ned had secured the wheel chocks, Terri had joined us. She rocked her father back and forth in an effusive hug.

"Nice to see you, Dad." With her three-inch heels, Terri stood nearly as tall as her father.

I extended my hand in greeting toward Terri, which she ignored, wrapping me in a bear hug laced with the fruity-spicy notes of Calvin Klein's Obsession.

"Another sister. Welcome to the crazy clan, Liz. I hope Dad warned you about Sandi. She's meeting us for lunch."

"Maybe Sandi will be on her best behavior." Ned offered while placing one arm around Terri and the other arm around me as we walked into the dinky terminal.

"I'm not sure Sandi has any best behavior, but hopefully, she's not already plastered," Terri said.

I took a deep breath, wondering how interesting and uncomfortable this lunch might be.

Terri sped down the two-lane road in her black Jeep Wrangler. I watched the ease of her interactions with Ned from the back seat.

"Where are we going for lunch, Terri?" Ned asked. "I'm hungry."

"To a restaurant in Kihei, about twenty-five minutes away. It's genuine Hawaiian-style, peaceful, and not touristy. I hope that's okay," Terri said, glancing back at me.

"It's fine with me as long as we don't have to take the road to Hana to get there," I said. I recalled the punishing nausea of the long, circuitous drive to Hana some nine years ago. Joe and I had been on our honeymoon back then.

Terri laughed. "Kihei is on the opposite side of Maui, the leeward side, just below Kaanapali Beach. Few tourists make it down as far as Kihei. Its sandy beaches and easy waves are a great place to learn to surf," she said. "Do you surf, Liz?"

"No, maybe in my next life," I said. The idea of being in the ocean terrified me. Being on the beach, where it was safe and predictable, was my style.

"Liz, can you hand Dad the photo album next to you on the back seat?"

As Ned flipped through the pages, Terri detailed her plan to become a professional fashion photographer. She planned to move to Milan, Italy, to create her inaugural portfolio. After getting her footing in Milan, Terri hoped to bring her two children over. In the interim, they would stay with her ex-husband in Maui.

"Why not dream big? Milan is where it all happens," Terri said. "I'm tired of being the one in front of the camera. I'm ready to get behind it."

An angular chin and green eyes, gifts from her father, anchored Terri's face. Surfing had imparted a vigorous, muscular look about her, although buxom and wide-hipped imparted a feminine finish.

According to Ned, Terri was the most motivated of his daughters. She had graduated from high school a year early, ready to take the world by the tail. Terri seemed intelligent, motivated, hands-on, and went after what she wanted. I liked all those things about her.

Ned handed the photo album back to me, complimenting Terri's photographic skill. I paged through the images of the island and its people in color, sepia tones, and black and white.

"Terri, these are exceptional. Did you teach yourself all this?" I asked halfway through the album.

"No, sweat equity. I traded modeling hours for training hours. The photographer that I model for taught me."

Sure enough, at the album's end were a series of photos where Terri was the *objet d'art.* She was the perfect photographer's model: long hair, tall, tanned, an hourglass figure, and no reluctance to expose her assets.

Terri parked her Jeep outside a restaurant with a lovely ocean view, and we walked inside.

"Get ready for Sandi," Terri muttered under her breath as she nodded toward a woman with light blonde hair falling in long layers about an angelic face. Sandi jumped up from the table and ran to Ned. Throwing both arms around his neck, she kissed his cheeks.

Sandi shared little resemblance with Terri. Sandi's saucer-like azure eyes imparted an innocence and softness. That is until she spoke, then she sounded like an old sailor.

"It's so good to see you, Commander!" Sandi effused in her husky, "whiskey" voice.

Commander? Terri turned to me as I looked at her in surprise.

"Sandi calls Dad 'Commander,'" Terri whispered and rolled her eyes.

Sandi was shorter, even in high-heeled strappy sandals. She wore a short, black leather skirt and a white, ruffled poet's blouse with a plunging neckline, barely corralling two fleshy cantaloupes.

She moved over to me, imparting a warm, enthusiastic hug, "Welcome to the family, Sis." Sandi smelled of cigarette smoke, ethanol wafted from her pores.

She held me at arm's length and scanned me head to toe. Her visual inventory reminded me of how women size up another, on the sly, hoping to be prettier or sexier than the other. I felt my face go red, self-conscious about my jean shorts, red knit polo shirt, flip-flops, and boyish figure.

"Liz reminds me of Joni," Sandi said, her words slightly slurred.

Sandi had dropped out of school by fourteen and had moved in with her boyfriend, according to Ned. She had made her living via street smarts and her looks.

More recently, however, Sandi had qualified for financial help through a rehab program, courtesy of the state of Hawaii, as long as she kept her therapy appointments. She bragged that her "shrink" wanted to take her to bed.

By Sandi's second vodka martini, we heard how her fourteen-year-old son was in trouble with the law again and was living in a juvenile detention home. And by her third martini, I learned that she'd reported her ex-husband to the IRS for tax evasion.

Terri punctuated Sandi's yarns with acerbic comments, head shakes, more eye rolls, and another order of Patrón Tequila on the rocks.

Although I wanted nothing of my half-sisters' lives, I felt a pang of jealousy for the many years they'd shared with Ned. I had voiced this feeling once, during an intimate moment with Ned. He had replied, "If I'd raised you, we wouldn't have what we do now." But still, part of me wondered how different my life might have been to have received his love without the heavy guilt I now lugged around.

After Ned asked for the check, he announced, "Well, girls, I have some big news. I'm leaving Hawaii. Moving to the mainland."

"What? Just because you and Karen got divorced?" Sandi pouted, jutting out her lower lip.

"No, that's not it at all. I'm retired and feeling 'rock happy.' I want to travel, and it takes too long to get anywhere from Hawaii."

"Where and when will you go, Dad?" Terri asked with a curious tilt of her head.

"I'm not exactly sure when. But probably sometime in the next six months. There are lots of options regarding where. I may rent somewhere and then decide where to plant roots. Initially, I bought that land near Lake Tahoe with the idea of retiring there, but now I have second thoughts about the winters there. There's always San Diego which has the best climate in the world as far as I'm concerned. Maybe I'll spend some time in Washington state."

"Well, hell," Sandi said, holding up her empty glass and announcing to everyone in the restaurant in a boisterous voice, "I'll have another and make it a double."

"Sandi, you've had enough. The bar tab is closed," Ned said.

"I'm leaving Hawaii, too, Sandi. I'm starting a new career in Milan," Terri chimed in.

"Milan? Where's Milan?" Sandi asked, looking confused and disoriented.

"Italy, of course," said Terri in a condescending voice.

"Nobody loves me," Sandi whined. "Do Vicki and Joni know you're moving, Commander?"

"No, I told you and Terri first," Ned said.

"Well, aren't we the lucky ones," Sandi said, glaring at me as if Ned's departure was my fault.

Sandi was right; it was all my fault.

THOUGHTS OF NED BLEAU and Fred Schmidt jockeyed for first position as I flew back to Seattle from Honolulu. Moving in with Ned was what I had wanted, and it was finally going to happen. Our living arrangement would appear to the world and my children as a sweet story of a reunited birth daughter and birth father. That story was part truth and part deception.

Yet I wondered, had I grown up living under the roof of deception as well? Had my adoptive father, Fred Schmidt, been Jeannie's biological father? Was this why Jeannie had been accepted more by the Schmidt side of the family?

Jeannie had done nothing to sort out her paternity since her first conversation with her birth mother. I'd waited long enough and decided to take matters into my own hands.

The very next evening, I phoned our cousin Penny. She knew nothing beyond what Mom had told Jeannie and me. Hazel had delivered Jeannie. Period.

Strike one for my sisterly sleuthing. That left the neighbor Trixie Dixon and cousin Melanie. If they knew anything about Jeannie's birth father, I'd wrangle it out of them.

I was a woman on my sister's mission, even if she wasn't.

The following Saturday, I drove to the old neighborhood where Jeannie and I had grown up and parked in front of Trixie's house. I hadn't seen Trixie since Mom's funeral. A car in the driveway assured me that Trixie, who was retired and lived alone, was home.

Widowed for three decades, Trixie had never remarried. At seventeen, she and Clay had married in Arizona and then moved to Pasco, where Clay found employment on the Hanford nuclear reservation. Clay was the age of Trixie's mother and had initially been dating Trixie's mother.

In broken confidence with Trixie, Mom had told me about the mother-Clay-daughter triangle, and, as promised, I'd never told a soul, including Jeannie. Yet, that shared secret between the two women led me to hope that Mom might have shared information about Jeannie's adoption with Trixie. Marie Schmidt and Trixie Dixon had at least one big secret; why not two?

I climbed the five concrete steps up to the front door and knocked several times. Trixie opened the front door beaming ear to ear.

"Well, I'll be doggoned. Lizzie Schmidt, you come right on in," she said with eyes clear and bright. She wore grey sweat pants, a purple sweatshirt that read, "Loving the GRANDMA life," blue fluffy slippers that made her feet look enormous, and pink sponge rollers in her grey hair.

"I hope you don't mind me just dropping by."

"Of course I don't mind, you silly goose. Get on in here!" She folded me into a hug. I followed her inside through the narrow hallway to the living room.

Trixie's youngest daughters had been my favorite neighborhood playmates, and I knew the Dixon house inside and out. Very little had changed. The antique organ was still in the living room, and the vintage bowl and pitcher remained in the center of the drop-leaf oak table in the adjacent dining room.

I asked about her daughters, who had long since left their hometown for bigger and better things, and relayed the Reader's Digest version of the search for my birth parents. Trixie had heard none of this before. Her fascination only increased when I produced pictures of Liddy and Ned. Those photographs greased the transition to the real reason for my visit.

As Trixie returned from the kitchen with a refreshed cup of coffee, I pulled the photocopy of Jeannie's birth certificate out of my purse.

"After Mom died, Jeannie and I found this among Mom's things," I said, handing her the photocopied document.

Trixie took the document in one hand and walked over to the dining table to put on her reading glasses. She walked back to her overstuffed armchair, scanned the document briefly, and looked at me with questioning eyes. "Jeannie's birth certificate. What am I not seeing, Lizzie?"

"It's the birthdate. We've always celebrated Jeannie's birthday on October 23rd. The birth certificate you're holding shows my sister's birthday as October 21st. Jeannie has a Washington state certified birth certificate that shows her birthday as October 23rd, as does her driver's license, and everything else that identifies who Jeannie is."

"Hmm." Trixie knitted her brows and cocked her head to one side, massaging the back of her neck.

"It gets stranger. Before Mom died, she gave me some information about Jeannie's birth father. Jeannie used that information to find her birth mother. That woman told Jeannie that she was born on October 21st, not the 23rd."

Trixie's mouth hung open. She leaned forward as I continued.

"Jeannie's birth mother claims that the medical staff told her that Jeannie had cerebral palsy. Since she already had one daughter with cerebral palsy, the birth mother said she sent the baby, Jeannie, off to a foundling home in Spokane. Obviously, Jeannie didn't have cerebral palsy and never went to a foundling home. She went home with Marie and Fred with a new birthday. Did Mom ever say anything to you about Jeannie's adoption?"

An uneasiness replaced Trixie's earlier carefree mood. "I don't know anything about changed birthdays or cerebral palsy or foundling homes in Spokane. But when your folks moved to Spokane, Marie told me that something about Jeannie's adoption had concerned her. She was a happy camper to get out of Dodge."

"Didn't that strike you as," I paused to choose the right word, "odd?"

"Well ... maybe." Trixie took a deep breath and exhaled it loudly.

"Mom told me that Aunt Hazel delivered Jeannie at Lourdes and through Hazel, Mom and Dad 'got' Jeannie. Mom also said that when Hazel called about Jeannie, she had to make up her mind immediately."

"To my knowledge, all that is true, Lizzie. But Marie told me a tad more."

"Like what?"

"That your Aunt Hazel handed Jeannie to Marie via the fire escape stairs."

"You mean like they were sneaking around or something?" I said, shocked.

"I made no judgment, Lizzie. I just listened."

"When did Mom tell you that?"

"A long time ago. You girls were small. Why don't you just ask Hazel? It was long ago, but I'm sure she can explain everything."

"Not possible. Hazel's been dead for years. But I did ask her daughter, Penny, what she knew about Jeannie's adoption. All Penny knew was that Hazel delivered Jeannie when she was the nursing supervisor of the maternity ward. No more."

Before heading back home with a heavy heart, I gave Trixie my phone numbers for work and home. I thanked her for sharing what Mom had told her about my sister's adoption. As we hugged goodbye, she promised to call me the next time her two younger daughters came back into town to visit.

Trixie's words had added uncomfortable creases to the bits of information that Jeannie and I already knew. But still, Jeannie's birth mother's claim that Fred Schmidt was Jeannie's biological father was far from proven for me.

❀❀❀

DAD AND HIS BABY sister, Pearl, had been like two peas in a pod. So close that Mom sometimes felt like an outsider. If Dad were Jeannie's biological father, perhaps he had told Pearl; they were that close. But people talk, especially in families. Melanie was my last hope. Melanie might have overheard something growing up if Maisie's story was true.

With or without Jeannie, I decided to drive to Northern Idaho to visit cousin Melanie. I wanted Jeannie to come with me, but her absence wouldn't stop me, not after Trixie's story.

Jeannie's band never worked Monday nights. Hoping to catch her at home, I dialed her phone number. I tapped my fingernails impatiently on the counter, waiting for someone to pick up.

"Hello?" My sister's voice sounded flat. Something was off.

"Jeannie?"

"Yeah, it's me."

"Is this a good time to talk for a few minutes?"

"Sure."

"Something's wrong, Jeannie. I hear it in your voice. What is it?"

"Maisie's dead."

"Oh, no. That's awful. I'm so sorry." Although devastated for my sister, I felt a loss, too. Only Maisie knew the real story of Jeannie's paternity.

"When? What happened?" I asked.

"Months ago, but I just found out. Pneumonia. She'd been diagnosed with lung cancer right after I found her. Nobody bothered to tell me that either. I kept hoping Maisie would want to see me, but I didn't know she'd been sick. I called Mark, my brother or half-brother, whichever he is, last week to suggest that the three of us meet up. That's when he told me that Maisie was gone. I never even had the chance to go to her funeral." She sucked in air and sputtered, "I never even saw my birth mother's face.

"I can't believe Mark didn't let me know. We had spent quite a bit of time together after I first talked to Maisie. I thought we were close. Why didn't he reach out to me?" Jeannie sniffed.

"That would really hurt, Jeannie. If I'd given a child up for adoption, I would have wanted a meeting right away, even if you hadn't reached out to her. And especially once I knew I was dying. I don't understand Maisie or Mark, either." The contrast between Liddy and Maisie was mind-boggling.

"It's not all her fault, Lizzie. I was a complete chicken. You know me, the last of the great procrastinators."

"Gosh, it's so sad that you never met her. Given what you just told me, right now is either the worst or best time to run my idea by you."

"Just say it, Sis."

"I contacted Penny and Trixie Dixon about your adoption. I didn't tell them that you found Maisie or that she'd said Dad was your birth father."

I paused, waiting for Jeannie to say something. Silence.

"Penny knew nothing, but Trixie had some new information. It's time to have a powwow with Melanie."

I PICKED JEANNIE UP at the Spokane airport and drove forty miles east to meet Melanie for lunch. Our cousin, wearing a navy-blue business suit, was waiting for us in the lobby at the Coeur d'Alene Resort. Melanie was fifteen years older, but her chin-length fashionable bob and line-free countenance minimized our age difference.

Her face broke into a broad smile the instant she caught sight of us. Although taller and bigger-boned than her mother Pearl, Melanie had her mother's vibrant, charismatic personality, which had served her well in real estate.

Jeannie fairly ran into Melanie's open arms. I stood back and gave them space to gush over one another. Melanie then pulled me into her arms.

"What a treat to lunch with you two girls," Melanie said as she enthusiastically pulled Jeannie back into a threesome hug.

Jeannie grabbed my hand as we followed Melanie through the resort's giant lobby to the restaurant to be greeted by unobstructed views of the pristine, sparkling blue lake.

By the time we consumed a good portion of our entrées, the small talk was grating on my nerves. We didn't have all afternoon; Melanie had a showing at two o'clock. I knew it, and Jeannie knew it, too.

"Mel, there is a reason we wanted to meet today beyond just enjoying our time together. Right, Jeannie?" I nudged Jeannie's foot under the table, encouraging her to pick up where I'd left off. I nodded at her when she looked at me.

"Yeah. There is something I want to ask you about." Jeannie grasped my hand under the table.

"Fire. I'm all ears." Melanie said, scooping up the last slivers of parmesan cheese from her chicken Caesar salad with her bread crust.

Jeannie eventually delivered the main points: the alternative birth certificate, finding her birth mother, her actual birthday, Trixie's story about the fire escape handoff from Hazel to Marie, and finally, Maisie saying that Fred Schmidt was her biological father.

As she spoke, I searched my sister's face and found none of the angst churning in my heart. I knew that Jeannie had agreed to the meeting with Melanie as a favor to me, sweetened with a paid airline ticket from Seattle to Spokane. My sister could flop about in ambiguity, leaving her to believe what she wanted. We were so different.

"Mel, what we want to know," Jeannie said, "is did you ever hear anything about who was my real father? I mean, my biological dad."

Melanie's eyes darted between Jeannie and me and then locked her chocolate brown eyes onto Jeannie's own chocolatey eyes. She reached across the table to take Jeannie's free hand in hers.

"Mom, your aunt Pearl, swore me to secrecy. But I guess the cat's out of the bag now. Fred Schmidt wasn't just your adoptive father; he was your biological father."

The conversation percolated back and forth between Melanie and Jeannie. As I watched the ensuing love fest, one loose end goaded me.

"Melanie, Mom told me that the last name of Jeannie's birth father was Savoca. If Dad was her biological father, how is it that Mom didn't know?" I asked.

"Nobody wanted to hurt Aunt Marie," Melanie said. "To my knowledge, your mom never knew."

After telling Melanie goodbye, I drove Jeannie back to the Spokane airport to catch her flight back to Seattle. On my drive back to the Tri-Cities, the feelings I'd dammed up after Melanie's disclosure rushed into my head and heart like a cloud burst.

It now seemed irrefutable: Fred Schmidt, my adoptive father, was Jeannie's biological father. Jeannie was a Schmidt.

I finally understood the backstory. Jeannie had been an excellent fit to the Schmidt clan because she was one of them. No wonder she had the signature Schmidt chocolate brown eyes. No wonder she had loved to go fishing with Dad. No wonder she sketched all the time as Dad had. No wonder Jeannie hit puberty at eleven like the rest of the Schmidt female cousins. The similarities fell like ripe apples from the Schmidt family tree.

I had achieved the desired validation but not the desired conclusion. Tears of disappointment coursed down my cheeks and blurred my view of the road.

The disconnection I'd felt as a young child had matured into the search for my birth parents. But finding Liddy and Ned had been more than an intellectual curiosity. My need to know had been driven by an instinctive need to belong, fit in, be recognized as family, and fill a void that my sister Jeannie had never experienced. And now I knew why.

Like a hungry, lost kitten, I lapped up every bit of love and acceptance that Liddy and Ned sent my way. That my adoptive father had been Jeannie's biological father only made my connection to Ned stronger.

Big House

My LIFE WAS ORGANIZED like an intricate domino run, a monotonous sequence of responsibilities lined up one after the other in close succession. A precarious balance held everything in place. The dominos began wobbling after I found my birth parents, but the first domino had tumbled the day my mother died. Her death had severed the organizing principle of my life.

The second domino fell when Leah left home, moving to Seattle the week after turning eighteen and, sadly, less than two months before her high school graduation. The lure of two hundred fifty dollars per hour for modeling was irresistible, as was the siren call of the hockey-player boyfriend whose team had relocated to Seattle.

Helplessly, I had watched as my firstborn committed the greatest of all sins in my survival bible, dropping out of high school. I blamed Charlie Davis's DNA for her foolish decision, but I knew my headstrong DNA was partly to blame.

The last domino fell when Ned decided to move to eastern Washington. Subsequently, I moved out of Joe's house, filed for divorce, and moved into a nearby rental. Since joint custody had worked out well enough between Leo and me, Joe and I had followed the same pattern. Joe kept Abby and Noah on the days that Leo kept Jonah and Hannah.

From the first moment that Ned had joined us in the rental house that fall, the kids experienced a mother who laughed and enjoyed life and them more than ever before. We were a happy, albeit non-traditional, family. The kids adored their charismatic grandfather, who remained adamant that he was to be addressed simply as Ned, not Grandpa. They were programmed to love him, as was I; it was in our DNA.

AFTER FOURTEEN MONTHS OF cramped living in the rental house, our custom home was move-in ready. The Big House, as the kids and I called it, was located on a hilltop perch with expansive views of the undulating, brown terrain dotted with silver-green sagebrush. Looking west, the wind-worn Horse Heaven Hills traced purple silhouettes at sunset. Some people loved the open starkness of the high desert. I struggled to see any beauty, its gritty winds like sandpaper to my soul.

From Ned's perspective, the acre-and-a-half homesite was inexpensive compared to the volcanic dirt of Honolulu and was fee-simple to boot. From my perspective, the location was sufficiently close to both Leo and Joe, and the kids didn't have to change schools.

The Big House broke all the rules of sensible real estate investment. But "breaking rules" was hardly an unknown infraction to me at age forty, some three-and-a-half years after finding my birth father. With eight bedrooms, four bathrooms, an office, a recreation room, a family room, a formal parlor, a dining room, a breakfast room, and a dream kitchen, everyone had their own space.

Joe, the kids, and I continued to attend Mass together while Ned stayed home. My birth father had no use for churchgoing, plus Catholic rituals were foreign to him. After Sunday Mass, Joe always came up to the Big House for a late breakfast.

We gathered for French toast, pancakes or waffles, scrambled eggs, link sausage or bacon, orange juice, and coffee in the dining room. Joe thought Abby and Noah were thriving, given the time away from Jonah and Hannah. He could lavish attention on them without the competition of Leo's kids.

On the days and nights that the four kids were with Ned and me, we lingered around the dinner table discussing the best and the worst parts of our respective days, starting with Noah, the youngest, and working our way up, age-wise, to Ned. After the evening meal, which occasionally Ned prepared, he retired to his part of the house, leaving me to spend time with the kids with no distractions. The kids saw nothing that would lead them to believe that Ned was anything other than a doting father and grandfather.

Certainly not their mother's lover.

As a child, my vacations had been limited to overnight road trips to Granny and Grampa Schmidt's house in Clarkston. But with Ned, the kids and I enjoyed holidays in Hawaii and along the Oregon Coast. Ned and I spent four weeks in France and a week in the Caribbean without the kids. As my birth father threaded his life and finances into ours, the children and I experienced the finer things in life.

Ned hooked into the core of my emotional need and want. His intimate acceptance of me convinced me that I was worthy of love and, dare I say it? Beautiful. It seemed that loving him was inseparable from finally accepting myself. Ned and my relationship sat squarely in my blind spot of what I wanted. No longer a throw-away, I was Ned's beloved.

SUMMER 1994

JEANNIE SHOULD HAVE ARRIVED by now. She'd phoned last night saying she'd be here by noon, and it was now close to one. She was always late, but I'd hoped each time would be different.

I relished the idea of showing off the Big House to my sister. She had yet to see it. I knew she'd be happy for me. I felt a twinge of guilt. Jeannie had never lived in anything but a rental, but I knew who had worked her butt off in school for umpteen years and who had not.

She could have made different choices, I told myself. I remembered her watching TV while stuffing popcorn in her mouth instead of doing her homework. Then there were her feigned headaches in elementary school. Mom always let her stay home. By junior high, Jeannie didn't need Mom's cooperation anymore to cut class and hang out with her deadbeat friends.

Jeannie and I existed in different orbits. Our paths mainly crossed when she needed money.

I bid my time reading a book from the window seat on the second floor overlooking the front circle drive. I heard a car pull up and then stop. Peering out the window, I saw Mom's Buick Special parked on the street in front of the house. I put my book down, rushed down the staircase, and out the front door to greet my sister. I tucked away my sense of dread and put on a cheery disposition.

I surveyed the sad state of Mom's car; the five years of my sister's ownership had taken their toll. The tires were nearly bald. And what was with the radio antennae taped to the car's passenger side?

"Well, you made it," I said to Jeannie through the rolled-down car windows.

"Yep, four hours in this heat." She stubbed out her cigarette into an ashtray overflowing with old butts and ashes.

"But Mom's car has air conditioning."

"Stopped working a while back. I can't afford to fix it."

"Still smoking, I see," I said, unable to swallow my disproval.

"I'll quit when I'm ready, Sis." Jeannie pushed the car door open with her shoulder.

Jeannie rounded the front of the car to give me a hug. Her signature scent careened up my nostrils: cigarette smoke and spearmint gum. She'd dyed her hair black and cut it into multiple lengths with a ratted mound on top, a style befitting the disarray of my sister's life. But maybe the windblown bedhead look was sexy; I was a poor judge of such things.

Still buff yet curvy, the stage dancing and singing had kept her in great shape. She looked ready to hop on stage with her clunky hooped earrings, multiple chains and necklaces, black crop top, leopard print leggings, and black high heels. Jeannie could wear that kind of getup and look cute and not sleazy.

However, at age thirty-eight, the late nights and worries that came with eking out a living playing in clubs had extracted its toll. Thick black eyeliner didn't hide Jeannie's puffy eyes or new outcropping of facial lines.

"Oh, Sis, look at your house! It's gorgeous." She stopped with her arms outstretched to take it all in. "Your house is a mansion! It must have cost a fortune."

I imagined looking at the Big House for the first time as Jeannie was. The Tudor-style home had high-pitched rooflines and multiple river stone chimneys. The front façade had a lower level of antique brick and a stucco upper level with painted cross boards. Tall windows with diamond-shaped panes imparted a castle-like aura. The attached garage had four wooden carriage doors, each tucked under a brick arch and crowned with a keystone. A storybook-worthy front door was flanked by leaded light panes and crowned with a lunette.

"Wow! Just wow. I love the circular drive and how the second floor sticks out over the first," Jeannie said.

"There are actually three levels. Follow me." I led Jeannie around to the back of the house, past the terraced rose garden and the white gazebo, and through an arbor wrapped with purple wisteria in full bloom.

The view from the backyard showcased the white-painted deck, which extended the length of the longest dimension of the house, creating a shaded patio underneath for the daylight basement level, hidden from the street level. A smaller balcony extended from the top floor from the French doors of the master bedroom, Ned's room. A turret ran from the ground level up through the other two stories in the center back of the house.

"Ned paid for everything except for two of the four lots I bought." I laughed as I spoke but was deadly serious. Jeannie needed to know that Big House was not on my dime. It had all been a gift from Ned. There was no way I could afford this kind of extravagance.

"My gosh, the backyard is crazy huge!"

"It is a whole lot of grass to mow. But the kids love it. Room for a pool and tennis court, I suppose, at some point."

I took Jeannie back to the front of the house to enter through the front door. She needed to experience the grand effect of the towering entryway. We walked through all three levels of the 6000-plus square feet of interior space.

"This house looks just like you, Lizzie. Did you decorate it yourself?"

"I had some help. Ned hired an interior designer to help me, his way of exerting some quality control over my decorating ideas. I don't think he completely trusted me with a project of this size. And to tell you the truth, I appreciated the security of working with someone else."

"You are so good at decorating," Jeannie said once we were back on the main floor, standing in the kitchen. "I don't recognize any of the furniture. Is it all new?"

"Most of it is new. We bought a few of the more interesting antique-looking pieces, including the big oil painting you saw when you came in the front door at auctions.

Jeannie retrieved a cigarette and lighter from her purse. I put my hand on hers before she lit up.

"Let's go out on the deck if you want to smoke. We don't allow smoking in the house."

"Sure, fine. Got anything to drink? I'd love a cold beer or a Coke."

"I've got water, milk, juice, ice tea, or wine."

"How about an ice tea with lots of sugar," Jeannie said as she let herself out to the deck, lighting up immediately.

I brought out a tray with two tall ice teas, the sugar bowl, long spoons, lemon wedges, a bowl of mixed nuts, cheese, and crackers, and a small ashtray. We sat at the patio table under the shade of an umbrella that Jeannie had cranked open.

"Let me know if you want me to make you a sandwich or anything. I've plenty of food, just no beer or Coke. Sorry."

"How are things going with Travis?" I asked because things had been rocky between them for months, but other than knowing they were no longer in the same band. I knew little else.

"Travis is divorcing me."

I couldn't tell if this was good or bad news by her manner of delivery. But I was pretty sure the economic ramifications would be devastating for Jeannie.

"He moved out last month and in with the female singer in his new band."

"Yikes. Sorry, Jeannie."

Ten years ago, Jeannie and her first husband, Jay, were in the same rock band with Travis. When Jeannie found out about Jay's infidelities, Travis was there to comfort her. That comfort led to the creation of a love child, Mia. They got married a year later. Travis was nineteen, and Jeannie was thirty-one.

"In some ways, it's a relief. But money is a nightmare. I'm scared. I don't know how I'm going to make it financially. Travis's parents have been watching Mia when she's not in school while I work waiting tables during the day."

"Will Travis's parents still watch Mia when you and Travis are divorced?"

"I think so. They're super good people, and they love Mia to death."

"Who watches Dex?" Dex was Jeannie and Jay's son. But Jay lived hours away in Spokane.

"Dex is old enough. I can leave him by himself. He's just not old enough to watch Mia."

"I'm so sorry, Jeannie. How much money do you need?"

"I don't want you to give me any money." Jeannie sucked in her quivering bottom lip.

"Right, but how else will you get along if I don't help you?"

"I don't know. But I haven't paid you back from the last time."

Or the time before that, or the time before that, or ever, I thought to myself.

I pushed back from the round glass table and headed into the house to get my checkbook. Thankfully, Ned was still out of the house on the lunch date with himself. He'd told me more than once, "You're just going to have to cut Jeannie off financially like I had to do with Sandi. The cash outlays will never end. Otherwise, just give the money as a gift and don't expect repayment."

Perhaps Ned was right. But I didn't want my sister out on the street. Mom would have wanted me to take care of Jeannie. Besides, what was the alternative? That she and her two kids came to live with me? That was worse, and Ned would never allow it.

Taming my resentment towards helping Jeannie carry her burdens was a continual work in progress. Yet my frustration wasn't entirely directed at Jeannie. What divine design placed me into the arms of Marie and Fred Schmidt in the first place?

"I promise I'll pay you back when I get back on my feet." Jeannie swiped at the stream of mascara-tinged tears running down her cheek with one hand while she took the check for a thousand dollars with the other hand. She exhaled loudly and then took a long drag on her cigarette before stubbing it out in the ashtray. At least it was filtered, I thought.

I heard the footsteps from inside the kitchen. Ned was back.

"Jeannie, please put the check inside your purse. Now." I didn't want Ned to see the check I'd written out. Yes, it was out of my checking account, but I didn't wish to discuss this latest "loan" either.

Ned wore his sunglasses and a tan baseball cap with a Veterans of Foreign Wars decal as he stepped from the kitchen nook out onto the deck. He still cut a dashing figure in his blue jeans, blue and white checked shirt, and braided leather belt. Although sixty-five, he could easily pass for twelve years younger, half of our actual age difference.

"Jeannie. How nice to see you. Are you staying for the weekend?"

"I wish. I have a gig tonight. What time is it anyway?" Jeannie smiled sweetly but began fidgeting with the strap of her purse.

Ned checked his Rolex with the diamond bezel. "Two twenty-seven," he said.

"I need to get going. I know I just got here, Lizzie. I got a late start this morning. I'll come back when I can visit longer and bring the kids."

My sister had made the four-hour drive to get money and was heading back having achieved her goal. I had assumed that she would spend the night.

"What do you think of the house?" Ned asked Jeannie as he made a sweeping gesture with his hand. He couldn't imagine what Jeannie's life was like: no security, no bank account, living paycheck to paycheck. Jeannie would have to cash my check at a check-cashing store that would gouge its worth.

"It's a mansion. I love everything about it." Jeannie stood up and downed the last of her sweet tea.

"Lizzie did a great job of making it all work and designing the landscaping," Ned said.

"That's Lizzie for you. She has always loved decorating any and everything," Jeannie replied.

"Jeannie, can I at least make you a sandwich to take back on the road with you to Seattle?" I didn't want her to have to spend money on food.

"No, but thanks. I'll use the bathroom, though, and then head out."

Before she got back in Mom's car, I slipped her a couple of twenties for gas. What a nightmare her life was. I wondered if I would forever be my sister's keeper.

THE PATERNAL HALF-SISTER THAT I was supposed to resemble, Joni, came for a short visit without her husband or kids during our second year in the Big House. She had black hair, a light complexion, and shared a bit of my lankiness. Pretty and reserved, Joni lacked the self-confidence of globetrotting Terri and possessed none of the coarseness of Sandi. A mother of four children by three different husbands, I understood the complications Joni juggled.

Two months after Joni's visit, Ned's stepdaughter, Vicki, and her family arrived to spend a week at the Big House. Early on, Vicki had given Joni, Terri, and Sandi a choice: "Liz or me. Not both." Ned had speculated this was because he had never adopted her. But after almost four years of our shared half-siblings demonstrating no interest in relating to me as another sister, Vicki waved a cordial white flag.

Uncle Henri and his wife even came to spend a week at the Big House and met my children. Henri remarked several times that he'd never seen his brother happier.

The trips that Ned and I took together alone became less and less frequent after a couple of years in the Big House. Shuffling the kids back and forth to their activities and my work-related trips sated my appetite for travel. To escape small-town life and Eastern Washington's cold winters, he took several trips a year alone, back to Hawaii or his favorite haunts in California.

When Ned was gone on his trips, Liddy would come to stay with the kids and me. I think she loved the Big House as much as we all did. We would drive to auctions where Liddy tutored me on what was junk versus a bargain and worth bringing home. Liddy enjoyed being around the only grandkids she would ever have and no longer asked about Ned.

As perfect as my life was, I still daydreamed about leaving Eastern Washington for San Diego once I'd safely launched Jonah, Hannah, Abby, and Noah into college. But that was eons away.

SPRING 1998

"CHECK OUT TODAY'S NEWSPAPER: front page, bottom right," I barked.

Ned unfurled the Tri-City Herald. A picture of Bob Symons, the staff scientist who had assumed management of my research project a month ago, occupied the bottom right front page. I'd nurtured that project from inception to infancy to intellectual property development and had garnered stable funding for the team over the last several years.

"Read it out loud."

Ned began reading obediently, but I cut him off as soon as he read the quote from Dr. Symons.

"That's my pet project. The lab waits until they formally assign my project to a big-shot scientist, a man and a level above me, who has had nothing to do with the work or intellectual property development and then does a big press release. The article says nothing about me or my team. It's as if Mr. Big-shot did everything himself."

My pride was wounded, hemorrhaging all over the floor.

"I'm so sorry. How dare they do that to my little girl." He pulled me close and wrapped his arm around me. "I know it's not right, Liz, but aren't you happily engaged on a new project that's more to your research interest now?"

"Yes, but that still doesn't excuse it. I feel betrayed. And yes, you're right. I'm so ready to get out of here. I HATE it here." I cried and laughed simultaneously at the futility of the situation.

"You know I'm ready to relocate anytime you tell me you're ready. Say the word, partner, and we're gone."

Ned had struggled to enjoy the semi-rural area home. His brief foray into real estate had been a bust. It was too much work for peanuts after Honolulu's premiere home sales. Added to that were inhospitable winters with Honolulu as his baseline. The burgeoning wine industry in the area was attractive, but even reasonably good wine at rock bottom prices could only compensate so much.

Beyond the regional shortcomings, we were isolated as a couple without any real friends. Ned had organized a few social get-togethers but failed to mention that I was his daughter. I was quick to remedy Ned's omission, after which a second get-together never materialized. It was too weird to hang with a father and daughter combo.

It had been harder to make a life together than I had ideated. Our kind of love, apparently, did not conquer all.

WINTER 1999

WE FINISHED UP BREAKFAST late Sunday morning after Mass. Homemade cinnamon rolls had been my bribe: "No Mass, no cinnamon rolls." That had worked well for all the kids except Jonah. Four months away from high school graduation, I had little influence over Jonah. He'd received a double helping of brainpower, Leo's good looks, Ned's disarming personality, and a triple disdain for convention. Thankfully, Jonah looked up to Ned, who provided the only boundaries he respected in the Big House.

Ned and the kids excused themselves, leaving Joe and me at the table in the kitchen.

"I think I've found a job opportunity in San Diego through my current project at the lab." I'd groomed myself for this work opportunity for a year after the infuriating newspaper article about Mr. Big-shot taking over my research project.

Although Joe and I were divorced, we hadn't told any of the kids that we had divorced. We still spent every Sunday morning together: Mass and then breakfast unless he was out of town on business travel.

"I can't imagine moving to San Diego without Abby and Noah, although I'm sure they'd love it down there. Uprooting them from their homes here ... and from you ... seems a bit much." I said, gauging Joe's reaction to a physical separation from the kids and me. I remained his best and only friend. Poor fellow.

"I wouldn't stand in the way of the kids getting out of the area. It is culturally dead. I'd love for them to experience more of the world and access the California University system as residents."

"But wouldn't you miss them?" I was astonished by his casual response.

"Of course, I'd miss them. But there are vacations, and I assume that I could always come down and stay with you."

"You'd always be welcome. I'm so ready for a change, Joe."

"I certainly understand that. You've lived here your whole life, minus a few college years in Seattle and Pullman. There might even be opportunities in Southern California that would be attractive to me."

My fantasies hadn't included Joe moving down, but it would ease the transition for Abby and Noah. The prospect of Joe relocating grew more attractive by the second.

"You know you can do or learn anything," I said, leaning into the idea.

It was true. Joe was as brilliant as he was eccentric. He picked up computer languages, one of his preferred pastimes, like dogs picked up fleas.

"Jonah plans to attend college in California. Either at USC or Cal-Berkeley, depending on the scholarship and aid package they offer him."

"Would Hannah go with you?" Joe asked.

"She's got another two years in high school after this one. But I can't see her wanting to leave her friends, the track team, the cheerleading squad, or her dad. Besides, I doubt Leo would let Hannah move to California."

Joe waved his hand in the air dismissively, "Hannah's old enough to make up her own mind. She might surprise you if she had the chance to move to Southern California."

After Joe's tacit agreement to allow Abby and Noah to move to San Diego, I struggled to attend to the balance of our conversation. My mind was busy formulating a financial argument for Leo's consideration. When money talked, Leo listened.

But life without Hannah seemed impossible. I wasn't sure either Leo or I could bear to be away from her. The easiest of my five children, Hannah remained a pure delight even at sixteen. She had skipped over the adolescent stage of disliking her mother and remained as affectionate as a puppy. Maybe Leo would let Hannah choose, as Joe had suggested. But if given a choice, would she choose San Diego?

San Diego

SPRING 1999

WE LISTED THE BIG House with a realtor and received a firm offer from a cardiologist recruited by a local hospital a week later. Emboldened by a sizeable earnest money deposit, we made plans to house hunt in San Diego over the kids' spring break.

Everything fell into place like clockwork. Joe never wavered in his decision that Abby and Noah could move to San Diego with Ned and me. Jonah would attend Cal-Berkeley in the fall, and with my move to California, he would achieve residency status through me by his second year. Once Hannah announced her desire to attend UCLA, Leo didn't fight her decision to spend her senior year in San Diego. Leah, now married to her hockey player and with a baby and a high school diploma in hand, couldn't wait for a free place to crash for vacations in San Diego.

The gods smiled on me and granted my wish to move to paradise seven years before Noah was college-bound. My job in San Diego came through like a charm with a flexible start date. My world was good and getting better.

We made plans to fly down to San Diego to check out the housing market during the first week in early April when the kids were out of school on spring break.

A LOUD THUD OF the landing gear announced our imminent touchdown at the San Diego airport. I woke Abby and Noah, who had slept through the entire 6 a.m. flight.

We bypassed baggage claim with only carry-on bags and arrived at Janet's real estate office in La Jolla by ten o'clock. The temperature outside was a pleasing seventy degrees. Gentle rays of sunshine promised to bless today's house hunting adventure.

I guessed Janet's age midway between my forty-four years and Ned's sixty-eight years. Her grey, loose-cut designer suit and light blue silky blouse expertly camouflaged her thickened middle section. A stylishly short haircut with blonde gel-tipped spikes softened the wrinkles in her smiling, tanned face.

We had corresponded with Janet by phone and email several weeks prior. She had arranged for us to visit eight homes in La Jolla and a newly developed part of north San Diego, called Carmel Valley, all within our price range. I was optimistic that Janet's no-pressure, no-nonsense ways would make the most of our two days on the ground.

Ned sat upfront in Janet's silver Mercedes 300-CE. I sat in the backseat between Abby and Noah, devouring cinnamon Pop-Tarts and sipping from juice cartons, courtesy of Janet.

"Looking for a new home is hard work," she said, "and the last thing you want to be is hungry." She winked at me, nodding like a knowledgeable grandmother towards the kids. And, no, she wasn't worried about the kids eating in her immaculate car, which smelled of new leather and her Estee Lauder Pleasures perfume.

While Ned and Janet bantered real estate, I watched the kids' eyes take in their surroundings. Their enchantment mirrored mine some eleven years ago when Liddy first drove me into La Jolla for lunch at the La Valencia Hotel.

We began in La Jolla, starting with the least expensive homes and working our way up to the most expensive homes in our price range. Four hours later, and with my stomach screaming for lunch, I came to a depressing realization. Even if we used all the money from the sale of the Big House, we would end up with something I couldn't bear to live in, at least in La Jolla. Owning any house in that quaint and picturesque town was impossible unless we lowered our standards well below our comfort zone.

Ned had warned me before we had put the Big House on the market,

"We'll never have the kind of home we have here in San Diego." Now I understood, painfully so. The kids, ravenously hungry, needed a break. So, did I.

Over lunch, Janet talked up Carmel Valley, an upscale master-planned community, which had been farmland twenty-five years earlier. After eating, she drove us to a lookout point in the Carmel Heights neighborhood.

"Carmel Valley is only ten minutes from the Del Mar beach," she said, pointing northwest to the blue swath of the Pacific Ocean.

Next, she drove us by the new middle school Abby and Noah would attend if we bought in Carmel Valley. The next stop was the high school.

"Torrey Pines consistently ranks as one of the top 100 best high schools in the nation," Janet crooned. She handed me the datasheets touting the impressive stats for the Carmel Valley schools.

After looking at several homes in Carmel Valley, each newer and better maintained than any of those we'd viewed in La Jolla, Janet brought us to the final home of the day. Like the other homes we'd toured, the yard was small. I thought, less yard work for me, reaching for the positive side of homes packed in housing developments like sardines in a can.

A rectangular rose garden, in full bloom, was to our left as we walked up to the front door. The realtor turned to our little group before knocking. "The older couple who live here might be home. I've shown this home before, and they didn't leave." She smiled apologetically.

"Weird but fine," Ned shrugged his shoulders and shook his head slightly. His voice carried the discouragement I felt but hadn't voiced. The long day was wearing everyone out. Noah and Abby had their fill, too.

A short, hunched-over man with bushy white eyebrows answered Janet's brisk knock at the front door. His bespectacled, gray-haired wife stood behind him and peered over his shoulder. Janet attempted first name introductions for our viewing party as the man waved us in and talked over her.

"I'm Milt. This is my wife, Miriam." He gestured to his wife as he stepped out of the way and waved us inside with a gallant bow.

The travertine entryway opened into a formal living room with a two-story ceiling, flanked on the right by a maple staircase leading to an upper-level hallway. The living room and dining room were connected but visually separated by the nine-foot dropped coffered ceiling in the dining room. Glass-paned French doors in the dining room opened into the backyard.

"Look, Abby, there's a pool in the backyard," Noah exclaimed as he looked out the French doors.

A six-foot wooden fence enclosed a swimming pool surrounded by night-blooming jasmine, bougainvillea, agapanthus, and bird of paradise plants. The backyard was small, consumed mainly by the pool, but lovely.

"Mom, I want this house," Abby whispered while clutching my hand and pleading with her wide-eyed baby blues.

The house had great bones. The openness imparted an air of spaciousness to the four-bedroom home, while the kitchen area and adjacent family room felt cozy.

This was the best house we'd seen all day, and it was within our budget, but just barely and at the very upper end. Miriam's decorating lacked flair due to the absence of art that the empty white walls demanded. After a quick tour upstairs, I knew this house would work. More than work, it would be perfect. Already salivating at the interior design prospects, I mapped which pieces of the furniture from the Big House would work well in this house.

The kids had already decided which of the four upstairs bedrooms would belong to whom. The three of us were on the same page. This was "our" house.

Ned stood in the master bedroom, looking out at the purple hills off in the distance. I left him to his reverie and went back down to the formal living room, where the owners sat together on the couch.

Milt dropped a bombshell as our realtor entered the room. "We received an offer this afternoon right before you got here, but we haven't accepted it yet."

My heart dropped. This house would have worked so well for us. Although only half the size of the Big House, we didn't need that much space anymore, nor could we afford a home of that size in San Diego.

I bounded up the stairs to find Ned. He was seated in the office area loft, which overlooked the main living area. I motioned him into the smallest bedroom to talk privately.

"What do you think?" I hoped that Ned liked the house as much as the kids and I did.

"It's the best house that we've seen today, that's for sure. It could work, but—"

I didn't let him finish. "They already have an offer on the table. It just came in." I couldn't hide my disappointment or sense of urgency.

"Have they accepted the offer?"

"Not yet."

"I want this house. Everything is perfect. Abby and Noah can even walk to school."

Without further discussion, Ned headed downstairs. He charmed Milt and Miriam into telling us what ingredients a competitive counteroffer would have.

"I like you and would love to sell our house to you, but we'd need your offer tonight," Milt said, lacking the facial expression to reinforce his honey-coated words. Milt was all business, including his requirement to close in 30 days. The Big House had a ninety-day escrow period from which we were still fifty-nine days out. If we wanted this house, we would need a high-interest bridge loan, guts of steel, and faith that the sale for the Big House would proceed without a hitch.

Although not happy with Milt's conditions, Ned authorized Janet to present Milt and Miriam with our best offer for their home that same evening. We checked all Milt's boxes: full price, a 10% escalation clause, no contingencies, no inspection, and closing in thirty days.

After breakfast the following day, we drove to Janet's office. Once she got off the phone, she joined us in the waiting area.

"Sorry to keep you waiting. I was on the phone with Milt and Miriam's agent. Good news, folks, they accepted your offer. Congratulations! Full price, but at least no escalation in price." Janet's face beamed.

"So, did we get the house?" Abby asked, trying to make sense of the conversation.

"Yes! They accepted our offer," I said, clapping my hands together. "We are almost done, just a bit more work to do today to tie up some loose ends."

"Yay," Noah exclaimed as he jumped to his feet and swung at the air with his fist in jubilation. "A swimming pool in our backyard!"

Our move to San Diego was going to happen. Like a salmon, I'd nearly arrived at my spawning grounds. Not to die, but rather to start living life to the fullest.

WHAT WAS IT ABOUT San Diego? People seemed so happy here. Maybe it was the pleasant weather, the soothing balm of sunshine averaging 266 days a year. We lived so near the coast that we rarely ran the air conditioning or the heating system. Carmel Valley truly felt like home, and I vowed never to leave my little patch of heaven on earth.

My new job still involved research but focused on analysis support for pharmaceutical drugs in the early stage of development. The work stress was different but was considerably less than what I'd experienced at the lab. Here I was only responsible for my contribution, something that I could control, and not a team of people.

Noah and Abby adjusted readily to San Diego. I still had to travel for work, which meant Ned was responsible for the kids in my absence without Joe and Leo taking over. It was the price he paid for living in paradise.

The price I paid was dealing with San Diego's freeways, with up to six lanes of traffic in each direction. And the people drove as if their hair were on fire. It took a year before I could drive the half-hour to Liddy's house without my neck and shoulders aching from the tension.

As I had hoped, Hannah moved down for her senior year of high school. She made the cheerleading squad, earned straight A's, and attended UCLA upon graduation from high school.

Jonah flew down from Berkeley anytime he wanted, as flights from the Bay Area to San Diego were plentiful and inexpensive. And upon graduation, Jonah began a doctorate program at UCLA in applied mathematics. Leah and her husband came to stay with us for several vacations.

Everything was going along swimmingly, yet something had changed in the nine years since I'd found Ned. I had fallen out of infatuation with my birth father. I still loved him fiercely, but the nature of my love had evolved to a different place, imperceptibly at first but now undeniable.

Unfortunately, nothing had changed for Ned. Our mutual attachments were inversely proportional. The more I wanted to pull away physically, the more he seemed to need or desire me.

A simple love song on the radio sent my heart clamoring and grasping for a relationship that could be acknowledged publicly and not hidden. After leaving three husbands, I'd promised myself (and Ned) never to leave him even when our twenty-four-year age difference transformed him into an old man. And although my birth father had remained a vibrant man, physically and mentally, something had moved on inside me. Would I ever be free from my relentless searching? Never satisfied. Never at peace.

I drove to the beach at Del Mar when my anxiety pressed in on me. Symbolically casting my worries into the Pacific Ocean, I imagined the waves carrying them far away. But the waves didn't cooperate. As I walked the shore, dodging the slimy washed-up seaweed, one niggling worry returned to me like the wet sand clinging to my feet. What had started as a whisper in the Big House now awakened me in the middle of the night.

In a cold sweat, keenly aware of my heart pounding in my chest, I awakened in a panic about the state of my soul. A stern self-lecture about the harm of Catholic guilt and a cup of chamomile tea became my ritual to get back to sleep. If this was menopause, I wasn't a fan.

2001 CHRISTMAS EVE

NED AND I SAT in the family room companionably, watching the blue and gold flames dart between the artificial logs in the gas fireplace insert. I hadn't bothered with a Christmas tree or holiday decorations this year. What was the point with all five kids in Washington State? Abby and Noah were spending their two-week Christmas vacation with Joe. Jonah and Hannah were spending the holidays with Leo. Leah was busy creating Christmas memories alongside her husband for her three small children in their Seattle home.

I sifted through my best childhood Christmas memories: trying to nap before midnight Mass but being so excited that sleep was impossible; listening to Mom and Dad and Aunt Hazel's laugh as they drank hot buttered rums or Tom and Jerrys in the kitchen; fantasizing about the Christmas present that Aunt Pearl would give me Christmas morning when I would walk across the street to her house. That sense of anticipation and enchantment, I wanted it back. Was that possible at age forty-eight?

"I'd like to go to church tonight," I said.

Ned raised an eyebrow and looked at me curiously. He swallowed the last of his Merlot before answering.

"That's a change. You haven't gone to Mass since we moved to San Diego. But whatever you want to do is fine, Darlin'."

"No, not Mass. Candlelight service at Community Fellowship Church, just down the road. It starts at eight. It would seem more like Christmas." I'd seen the service advertised on their electronic sign on my way home from work last week.

"Would you go with me?" I tried to sound like I wasn't begging, although I was. I'd never been to a Protestant church service before and was reluctant to go alone.

"Is it important that I go with you?"

"I don't want to twist your arm, but yes. Would you, please?"

"For you, Liz, anything." He rose from his leather recliner and kissed my forehead on the way to refill his wine glass. "Consider it part of your Christmas present. But let's leave early enough, so I don't have to stand the whole time."

A couple of hours later, Ned and I pulled into the crowded parking lot at Community Fellowship Church. The night was crisp and seemed to resonate with the promise of good things.

"Merry Christmas and welcome," said the jolly man in the red-felt Santa hat. His silly Christmas sweater with a flashing Rudolph-the-reindeer red nose provided all the warmth needed against the slight chill in the evening air. He handed me a small white candle inserted through a round piece of cardboard.

We walked through the doors leading into a big room, which reminded me more of a multi-purpose room than a church sanctuary. There was no altar, no bay of stained-glass windows, and no statues of Jesus, Mary, or Joseph.

The Christian statement was proclaimed solely by a large wooden cross, absent a crucified Jesus, and centered on the front wall. Directly below the empty crucifix was a platform stage, upon which an electric keyboard, drum set, two guitars, and multiple amplifiers rested.

Off to both sides of the stage were two groups of risers facing each other and slightly angled towards rows of connected upholstered chairs that substituted for pews. Evergreen wreaths festooned with red ribbons and multiple Christmas trees decked out with red and gold ornaments and strings of twinkling lights were scattered about the room. I settled into my comfy chair next to Ned, delighted that we had come.

At eight o'clock, the overhead lights dimmed. Every available chair was filled with latecomers standing against the walls. Ushers transferred the flame from their burning candles to those seated at the end of each row. And they, in turn, shared their fire with those seated next to them until all candles burned brightly in the sanctuary. The musicians assumed their instruments on stage, and the choir ascended to the risers while softly singing "Silent Night."

When the choir sang, "All is calm, and all is bright," the flickering lights from the small candles provided the only illumination. After gentle renditions of "O Holy Night" and "O Little Town of Bethlehem," the overhead lights came back on, and we extinguished our candles.

With the bright lights came louder, electrified versions of Christmas carols that filled the room. Some choir members raised their hands upwards and swayed their bodies as if an extension of their voices. Other people rose from their chairs, swaying and singing in that same uninhibited way. I knew nothing of that kind of freedom, and a stab of envy washed over me.

After another half-dozen Christmas carols, the musicians and choir moved off to the side, standing as all chairs were taken. An energetic, smiling, middle-aged man took center stage and motioned for everyone to stand. He led the crowd in a short impromptu prayer.

The pastor, who introduced himself as Matt, extended a special welcome to visitors here for the first time this Christmas Eve. He asked each person to introduce themselves to those seated around them before they sat back down.

Matt preached about God's steadfast love and the promises embodied in the birth of the child Jesus on the first Christmas.

"Our loving Father never abandons his children, no matter what they've done," he said.

The pastor looked directly at me as if peering into my soul. However seductive those words, I doubted they extended to sins like I'd committed with my birth father over the last decade.

But he kept slathering on hope, like ointment on a burn. "God loves you just as you are, but he loves you too much to leave you that way. The Father's divine love culminated in the birth of his Son whose death on the cross and resurrection is the bridge from our brokenness to eternal life."

Later on, the musicians crept back on stage, playing soft music as Matt continued speaking. The cadence of his words slowed as his eyes swept over the crowd like a lighthouse beacon, searching for lost ships.

"It's never too late to find the only true peace on earth. If you have not yet invited Jesus into your life as your personal Lord and Savior, I invite you to do so tonight. In just a minute, you'll have the opportunity to do so. No one will embarrass you or point you out, this is between you and God.

"Would you bow your heads with me for a few moments? Jesus stands at the door, knocking, saying, 'If you hear my voice and open the door, I will come to you.' In the quiet of the next few moments, respond to his invitation, open the door of your heart, and begin a relationship with Jesus."

Gentle music floated in the air for the next thirty seconds. Finally, Matt said, "Father in heaven, thank you for the gift of your Son, whom we celebrate this Christmas season. Amen."

At Matt's "Amen," all heads bobbed back up, yet he continued. "Scripture assures us that if we confess with our lips that Jesus is Lord and believe in our heart that God raised him from the dead, we will be saved. My prayer for each of you tonight, especially those who have newly committed your lives to Christ, is that you will unwrap the extraordinary gift of your salvation in Jesus Christ this and every day going forward. Merry Christmas and many blessings in the coming year."

The young woman at the keyboard closed by singing a Christmas song unknown to me. Between her soothing, perfect-pitch soprano voice and the poetic lyrics, which reflected Mary's thoughts while looking into the face of the baby Jesus, I was mesmerized.

Ned tugged at my sleeve to divert my rapt attention. "Liz, it's over. Let's go."

"I know, I know. But I can't leave until the end of this song. You go on ahead."

I stole one last glance at the empty cross as I gathered my purse and headed to the car to join Ned.

"The pastor's invitation at the end of the service, asking Jesus in your heart and then getting saved, have you ever done that?" I asked, buckling my seat belt.

"Pastors didn't do that in the church I attended growing up. Whatever denomination Community Fellowship Church is, I can tell you that it isn't Methodist. But to your question, yes, once, when I was twelve. I went with Mom and Pop to a tent revival. I joined others up front and read a prayer on the card that some guy handed me. Afterward, the preacher, who reminded me of a snake-oil salesman, announced that we were saved."

"Did it change anything for you?"

"I'm not sure it took in my case," Ned chuckled, keeping his eyes focused on the road. "It was something that I thought my parents wanted me to do, so I did it."

"Do you believe you're saved?" I asked.

"Of course, I'm saved. And you're saved, too. Nobody is going to hell. Don't let your Catholic upbringing steal your joy and burden you with guilt."

When we got home, a quick search online produced the name of the closing Christmas song, "Mary, Did You Know?" I printed out the lyrics and placed them in my desk drawer, reflecting on Matt's words again. Could being saved be so simple as saying a prayer?

Being saved from the whipping of my conscience sounded mighty good to me. But I wasn't ready to drink the Kool-Aid that Pastor Matt offered. No words alone could extricate me from the complicated mess I'd made of my life. I'd have to change everything first and, for that, I wasn't ready. Yet.

Part Three: 2003 - 2006

For surely, I know the plans I have for you, says the Lord,
plans for your welfare and not for harm, to give
you a future with hope. (Jer 29:11)

Mortality

Fall 2003

PHYSICAL PAIN HAD NO place in my life. I'd plowed through the workweek as best I could, ignoring the constant ache in my lower back. One part stubborn and two parts pride, I'd made it to Friday with my usual coping skills—white knuckles and denial.

A splitting headache stuffed my brain with cotton as I stared blankly at my computer screen. *What was the name of the analysis macro I needed to run on the data?* I squeezed my eyes shut, trying to remember. My hands, poised at the keyboard, suddenly began shaking as I broke out in a cold sweat.

My entire body violently shivered. I glanced around, more embarrassed than frightened, hoping no coworkers had observed my out-of-control body. All the adjacent cubicles were empty. *Yes, of course, everyone had gone out to lunch.*

Something was wrong. I sent a one-line email to my boss, saying I was taking off the rest of the day.

I drove home on autopilot, grasping the steering wheel tightly amidst waves of uncontrollable shaking. *Why was it so cold?* San Diego was never this cold in late September.

Once home, I climbed the stairs to my bedroom at the end of the hallway and fell onto my bed, my purse slung over my shoulder. I pulled my bathrobe over my clothes. Minutes later, still freezing, I grabbed a blanket from the top shelf of my bedroom closet. Even the blanket didn't help. I found the thermometer in the upstairs bathroom that the kids and I shared. After rinsing it off, I stuck it under my tongue and lay back down on my bed.

Something poked me in my mouth as I rolled onto my side. The thermometer, I'd forgotten about it. I rotated the shaft toward the bright sunlight streaming through my bedroom window. A silver line of mercury ran from the tip of the bulb and up the glass shaft. 104.7 °F. *Impossible.* I must not have shaken down the thermometer.

Rummaging through my purse, I found the small bottle of ibuprofen. I took two pills with a sip of last night's water from the glass on my bedside table and lay back down.

Anxious thoughts roamed my mind freely, unopposed in my delirium, like unwelcome and uninvited guests. As I lay shivering, a sensation of hopelessness glommed onto me. The ensuing darkness transported me to a lonely place where nightmares are born and fears fester unabated.

The mess of my life pressed heavily upon me and whispered words of hopelessness in my ears. The exhaustion of living a lie washed over me, drowning me in waves of guilt. An inviting numb-like submission promised escape and beckoned me forth. The promise of a good, long, forever rest, with no worries to suck me dry. *Was I dying? Did it matter?* I was too tired to fight any longer. Death would be a welcome relief.

"Call the doctor," a woman's voice whispered. *Was that me?* It had to be. I was alone. I dug into my purse for the cell phone Ned had given me last Christmas, insisting that I carry it. *Why had I resisted?* I couldn't remember.

I found the doctor's number in my contacts and hit dial.

"This is Liz Schmidt ..."

"Hang up," commanded the angry voice in my head.

"Hello, are you still there?" said the voice on the phone.

"Something is wrong with me. The thermometer read 104.7, and I can't stop shaking. I need to see Dr. Larsen."

"Are you a patient of his?"

"Yes."

"Is this a good number to call you back on?"

"Yes."

"The nurse will call you back as soon as possible."

"Okay. Thanks."

Ned's voice. *What was he saying?* I opened my eyes. His hand stroked my forehead.

"My god, you're burning up. Darlin', what's wrong?"

"I called the doctor. They know."

"Why didn't you call me?"

"I don't know."

Then the ringing of a cell phone. Words. Many words, and then Ned's voice, "I'm bringing her in now."

I don't remember getting down the stairs or into the car, or walking into the doctor's office. Had my seventy-three-year-old birth father carried me?

I curled up in a ball on the table in the doctor's examining room.

"Do I need to catheterize you, or can you give a urine sample?" a nurse said.

After an examination and urine sample, the doctor announced, "You have a rip-roaring bladder infection. I'm suspicious that it may have progressed to your kidneys because of your flank tenderness and high fever. Do I send you to the hospital for IV antibiotics or give you a shot now and oral antibiotics?"

"No hospital ... please."

The nurse gave me a shot of something in my backside.

"If you're not profoundly better in twenty-four hours, promise me you'll go to the emergency room. You have let this go too long. You may need IV antibiotics to kick this," Dr. Larsen said.

"I promise," I said.

I SNUGGLED UNDER A cozy blanket on the couch in the family room downstairs. I listened to the sounds of Ned cobbling together dinner for the kids and himself. I didn't bother asking what he was fixing; I had no appetite anyway.

Twenty-four hours after the shot in the tush and taking the prescribed oral antibiotics, my fever was down to 102. My backache had lessened some, although my headache and nausea had not. My left arm had swollen up, but it didn't hurt. I dismissed my elephant arm, more concerned that I might miss work come Monday morning.

While everyone else ate, I went upstairs to bed and eventually fell asleep until 3:17 a.m. I awoke to a crushing, squeezing pain between my shoulder blades, neck, and jaw that ran down my swollen left arm. I got out of bed and tried to walk off the pain, steadying myself against the upstairs wall. Nothing helped. I sat at the top of the stairway, deciding what to do. *Should I ask Ned to take me to the hospital?* Dr. Larsen's lecture about taking care of myself still stung.

Eleven months ago, I'd had chest pains. However, this squeezing pain was different, as if someone was choking me. I didn't want to overreact, but the thought of death terrified me.

It was my fear of dying that led me into Ned's bedroom. I gently shook him awake.

"Ned. Ned, sorry to wake you up." I stood next to his bed, dressed in jeans, a t-shirt, and my running shoes.

"Uh, ... what?" Ned sputtered as he woke up.

"I'm having pain in my back, jaw, and down my left arm. I need to go to the hospital to get it checked out, but I can call a taxi." I tried to sound calm.

"No need for a taxi. I'll get dressed right away."

While Ned dressed, I grabbed my bottle of antibiotics, cell phone, and charger, stuffing everything in my purse. I returned to the top of the stairs and sat down to wait for him. Healthy women at forty-nine years old didn't have heart attacks. *Did they?* That couldn't be happening to me. *Could it?*

Ned and I spoke little on the way to the hospital. Anything I said would only add to his concern and amplify my anxiety as my pain continued unabated. Finally, exit 29. Minutes later, Ned turned onto Genesee Avenue, and La Jolla Memorial hospital came into view.

"Don't come in. Just drop me off."

"Are you nuts? Of course I'm coming in."

"No. Please. I'd rather be alone." I touched his arm. "Go back home, so the kids aren't alone." The clock in the car showed 4:20 a.m. As a mother of five kids, I'd spent enough time in hospital emergency centers to know that everything progressed slowly.

"It will be after breakfast before they decide what to do with me. I promise to text you when I know something. But, please, go back to bed if you can. It's probably nothing. Perhaps a reaction to the antibiotics." I forced a smile of false confidence. Besides, he knew better than to argue with me.

I walked into the hospital's emergency entrance as Ned drove off. Not a single person was in the waiting area. Steadying myself against the unrelenting squeeze, I described my pain to the woman sitting at the admitting desk.

Moments later, a nurse in lavender scrubs came through a swinging door pushing a wheelchair. She ferried me to a room with four walls and a door, not a makeshift pseudo-room created from sliding shower-like curtains hung from a metal rod where patients overheard each other's business.

"Chest pains?" she asked, patting the exam table covered with white paper where she wanted me to sit.

"Not exactly. Pain between my shoulder blades, neck, and down my left arm." I held out my left arm for her inspection. "The swelling began yesterday, the day after I started antibiotics for a bladder infection."

She wrapped the blood pressure cuff around my right arm and pumped it up, letting it out slowly. "Have you been told that you have low blood pressure before?"

"All the time."

"Are you nauseated or have a headache?" She asked as she stuffed a thermometer in my mouth and snapped a pulse oximeter on my fingertip.

"Both," I said once she removed the thermometer.

"The doctor should be in right away. You picked a good night; we're not crazy busy." She made several notations on her pad, exited the room, closed the door, and left me sitting on the exam table. I fished the antibiotics out of my purse to show the doctor when he came in.

A minute later, a doctor in blue scrubs joined me in the exam room. "I'm Dr. Rhodes," he said.

"Liz," I said back. I studied the badge clipped to his shirt pocket. Jason Rhodes was prematurely gray.

He peppered me with questions about my pain's location, intensity, onset, and duration. His manner was reassuring and personable.

He moved his stethoscope around my chest, neck, and upper back. "Any relevant history of heart issues, you or your immediate family?" He hung the device around his neck when he finished listening and palpitated my neck.

"Eleven months ago, I had some chest pain." I paused, closing my eyes and gritting my teeth through the pain, struggling to regain my train of thought. "My EKG was normal, but my cardiac troponin levels were slightly elevated.

The follow-up catheterization was perfectly clean. My mother has congestive heart failure. She smokes; I don't. Her father died of a heart attack in his fifties."

I held out the bottle of antibiotics toward Dr. Rhodes. "Been taking these since Friday, late afternoon, for a bladder infection."

Just then, Dr. Rhodes noticed the difference in my arms. His eyes narrowed as he held out both of my arms for comparison.

"That started last night. It's less swollen now." My feeble attempt at stoicism was rapidly cracking like a calving iceberg.

The doctor read the label on the bottle and handed it back to me. I grabbed his hand and the bottle, sandwiching them between my hands, clinging for reassurance.

"Am I going to die?" My voice broke with emotion. Death—no longer an inviting, restful vacation—now terrified me.

"Everything will be okay. You're in good hands. Mine." Jason Rhodes did not pull away from my grasp. A gentle smile moved from his lips, resting in the crinkly, outside corners of his steel-grey eyes.

Embarrassed by my show of emotion, I released his hand back into service, "Sorry."

"No need to apologize. It's okay to be frightened."

He brought the top half of the exam table up. "Let's get you more comfortable. Sitting up can help with this kind of pain. You will have to lay down for the EKG, but it is quick. Five minutes.

"Someone will be here shortly to draw your blood. In the meantime, the nurse will start an IV to get some fluids in you. Once I start getting your labs back, I may need to add some meds to your IV."

"I'll be back shortly," he said, touching my shoulder briefly before exiting the room.

I liked Dr. Rhodes. And I'd like him a lot more if he could make my pain disappear.

"Let's get you into this sexy yellow gown," the nurse said when she returned. She attached sticky electrode pads to my chest, arms, and legs. The nurse pulled up my gown, just as a young woman showed up with a wire basket of test tubes, alcohol pads, needles, and elastic bands.

The nurse stepped out as the phlebotomist decided which arm to poke.

She wrapped a tight band above my right elbow and flicked the skin inside my elbow, choosing her target vein. "Hold still. Stick coming." I watched as she filled the first tube and then another.

The nurse returned to finish connecting me to the EKG machine. "I'll start the IV once we get the readings. Don't move a muscle for five minutes while the machine takes its readings. Okay?"

As the EKG machine took its readings, I counted the perforated holes in the white, square ceiling tiles above me, desperate to refocus my mind away from the constant pressure that hammered my body and my raw fear. I tried to talk myself down the flagpole of panic I was busily scaling.

My rational self presented the evidence: You can't be having a heart attack because the doctor and nurse are too calm. They wouldn't leave you in this room to die by yourself. Besides, people don't walk into the ER while having a heart attack. They come in by ambulance on a stretcher.

My irrational self countered: But doctors and nurses see this kind of thing every day. This is only an emergency to you, not them. Remember the last trip you made to ER? Your mother Marie was pronounced dead; not everyone makes it out of here alive.

The nurse mercifully returned to muzzle the debate, disconnecting the leads from the electrodes but keeping the sticky pads on my chest. She found a cooperative vein for the IV needle and attached a saline drip.

Minutes later, Dr. Rhodes walked in the door. "Part of your labs are back. Your cardiac-specific troponin level is way up."

"Am I having a heart attack?"

"I don't think so. No blockage or abnormality shows on your EKG, plus your heart catheterization was negative eleven months ago. I found your previous medical records in the system. My best hypothesis is that your infection made its way to your kidneys, entered your bloodstream, and hit your heart. What I can say is that your heart is under stress.

"I'm going to apply this patch to your chest. I'm adding an antibiotic to your IV and another medication, verapamil, to relax the blood vessels in your heart. Your pain should subside very quickly."

Dr. Rhodes stayed with me, distracting me with small talk as my pain ebbed away with astonishing speed. Once he left the room and I was alone again, my anxiety melted into tears of relief.

A short time later, Dr. Rhodes returned. "The rest of your labs are in, and there are some additional red flags. I'm admitting you to the hospital. You'll spend the next twenty-four hours in ICU and on IV antibiotics. And, assuming all goes well, I want you monitored for another day or two before being discharged. I'm referring you to an excellent cardiologist, Dr. Briggs, a friend of mine. Before leaving the hospital, I want him to check out your heart.

"It's providential you came in tonight, Liz. Once an infection hits the bloodstream, a patient's condition can deteriorate rapidly. Things could have turned out very differently," Dr. Rhodes said. When he reached the door, he hesitated and turned back towards me.

"Your guardian angel was watching over you tonight," he said and walked out the door.

I arrived in the ICU ward to a flurry of activity as the day shift staff relieved their weary graveyard counterparts. An orderly rolled me and my IV into a small fishbowl of a room. The front wall, comprised entirely of glass, faced the nursing station. I listened to a stream of beeps and soft soles padding down the hallways.

Although impossible to view with no outside window, the sunrise would soon announce another glorious day in "paradise." But this was not a typical morning, and I wasn't in paradise. Exhausted but too adrenalized for sleep, my unsettling thoughts taunted me. *Had I almost died? And what if death had claimed me, then what?*

I left a message at work saying that I wouldn't be in for a couple of days and then called family, letting them know that I was in ICU for observation and didn't want any visitors. Each one worried in their own way. Ned assured me that he'd take care of Abby and Noah and that he would contact Leah. I asked him to say nothing to Jonah or Hannah until the cardiologist ran his tests. Liddy offered to pray the Rosary for me. There was no way to contact Jeannie, which was probably for the best

When the phone rang late afternoon, I still hadn't slept a wink. I considered just letting it ring but finally picked up.

"Liz Schmidt?" There was something familiar about that voice.

"Yes..."

"This is Jason Rhodes, the doctor from ER. Just checking in on you. How are you feeling?"

"I'm fine. Just tired." A painful lump formed in my throat, and my eyes stung in response to his concern. "Your IV cocktail was magic," I said.

"You were so frightened this morning. I wanted to check in with you before starting my shift tonight."

"More like terrified. What a fool I must have made of myself."

"You were frightened, a completely normal response. Dr. Briggs will check in on you tomorrow morning. Just do what he says, and you'll be fine."

"Thank you for taking care of me this morning and calling to check on me."

"No problem. Take care, and God bless you."

After we hung up, I thought about that call for a good while. Wholly unexpected and comforting, Dr. Rhodes was a different kind of doctor.

When Leah phoned later, she sounded tearful, "Mom, you can't die."

Poor, tender-hearted Leah. She was the child most in need of an affectionate, cuddly mother that I had never been.

"I'm not going to die. The ER doctor simply admitted me for observation. Just a bad bladder infection that got out of control because I waited too long to go to the doctor."

Leah asked if she could pray for me over the phone. And for once, I wasn't offended that my oldest daughter was pushing her born-again Christianity down my throat. Her words seamlessly flowed as she asked God to heal me and bring me to complete physical and spiritual recovery. I felt no irritation, just her love.

THE HEART SPECIALIST, DR. Briggs, was neither as pleasant as Dr. Rhodes nor half as handsome. His bedside manner had an irritable edge. Perhaps he thought I should only answer his curt questions. But after thirty-six hours caged in a hospital room, I wanted answers to my questions.

His cutting-edge imaging technique found no damage to my heart muscle. That surprised Briggs, given my labs from the ER and the ones drawn 12 and 24 hours later. "You're damn lucky," he barked at me.

He prescribed a daily beta-blocker and tiny white nitroglycerin tablet should the pain return. Once I got off the IV antibiotics, Dr. Briggs instructed me to finish my capsule antibiotics. I bellyached about the beta-blockers. I was too healthy to take a pill every day; I didn't even take vitamins.

Dr. Briggs instructed me to make an appointment to see him in six weeks, barring no further episodes. I'd be discharged in the morning and could return to work when I felt well enough.

I greeted my first non-medical visitor that evening. Ned and I had spoken on the phone numerous times, but I hadn't seen him since he dropped me off in the wee hours of Sunday morning outside the ER.

"You don't look any worse for all the wear and tear." Ned leaned over, kissed me lightly on the lips, and then seated himself in the lone chair in my half of the hospital room. My roommate, an older woman, who loved gabbing on the phone to someone named Clarissa, had been discharged earlier in the day.

"That's surprising; I've not had any decent sleep for two days. I can't wait to get home to my own bed."

"I hear you. The hospital is the last place I want to be if I don't feel well. But seriously, how do you feel?"

"Other than stressed out, the same as always. The cardiologist says my heart sustained no permanent damage."

"You will take a few days off work, won't you? Please don't push it, Liz."

"I'll probably take the rest of the week off. I'll see how I feel once I'm home."

"Glad to hear you are going to be reasonable with your recovery. You push yourself too hard."

I'd had too much to think over the last day and a half, and my worried tangle of thoughts needed to graze free in Ned's pasture.

"I think God might be angry with me," I said.

"That's completely ridiculous. Why would God be upset with you?"

"You know, because of ... us ... our relationship. When I was in ER Sunday morning, I thought I would die and end up in hell."

"Liz, there is no such thing as hell or the Devil. That's fantasy. God is too good to send anyone to hell."

"Maybe God doesn't send people there. Maybe they send themselves there."

"That's your Catholic Church indoctrination speaking." Ned shook his head and exhaled loudly in exasperation. I couldn't tell if he was upset with me or simply pitied me. Perhaps both.

The realization that Ned had never shared the slightest shred of guilt—a guilt that I'd lugged around since our first kiss in Tiburon and after a decade of living a lie—hit me like a ton of bricks. My body shuddered as if defibrillated by a pang of anguish-tinged regret sent to resuscitate my limp, seared conscience.

Although my birth father had no concern that he might be endangering his soul by our relationship, I was amply concerned for both of us. His assertion of an empty hell and a non-existent Devil rang hollow as if emptied of truth. The sound of that emptiness sent shivers through me like so many fingernails on a chalkboard.

The Dream

I'd BEEN BACK AT work for a week when Aunt Alice called to check in on me. Our conversations had become progressively more irksome, particularly over the last year. She hadn't changed, but I certainly had.

To my aunt, I remained the same sweet niece she had connected with Liddy after much prayer and the "miracle" of roses from a disappearing boy named Martin some fourteen years ago. My super-Catholic, naïve aunt could never imagine how far I'd strayed away from all she cherished.

"Liddy told me about your time in the hospital. I am so glad that you are okay. Did you ask for the Last Sacrament?"

Aunt Alice and her religiosity! I had no stomach for it anymore. She would never stop unless I clarified where I stood on religion, Christianity, and Catholicism.

"Aunt Alice, I know that you mean well, but I don't go to the Catholic Church anymore. And I don't force my kids to go either."

I glanced over at Ned, reading the newspaper nearby. A surge of anger and impatience welled up inside me like gathering storm clouds. At what? Any and everything, myself included, triggered by Aunt Alice's mention of the Last Sacrament. I was on a roll.

"And honestly, I not sure that Jesus Christ is God."

Aunt Alice gasped, the blow of my sucker punch stealing away her words. She struggled unsuccessfully to regain her composure.

I ended the call, knowing that our short conversation would keep her on her knees for months to come.

After we hung up, my agitation continued. I remained seated at my desk with my swivel chair facing Ned. He lowered his newspaper and met my eyes.

"You were a little rough on Alice, don't you think?"

I didn't reply. After a few seconds of silence, Ned raised an eyebrow, shook the newspaper once, and continued reading, his face hidden. I was utterly disgusted with myself. Not for what I'd said, for that was the truth, but for my delivery. The venom behind my words shocked even me.

Her "preaching" had become unbearable, unleashing a firestorm in my soul. I seethed in a prison of self-loathing, created by my choices, with no way out and no one to blame except myself.

DR. BRIGGS KEPT ME waiting for a long time, first in the waiting room and now in the exam room. Where was the self-important doctor? He wasn't the only one whose time was valuable.

I'd been taking the beta-blockers that he'd prescribed for six weeks. While less anxious, I crawled through my days like an over-medicated slug. My primary sign of life was free-ranging anger seeking any target outside myself. I still carried the nitro pills, although I'd no reason to use them.

The door opened. In came Dr. Briggs with his unsmiling countenance and eyes glued to the summary of our last contact, excusing him from unnecessary eye contact.

"Six weeks ago, you had a cardiac event when I saw you at Scripps Memorial. How do you feel?" he said blankly.

"Like I don't need to take the beta-blockers. They're depressing."

He knit his brows. "I'd like you to take them for six months. Though no permanent damage showed up on the imaging, your heart needs time to recuperate. The beta-blockers keep your heart from getting overworked," he said, listening to my heart with his stethoscope.

I waited for him to finish. "I know what they do. I just don't think they are necessary in my case. Couldn't I pop a nitro if I have any pain symptoms? Which, by the way, I have not had."

"Look, I'm not going to argue with you. It's your body. I know what the research shows, beta-blockers after cardio-vascular events reduce their reoccurrence." He stepped back away from me, matching my stubborn gaze.

"Have you any idea how close you were to death six weeks ago?"

Like a deer caught in the headlights of an approaching car, the doctor's words forced me to unflinchingly face what I had never admitted to anyone, including myself.

"You were slipping under the line that hangs between life and death. You're here today only because the angels pulled you up by the shoulders," he said.

What? Had I heard the man correctly? His mouth, his voice, yes. But Dr. Briggs would never say such a thing. I was dumbfounded. Was I hallucinating?

"See me in six months, and we will reevaluate the beta-blockers." And he was gone.

I remained on the examination table going back over our brief conversation, stunned, in a daze of disbelief. I threw the beta-blockers in the garbage can on my way out and walked past the receptionist's desk without making a follow-up appointment.

ALTHOUGH I STOPPED TAKING the beta-blockers, my mood continued its downward spiral. My boss gave me a pass from international travel for six months, eliminating a major work-related stressor. Nothing had changed that I could tell at home, other than me. My secret life pressed in on me with bone-deep loneliness and consuming guilt, crowding out the initial joy that I'd felt when Ned and I first moved in together.

My love for my birth father continued to migrate to a place that didn't need or desire sexual expression. This shift in my feelings was not one that I could share with Ned, for his desire had not changed.

In my fantasies, our life together would continue with the one fundamental change of celibacy of a normal father daughter relationship All my living benefits would remain, and my guilt would magically vanish.

If one is as sick as their secrets, I was critically ill. But who could I tell? No one would ever understand, and the shame of disclosure was paralyzing. Since Ned came into my life, I'd distanced my few friends. I knew Liddy loved me, but I could hardly admit what I had done. Least of all to her. How could she forgive me? I wasn't sure that I could forgive myself.

Nightmares that had plagued my childhood returned in force. Although they never completely stopped, I'd conditioned myself to awaken before the terrifying visions burned their way fully into my dreams.

The holidays came and went as I bid 2003 goodbye. The prospect of the new year didn't feel so joyous, stuck as I was in the joy-sucking muck of the last three months.

The phone rang. "Happy New Year, Mom. How are you feeling?" Leah asked.

"Fine physically ..." My voice trailed off. A dark cloud devoured the remainder of my words.

"Look, Mom, you can't pretend everything is okay. You don't sound right, and you didn't the last time we spoke either. What is it?"

Leah called out my charade. But she couldn't help me carry my burdens, especially when I couldn't be completely candid with her. I grappled for my words, but they were locked away in a prison of shame with no key.

"Mom, please. Talk to me."

"... I just feel like there's no hope for me." I heard the empty, flat intonation in my voice.

"Mom, listen to me. That's exactly what Satan would have you believe, that your situation is hopeless. But it's a big fat lie. No one is beyond hope. That's what Jesus is all about. Second chances, third chances, seventy-seventh chances."

Would anything less come out of Leah's mouth? She'd given me a copy of *The Spirit-Filled Life Bible for Students* for Christmas four years prior, with the inscription, "For Mom, forever a student! 1 Pt 1:3-5," knowing full well that I had no use for a Bible.

I couldn't remember exactly how our conversation had ended. I'd fixated on the life-preserver Leah had tossed me: "That's exactly what Satan would have you believe." Who held the keys to my self-made prison of lies? Was it me or someone or something else?

MOONLIGHT FILTERED THROUGH THE sides of the blinds, covering the three small windows above my bed. Something had awakened me. My hair and pajamas clung to me, damp with perspiration. My heart pounded as if I were being chased. The metallic tang of blood flooded my tastebuds from where I had bitten my tongue. My eyes blinked open, adjusting to the few slivers of light. Then I saw it, the very same as the night before.

A bodiless face, half-animal and half-human, hovered above me as I lay in bed. Menacing red eyes with amber pupils glared at me. Its lion-like mouth opened and closed as if ready to devour me with triangular, pointy teeth. Its putrid breath burned on my face and smelled of sulfur. Curved horns emerged from a beast-like head.

Was I awake or asleep? "No!" I shouted, pulling my bedsheets over my head, hiding from the nightmarish creature. I turned on the light on my bedside table with trembling hands, knocking my glass of water onto the floor.

Was I losing my mind? Rising, I changed into dry bedclothes and went downstairs to make a cup of chamomile tea.

When I got back to my room, I popped a sleeping pill, dreading the hangover-like feeling I would take into work in five hours. But that was better than lying awake the rest of the night. I kept my night-light on until the sleeping pill started to take effect.

The next night, I experienced something entirely different. A brilliant light awakened me from my sleep. I sat up in bed, mesmerized by its source: a man dressed in a long white robe, sitting in the same green rocking chair that Grandpa Schmidt had rocked me in as a child.

The man's shoulder-length, wavy, dark brown hair framed his olive-toned features. His eyes trained on a woman and young female child who walked hand-in-hand towards him and with their backs to me.

The child had short raven hair and, based on her height, looked about three or four years old. She wore a filthy red nightie that fell mid-calf. Foul matter covered her arms and legs, emitting a putrid stench.

The woman wore a floor-length blue tunic, cinched at the waist with a long veil covering her long dark brown hair. Her translucent shimmery veil, held in place by a wreath of purple violets, rested atop her head like a crown.

The man's dark expressive eyes teared up as they focused on the child. He opened his arms to the child, beckoning her to come to him. The woman stood behind the child and gently prodded her towards the man. His eyes momentarily left the child and peered upwards in the woman's direction. He nodded slightly and smiled at the woman, saying, "Thank you, Mother."

In a quavering yet familiar voice, the little girl said, "Rocker me." Dazzling as sunlight, the man picked up the filthy child as if she were his most priceless treasure. He held her in his lap while pressing her close to his heart and began to rock her gently. The longer he gazed into the child's face, the cleaner she became until all vestiges of grime vanished. A soft powdery, clean scent now filled my room. The unmistakable fragrance of violets.

The man held the child tenderly, bathing her with his light. When the child turned her face towards me, I recognized her immediately, for she was me.

My eyes traveled up to the man's face. He lifted his eyes to meet mine. His gaze held the unconditional love and acceptance that I had sought my entire life and never truly found.

And with his gaze came an infusion of knowledge and certitude as powerful as water crashing over a spillway. As I had done nothing to earn or deserve that love, neither was there anything I could do to destroy it. Freely offered, I could accept or reject his love. But if accepted, he would be there to wash me clean.

My alarm rang at 6:30 a.m. as any other workday, except that this was Saturday. I'd forgotten to turn my alarm off the night before.

I blinked open my eyes, wishing only to be in the man's presence once more, to feel his eyes upon my face. His light had chased out a darkness that, only in its absence, was possible to comprehend fully.

Falling to my knees at my bedside, I shed tears of pure joy. A short prayer fell from my lips. "Jesus, you are real! Show me your way, for I am weak and unwise. Lead me to the help that I need." I remained on my knees, basking in the love and peace I'd received during the night.

Was it all a dream? It remained palpable. Everything around me was the same, yet everything was different.

Filled with a boundless faith, I had a ravenous hunger to know Jesus, this God-Man, whose love for me could not be diminished and who would be there to wash me clean.

I walked downstairs and stopped in front of the bookcase in my office. I ran my fingers down the spine of the Bible that Leah had given me. Other than reading her inscription to me, just inside the front cover, I had never turned a single onion-skin page.

I removed the book, walked into the kitchen, and started brewing a pot of coffee. The hardback binding was stiff, and the pages smelled of newness as I opened the book.

I'd never read the Bible before on my own, nor had I desired to do so. However, my exposure to Scripture was not insignificant. I had decades of listening to the readings at Mass. The words had gone in one ear and out the other, lacking the seed of faith to bind them to my heart. All I had heard were words written by men. But this morning, those words took on a new significance. They became a beacon of light, leading me to a Jesus who loved me, warts and all.

Noah and Abby were still sleeping when Ned made his way downstairs in his plaid bathrobe. I'd been awake for several hours. In my pajamas and robe, I sat at the breakfast table in the kitchen. The Bible that Leah had given me lay open to the verses from 1 Peter that she'd highlighted in yellow:

> *Blessed be the God and Father of our Lord Jesus Christ! By his great mercy he has given us a new birth into a living hope through the resurrection of Jesus Christ from the dead, and into an inheritance that is imperishable, undefiled, and unfading, kept in heaven for you, ...*

"Morning, Liz. Good book?" Ned kissed the top of my head. "What's this? The Bible?"

"Yep. A surprise, isn't it? The first time with my nose in the Bible. Ever," I said.

I stood up and wrapped my arms around my birth father. "You aren't going to believe what happened last night. I have so much to tell you. Grab a cup of coffee, and when you're awake and ready to hear about it, let me know."

And so, as a "baby" Christian, I began my sojourn into the light, with no idea how arduous and steep the climb would be, for the wake of my sin was wide. The only thing I had to change was everything. There would be no magic on the road to recovery. I would scale my own Mount Calvary.

The date was January 24th, 2003, thirteen years to the day that my mother Marie had died.

Studies

MY DREAM, OR WHATEVER it was, and the memory of Pastor Matt's Christmas sermon from thirteen months ago had drawn me back to Community Fellowship Church like a thirsty woman to a well.

The usher had handed me a bulletin as I'd entered the sanctuary the following Sunday. Alone. Tucked inside had been sermon notes, a separate sheet containing bulleted take-away points with fill-in-the-blanks. What a great idea, I thought. Organization and clarity were right up there next to godliness. The back of the bulletin had included notices and announcements. I had zeroed in on one, "New – Singles Bible Study. Come check us out! Tuesdays @ 7 p.m. in the church sanctuary."

I approached my nascent interest in the Bible academically, much as I would approach a project at work. But lacking even the basics of studying or reading the Bible, I had many questions and few answers. Should I begin reading from the first chapter in Genesis and end up at the last chapter of Revelation? And which version of the Bible should I use; there were so many.

Hobbling along, using trial and error, was not my style. I would learn from people who possessed some expertise. The Singles Bible Study was the perfect place to start. I could also observe how Christians interacted with one another.

I arrived at 6:59 p.m. with Ned in tow, ready to begin my research into the "materials and methods" of Bible study. The sanctuary had been reconfigured slightly from Sunday's service. About fifteen people sat around the three folding tables placed end to end. At forty-nine, I could pass for a few years younger. However, at seventy-three years old, my birth father stood out like a sore thumb in a sea of mostly thirty- and forty-year-olds.

It was the second meeting of the newly organized group, and they were studying the book of Nehemiah. On an intellectual level, I didn't know enough about the Bible to have any interest or disinterest in any particular book. Beyond that, I'd hoped the singles group would help me meet people who were part of the new church that I planned to now attend regularly. Making new acquaintances would best happen for me within a structured situation, especially in a classroom-like setting.

Ned and I took two of the three empty seats interspersed amongst the other attendees. A woman with short brown hair seemed in charge. She asked a man, sitting at the far end of the table and wearing a black leather jacket, to "lead us off in prayer." The group jumped into their study without any introductions. No one wore name tags, but they all seemed to know each other.

I'd brought the Bible Leah had given me, but everyone else had a study booklet. An attractive Latino woman sitting to my right let me look on with her. As my interest flagged, I studied the group dynamics, which held more appeal than a book in the Old Testament I'd never read.

Ned sat further down from me, on the opposite side of the table. Before long, he lost the battle to fain interest and nodded off. I felt guilty for begging him to come with me. I wished that new things weren't so uncomfortable for me. He had been kind to go with me.

At eight o'clock, the woman with short brown hair, who I now realized was the group leader, announced that we had to switch meeting nights. Some sort of conflict required the switch from Tuesday to Wednesday evenings. Either day was okay for me.

A period of sharing followed. As led, members of the group shared their fears, failures, and struggles as they asked for prayers. When good things happened, they gave glory to God and called it a "praise report." Although I cared no more about the book of Nehemiah than before, I was intrigued by the group's vulnerability, openness, and fellowship.

With the final "Amen," Ned stood, got my attention, announced quietly, "I'll meet you in the car," and promptly left. I'd begun my study of Christians: what they could teach me, how they interacted and prayed. I was elated by my tiny step in the positive direction.

I introduced myself to the group leader named Lisa and gathered up my things to rejoin Ned outside. A chatty fellow, intent upon making my acquaintance, delayed my exit. Finally, I said, "My father is waiting for me outside in the car, but it was nice meeting you." I rarely disclosed that Ned was my birth father; it was too complicated. I smiled and turned towards the door.

"Wait! Hold up a minute," called a different male voice. It was the man in the black leather coat that had led the meeting off in prayer. Although he had spoken infrequently, he possessed a quiet authority.

He caught up with me, "Did I overhear you say that you're heading to the car to meet up with your father? Was that the older gentleman you came in with?"

"Yes, and yes." It was becoming difficult to make my escape.

"Jonathan Williams," he said, extending his hand in greeting, "and you are?"

"Liz Schmidt," I said, looking at my wristwatch before shaking his hand.

"I don't want to keep your dad waiting, but I stood in line to meet you. You have to give me five minutes," he teased, flashing an infectious grin. He opened up a small tin containing small brown round tablets. "Would you like a breath mint?" He held the container towards me and placed one in his mouth.

"Why? Do I have bad breath?" I asked in horror.

He laughed softly. "No, I just want to ensure that I don't." His blue-grey eyes twinkled. "My friends call me Jon."

"Okay ... Jon." I popped one of his mints in my mouth. With my ultra-sensitive sense of smell, this guy got points for prophylactically fighting bad breath.

I'd already pegged Jon as a person of interest, but not because I was physically attracted to him. I wasn't. Not that he was unattractive. Sandy-brown hair, pale skin, and under six feet on his tip-toes wasn't my idea of tall, dark, and drop-dead handsome. But Jon did have something going for him. He was hands-down the most knowledgeable, intelligent, and articulate group member. And competence was very attractive to me.

"It would be fun to get to know you better," Jon said as he closed the tin and placed it back into his coat pocket.

What did that mean, "get to know me better"? I wasn't ready for anyone to know too much about me. I was the one studying them.

"Look, I'm older than you, and I have lots of kids," I said, dousing any romantic interest he might have upfront.

"I'm probably older than you think, and I like kids. I even have one of my own," Jon protested with levity.

I knew Jon was younger, but why argue with him? Besides, maybe he was someone who could answer the questions that I had. Not about Nehemiah but about Jesus, Christianity, salvation, and how to plumb the depths of the Bible as I set out to fix my broken life.

Trying to be smooth over my rough edges, I asked, "What do you do? I mean, for a living?"

"I work in computer networking."

Okay, Jon passed my deadbeat filter.

"And you?"

"Pharma drug discovery. I need to go, though, my father is waiting. We can talk more next week."

I departed my first Bible study with a skip in my step and a lightness in my heart.

BY THE THIRD MEETING, I felt very comfortable with the singles group and had learned everyone's first names. Jon had been absent the week before. I'd missed his astute comments and wondered why hadn't he returned.

Tonight, I arrived early and helped rearrange the tables and chairs into a square. Jon Williams was last to arrive. Two empty seats remained: one next to me and the other next to Kellie, a pretty blonde. I surreptitiously monitored Jon's interactions from where I sat, noting that his attention never wandered my way.

Why should I care? He wasn't why I'd taken extra care with my appearance before showing up for the last two meetings: fixing my hair and applying mascara and a bit of lip gloss. Those things were an outward manifestation of the renewed hope that percolated within.

At the end of the study, Lisa asked if anyone had anything to share. With a dimpled smile, Kellie announced that she was visiting a nearby nursing home to celebrate Valentine's Day.

"I've got no sweetheart. But rather than feel sorry for myself, I'm baking heart-shaped cookies to give to the residents. If anyone wants to help out, show up this Saturday in the church parking lot at three-thirty," Kellie said.

After the closing prayer, Jon stayed put, gabbing with Kellie, the embodiment of cuteness. I dawdled in place, talking with Sam, a red-headed pharmaceutical salesperson seated next to me. I hoped Jon might make his way over to me. He did not. *So much for getting to know me better,* I thought, confused about why I felt miffed.

Kellie finally gathered her things, stood up, and headed towards the door. I caught up with her.

"I'd like to join you this Saturday at the nursing home. I'll bake some sugarless cookies for the folks who have to limit their sugar intake."

"Excellent, glad you can come! We can ride over together. See you then."

I ARRIVED TEN MINUTES early at the church parking lot to meet up with Kellie for our field trip to the nursing home. The smell of vanilla filled my car as three dozen freshly-baked cookies exhaled their last warm breath. I finished tying the pink ribbons around the cellophane bags, each holding a single heart-shaped cookie.

Promptly at three-thirty, Kellie pulled up in her car alongside mine. I grabbed my basket filled with cookies and boxes of candy conversation hearts, exited my car, and locked it. After I placed my treats in the back seat of her car, she drove us to the nursing home.

The receptionist handed us property maps, blank stick-on name tags, and a black marker once we arrived. I wrote "Liz, Community Fellowship Church" before placing it on my sweater. It felt good to be part of something bigger than myself.

We divided up the hallways with the aid of the maps, splitting the regular and sugar-free cookies we'd baked and the boxes of conversation hearts between us.

"Let's meet back at the front desk in two hours," Kellie said.

"Sounds good. See you then."

Praying for a temporary bout of anosmia, I put my self-consciousness aside and set about to create a memorable Valentine's Day for the elderly residents who meandered through the hallways or sat in wheelchairs staring blankly out windows or lay alone in their rooms.

Handing out cookies and candy gave me the confidence to interact with the residents. They took treats, but what they hungered for was my company. I asked them where they'd grown up, about their children or grandchildren, and what their favorite memory was. And more often than not, their stories and words of wisdom captivated me. Something extraordinary unfolded before me that afternoon. What I received far outweighed what I'd proffered—the gift of losing myself in the world of another.

When I returned to the front desk, Kellie was waiting for me. "Not bad for sugarless cookies, Liz," she said, swallowing the last bite before handing the remaining bagged goodies to the receptionist.

When Kellie drove me back to the church parking lot, people had started arriving for the six o'clock worship service. Although I hadn't planned on attending that evening, I thought, why not? I wanted to prolong my emotional high.

I dialed Ned on my cell phone. "Hi. I just got back to the church parking lot from the nursing home. I think I'm going to stay for the worship service. Want to join me?"

"No. I'll pass, but thanks for checking in."

"I'll be home right afterward to cook dinner."

"Okay, see you then."

"Bye."

I had hoped that Ned would somehow weather the change in our relationship, but he had felt abandoned in the month since "The Dream," as he called it. I wanted to believe that I could simply close the door to the illicit part of our relationship, hit a reset or erase button, and pretend it had never happened.

Although Ned honored my wishes for a platonic relationship, that was not his desire. No longer lovers, what were we to be? Father and daughter. What was even possible?

I entered the sanctuary early and listened to the praise band as they warmed up. As people filed in and took their seats, I counted three people from the Singles Bible Study. They all sat together: Lisa, the group leader; Sam, the red-headed pharma sales guy; and Lindy, who rode a motorcycle and had a cross tattoo on her forearm.

Keenly aware that I sat alone as the empty seats filled in around me, I buried my face in Pastor Matt's sermon notes. Suddenly, the air stirred next to me. There sat Jon, with a single empty chair between us. "Hi, Liz. Mind if I sit here?" He pointed to the open seat right next to me.

"That would be fine," I said, genuinely delighted.

Throughout the hour-long service, I studied Jon through furtive glances. His sandy-brown hair was thin and receding in front. It was clean but in dire need of a trim. His wire-rimmed glasses, though outdated, were expensive. He smelled of the brown cinnamon mints he had offered me three-and-a-half weeks ago.

He closed his eyes during the worship songs and held his hands out and upward, making a prayer of his entire athletic body. A runner, I surmised. An agate in the rough, Jon only lacked the polish to bring out his luster.

After the service, Jon and I remained seated and looked at one another simultaneously.

"I haven't seen you at this service before," he said.

"This my first time at Saturday night Mass. No, not Mass, I mean service."

Lisa, Sam, and Lindy walked over to where Jon and I sat.

"We are thinking of heading over to the Piazza and for dinner at Souplantation. Would you two like to join us?" Lisa asked.

Jon replied enthusiastically, "Sure, why not. I don't have my son this weekend. It saves me puzzling over what to have for dinner." He then turned to me, "What about you, Liz? Can you come?"

"I think so. I just need to make a quick phone call to check on things at home."

Noah and Abby were happy to have an excuse to eat dinner with their friends, but Ned wanted to join me. I told him that I'd wait for him out in front of the restaurant.

I couldn't remember the last time I felt so giddy, and it wasn't about the meal. It was about getting to spend some time with Jon. I wondered what his story was.

Ned had no trouble finding me as all five of us were still outside, standing in a slow-moving serpentine line, waiting to make our way inside. I introduced Ned as my father, although everyone remembered him from the one meeting he'd attended.

The forty-foot, two-sided self-serving station split our group as we entered the restaurant. Lisa, Sam, and Lindy queued on one side while Jon, Ned, and I went to the opposite side. I grabbed a tray and began to load my plate with salad, fresh veggies, and fruit.

With the clamor and clatter of the Saturday evening dinner rush and Ned standing between Jon and me, I struggled to continue my conversation with Jon. Halfway to the cash register, Ned moved behind Jon so that we wouldn't have to talk over him.

Initially, I didn't notice that the cashier had added Jon's meal to Ned's and mine. Surprised and somewhat embarrassed, I shrugged when Jon looked over at me.

"That was nice of you to pay for my dinner. That means I have to sit with you," Jon said with an ear-to-ear grin, milking my lack of attention and the cashier's mistake for its full worth.

I spotted Lisa, Sam, and Lindy sitting at a long table toward the back of the restaurant. Once joining them, I placed my tray down and went to get soup and muffins. When I returned to the table, Jon, true to his words, sat to my right. Ned sat to my left. Jon and I monopolized each other's attention during the meal, as Ned would point out to me later that night.

"Would you like to get a cup of coffee and continue our conversation?" Jon asked when everyone stood to leave.

"Sure. I know the perfect place, Champagne," I said.

The little French shop was nearby. One side was a patisserie, and on the other side, a small cozy café. It reminded me of what I loved best about the month I'd spent in France with Ned: the desserts and sidewalk cafes.

Ned overheard us and said to me quietly, with a wounded look, "I'll see you at home," and then left.

Jon held the door for me as we entered through the patisserie side. Antique-looking chandeliers of black wrought iron and amber alabaster globes hung throughout. A half-dozen small, glass-topped bistro tables and chairs sat between the storefront glass windows and an impossibly long refrigerated glass case, displaying every kind of exquisite pastry temptation.

I walked in front of the refrigerated cases admiring the creations, counting those I had tried before and, more importantly, those I had yet to savor. Jon stood patiently at the counter, waiting for me to order my coffee.

"Have you already ordered?" I asked, realizing that I was alone in my dessert reverie.

"No, I was waiting for you. But please order something to eat, too!"

"A decaf cappuccino and a Mille-Feuille," I said to the waiter standing behind the counter. Already, I tasted the alternating layers of puff pastry and crème filling, topped with royal icing and chocolate zig-zags."

"A chamomile tea. That'll be all for me," Jon said.

"What? You had me order a dessert and then didn't order one yourself?" I turned to the young man that took our order, "Two forks, please, and a knife."

I followed Jon to a table tucked away in a secluded corner away from customer traffic.

"You asked me out for coffee, but you ordered tea," I observed.

Jon smiled sheepishly. "I don't drink coffee or real tea, just the herbal stuff. My friend told me that I couldn't ask a woman out for tea. I had to ask her if she wanted to get a cup of coffee. You're my first test case."

"Do you think caffeine is a vile drug or something?"

"No, nothing like that. I just never developed a taste for coffee or black or green tea."

"What about chocolate?"

"I love the stuff, especially if it's dark!"

"Good, because I don't trust anyone who claims they hate chocolate." I laughed but was halfway serious. Jon passed my chocolate filter.

"So, tell me about yourself." Jon asked as the server delivered our tea and single pastry.

"That's too broad, Jon. What's important for you to know about me?" With no idea where to begin, I pushed the Mille-Feuille halfway between us and carefully bisected its luscious layers. "Your half," I said.

"Fair enough," Jon said, taking the fork I handed him. "Okay, why did you start attending Community Fellowship Church? I've been involved there for ten years and only recently noticed you when you started attending the

Singles Bible Study."

I speared my first bite of the pastry. Jon followed my lead and nodded approval of his first taste.

"The church is close to my house. I'd gone there the Christmas before last and liked what Pastor Matt had to say." I wanted to be honest with Jon, but total transparency wasn't possible. "I had a strong desire to attend church again after a ... long dry spell."

"Were you raised Catholic? I noticed you mentioned Mass inadvertently after the service tonight."

With another mouthful of pastry, I nodded my head. "Yes, but I haven't been inside a Catholic church for a decade."

"My ex-wife was raised Catholic. I met her when I was in seminary."

"Wait, are you saying you studied to be a priest?"

"No, not a priest. Protestant pastors go to seminary, too. I have a Master of Divinity degree, the same as a Catholic priest. But obviously, the curriculum differs some."

Everything was making sense now. No wonder Jon's knowledge and insights soared head and shoulders above everyone else in the class.

"What prompted you to attend the Bible Study?" Jon asked.

"That is a long story. The short version is that I've never been motivated to open the Bible until recently. I heard bits and pieces of the Bible during Mass while still attending the Catholic Church, but I didn't have the faith to hear or the heart to understand back then. I'd hoped to get hints on digging into the Bible from the Singles Bible Study. I like listening to the people in the group share their passion for their faith and their struggles." And then added, with a teasing smile, "Especially you, Jon, that is when you decide to show up."

"Yeah, about my spotty attendance. My son is with me every other Wednesday evening, so when Lisa changed the meetings from Tuesday to Wednesday, that cut me out half the time."

"Okay, you're forgiven. What about you, Jon? Why did you start attending the small group? You could teach the group and don't need to attend to increase your knowledge. That's pretty obvious."

"This was the first time Community Fellowship has tried a singles group, and it is the first time since joining that church that I have been single. Well, more precisely, divorced for a year and a half now. I felt prompted, like God wanted me involved, not to facilitate the group but for some other reason. Perhaps, I'll eventually find out."

Jon spoke slowly and deliberately. He had gentleness and patience about him. Perhaps because I lacked both virtues, those traits strongly attracted me. There was so much I wanted to ask Jon about himself. I hoped there would be more opportunities in the future.

"Did you grow up around here? Sometimes I think I hear a tiny accent in your voice," I said.

"After being in California for eighteen years, most of my Tennessee accent has washed out. But I suspect if I spent a couple of months back in the little town that I grew up in, my accent might come roaring back."

Funny, Jon dressed more like he was ready for a hike on Mt. Rainier with his convertible-to-shorts hiking pants and trail-ready shirt than a Tennessee native. Where were the boots, big belt buckle, tight jeans, and cowboy hat? He sure had the body for it. I suspected his polite, slow, door-opening ways spoke to his Southern pedigree.

"Tennessee is a long way from California. Why'd you move west?"

"After college, I worked for a year, knowing that I'd be going on to seminary for the ministry work that I wanted to do. I needed to spread my wings. Attending seminary in L.A. accomplished that. When I finished seminary, I got married and went to work as an assistant pastor for about eight years."

"But you got out of the ministry. You work in technology now."

"Yes. My ex-wife hated me being a pastor: the pay, the time commitment, the pressure on her when she lost interest in anything to do with her faith. She was a different person than when I met her."

"That'd be hard. From what I see at Community Fellowship Church, it seems like the pastor's wife has a critical role in a Protestant Church."

"It was heartbreaking. Thankfully, I retrained in computer networking because I would have been out anyway when my ex-wife left because of 1 Timothy 3:4."

"What do you mean, 1 Timothy 3:4?"

"'He must manage his own family well and see that his children obey him, and he must do so in a manner worthy of full respect.' My ex-wife and I couldn't even agree on how to raise our son, to his detriment."

There was no way I wanted to get into my messy history of divorces and joint custody issues and Ned. I needed to change the topic and head home. At this point, Jon only knew that I was divorced and had five kids, but not even their ages. He had no idea that I'd divorced three times. He didn't know that the parents I spoke of were my birth parents and not the parents who had raised me, nor, most damning, the extent of my tangled relationship with Ned.

"Speaking of kids, I should head home to check in with mine." I drained the last bit of cappuccino foam from my cup.

"You got it. Off we go." And with that, we walked back to his car in the crisp evening air. "By the way, Liz, I'd suggest starting your private Bible reading with the Gospel of John. Nehemiah's a tough place to start. Everything makes more sense if you start with Jesus. The Bible is one continuous story of God's plan to fix humanity's brokenness."

It was as if Jon sensed something in my heart. Although my heart radiated the joy of God's love for me, so much in me was messed up and flat-out broken.

Jon dropped me back off at my car at the Piazza. "Thanks for going out for 'coffee' with me. I enjoyed our time together. I won't be at class this Wednesday because my son will be with me. Do you have this Monday off for President's Day?"

"Yes. Why?"

"I'd like to take you out to lunch if you're available."

"That would be lovely. I'd like that."

I typed my phone number into Jon's cell phone. He would call Sunday evening to confirm the time.

As I drove home, I prayed aloud. "Thank you, Lord, for sending me a teacher. How awesome you are!"

That night, I began reading the Gospel of John. I planned to have my questions ready by Monday lunchtime.

Chapter 21

Los Angeles

I HAD PURCHASED A new outfit for my outing with Jon. Yes, an outing, not a date, I told myself. It had been so long since I'd bought any new clothes. My dated wardrobe was not for lack of means but rather a lack of interest in my feminine appearance. But this was a new season; out with the old and in with the new. Joy had found me.

Jon picked me up at noon and drove us to the seaside village of Del Mar. Finding a parking space was more difficult than usual due to the holiday. We were lucky with the crowds to find a table on the outside patio of Jake's, a popular beachfront eatery. The weather was perfect, sixty-five degrees with the hint of a breeze

After we ordered, I nervously twirled the ring around my finger. The sun glinted off the 2-carat oval-cut tanzanite ring. "A purple condominium for your finger," my half-sister Lily had exclaimed when I unwrapped Liddy's extravagant birthday gift. I'd always admired the ring when Liddy had worn it, never imaging she would give it to me. On my hand, it looked almost ostentatious with its apron of diamonds set within its wide band of polished gold.

"That's quite the ring," Jon said, pulling me back to the present.

"It's a bit much, isn't it?" I pulled my hand onto my lap self-consciously.

"That's not what I meant. It's beautiful."

"I'm still getting used to wearing it," I said, feeling my face grow red as the server brought our lunch.

We ate our fish tacos with the Pacific Ocean as our backdrop. Our easy conversation blended with the sound of the surf and the soft buzz of nearby conversations. An hour later, we left the restaurant for the beach, stuffed to the gills after splitting a giant slice of hula pie, a fudgy, macadamia mountain of ice cream yumminess.

Mounds of purple statice, wild buckwheat, and clusters of purple-pink ice plant bordered the foot-worn path of sand we took down to the beach. A few hearty souls lay on the beach in swimsuits, hoping to catch a tan. We strolled along two miles of soft, sandy beach from Powerhouse Park to the coastal bluffs of Torrey Pines State Park.

As we walked along, Jon shared his greatest disappointments: the failure of his marriage, his departure from the ministry, a two-year expensive divorce battle, and his ongoing struggle to finalize custody arrangements for his son. An anxiety-driven eating disorder had been the catalyst for a teenage Jon to turn to the Lord when all else had failed. That experience had birthed a dependence on the Lord and a faith that remained his guiding light and strength.

If Jon was shocked when he learned that I'd been married and divorced three times, he hid it well. I painted a picture of my life in the Schmidt household and how I came to search for my biological parents, first Liddy and then Ned.

"So, Ned isn't the father that raised you?" Jon asked in astonishment. "Then how did you two end up living together?"

"That is a complicated story and one that will never make sense to anyone else. I was obsessed with my biological parents. I felt an instant bond with them, first with Liddy and then with Ned. My best analogy is how I felt when I first held my children as newborns. I doubt if I ever truly loved my third husband, but I did love him loving me. After Ned's divorce, I jumped at the chance when the opportunity presented itself to build a house with him."

Explaining why I'd left my marriage to Joe required some pretty fancy footwork. While I didn't say anything technically false, what I left out mixed the purity of truth with the stench of falsehood. The worst part of my story, my secret life with Ned, and the best part, a divine gaze of unconditional love that had turned my life around overnight, remained behind a locked door. A door to which only Ned and I retained the key.

Two opposing forces waged war within me: the desire to be known fully and the fear of being known completely. I'd no idea how to bridge the chasm, but my budding friendship with Jon placed me on the precipice.

"Thank you for lunch and the great time today. I should probably be heading home soon," I said, abruptly changing the subject.

"Of course, it was my pleasure. Do you have time for me to show you where I live? I could have walked to your house almost as quickly as I drove there."

"Sure, now you've got me curious."

We rounded the corner into the cul-de-sac where Jon lived on the way home. He pulled into the driveway of a two-story earth-toned stucco home with an orange tile roof, the largest of the four models in the housing development. He was correct; we did live very close to one another. I could walk there in under ten minutes.

"Hey, you live practically next to the athletic club. I work out there most evenings after dinner. I've never seen you there. Do you belong?"

"No, too busy. I'm finishing up the requirements for my black belt in Tae Kwon Do."

"Whoa, that's impressive. All I do is walk on the treadmill for thirty minutes each day while reading the Bible. Speaking of which, I have some questions for you on the Gospel of John if we do this again sometime."

"Why don't you stop by my house tomorrow evening when you finish at the gym. We could go over your questions then."

"That would be great. But be prepared; I'm a serious student."

"I already know that about you, Liz. I've watched you in action in the singles group."

Jon shifted into reverse to take me home and then suddenly shifted back into park. "Do you have time to come in for a minute?"

"Sure, why not?" I was curious to see Jon's taste in décor. I saw my home as a reflection of me and loved seeing how other people decorated their homes.

I noticed that his yard needed some serious attention as we walked from the driveway to the front porch. He had a brown thumb, lacked a landscaper's vision, didn't care about his yard, or all of the above.

The front door opened onto a light pink and cream limestone entryway that opened into a long hallway. A short distance to the right, a gently curving staircase wound to a second floor. I followed Jon to the left, stepping down into the sunken living room.

From the moment I walked into the living room, an emptiness pressed in on me like a raided tomb. No pictures hung on the turquoise walls, and not a single stick of furniture sat upon the purple wall-to-wall carpet. Two dated Doric-style columns delineated the living and dining rooms. A chandelier, with purple and turquoise and orange globes in various sizes, hung like a discombobulated solar system over the space where a dining table would sit, had there been one.

While not updated, the kitchen had a serviceable island covered with dull four-inch white tiles. The light oak floor extended into the family room and provided visual relief from the purple carpeting. Four folding chairs surrounded a small square table, shedding layers of old white paint like a molting snake in the eating nook.

On the plus side, Jon's house was of high construction quality, and it had an excellent floor plan from what I'd seen downstairs. The problem was that the home wore the ugliest "clothes" imaginable. And if a house could be in a state of clinical depression, this house qualified.

"Please sit down," Jon said as we entered the family room. He pointed to a pink, modern sectional sofa, the only piece of upholstered furniture downstairs. A fringed area rug with a geometric design in southwestern colors lay in front of it.

I complied, hoping that the tour had ended. My ugly quotient for the day was full.

"The house is pretty empty, isn't it?"

"You can say that again. Did your ex-wife take all the furniture when she left?"

"She did. At that point, I was more focused on just keeping the house."

"Who loves the southwestern color palette? You or your ex-wife?"

"That's all her. The master bedroom upstairs is pink and has the only picture remaining in the whole house. I guess she decided it was too ugly to take."

"When my father and his wife came to visit at Thanksgiving, they were appalled, as I suspect you are. My father is footing the bill to remodel and redecorate the house. I think my stepmother talked him into it."

"Wow. That's a very generous gift. I hope you don't mind me saying so, but your house needs help desperately and an interior facelift."

"That's all going to happen. I'm going to Los Angeles to meet with my brother in a couple of weeks. He is very artsy and great with interior design. My stepmother wants me to check out a furniture showroom there."

"How fun! I love decorating," I said.

"I'd love for you to come with me if you are interested."

"You may want to check out my taste in décor before you decide to bring me along. I have pretty strong decorating opinions. Be forewarned, I'll bombard you with my opinions."

"Well, that's one way to get to know you better." Jon smiled as he spoke.

I'D NEVER BEEN WITHIN the city limits of Los Angeles until I traveled there with Jon. Nothing prepared me for the grinding traffic. San Diego freeways were tame by comparison. Although the congestion set my teeth on edge, Jon wasn't the least bit frazzled by the gridlock. He had insisted that we leave by 6:00 a.m. I had complied, but my body still protested the 5:00 a.m. alarm on a Saturday morning.

After spending the night in L.A., the plan was to return home Sunday afternoon. Jon would spend the night at his brother's place while I would overnight at a nearby motel. Jon's brother had made the reservations.

Three-and-a-half hours later, we arrived at a Spanish-style, single-level home where Jon's brother, Jackson, lived. We walked up redbrick steps and passed under a cream-colored stucco archway into a well-groomed, lush courtyard.

The moment Jackson opened the door for us, I understood why he'd abandoned small-town Tennessee life for an acting career in Hollywood. One year older than Jon, Jackson was classically handsome. They shared little resemblance, but their blue-grey eyes and warm, gentle personalities identified the two men unmistakably as brothers.

"Jackson, my friend, Liz," Jon said as he stepped out of his brother's embrace and to my side. "Liz, my brother, Jackson."

"Very nice to meet you. Please come inside." Jackson extended his hand to me in a firm handshake.

Jackson's decorative style was eclectic, impeccably balanced, and very masculine. No wonder Jon wanted his input. As I found my way to the bathroom, I peeked into the various rooms. Each was stunningly appointed, a perfect harmony of space, form, line, earth tones, texture, and pattern.

The three of us visited a half-dozen stores and spent hours in the enormous Baker showroom. Jon amassed an armload of catalogs as the day progressed. And although Jon made no purchasing decisions, he discovered his taste in furnishings.

By the time we stopped for lunch, it was late afternoon. I was hungry enough to eat the menu and mentally exhausted from the window shopping. As Jon and Jackson talked, I learned a great deal about their lives growing up.

After lunch and a short respite at Jackson's place, Jon agreed to take me to the hotel for a short rest before we would have dinner later on our own.

"It was wonderful meeting you, Liz. I still can't believe you had five kids. Good genes. I liked watching you and Jon today. I think you are good for him," Jackson said.

I searched Jon's face for a reaction to his brother's words. In the weeks since President's Day, Jon and I had seen each other most days, and on the rare day that we didn't, Jon phoned to check in with me. On work nights after my gym workout, I often stopped by his home for fifteen or thirty minutes, asking questions about my Scripture readings that day.

On weekends, when his son wasn't with him, we would spend many hours together. We hiked the open spaces near our homes where the natural terrain remained untrampled and often went out to dinner. We arranged to attend the same church services and sat together, and I saw him every other week at the Singles Bible Study.

Jon and I were friends, that much I knew. But he was a man and a lonely one at that. And I was a woman, becoming more aware of a growing attraction to him that so far had defied definition.

"I'll see you later," Jackson said, turning to Jon. Then he added, "By the way, Jon, you don't need me to help you decorate. Liz is quite competent. I'm busy, and L.A. is well ... L.A. Liz is in San Diego. I leave you in her talented hands."

I thanked Jackson for his vote of confidence and said, "That's up to Jon."

"That's up to Liz," Jon said.

Within minutes, we traded Jackson's serene residential neighborhoods for the chaos of Wilshire Boulevard. I pulled my phone from my purse to check for messages and immediately realized what was missing from my finger.

"My tanzanite ring, it's gone! I must have left it in the restroom at one of the furniture stores. I always remove my rings when I wash my hands." A sinking feeling told me that I had seen the last of it. After all, this was L.A., the city of the lost and not found.

"Oh my gosh! I'm so sorry, Liz. We can call the stores tomorrow to see if anyone turned it in."

"I bet I left it at Baker Showroom." We had stayed there the longest, and I remembered visiting the ladies room.

"We can stop by on our way out of town. If they are closed, we can call on Monday. I know Jackson would pick it up if you left it there."

"I guess someone needed it more than I did," I said. The memory of the extravagant token of Liddy's love would remain mine, even if the ring were permanently gone.

My baseline for loss had been recalibrated. I counted my years of not following the Lord as my true loss. A ring was just a ring. Besides, it was out of my hands. Literally and figuratively.

Jon turned into the parking lot for my overnight accommodations. Hopefully, the motel didn't charge by the hour, but I wasn't too sure by the looks of the place. Jackson had made the motel reservations sight unseen, and Jon had already paid for my lodging. I waited in the car until Jon got the room key.

"Do you mind if I come in, Liz?"

"Not at all. Please, do."

A single exterior door separated me from the traffic that ran like a raging river twenty yards away, but the room was adequate and clean. The large picture window next to the double bed had a great view of the motel's flashing signage but no blackout drapes.

"Not very fancy, is it? Will it work for you?" Jon said. He placed my overnight case by the closet.

"I hope so," I said, competing with the sound of a police siren.

Jon sat on one side of the double bed and kicked off his shoes. The bed sunk as the springs complained. He swiveled his legs onto the bed and laid back on the pillow. I pulled the wooden chair out from the small desk and sat down.

"Can you lay down here, next to me?" Jon lifted his hand in invitation towards me.

I took off my shoes and walked around to the other side of the bed. Jon rolled onto his side, watching me as I lay down on the other side of the bed.

We just lay there quietly amidst the chaos outside, gazing into each other's eyes. The soul-bearing intimacy of the moment was terrifying for me, a woman with secrets, yet spellbinding.

"Thank you for coming with me today." Jon moved a strand of loose hair away from my face and tucked it behind my ear.

His touch felt very intimate, as there had been nothing physical between us besides an occasional one-arm shoulder-to-shoulder hug.

"Doesn't it bother you that I'm almost nine years older than you are, Jon?"

"Not at all. Does it bother you?"

"A little, I guess, because I said something."

"I think we look the same age. Regardless of your age, you are beautiful."

He removed my eyeglasses, then his, setting both on the bedside table next to him. He rolled back to face me and moved his hand to my small back, pulling me closer.

His cinnamon breath warmed my face. My heart pounded like a drum in my ears, wild with anticipation.

"Would it be okay if I kissed you?" he asked.

I nodded. A fire whipped through me as our lips melted into one. One kiss led to another and another, a passionate union of mouths and tongues. Blood rushed to places that I'd long ago buried as dead.

"We seem to fit together well, don't we?" Jon whispered as he kissed the end of my nose.

"Please feel at ease with me. I don't want to rush anything, Liz, but know that I wouldn't have kissed you if I didn't feel that our relationship could have a future."

Our kisses opened a Pandora's box of feelings for Jon and fears for myself. The strength of both pulled me in opposite directions. I knew my history in a way that Jon didn't. I pulled away from Jon and stared at the ceiling.

"Jon, you need to understand something about me. I had sex with all my husbands before we got married. Once we had sex, I felt bound to them in a way that demolished my better judgment. I refused to see red flags that should have sent me running."

I desperately wanted to add, "And the pinnacle of my failed judgment was a decade-long disordered relationship with my birth father," but the shame of my sin tied my tongue. I knew God's infinite mercy and forgiveness were boundless, but human mercy and forgiveness were stingy by comparison. And I wasn't ready to tell Jon "goodbye" when we had just said "hello."

"I didn't have faith in God to hold me to a higher standard of behavior, but I do now. I don't know where our relationship is headed, Jon, but I can't do anything that jeopardizes my relationship with Christ."

"I'm glad to hear you say that, Liz. I don't want to be an occasion of sin for you. God is not opposed to intimacy but, of course, sexual intercourse is reserved for marriage."

"But how do you know how far is too far?" I didn't know. Was it okay to kiss Jon as I'd done when it filled me with such desire?

"The Bible isn't completely clear on that," Jon said. "My personal opinion is that each person has to pray and discern the boundary for their chastity. And from there, a couple should back up even further to preserve them from temptation."

I wanted a list. Something that I could keep track of and use as a fence to keep me from going out of bounds, especially given my history. Jon's way sounded vague and unclear; how could I know for sure? With the feelings I now admitted I had for Jon, we'd have to back up pretty far.

I TOSSED AND TURNED like a dinghy on a stormy sea throughout the night. The combination of street noise and flashing lights, the taste of Jon's kisses, and the worry that I shouldn't have kissed him worked in concert to rob me of restful sleep. I worried that until he knew my deepest, darkest secret, a relationship with Jon was unfair. But if I had confessed to God and he had forgiven me, who else needed to know?

My morning shower revived my body and helped to declutter my brain.

I threw on my clothes, camouflaged the dark circles under my eyes, and sat down at the desk with my Bible. Psalm 32, verses 1-5, was where I'd left off. The words of David pierced me to my core. His song was my story, too:

Happy are those whose transgression is forgiven,
whose sin is covered.
Happy are those to whom the Lord imputes no iniquity,
and in whose spirit there is no deceit.

While I kept silence, my body wasted away
through my groaning all day long.
For day and night your hand was heavy upon me;
my strength was dried up as by the heat of summer.

Then I acknowledged my sin to you,
and I did not hide my iniquity;
I said, "I will confess my transgressions to the Lord,"
and you forgave the guilt of my sin.

Shutting my Bible, I laid my head down on the desk and sobbed. "Thank you, Lord, for never giving up on me. Help me, Lord, to the path of repentance and healing. I know where I want to go but not how to get there. Send your Spirit to guide me," I prayed aloud.

I stowed my Bible in my overnight case and opened the flimsy drapes. Rays of sunlight danced on the bed where Jon and I had shared our first kiss. The memory of his touch sizzled through me and stole my breath anew.

The knock at the door jolted me back to the present. Jon, bright-eyed and bushy-tailed, looked even more desirable and sexy than last night. *What a difference a kiss can make*, I thought.

"Look what I found." Jon proudly held up his right hand, wiggling his little finger adorned with my tanzanite ring.

"You found it! Where was it?" I pulled him into a happy-dance hug.

"You left it on the sink in the guest bathroom at Jackson's house, where it remained safely all day."

"Thank you, Lord!" I said.

"I have to say, Liz, your reaction to losing that ring impressed me. A whole lot of women would have been distraught, including my ex-wife. It was a window into your heart, and I liked what I saw."

OVER THE NEXT SEVERAL months, Jon's house began its much-needed transformation. Ordering new furniture was just the beginning as workers started renovating the interior. Although Jon acted as his general contractor coordinating the subs, I functioned as the primary consultant on every artistic decision. We were a dynamic duo.

Jon's home projects required a great deal of my time, but what did I care? The more time with Jon, the better. A hot guy was letting me turn his home from an ugly duckling to a graceful swan and leading me to Christ in the process. What could be better?

We observed each other's strengths and weaknesses as frustrations with slipped schedules mounted and miscommunications arose. Yet everything worked synergistically to strengthen our bond of friendship. Our romantic feelings blossomed into a beautiful rose that remained chaste through our joint commitment and effort. Lots of effort.

THE KIDS RACED UPSTAIRS to start their homework (or call friends) while Ned remained at the dinner table. I began clearing the dishes, wondering if he was feeling ill. He had been quiet during dinner and had just picked at his food.

"Heading off to the gym after the dishes?"

"Yes, then to Jon's house briefly. The contractors installed the French doors in the dining room today. I can't wait to see how they look."

The sound of two closing bedroom doors, followed by silence, assured me that we could speak candidly.

"How did your session go today with the therapist?" I asked.

Ned had been in psychotherapy and on antidepressants for two months now, navigating the wasteland of his shattered heart as best he knew how. I was responsible for his suffering. Yet I had to terminate the physical component of our relationship for my spiritual and emotional health. It had been wrong. Someday, I hoped he would agree.

"I want to talk to you about that, Liz."

Ned's grief-stricken eyes latched onto mine. I turned off the hot water, stopped loading the dishwasher, and sat down across from him at the table.

"What is it?"

"I like my therapist a bunch. I feel very comfortable being honest with her."

"Did you tell her about us...that you're my birth father?" My heart jumped in my chest at the thought of anyone else knowing about us.

"No, she doesn't need to know that. But she knows that you are the love of my life and that I feel like I'm dying without you. Whether we are biologically related or not doesn't matter. She knows that we continue to maintain a common household, that you've decided we'll never have the shared intimacy of lovers again, and that you are seeing someone else." Ned wiped away the tear that wandered down his chiseled cheek.

"I'm sure she thinks I'm a total monster. I feel horrible. What a tangled mess we've created."

"She's helped me see that I need to sell this house and move on."

Sell the house? I was terrified by what should have been obvious. Did I think I could have my cake and eat it, too?

"Can't we hold off until Noah graduates from high school? Or until Abby heads off to college in the fall? Or at least until Abby finishes her senior year in two months?"

"No, I can't wait. I've put all my eggs in your basket for the last twelve years. Today I contacted a real estate agent. She's coming over tomorrow to look at the house."

The finality of Ned's words sounded like glass falling to the floor, shattering the security of my physical world. The kids and I would lose our beautiful home.

"I see. I don't want to be any part of the sales process. For each dollar I've invested, you have fifteen in the house. I've no say in this except to voice my displeasure. Do what you need to do."

The remnant of me, not consumed by fear, knew that Ned was doing the right thing for him. There had to be a cost associated with cleaning up my life. Losing my home was merely the first installment of my long-overdue bill. God had never abandoned me, even when I had abandoned Him. He would help me get through this, one day at a time.

But how would I spin this development to my children and Jon when the truth could not be told?

Truth

MAY 2004

"NED IS OLDER NOW and wants a smaller place all to himself," I told Abby and Noah the day before the real estate agent hammered the "For Sale" sign into our front lawn. They didn't press for details or ask why suddenly their grandfather no longer wanted to live with us after ten years. Their only question was whether they would have to change schools.

"We will stay close by, no changing schools," I promised. And with that assurance, they adjusted to the news with more equanimity than I could muster.

Jon saw the "For Sale" sign when he picked me up for Singles Bible Study that week. I'd dreaded the inevitable questions, knowing I'd have to spin another lie onto the sticky web I'd built to conceal my past relationship with Ned. I made Ned out to be the bad guy.

"The kids are getting on his nerves. You know how older people can get," I said, failing to disguise the cutting edge of my voice and averting my eyes away from Jon.

"I can tell you're upset about this. I'm sorry this is so hard for you."

"Yes, I am upset. You'd think my father could wait six weeks until this school term ends. But, no." I felt my face tighten while the tears of a spoiled, petulant adult-child gathered like an impending storm.

"It's not like the end of a marriage," he said, squeezing my hand before turning into the church parking lot.

In some ways, it is, I thought darkly while looking out the car window.

STANDING ON THE FRONT porch of the condo, I watched the two brawny men drive off in their now-empty moving van. And with them, so went my angst over losing my home, evaporating like dew on a summer morning. In its place, a calm, cleansing feeling descended upon me.

Barely five weeks passed between when Ned listed our home and its closing. Ned moved into an upscale two-bedroom place in Solana Beach, less than half an hour away from the condo. He'd made a killing on the sale of the house, getting back a hundred fifty percent of the purchase price, enough to cover every dime that he'd lost on the Big House and a tidy down payment for his new home.

I signed a year-long lease on a tired, three-bedroom condo smelling of mildew and vibrating with the sound of constant traffic from nearby I-5. But the location permitted Abby and Noah to remain at the same high school, and the rent was semi-reasonable. At least the rooms were decently sized, one advantage of an older complex, and the place did have a Del Mar zip code, but just barely.

I walked back inside, moving from room to room, visualizing how to bring beauty to the space. Patches on the walls, worn places on the carpet, nicks and scratches in the woodwork, and tired vertical blinds dated the condo and screamed "rental." I smelled the musky passage of time.

My "new" home was a bit battered like me. It mirrored my failures but also held the promise of a fresh start: the gift of God's grace to make all things new.

NEAR THE END OF the 11 a.m. Sunday service, Pastor Matt introduced Kellie from the Singles Bible Study. She stepped up to the podium dressed in pink twinset and black slacks. A small strand of pearls hung around her neck; her blond hair swept back in a ponytail. Her confident eyes swept the room, her endearing smile never wavering. "Hi, I'm Kellie, and I'm an alcoholic."

Whoa, that was the last thing I'd expected Kellie to say. For the next five minutes, Kellie described how she had first denied her problem, hidden her addiction, and finally how it had controlled her life to rob her of the joy and freedom that redemption in Christ offered. Raised Catholic, I knew nothing of personal testimonies. Kellie's was the first I ever heard.

"We will meet every Thursday evening at 7:30 in the third-grade classroom. We start this week. All women are welcome. I'll be outside after the service if anyone has any questions."

As she finished, the entire congregation applauded. That Kellie's delivery had been passionate and articulate but not emotional had stunned me.

I wanted to support Kellie's efforts and had yet to cultivate a friendship with her outside the Singles Bible Study and beyond our time together at the nursing home. A couple of women that I didn't know were talking with her. Once they left, I waved to her. She waved back enthusiastically as I joined her under the awning.

"Kellie, I was blown away by your honesty. Gosh, to be so free that you can share such a personal struggle." I shook my head in awe.

I didn't need to know anything about Kellie's small group beyond that she would be leading it and that other Christian women would be there. My chance to get to know Kellie better had arrived.

"I'll be there," I said enthusiastically.

"Great! I'll see you on Thursday, Liz."

KELLIE AND EIGHT OTHER women gathered in the third-grade classroom. They sat in a circle created from child-sized tables and chairs pushed together. I took one of the small orange plastic chairs to the left of Kellie.

"Hey, Liz. Thanks for joining us!" Kellie handed me a booklet with "Overcomers Anonymous" printed on the yellow front cover. I had no idea what that meant but was delighted to be part of a group with Christian women. I placed the booklet down in front of me without peering inside and chatted with Kellie until the small group started.

Kellie began the meeting with an impromptu prayer. She then asked us to turn to the first page of the booklet and read the preamble aloud. After the first sentence, "Overcomers Outreach is a fellowship of women who have been affected directly or indirectly by the abuse of any mood-altering chemical or compulsive behavior," I realized this was no Bible study.

Panicking, I scanned the preamble's five organizing principles: fellowship in recovery, reconciliation with God and family, understanding addiction, strength derived from faith in Jesus Christ, and service to those suffering "as we once were." That sounded like Alcoholic Anonymous, albeit focused on Jesus instead of some nebulous higher power.

I didn't belong in any recovery group.

Kellie introduced herself just as she had at church. The women to her right began ticking off their introductions. All I heard was a mélange of addictions: cocaine, alcohol, oxycontin, hydrocodone, food. The women's names were lost in a fog.

I realized coming had been a big mistake, but I could hardly run out of the room. How could I explain my attendance at this meeting? I'd never taken any illegal drugs, abused pain medication, or even been drunk. Overeating was hardly an issue for me.

Compulsive behavior? Maybe. My mind searched for a common thread running through my most shameful behaviors as my turn approached like a speeding train.

"Hi, I'm Liz." I paused, waiting for my words ... something ... anything. "I've had multiple marriages and another inappropriate relationship. I chase after love that never satisfies."

Willing my breath to slow, I cooled my hot face with the sweat of my palms. When I finally looked up, no judging eyes looked my way.

The buzzing in my ear quieted as Kellie explained the group's rules: what was said in the group stayed in the group, no dialog or advice was allowed when someone shared, there was no pressure on anyone to share.

The woman began their litany of trials, failures, and small wins with heroic humility. A near relapse when a husband moved out. The purchase of a bottle of vodka. Another week without binging, and so it went. Somehow simply being in the room together held these women accountable and gave them strength. They had left their pride at the door when they walked in; I had brought mine in with me. I offered nothing beyond my introduction, grateful that I found any words at all.

I sat alone in my car in the church parking lot under cover of darkness, marveling at what I'd just witnessed. These women had escaped the prison of their shame by confessing their weakness before the Lord and to one another. They owned their behavior without excuses. I would be back next week.

THANKSGIVING DAY 2004

IT HAD BEEN JON'S idea to host the Thanksgiving feast at his place, blending our two families. His only condition was that he purchase all the food and that I orchestrate the meal preparation. Cooking for a large crowd was my specialty and something that Jon knew I enjoyed. Cooking for ten or fourteen made no difference to me.

We should have been fifteen, but Jon's ex-wife had their son for Thanksgiving that year, and negotiation wasn't an option with her. Jon would have his son on Christmas Day, and that was that.

I'd left for Jon's place to start the dressing and get the turkey in the oven early that morning, grateful for a double oven and an updated kitchen. I brought over the pies and rolls I'd made the day before amidst the unfolding chaos as my out-of-town children had filtered into the condo.

Hannah and Jonah had driven down together from UCLA. Abby had flown down from the University of Oregon at Eugene. Leah's family had flown in from Seattle. Since Jon had plenty of empty bedrooms, he invited Leah's family to stay with him.

"Dad and his wife always insist on staying at a nearby hotel. They like their privacy and don't want to be any trouble," Jon had said. I'd warned him that my three young grandsons generated a full decibel more noise than an only child.

But Jon, smiling, said, "My son equaled three. Trust me."

Finally, everyone arrived, including Jackson, who drove down from L.A. that morning, and Ned, who Jon had insisted we invite. Jonah, Noah, and Jon rearranged the living room furniture to increase the functional space of the dining room. They placed two rectangular folding tables, side by side, at one end of Jon's new dining table. Six folding chairs were added to the eight already flanking the dining table.

The girls helped me move the food to the table. I placed my homemade pumpkin and pecan pies on one of the four lazy-susan turntables running down the middle of the table as a reminder to save room for dessert. When everything was perfect, I announced that dinner was served.

Jon sat at the head of the elegant oak table in the dining room. To Jon's left sat his father, stepmother, Jackson, and Ned. I sat to Jon's right, flanked by Jonah, Noah, Hannah, and Abby. Leah's family occupied the end slots, with the three wiggly boys parked between their parents.

Fourteen smiling, hungry faces huddled around the elegant oak table and its makeshift extension. Buttery, spicy, yeasty aromas of turkey, cranberry sauce, sweet potato casserole, mashed potatoes and gravy, onion and celery stuffing, green beans, ambrosia fruit salad, and dinner rolls filled the house.

Jon invited everyone to hold hands as he said the blessing, ending with a "God bless the cook," planting a big smooch on my lips as I turned towards him. "Especially the cook," he said softly to me.

The thrill of Jon's small but public display of affection tingled through me. I avoided my birth father's eyes until several minutes had passed, relieved that he appeared fine and fully engaged, talking business with Jon's father. Somehow, we all fit together like different ingredients thrown into a big pot to make a delicious soup, each distinct but complementary. Hope and promise floated in the air.

"Mom, Jon is crazy about you," Leah whispered when we were cleaning up afterward. "How'd you get so lucky?"

I replied, "No luck involved. Just the grace of God." Leah smiled and hugged me.

"He seems like a great guy," she added.

Later that evening, my four youngest headed back to the condo with half the leftovers. Once Leah and her husband went upstairs to put the boys down for the night, I gathered up my things to head back home.

Jon's father followed me outside. "Thank you for everything you've done for Jon."

"Oh, it was no trouble," I said. "I love decorating."

"It's more than that, Liz. I've never seen my son so happy. Keep up the good work," he said with a wink. "We hope to see a lot more of you and your family. It was a lovely day."

THE MONDAY AFTER THANKSGIVING

I SAVORED MY LAST cup of coffee before getting ready for work. The sound of Noah's morning shower assured me that he was up and getting ready for school. I glanced at the clock on the stove, 6:37. Although grateful for a wonderful weekend with family, my brain and body were uncooperative and slow-moving. The condo had burst at its seams with wall-to-wall loud, energetic bodies. It was quiet again, just Noah and me. Maybe in a week, I'd catch up on my sleep.

The first flares of a brilliant red-orange sunrise announced the new day through sliding glass doors between the kitchen and the back patio. My Life Recovery Bible laid open on the kitchen table to the verse I'd highlighted in yellow months ago. I kept coming back to 1 Corinthians 4:5:

> *Then God will give to each one whatever praise is due. Therefore do not pronounce judgment before the time, before the Lord comes, who will bring to light the things now hidden in darkness and will disclose the purposes of the heart.*

I loved the part about not pronouncing judgment, but the part about bringing to light all things hidden in darkness stabbed at my conscience. While Jon and I had become a fixture in each other's lives, I still hadn't told him everything he needed to know about me.

How could Jon and I have a future together if I couldn't be honest with him about my past? But I feared that I'd never see him again if he knew the truth. Not that I blamed him, but I didn't want to lose him.

He knew how I felt about him. Although I tried to seal up my feelings inside, an "I love you" bubbled to the surface more times than I wished to count. Jon was more measured. He guarded his heart, one of the many reasons I admired and loved him.

After five months in Kellie's recovery group, the roots of addiction and patterns of relapse were now clear. Relapse was most likely when one was hungry, angry, lonely, tired, or hurting. The drug of choice blunted one's pain. The false comfort of addiction would remain forever a temptation, and recognizing the triggers for one's destructive behavior would be the work of a lifetime.

While sharing very little of my story, I never missed a meeting. At least I now recognized my need to control everything in my life but still lacked the trust in the Lord to do the actual work of recovery.

I ran from my pain, whether it was a bad marriage or disclosing the whole truth to Jon about Ned and me. I'd denied the common thread running through all my "love 'em and leave 'em " decisions. It was easier to blame everyone else than myself. But this current mess was my fault. Would I ever stop running? I was the problem.

I stumbled along like a blind, crippled woman towards the Truth and Light but was unwilling to do the work transformation required. Exactly what recovery would look like for me was unclear. But telling Jon the whole truth about Ned felt like the place to start.

"...bring to light the things now hidden in darkness," my eyes rolled over the words again. Didn't that Scripture imply that not only Jon but everyone else that had ever lived would know all my sins at the second judgment? So, in the end, Jon would know anyway.

"Lord, open a window of opportunity, give me the courage to come clean with Jon. No matter the cost," I whispered, closing my Bible.

It was time. I didn't want to hide anymore, and I was tired of running.

JON LOADED THE DINNER dishes into the dishwasher and placed the leftover spaghetti sauce, pasta, and salad into containers. He often ate dinner with Noah and me at the condo on the nights that his son was with his ex-wife.

"See you later, Mom," Noah hollered on his way out to a classmate's house to study for a physics test.

"Okay. Don't stay out too late."

That evening, I had Jon all to myself, without an audience. And like a high school girl, I dreamed of his arms around me, already tasting his lips on mine. The last thing I wanted was to spend the evening listening to Jon air his grievances about his ex-wife, now that we were alone, but that was how the evening was shaping up.

"The biggest regret of my life is marrying her," he said, shaking his head somberly. "One thing I have learned is never to marry anyone who doesn't bring you joy. Marriage is hard work even in the best of circumstances, you need to enjoy one another." Jon took me by the hand and led me into the living room, pulling me onto his lap. "That, and sexual compatibility," he added, winking at me. I'd heard all about those problems in their marriage, too.

Because we'd remained committed to no sex, I never had to worry that we would go too far. There was safety in our intimacy. I wrapped my arms around his neck and waded into his blue-grey eyes.

"I experience more joy with you, Liz, than I've ever felt with anyone in my life. I married the wrong person, but I feel like I've met her now. Where were you fifteen years ago?"

"Unavailable: married, raising five kids, and not walking with the Lord. You wouldn't have liked me."

"What is your greatest regret, Liz?"

If Jon truly loved me, he deserved to know all that I had been, even if it was the end of us. I became conscious of each breath; every heartbeat pounded in my ears. How could I have been so selfish over the last ten months? What future could there be with a man if I had to hide my past?

"Do you really want to know? You may not like what you hear."

"I want to know everything about you, Liz," he said, planting a soft kiss on my lips.

I scooted off his lap, turned towards him, and took a deep breath. His unsuspecting gaze ripped at my heart. There was no backing down. The window of opportunity was thrown wide open.

"I lived with Ned, as his lover, for a decade. I ended that relationship several weeks before I started the Singles Bible Study. That's why Ned sold the house and why I'm renting this place."

I had finally dropped the bomb. I listened for the explosion. Instead, shards of sterile silence encompassed us. Jon's eyes reflected confusion and disbelief.

"Are you telling me that you were having sex with your birth father for all those years?" The unmistakable sting of a betrayal as his eyes searched mine.

"Yes. I wish it weren't true. But you need to know before our relationship goes any further. So ... so you can break it off."

Time slowed to a surreal crawl. I was ready to be apprehended like a fugitive tired of running from the law.

"Is that what you want, Liz?"

"No, of course not. I love you, Jon. But I can't hide this from you any longer. I should have told you sooner, but I was afraid. I'm sorry."

Jon leaned forward, cradling his head in his hands, staring at the floor. "I'm glad that you finally told me."

Minutes of silence piled up between us, pushing him further away from me. Slowly he stood up.

"I'm sorry, but I need to go." He walked to the hall tree, removed his jacket, and walked out the front door.

Alone and terrified, I groped for some way to fill my emptiness. I reached out for my drug of choice: Ned.

He didn't pick up, so I left him a voicemail. "Jon knows about us. I told him tonight. I don't want to talk about it. I just thought you would want to know." I turned off my cell phone.

Remorse, shame, embarrassment, disgust wrapped their greedy tentacles around me, pulling me towards the darkness of self-hatred. I wept until there were no tears left. "God have mercy on me," I cried.

But God had me where he wanted me. It was just the two of us now. And I was not in control. He was.

RESTFUL SLEEP ELUDED ME through the long, torturous night. The few times I drifted off, I awakened with a start, my heart beating wildly. The hurt I'd inflicted on Jon, the pain in his eyes, played cruelly on my mind.

When the fear of what lay ahead threatened to crush me, I replayed my dream of eleven months ago. I entered the loving gaze of Jesus and cloaked myself in the peace I'd felt when our eyes had met. I imagined that he cradled not a younger version of myself in his arms but as I was now.

In the morning, I forced myself to eat half a piece of toast and drink a cup of coffee. I opened my Bible, searching for the verse in Isaiah that called my name. There it was, chapter 42, verse 16:

I will lead the blind by ways they have not known, along unfamiliar paths I will guide them;
I will turn the darkness into light before them and make the rough places smooth.
These are the things I will do, I will not forsake them.

The honeymoon phase of my relationship with Jesus was over. I'd received the gift of faith in a dream, but trust in God's providence was an entirely different thing. I wanted the highway of my future lit up for miles down the road, but instead, I could barely see my next step. Trust would be my shield between hope in a future and the despair of my shame.

After my shower, I put on my work clothes, pretending this could be just another day. It didn't work. Grieving the loss of Jon, I couldn't bear to be around my work colleagues. I was a basket case, an empty zombie one minute and weeping the next. Finally, I sent an email to my boss stating that I'd work from home in the morning and take the afternoon off.

I didn't expect to hear from Jon again. Ever. Although my foolish heart wanted everything as it had been. Trying to avoid thoughts of Jon, I booted up my work computer. Work had always been my lifeline. I'd survived more than one crisis by losing myself within its demands. This morning I needed it to transport me far from my heartache and problems.

About noon, there was a knock at the front door. I opened the door to find a barely recognizable, disheveled-looking Jon. His entire posture was stooped as if he carried the world's weight on his shoulders. His eyes were bloodshot and swollen, and his hair was matted.

"Jon, are you okay? You look horrible." I stepped outside onto the porch where he stood.

"My boss said that, too. I'm not feeling so hot. I couldn't work." Jon's voice sounded flat.

"How'd you know I was home?"

"I didn't. I drove by on my way home from work and saw your car."

"Do you want to come in?"

"Please."

"Why don't you go upstairs and lie down in my room." I hadn't expected to see him.

He walked up the stairs to my bedroom like an old man. I went back to my desk, logged out of the database, and joined him upstairs.

Jon lay in the middle of my bed, still wearing his jacket and shoes and arms stiffly at his side. Before last night, I would have lain down next to him, taken off his glasses, and looked into his eyes. Whether we spoke would have mattered little, our connection had been so strong. But now, everything was different.

I curled up next to him, placing my arm over his chest and my face next to his tear-stained cheeks. He could push me away if he wanted to, but he didn't. Instead, he rolled towards me and held me in a clutching, desperate way like a lost child. Even in his distressed state, I never wanted him to let go of me.

"I had to tell you. I was worried you might want to marry me, and you had to know what you'd be getting."

"You were right to tell me. But, Liz, we should never have been dating at all. I thought you were more emotionally healthy than you are."

At his words, the well of my tears spilled over, mingling with his. We lay there in silence as I puzzled over his words, "emotionally healthy."

"What do I need to do to get emotionally healthy?"

"At a minimum, you need to get into therapy as soon as possible. You shouldn't be seeing or dating anyone, including me."

He looked at me vacantly, emptied of the intimacy that had once characterized our relationship.

"What kind of therapy?" *Yes, I was a big fat sinner, but did that mean I was crazy, too?*

"Christian counseling. And hopefully, someone who has expertise with sexual sin and incest, Liz."

When Jon said "incest," my stomach churned and spasmed. But what other way was there to think about the years that Ned and I had lived as secret lovers? I hadn't been a child that my father had seduced. I'd been a willing participant, a grown woman and mother of five, wanting to be close to him in every possible way, coveting his attention and craving his physical affection.

While intellectually, I always understood that Ned was my father, some part of my brain had refused to acknowledge that truth and restrain my actions. Yet what we had done, given our biological relationship, was the source of my most profound shame.

"I'd recommend starting with the Dayton Christian Counseling Group in Mission Valley. I used them for marriage counseling with my ex-wife. They should be able to recommend someone for you."

"Okay."

"Liz, we can't see each other anymore. Not for a while. Maybe not ever. I loved you, and you lied to me. I believed that you hadn't been with anyone since you left your third husband. You misrepresented yourself. I invested ten months in a relationship with you. How could I have been so wrong?"

What could I say? Jon's words were soft, gentle even, compared to what I deserved and my internal dialogue.

"I'll see myself out," he said, leaving me alone with my grief and shame.

Chapter 23

Appointment

AFTER JON LEFT, I found Dalton Christian Counseling Center online and jotted down their phone number and address. I memorized the image of their office building in Mission Valley, a part of San Diego unfamiliar to me. I scrolled past the details of their counseling philosophy, searching for the names and faces of the therapists who worked there. But that information wasn't posted.

Therapy sounded scary, but what other safe options did I have? I wasn't about to pick up the phone and pour out my sins to anybody else. I was too ashamed. After a half-hour of pacing and picking at my lunch, I dialed the counseling center.

"This is Dalton Christian Counseling Center. Please leave a message at the sound of the tone with your name, phone number, and how we may help you. Someone will call you back as soon as possible." Beep.

"My name is Elizabeth Schmidt. I need to make an appointment with a female therapist who has experience with incest." I left my phone number and hung up.

That was the easy part. When the receptionist listened to the message, she'd figure something happened to me when I was a kid and that I was finally trying to sort through the mess. If only my problem were so straightforward.

"Incest" didn't feel like the correct word, but I didn't know what else to call ... it. In my mind, incest implied an innocent victim and an evil perpetrator. Neither applied in my case. Yet my relationship with Ned satisfied the functional definition of incest, and the burden of my shame and intricate web of deceit testified to its wrongness.

I walked about the condo like a zombie, reliving the horrors of the last twenty hours. By mid-afternoon, I had to get outside and focus on something else, or I'd go mad. I drove to the beach, my go-to place for solace and sanity. I pulled the hood of my sweatshirt over my head, hiding within its warmth, cocooning myself away from ... What? The mess of me.

From a green park bench perched on the grassy knoll, I looked out over the train tracks and onto the beach. The waves sparkled like diamonds, rhythmically kneading the caramel-colored sand. The Coaster train chugged its way down the tracks running parallel to the shoreline, briefly interrupting the soothing view of the breakers. The only therapy I knew or trusted was the beating of the waves.

My phone buzzed. Five minutes later, I had an appointment with a therapist named Angie Bell. The earliest available time slot was one week from today. I'd have to leave work early to make a four o'clock appointment, but so be it.

A pleasant female voice said, "Do you need the address?"

"No, I got it off the website."

"Great. When you arrive, take the elevator up to the second floor. We're in suite 210. When you enter the waiting room, knock on the inside door a couple of times soundly and then have a seat. Angie will come out to get you when she is ready to see you."

"Okay. Thank you."

At least that much was settled. Meeting with this Angie Bell couldn't be any worse than telling Jon, could it? But my mind and body buckled with fear as I considered the upcoming meeting. Could I bear Angie Bell's condemnation when added to the weight of my own?

I removed my composition notebook and pen from my leather shoulder bag with jittery hands. The empty, white-lined pages promised safety and release. Writing whatever came to mind, I poured out my heart to the only One who would never abandon me. My thoughts were too scattered to be called a fearless moral inventory, but my journal entries that day formed a crude start. I couldn't fall apart; I had responsibilities. I had to keep going.

A list of my regrets and moral failures began to wind its way down the page: conversations where I'd misled others about my relationship with Ned, half-truths where I'd left out relevant detail. All lying if I was honest with myself. Each item reflected another facet of the same defect in my character, and each would require that I apologize, ask for forgiveness, and make amends. But how would I make amends? Was it even possible?

I wrote "May 2004—Meeting with Pastor Matt," pressing my eyes closed, unable to blot out the now painful memory as the cold hand of remorse clawed at my soul...

Jon had insisted that we meet with Pastor Matt before our relationship had progressed any further. I liked Matt a whole lot but didn't understand why Jon needed his approval for us to continue seeing one another. Jon was 41, and I was 49, for pity's sake.

But Jon didn't want a rebound relationship, and the Bible forbade divorce. Jon had a stringent dating philosophy: never date anyone unless you consider them marriageable material. He wanted to know if Matt had any reservations about our being in a dating relationship open to the possibility of marriage.

Jon possessed a level of accountability and openness that was foreign to me. The good news was that marriage was on Jon's radar, and the bad news was that Matt seemingly had the power to quash my relationship with Jon.

"You don't have to be so nervous, Liz," Jon said as he pulled into the Community Fellowship parking lot.

"Easy for you to say. You haven't been married and divorced three times." But that wasn't really what worried me. The façade of half-truths and outright lies shrouding my past with Ned required continual care and feeding. I feared what Matt might ask me and dreaded another lie.

"It's as much about me as you. Try to relax." Jon opened the car door for me as I got out.

After exchanging pleasantries, Jon explained to Matt why he'd requested a meeting and that we'd been seeing one another since Valentine's Day. Matt knew Jon well, but not me.

"Although raised Catholic, I never truly believed nor had a personal relationship with Christ until recently. That's what brought me to Community Fellowship Church," I had said when Matt asked me about my walk with Christ.

He had asked about my personal life. Cringing inside, I'd relayed my marital history and that I had moved in with my birth father after leaving my third husband.

"Besides Jon, have you dated anyone else after leaving your third husband?"

"No, I haven't." I weaseled my way around the lie by rationalization. Of course, I didn't date anyone else; I'd been in love with Ned. But like Jon, the perversity of my relationship with Ned failed to cross Matt's mind. By then, my palms had been sweating.

Matt said something about being a new creation in Christ, but the buzzing in my ears was louder than his words.

"Well, I don't see any issues for you two. Liz hasn't been in a relationship for a long time. And, Jon, I don't get the sense that this is a band-aid relationship for you to get over the losses in your first marriage. Just take it slow and keep things pure." And so, Matt had pronounced his blessing on the bud of our blooming romance.

I SPENT SATURDAY MORNING at my office in the Torrey Pines Science Park, something I'd not done since Jon and I had been seeing each other. Staring into my computer and puzzling over data patterns temporarily crowded out thoughts of Jon and evaporated my shame.

Midday, I shut down my work computer and headed to my car to begin my practice drive to Dalton Counseling Center. Directionally challenged, I compensated by driving unfamiliar routes beforehand to minimize the chance of my getting lost or arriving late.

Ignoring the honks of drivers signaling their displeasure at my slow speed, I followed my printed MapQuest directions. Some thirty minutes later, I arrived outside a big office building matching the picture I'd seen on Dalton Counseling Center's website. The parking lot was empty. Of course, today was Saturday. Nobody worked on a gorgeous Saturday besides me when they could be outdoors.

I folded up the directions and placed them in the glove compartment. Monday afternoon, I would need them again.

TOO NERVOUS TO CONCENTRATE, I packed up my things and left my cubicle an hour before my counseling appointment. Traffic would be heavier on a Monday than on Saturday, but I'd wait in my car out in the parking lot if I arrived early.

"One step at a time. You can do this, Liz." I said to myself, buckling my seat belt with a trembling hand. I popped my *Kristy Starling* CD into my car's player, singing along with her and praying for courage and honesty. When the track "Broken" finished playing, I had to pull over. The freeway and the zooming cars dissolved into a wet blur as my resolve melted into a bottomless pool of grief. Only God could pick up my pieces and put me back together as the song's lyrics suggested.

I gripped the steering wheel and leaned my forehead into the leather-covered circle. My tears merged with the flawless soprano voice, lifted in prayer to the Lord. Each succeeding song interceded for me, supplying the words from deep within the groanings of my broken heart.

When "You Love Me Like That" began playing, I wiped my face and pulled back on the road. The broken pieces of my life coalesced into a picture bigger than myself. Everything I'd been running toward, even my sins, purified through grace, had been a circle leading back to Him.

I pulled into the parking lot with a splotchy face and renewed hope with ten minutes to spare. But something was wrong. Why was the parking lot empty, mid-afternoon on a workday? I drove up to the front door and saw the "For Sale" sign. The building was vacant. How did I miss this on my test run?

Shivering with alarm, I dialed the Counseling Center. I needed a person but got a recording. I wailed my message, "This is Elizabeth Schmidt. I have an appointment with Angie Bell at four today. It's three-fifty now, and I'm at the address I got off your website, but it's an empty building. I need someone to tell me how to get to your office." I left my phone number with a long sob. There was nothing I could do but wait. At ten past four, my phone rang.

"This is Dr. Angie Bell. Is this Elizabeth?"

"Yes. Thank God, it's you!" Rattled to my core, I croaked, "How do I get to your office? The address on your website is wrong."

"I know exactly where you are. You're no more than ten minutes away. Don't panic. I can talk with you on the phone as you drive to my office. I'm so sorry that the website hasn't been updated." The woman on the phone steadied me with her reassuring, calm voice.

"I am so bad with directions. You have no idea," I moaned.

"That's okay. I'm patient and good at giving directions. I don't have anyone after you; I can stay over. We will meet as planned whenever you get here. Now take a deep breath and let me know when you're ready to get back on the road."

Twelve minutes later, I was in the elevator heading up to the second floor. After turning down the wrong hallway, I made my way to Dalton's Christian Counseling Center. No receptionist sat in the waiting room. There were only empty chairs, end tables, lamps, some plants here and there, and several sedate pictures hanging on the light green walls. I knocked at the door, waiting there instead of sitting. Moments later, a tall woman with gentle brown eyes and light auburn hair, falling to her chin in loose beachy waves, opened the door.

"Elizabeth?"

"Dr. Bell?"

We both shook our heads affirmative, and she smiled warmly.

"I desperately need to use your lavatory after my little anxiety attack. Can you point me to the restroom?"

"Of course. It's down the hall to your left, but you'll need a key. Go ahead and put your things in my office. I'll get the key for you."

I splashed cold water on the itchy hives that had cropped up on my neck and soon returned to Dr. Bell's office. Her office resembled an inviting parlor. I sat on a plum upholstered couch with tapestry throw pillows, and Dr. Bell sat across from me in a burgundy wingback chair. A coffee table with a basket of silk flowers separated us.

"You're here now. Just relax as best you can."

"Thank you so much for getting me here."

Dr. Bell wore an ankle-length, crinkled skirt and a loose, hip-length green sweater belted at her waist. Dangly earrings and a matching necklace with multiple strings of multi-colored beads completed her Bohemian look. A copper-like medallion in the shape of a stylized cross hung from her necklace.

"Do you feel up to going ahead with our session today, Elizabeth?"

"I think so. Please call me Liz."

"Let's start with a short prayer. Okay?" I nodded, and she began. "Father God, we ask you to send the wisdom and healing of your Holy Spirit into our session today. Give us the mind of Christ to respond to your will. We ask this in the Precious Blood of your Son, Jesus."

"Amen," I said.

"Can we start with a tiny bit of introduction?"

"Sure." I felt an itchy welt crop up on the side of my face.

"Okay, I'll go first. I have a doctorate in clinical psychology and have been practicing for about eight years. My research was on bonding and attachment disorders and their impacts on the brain's neurochemistry. I have worked with many clients of sexual trauma and incest. I'm married and have two teenagers, a son and a daughter."

Dr. Bell looked at me expectantly, waiting for my words. My stomach twisted and pulled as I began.

"I'm an applied mathematician and work for a biotech company. I have five kids, ranging in age from twenty-nine to seventeen, from three different marriages. I'm here because my ex-boyfriend told me I needed to get into therapy when I told him that ..." I struggled to continue.

Finally, I cracked open like a raw egg thrown to the floor of Dr. Bell's office. "... that I lived with my birth father for ten years and started having sex with him about six months after I found him ..."

The sound of my wailing filled the room and echoed off the walls, stealing my strength and pulling my body downward. I fell to my knees, rocking back and forth, crouched between the couch and coffee table. My forehead lay upon the floor, and my arms wrapped tightly around my head as the keening sound of remorse escaped my lungs, floating past the boundaries of time.

Arms folded around me, rocking with me. "We can deal with this, Liz. Let the feelings out."

"I deserve to die. I'm the worst person in the world."

Dr. Bell gathered me into her arms, my shame extruding like an infected pustule. She pushed the coffee table away and gently propped me up next to the couch into a sitting position. Kneeling in front of me, she gently lifted my chin. But I couldn't look at her.

"Liz, I'm with you. You're not alone. This kind of thing happens. Look at me, Liz. I need you to hear me."

Finally, I met her gaze.

"You are not the only person in the world that this has happened to. Less than two weeks ago, I read the results of a research study reporting on the prevalence of sexual relations between birth parents and adult children separated by adoption and first reunited as adults. Sex happens as a way to form intimacy, usually after intense feelings of falling in love." Dr. Bell handed me the box of tissue.

"I'm not the only one?" I hiccupped, catching my breathing and wiping my snotty face with tissues.

"No, you're not. I'll make you a copy of the article; it might help you process this." As I calmed down, she remained on the floor, sitting before me, talking softly and confidently.

"Sex is something we humans do to feel connected to others. The attachments aren't always healthy or what God wants for us, but it is a way we try to establish intimate connections. I've had clients who grew up in orphanages tell me that the kids had sex with one another to feel close.

"Everyone is broken in some way or another. You can work through this, Liz, and I can help you. It will be hard work, but God has brought you this far. He will not abandon you."

By the end of that first session, Dr. Bell had compassionately reached through my pain, accompanying me without judging me. She was no longer Dr. Bell. She was Angie and my lifeline.

In two days, I would see her again. She gave me her cell number to call if I felt out of control.

KELLIE'S RECOVERY GROUP WAS due to start less than an hour after I arrived home from my second counseling session with Angie. Although not as traumatic as the first session, the second had been taxing and left me feeling like I'd been in a car wreck. Getting "emotionally healthy," as Jon had called it, felt like running a marathon after being a life-long couch potato.

With no energy to fix dinner for Noah and me, I ordered a large Hawaiian pizza and Caesar salad to be delivered to the condo. Bushed or not, I couldn't afford to miss the camaraderie and accountability of the recovery group. Not this week.

The food arrived as I was on my way out. "Hey, Noah," I hollered, waiting at the base of the staircase, looking up at his closed bedroom door.

"Yeah?" he replied, poking his head out the door.

"Pizza's here. I'm heading to church."

"Alright! Heading down."

"See you in an hour and a half, max. Put the leftovers in the fridge, okay?"

"Sure thing. Later, Mom."

"Thanks. Bye."

I arrived with five minutes to spare, wishing I'd grabbed a second piece of pizza. The church parking lot was empty, except for Kellie's car and mine. The number of women attending varied from week to week, but the number had never increased beyond that first night's meeting when I had first joined the group.

Kellie and I were the regulars. A couple of times, we were the only two that had shown up. On those evenings, which I relished, especially since Kellie no longer attended the Singles Bible Study, we had an informal Overcomer's Outreach meeting. She knew about Jon, and I knew about her boyfriend in Orange County.

When I entered the third-grade classroom, Kellie appeared to be studying the artwork taped on the walls. She heard me come in and turned toward me with her dimpled smile.

"Hey, Liz. It looks like it may be just the two of us tonight."

"Okay by me. It's been a long week," I said.

Kellie hadn't bothered to rearrange student tables and chairs into the typical meeting configuration, so we sat on a small platform in the back corner of the classroom, with our feet resting on the two stairs leading up. I leaned back, bracing myself with my extended arms, resting on the palms of my hands.

After an impromptu prayer, Kellie turned to the back of her Recovery Bible. "Are you okay if we simplify the format and just read a devotional based on one of the twelve steps tonight?"

"That's perfect. Which step?" I turned to the very back of my Recovery Bible.

Kellie scanned the two pages listing the twelve steps. Each step had seven suggested reflections.

"How about 'Step Five: We admitted to God, to ourselves, and to another human being the exact nature of our wrongs.' Want to pick which reflection?"

I scanned the choices and kept returning to the same one. "How about 'Freedom through Confession'?"

"Ah, my exact choice." Kellie gathered her hair into a ponytail with the elastic she pulled from her wrist and began reading.

The truth contained in the four short paragraphs pierced my soul like a hot knife cutting through butter. There would be no true freedom until I owned and admitted all my past sins. I was accountable for every single one of them. I had spent a lifetime running from God's mercy and forgiveness by trying to silence the built-in alarm system he'd given me: my conscience. But the signposts of right and wrong had always been there, regardless of how I'd tried to rationalize my choices.

As Kellie read the last five words of the reflection, "one step closer to recovery," her voice faltered. Between her sobs, she unloaded her burden: she and her boyfriend had been sleeping together. Spending weekends together at his place in Long Beach had created the perfect environment for temptation and subsequent fall. She felt convicted but powerless to change things. Her boyfriend, though Christian, did not share her guilt.

Kellie's tears loosened a flood of my own as I entered her pain. Her honesty and my last four days of hell triggered my confession to her. I explained that Jon and I were no longer an item and the sordid reason why.

Kellie moved next to me, placing her hand on my back, saying nothing. But her clenched jaw, furrowed brows, and intense gaze spoke volumes.

"I can't believe your dad did that to you."

"Kellie, I'm every bit as guilty as my birth father. The problem is that Ned never seemed like my dad, and I never seemed like his daughter." I walked over to the teacher's desk, pulling a handful of tissue from the dispenser to clean myself up.

"I disagree. He is your father; you are his daughter, whether you were eight or thirty-eight."

"Do you hate me, Kellie?"

"No, Liz. I am proud of you for breaking it off and telling me. I will pray for you, and I'll try to pray for your dad. Which, I have to tell you, will not be easy. I'm so angry with him."

TWO WEEKS REMAINED BEFORE Christmas, but there was little joy in my world. A wave of sadness washed over me as I eyed the box on the chair next to my dresser. I needed to return the no-longer-needed Christmas gift I'd bought for Jon. The V-neck cashmere sweater matched the smoky blue of Jon's eyes. What fun Leah, Hannah, Abby, and I had on that shopping expedition the Friday after Thanksgiving. A whole lifetime ago.

I performed my final pre-church self-check in the gilded mirror hanging over my dresser. Tucking my hair behind my ears, I inserted the pink tourmaline earrings that Aunt Maura had sent me ten years ago, only months before her breast cancer roared back, claiming her life.

When I had phoned to thank her for the earrings, she had cautioned me about moving in with Ned. Liddy had told her of my plans. Aunt Maura's words now rippled through my mind, "You're on uncharted waters, Liz. Be careful; go slowly. Don't do anything you'll regret." If only I'd listened to her. But nobody could ever tell me anything that I didn't want to hear. I was my own worst enemy.

Maura was gone, but Liddy was not. Driving to the 11 a.m. Sunday service, I thought about how Liddy had stood patiently in line behind Ned and then Jon for crumbs of my attention. I owed my birth mother a giant-sized apology for lying, for everything.

When I pulled into Community Fellowship Church's parking lot, I saw Jon's car and parked my car away from his. Tomorrow would mark the two-week anniversary of our split.

Upon entering the sanctuary, I chose a seat on the opposite side and further back than where Jon sat with his son. My eyes darted back to Jon throughout the service. He looked so much thinner. How could anyone drop that much weight so quickly?

As the praise band finished their last song, I fished the car keys out of my purse. I still had the key to Jon's house on my key chain, and he still had a key to my condo. Loose ends of our broken relationship that we had yet to tidy up.

I exited the sanctuary quickly to avoid Jon. Several friends from the Singles Bible Study stood off to the side, just outside the double doors, chatting and laughing. My plan to go directly to my car was interrupted when someone from the group waved me over.

They were going out to lunch and asked if I wanted to join them. Though lonely, I didn't want to be around anyone else. My smiles felt phony, and my laughter feigned. I politely passed and walked towards my car.

"Liz, hold up a minute." Jon's voice stopped me in my tracks. "Do you have five minutes? I'd like to talk to you about something."

"Sure ... but out here in the parking lot isn't very private." Several cars remained parked near my vehicle, and many people continued to mill about.

"Agreed. Let's talk in your car. I need to open up the car for my son, but I'll be right back." Jon's son leaned up against the passenger side of his car, with the black hood of his sweatshirt hiding all but the shock of long bleached-blond bangs that forever hung in his eyes.

I unlocked the car, cracked the windows, and waited for Jon while inhaling and exhaling slowly. Remembering his house key, I removed it from my key chain, placing it in the cup holder next to me.

Jon sat across from me in my car a minute later, his cinnamon scent a familiar yet painful reminder of what was no longer. He pushed the passenger side bucket seat back before turning to me. Scouring his face for hints of old warmth, I saw only dark circles beneath his eyes and a new crop of fine lines surrounding them.

"You doing okay, Liz?"

"Trying."

"Did you find a therapist?"

"I did. I love her, but I hate going." I forced a smile.

"It's hard work, not fun. I know."

"Jon, you've lost so much weight. What's going on?"

"I'm having trouble eating and can't keep much down."

"Like when you were in high school?"

"The very same. If it doesn't ease up soon, I'll get professional help."

"It's my fault. You'd have been better off if you never met me." I looked away as I spoke.

"That is not true, Liz. My eating problem is my brain and body's response to stress and anxiety. That's not your fault. But my stomach issues aren't what I wanted to talk with you about."

He paused until I looked back into his face. Once our eyes met, he continued in a gentle but firm voice. "You need to tell Pastor Matt that you lied to him back in May when we met with him. He asked you if you had dated anyone when you lived with Ned, and you said you hadn't. Apologizing, asking for forgiveness, and making amends are important steps in recovery. Your therapist can help you decide when you're ready to meet with Matt. I hope you stay in Kellie's recovery group."

My eyes stung. I fought to maintain control.

"That's all I wanted to say, Liz. I pray for you every day." He reached over and squeezed my hand gently.

"Thank you, Jon, for ... checking in." I swallowed the golf ball-sized lump of misery lodged in my throat. "I'm so sorry for everything."

He pulled on the car door, readying to leave.

"Wait, Jon, ... before you go. I need the key to my condo back. I don't want to bother you for it later if and when I find another place." Jon had been the primary reason I'd rented instead of buying a small place when Ned had sold our house in Carmel Valley. The reality of my once-imagined future with Jon had dissolved in the acid of my secrets.

He pulled his key chain out of his jacket pocket and removed the key to my condo, handing it to me. "Thanks," I said, taking it. "Here's yours." I picked up his house key from the cup holder and held it out to him.

He held the palm of his hand towards me. "Please keep my house key for a little while longer. That is if you don't mind."

"All right." I watched him walk back to his car. My fingers closed around the cool brass of his house key, a shred of hope in my hand.

First Confessions

CHRISTMAS EVE SPREAD BEFORE me like cold, bitter sap as I unlocked the front door. Walking into the kitchen, I dropped my purse on the table and started brewing a pot of coffee. Breakfast could wait indefinitely; I had little appetite these last few weeks. But coffee, I needed. My fragmented sleeping had only worsened.

The early morning traffic had been light, both going and returning home from the San Diego Airport. Hannah and Noah were now airborne, flying to the Tri-Cities airport to be greeted by two different dads. I imagined Joe and Leo standing near one another at the arrival gate, failing to acknowledge each other while keenly aware of the other's presence.

Hannah had arrived on Monday to spend the first part of her college break with me before flying north. Her effervescent personality was a welcome vacation from my inward focus. Noah's high school had only let out for Christmas vacation after classes yesterday afternoon.

Last evening Ned had taken the kids out for a fancy Italian dinner at Il Fornio in downtown Del Mar. My invitation was delivered secondhand through Hannah, "Ned really wants you to come, Mom," she had said, pleading his case.

"Another time," I'd said. "I can see Ned any time. You two go on without me," I'd said, sending Ned's Christmas present along with the kids.

The last time I'd seen my birth father was Thanksgiving dinner at Jon's house. Based on Hannah and Noah's chatter in the car this morning, Ned seemed to be doing well and planned to spend Christmas Day in Orange County with his brother, Henri. I was grateful that he wouldn't be alone.

My children would be with their fathers over Christmas, my annual concession for having them together on Thanksgiving since they were small. This year their absence was more difficult. I'd never been entirely alone before over the Christmas holidays. In the past, at least I'd had Ned.

Noah and Abby would spend Christmas on the ski slopes in Sun Valley with Joe. Hannah, Jonah, and Leah's clan would be at the Trembley family cabin at the eastern base of the Cascades, surrounded by Leo, his newest wife, their many aunts and uncles, and an army of first cousins. Until I'd found Liddy and Ned, I'd had no way to compete with Leo's tight, extended family.

Christmas Eve through New Year's Day promised to be a long nine days. Hanging out at the office, pretending I had important work to finish, wasn't even an option. All employees were required to take the interleaving Monday through Friday as vacation unless an ongoing experiment required hands-on supervision. I could hardly make that case for myself. As a data geek, my "experiments" didn't involve monitoring cell growth or the care and feeding of mice.

All my usual evening activities: twice-weekly sessions with Angie Bell, weekly meetings with Kellie's recovery group, and the Singles Bible Study group, had been canceled until after the new year. The singles group had planned a New Year's Eve gathering, but I couldn't see myself attending without Jon. His absence from my life throbbed like a toothache.

Draining my third cup of coffee, I reviewed today's "pressing" activities: walking outdoors, picking up the fruit tart I'd ordered at Champagne before they closed, calling my sister Jeannie, and attending candlelight service at Community Fellowship. The tart was my contribution to Liddy's Christmas brunch, the extent of tomorrow's activities.

Liddy had invited both Jon and me to her Christmas Day brunch. "Jon won't be coming with me," I had said. "He's taking his son snowboarding at Big Bear ski resort on Christmas day." Those holiday plans had been long in the making. So, I wasn't exactly lying, just failing to supply relevant details. My modus operandi.

The appointment I'd made to meet with Pastor Matt next week unsettled me. I wanted it over and looked forward to scratching his name off the list of all the people that deserved an apology.

After swallowing my last bit of coffee, I moved to the living room and removed my journal from my desk drawer, turning to the list of names. I needed to come clean with seventeen people. Except for Matt, everyone belonged to my family, at least at one time by adoption or blood or a past marriage. I scanned my list, arranged by category of relationship to me:

Pastor Matt,
Liddy;
Leah, Jonah, Hannah, Abby, Noah;
Joe, Leo;
Jeannie, Lily, Joni, Terri, Sandi, Vicki;
Aunt Alice;
Uncle Henri.

Some of those names required that Ned first talk with his family: his brother, Henri; his daughters, Joni, Sandi, and Terri; and stepdaughter, Vicki. As much as I wanted to write the last chapter and close the book on my wrongful coupling with my birth father, I had to be patient with him. Ned was in a very different place than I was. Would it ever be possible to have a relationship with him, somehow cleansed from our past?

I believed the Lord had forgiven me, and I continued to work on forgiving myself with Angie Bell's help. But breaking the shackles of shame and permanently silencing the internal taunting voices required more: coming clean, asking for forgiveness, and trying to make amends, if possible.

LOCKING UP THE CONDO, I drove the short distance to the trail that Jon and I had walked for many months at the end of our workdays. Hiking along the paths, he had answered many of my theological questions. Occasionally Jon had said, "I can't answer that question, Liz," with a shrug of his shoulders. He'd been so comfortable owning the limits of his knowledge, his humility and honesty bolstering my trust in his words and amplifying my love for him.

I parked my car on a neighborhood side street a short distance from the trail's entrance, away from the main traffic arteries. The sun had burned off the remnants of the marine layer. I grabbed my sunglasses and visor and tied a light jacket around my waist. Leaving behind the stucco homes and their orange tiled roofs bordering the neighborhood streets, I turned onto busy

Carmel Country Road.

As I crossed the bridge over SR 56, streams of cars rushed beneath me like rows of carpenter ants on a food pilgrimage squeezed between tall concrete walls. I turned into the dirt trail to my right. Once used as the rural roadway to one-time farms and dairies, the path was barely wide enough for a single car. Native plants had reclaimed the road over time.

The trail wound through scrub brush, silencing the sounds of civilization. I headed toward the trailhead a mile and a half ahead. A man and a friendly Irish Setter passed me by, walking in the opposite direction. The smell of the vegetation filled my senses, familiar herbaceous scents that I recognized but couldn't name. A young couple on mountain bikes rode past as I stepped out of their way. I passed the old, dilapidated house about a half-mile in. Jon and I had often wondered about its story.

A runner off in the distance closed the distance between us, coming into focus. The red and gray athletic wear and the body movements sent a rush of adrenaline through me.

It was Jon.

He slowed down his pace as he neared me, stopping several yards in front of me. He leaned over, hands on his knees, trying to catch his breath.

"I didn't expect to see you out here on Christmas Eve morning. How are you?" Jon said, still breathing hard.

"I'm getting along. How about you?"

"I'm doing okay."

Okay? Jon still looked like he could shimmy through a knothole, skinny as a rail.

"Are you still going to Big Bear on Christmas with your son?"

"Yeah, he's pretty jazzed about it. Do you have any plans?"

"I'll spend tomorrow with Liddy and Andy. My half-sister, Lily, and her boyfriend will be there. The kids are all with their dads, as usual."

"Well, I'm glad you aren't alone."

I hadn't expected to see Jon, but I refused to waste the opportunity. "Jon, I know there is nothing I can say to change our past. But I want to apologize for hiding my relationship with my birth father. It was so wrong; I was a coward and selfish. Can you ever forgive me?"

"I have forgiven you already. I get that it was hard for you to tell me, and

I am grateful that you finally did. But had you told me early on, I could have helped you get into therapy, and we'd be in a different, more appropriate, and healthier place than we are now."

He was so right; he always was. The sting of tears burned my eyes, but I forced them back.

"I am grieving the loss of our friendship, Liz, and quite frankly, the death of an imminent future that I had imagined for us. You aren't ready for a relationship with me or anyone else. When I'm with you, like now, I feel anxious. Yet when we're apart, I feel depressed. I recognize that I need help, so I started seeing a therapist and began on some medication last week. It's a step in the right direction anyway."

"Is there any way that I can make it up to you, Jon?"

"Give me time and space. Keep seeing your therapist, Liz, and work to understand why this happened. Ask your therapist to decide how to talk to your kids about you and their grandfather. I'd encourage you to steer clear of Ned, other than encouraging him to get into Christian counseling. And, please, apologize to Pastor Matt. The sooner, the better."

"I promise to do all those things, and I have an appointment with Matt next week."

Jon nodded his head in affirmation. "Take care, Liz. God can use all of this to get us both to a better place, a place of healing."

FOR ONCE, REACHING OUT to Jeannie didn't feel like a sisterly duty. We'd had plenty of phone contact, usually when she needed money. But the last six months had been blessedly quiet, apparently no financial crises. We rarely saw each other face-to-face and then only for relatively short periods. But this afternoon, as I dialed her number, I wanted, no needed, something from her.

"Merry Christmas Eve, Jeannie."

"Hey, Merry Christmas to you, Sis."

"Am I interrupting any big plans?"

"Nope. You're interrupting my date with the TV."

Inquiring after each other's children, I abruptly changed the subject. "I don't want to ruin your Christmas, but I need to get something off my chest, something that I've hidden from you and a whole lot of other people. For years."

"Lizzie, don't you know you can tell me anything?"

"I want to believe that."

One by one, I unraveled the threads of the tattered cloth I'd hidden under for a dozen years, covering the illicit relationship with my birth father. My sister learned of the dream that had changed my life, how things had ended with Ned, and how things ended with Jon when he learned the truth.

"I've been living a lie, Jeannie. The sister you thought you knew never existed. She's a total fraud."

"Don't say that, Lizzie. You are the same sister I've always loved and looked up to, and I still do no matter what you've done. There's plenty of stuff you don't know about me." I heard my sister's voice crack with emotion.

"Now, I need to tell you something, Lizzie. Your feelings toward Ned, I felt the exact same way towards my half-brother Mark in the early months after finding my birth mother. We manufactured reasons to be together, and the only reason we didn't have sex was that we were both married. During the times that we were alone, we were very physical. The attraction and intimacy I felt were overpowering. If we'd both been single, let me assure you, things would have progressed."

"Oh, Jeannie ... What's the matter with us?"

"I don't know. But whatever bit you, bit me, too. I felt ashamed just like you did. But I got more to tell you, Sis. You know all the money you've given me over the years, not one dime that I've ever paid back? Guess where it went? Alcohol and drugs. I'm clean now and have been since you helped me get in that apartment."

"I had no idea. I'm so sorry you have been dealing with this."

"Of course you didn't. Do you think you're the only one that hides stuff? I've been hooked on pain pills since tenth grade when I had my tonsils out. After that, I started sneaking Mom's Darvocet, and being in the music business, it was easy-peasy access to all kinds of drugs."

"Would you believe that I've been in a recovery group for women addicts since May, Jeannie? I ended up there by accident, but it has been one of the best things ever for me. I'm not so very different from them or you. Their example helped me find the courage to tell Jon and now you."

"Wow, God works in strange ways. Get this. In April, I joined a Women's Celebrate Recovery Group at the church I've been attending here in Houston. Since May, I've had a full-time job, and I'm hanging onto it. This time is different. I am turning my life around, and I'm tired of asking you for handouts."

"WELL, IT'S ABOUT TIME you got here," Lily said as she opened the front door holding a tulip glass half full of bubbling champagne. She looked the personification of Christmas in her fitted and slightly flared red dress, matching red heels, bright red lipstick, and clunky gold jewelry.

"Merry Christmas to you, too, Lily," I said, leaning in towards her, planting a perfunctory kiss on her cheek. One of my hands clutched a carryall bag with Christmas presents poking out, and the other balanced the white box containing a fancy fruit tart.

"Here, let me help you." Lily took my bag of gifts and placed it beneath the Christmas tree. My gifts joined the remaining two presents, bearing tags with my name. Liddy's Christmas tree looked like something from a Saks Fifth Avenue department store window.

Doll-sized ceramic angels with feathered wings wore glistening white gowns. Delicate blown-glass roses festooned the boughs in shades of burgundy and mauve. White, silken poinsettias were tucked randomly within the branches. Fist-sized golden ornaments hung from the limbs, bearing shimmering crystal and pearl inlays. Velveteen ribbon, stripped in burgundy and mauve, fell from the star top piece, lacing through the branches.

I walked into the kitchen where Liddy grated parmesan cheese over a Caesar salad. The scent of lemon, anchovy, and garlic from her homemade dressing lingered. She had finally let her hair go gray and wore it short now and loosely curled; her seventy-year-old face never seemed to age and remained beautiful.

"Merry Christmas, Liddy."

"Oh, Merry Christmas to you, too. You know that this is the first time you have been with me on Christmas day since you moved to San Diego." She left her preparations to hug me.

"I know." Of course, it was. When I'd lived with Ned, we weren't both invited, and I couldn't very well leave him alone, or so I thought. I had dropped presents by on Christmas Eve, but I had never joined her on Christmas Day.

"Did you go to midnight Mass?" I asked, unboxing the tart. "Do you have an elevated platter for this to go on?"

"Yes, over in the armoire. No, we went this morning at eight-thirty. I can't stay up that late anymore."

Lily followed me into the kitchen, leaning against the refrigerator with her champagne glass in hand.

"Where's Jon? I thought he would be here to keep Damian company." Lily motioned into the family room a half-floor below the kitchen.

An attractive, tanned dark-haired man sat on the couch, keeping Andy company. Damian looked up when he heard his name and walked up the two stairs into the kitchen, toting his glass of champagne.

"Jon and his son are snowboarding at Big Bear," I said quickly, working at a smile.

"Damian, this is my sister, Liz Schmidt."

"Nice to meet you, Damian," I said.

As Lily pulled him over to her side, I noticed an engagement ring on her finger.

"Whoa! It looks like congratulations are in order. When did this happen?" I said.

Lily held out her tiny hand so I could better admire her ring. "Last night. Damian wrapped it up in a big box that contained a bunch of smaller nested boxes."

"It's lovely. I'm happy for both of you." An unwelcome surge of envy piqued me.

"Andy, turn off the TV. Everything is ready. Liz is here, and it's time to eat," Liddy called into the family room.

Andy got up from his recliner, grabbed his vodka glass, walked into the kitchen, and gave me a tight hug. "Welcome, Liz. You feel like a feather." He stood back, studying me. "Have you lost weight? Everything okay?"

"Yeah, fine. There's just a lot going on." I avoided Andy's gaze and helped Liddy move the food to the table: smoked salmon, baked brie in puff pastry, crackers, a fresh fruit platter, and salad. Liddy cut up the ham and cheese quiche into eight pieces and brought it over to the table while Lily filled or refilled champagne glasses for everyone but Liddy, who drank water.

Twenty-four hours after they had arrived, Lily and Damian headed back to the San Gabriel Valley. Andy returned to his favorite chair glued to the TV set without his hearing aids, the booming volume providing a privacy backdrop for Liddy and my conversation.

Liddy and I moved to the living room after cleaning up the kitchen. She sat in her favorite chair, sipping her diet cola through a straw, her smoking cigarette balanced on the cloisonne ashtray. The late afternoon sun shone through the French doors behind the tufted sofa, still brightening and warming the room.

I retrieved the last few gifts from under the tree as Liddy had wanted to wait until we were alone to exchange our gifts.

"You first." I pointed to the Christmas present on Liddy's lap.

She tore into her gift with the excitement of a small child. With delight, she studied the miniature reproduction of Bouguereau's "Song of Angels" in its gilded frame. Upon the lap of a slumbering Mary slept the child Jesus as three attentive angels serenading them with violin, lute, and the tiny keyboard of a virginal.

"I love all of Bouguereau's religious art. Thank you," she said, holding it out at arm's length and finally donning her reading glasses for a closer inspection. When she turned to me, her eyes shone with tears.

"The last thing you need is more artwork for this house, but perhaps you can find a place to hang it," I said.

Bouguereau was my favorite Pre-Raphaelite artist, and when I'd first seen the picture at a local department store months before Christmas, it had stopped me in my tracks. The image of the perfect mother cuddling her perfect child had slain me. I could not get the image out of my mind. It seemed to have my Catholic birth mother's name all over it. A few days later, I returned to purchase it, having decided it would make the ideal Christmas gift for Liddy.

"Now, your turn." A smile spread over Liddy's face as she brought her hands together under her chin, her ice-blue eyes dancing.

It seemed a shame to tamper with the box, wrapped in gold-colored foil with velvet-like burgundy stripes and a large matching bow. Everything my birth mother touched became a work of art. Inside were two cups and saucers completely overlaid in gold, protected in bubble wrap. I unwrapped one, amazed at its delicate beauty.

A three-quarter inch band of violets, engraved in the porcelain and then delicately painted in shades of purples and white, wrapped around the outside lip of the double handled cup and the outer rim of the saucer. A single, engraved heart-shaped leaf remained in the 22-karat gold, separating the face of each flower.

"I have never seen anything so beautiful in my life. Thank you." I turned over the cup and saucer, noting the marks. One identified the porcelain as antique Limoges, and another, "JED-E-AN," as the trademark of an artist unknown to me.

Liddy supplied the artist's details. Jesse Dean was renowned for his gold artwork in the late 1800s and early 1900s.

"Violets connect us, dear daughter, as they connect me to my mother, a mother whom I never knew."

She grasped my hand before continuing. "Their leaves, a perfect heart; their flowers, a symbol of purity and innocence, joined into a circle of everlasting love, as we are connected, my darling Liz, through a web of tangled violets."

I was utterly overwhelmed by my birth mother's little speech. Her love. My guilt. My shame. The emptiness of Jon's absence. Envy of Lily's engagement. Fear of the fallout that revealing and untangling my past would surely bring.

Moments later, I fell sobbing at her knees, searching her eyes. "Mother, I am so sorry. I don't know if you can ever forgive me."

"What's the matter?" Liddy asked, bewildered.

"Everything. Can we go upstairs to talk where Andy won't walk in on us?"

Liddy led me to the upstairs bedroom where I'd stayed during my first visit sixteen years ago. I confessed it all, sparing no detail and blaming no one but myself. She listened intently, her face calm, without interrupting and patiently waiting for me to finish.

"Dearest daughter, do you think I'm surprised to hear this? Let me assure you; I am not. I have prayed for you to come to your senses since you told me you were moving in with Ned. So many Rosaries I have prayed on your behalf, asking for Mary's intercession. The Lord has indeed answered my prayers."

"But you never said anything?"

"No, the risk of saying anything that might drive you away from me ... and lose you again ... I couldn't bear it. Other than sharing my concerns with my sister Maura, I have kept my worries and suspicions to myself." I instinctively reached to my ear lobe, touching the tourmaline earrings from Aunt Maura.

"I'm disgusted with your father, but what else is new? The reemergence of Ned after thirty-seven years brought an upheaval of feelings and temptations into my life. I did some things that I am not proud of as well.

"And who am I to judge? I've been married five times, five times, by the time I was your age, Liz. And I'm the sixth wife of a bipolar alcoholic. I've hit bottom many times and been a poor excuse for a Catholic for more years than I wish to remember. But I have brought my sins to the Lord; He has forgiven me many times as he will undoubtedly do in the future."

Liddy scooted next to me on the bed and wiped at my tears with her fingertips. She held both of my hands in hers. "You ask if I can forgive you. Absolutely. Forgiving you is much easier than forgiving myself for my failures."

"Is there anything I can do to make it up to you?" I asked.

"You don't need to do anything for me. But I want you to think about something for yourself. Consider meeting with a Catholic priest and making a full confession. I know you don't attend the Catholic Church anymore, but the priest at my parish is wonderful. He's been there for almost twenty years, and he helped Andy and me get married in the Catholic Church. He connected us with an advocate to apply for the many annulments we needed."

"What's his name?"

"Father Tim O'Malley. You've met him before. When you first found me, I introduced you to him. He knows our story. So you see, the way is already paved." She paused briefly, holding my gaze.

"I doubt that Jon has left you forever, Liz. Give him time to heal from his disappointment. Marriage is the process of managing disappointments. God will arrange all the details if you and Jon are meant to be together. Trust in Him. God wastes nothing, not even our sins, when we come to him with a repentant heart."

I ARRIVED AT ST. Martin of Tours parish office twenty minutes early for my appointment with Fr. O'Malley. Exiting my car and finding the front door to the church building unlocked, I passed through the narthex and entered the long narrow sanctuary. Empty, brown wooden pews stood like stiff soldiers at attention on each side of the marble aisle.

Directly above the rectangular golden tabernacle, a large crucifix hung on the yellow wall. A red lamp flickered on a stand, indicating consecrated hosts in the tabernacle. Panels of traditionally-rendered stained-glass windows admitted the late afternoon sunlight into the otherwise dark nave.

Many years had passed since I'd been inside a Catholic church. I genuflected before entering a front pew and lowered the kneeler. I recalled God's words to Moses as he stood in front of the burning bush, "Remove the sandals from your feet, for the place on which you are standing is holy ground." Immediately, I experienced the unmistakable aura of a place set apart, a sacred space for prayer and worship, never to be confused with a multi-purpose room.

My gaze moved from the tabernacle to the crucifix and back down to the tabernacle, remaining there. Faith in a merciful God had revamped my life, but did I believe in the mystery of the Real Presence, a crucified God present in a consecrated host? And there, on my knees, a warmth spread through my body like a consuming fire.

"Lord, I do believe; help my unbelief," I whispered as spontaneous tears washed over my face. The many Scriptures I'd pondered over the last year flooded my mind, forming the prayer that echoed aloud between a sinner and her God.

"'Unless you eat the flesh of the Son of Man and drink his blood, you have no life in you' were your words, Jesus. And when your disciples complained, 'This teaching is difficult; who can accept it?' did you run after them, saying, 'Wait, come back; I was just speaking symbolically?'

"No. You let them go, just as you let me run away. But Jesus, you came after me, waiting until my spirit was sufficiently broken so that you could reassemble me according to your good purpose."

A wave of gratitude washed over me like a tsunami. I knelt in silence now, imploring the Holy Spirit to carry the vague yearnings of my heart to the Father through the wounds of the Son.

And at that moment, I finally found the identity I'd searched for and hungered for my entire life. Before Liddy. Before Ned. It had always been there: I was the beloved daughter of the Father.

Having lost track of time, I now remembered my meeting with Fr. Tim.

As I rushed to leave, my eyes lifted to the life-sized mural in the back of the church painted above the choir loft. Transfixed in utter amazement, I froze. I knew well the painting that had inspired the mural. Spanning the entire width of the nave was Bouguereau's "Song of Angels," the very image I had chosen for Liddy's Christmas gift. My heart had been drawn to it then as it was now.

Remembering the mist in my birth mother's eyes on Christmas day as she'd unwrapped a tiny reproduction of the masterpiece, I was now confident of my next step. Somehow, my heart had known before my mind. It was time to come home to the Catholic Church.

I exited the church with great peace and resolve as I walked to the parish office. A kindly woman ushered me into Father Tim's office. He rose from his desk and extended his hand in greeting.

"Hello, Elizabeth. Liddy Anderson's daughter, right? The resemblance is quite amazing."

"Yes, Liddy's my birth mother." I smiled and shook his warm hand.

"Now, please sit down, and tell me how I can help you." He scratched his bald head and pushed up his wire-rimmed glasses from the end of his thin nose.

"I told your secretary that I'd need a whole hour. I hope you have time. I'm afraid this is going to be ... messy."

It had taken the better part of an hour when I'd come clean with Pastor

Matt last month. I expected meeting with a priest would take even longer.

"You can have two hours if you need it. Don't fret about the time. You're my last appointment of the day." He flashed a disarming smile, animating his dark eyes.

"I'd like to go to confession, the long kind that goes over my whole life. But before that, I need to give you some background." I removed my yellow composition notebook from my shoulder bag.

And background he received. Forty-five minutes later, he wrapped his purple stole around his neck.

"Okay, let's hear that confession now," he said.

He invited me to make the Sign of the Cross with him and began, "May God, who has enlightened every heart, enable you to know your sins and trust in his mercy."

"Bless me, Father, for I have sinned. My last confession was twenty years ago, maybe longer."

He nodded, closing his eyes as I reeled off my sins in reverse chronological order, turning the pages in my notebook where I listed every sin I could ever remember. Finally, I reached the end of my list.

"For these and all the sins of my past life, I ask pardon of God and penance and absolution of you, Father."

Father Tim was silent for a few moments before he spoke.

"Liz, it is not humanly possible to avoid sin or remake our hearts on our own. These things can only happen by God's grace. Know that God forgives and heals your past. He wants you to live in the present and look to your future. Pray for a heart open to God's grace, love, and mercy. When we bring him a repentant heart, God can transform our most painful moments and grievous sins into opportunities for spiritual growth and transformation."

I grabbed a handful of tissues from his desk, the water faucet of my soul leaking once again.

"For your penance, I'd like you to pray the Rosary. Now make an Act of Contrition. If you don't remember, I can help you."

I prayed the words that Sister Marie Clare had taught our class in second grade, meaning them from the bottom of my heart. Afterward, Father Tim raised his hand toward me.

"God the Father of mercies, through the death and resurrection of his

Son, has reconciled the world to Himself and sent the Holy Spirit among us for the forgiveness of sins; through the ministry of the Church, may God give you pardon and peace, and I absolve you from your sins in the name of the Father, and of the Son and of the Holy Spirit. Amen."

"Thank you, Father."

"Your future is ahead of you, Liz. Go in peace and sin no more."

Second Confessions

I HAD RESISTED ANGIE'S suggestion for months but finally gave in. She had explained, "Something had to be missing in your childhood to connect so deeply with your birth father and to have stayed with him for all those years. My Pesso-Boyden therapy group might help you uncover that hole, plug it up, and make it easier to move forward. To forgive yourself and heal."

Angie's words echoed in my mind as I entered the meeting room and claimed the last available chair. Her words, "forgive yourself," finally convinced me to give it a shot. "Okay, I'll try it for six weeks," I'd said.

The fear of airing my dirty laundry in front of a small group of women was not what troubled me. As a left-brained mathematician, I struggled to embrace the theory of psychomotor therapy.

Using the method, specially trained therapists, like Angie, used dramatization and props to help a client create new, believable memories somehow anchored to the ego. Those therapeutic memories were supposed to correct and positively restructure early traumatic events and plug emotional deficits. It seemed pretty far-fetched, and I'd told Angie Bell as much.

After three sessions of observing other women spend an hour reworking their past in the present, I well understood the logistics. Tonight, however, promised to be different. I was the central actor on a virtual stage, reliving my memories. The security of simply witnessing or playing an idealized role in another woman's drama was gone.

I sat in the middle of the floor in a room twice the size of Angie's office, my back to the windows. The other five women sat on chairs on either side of her. I closed my eyes to block them out.

"Can you tell me where you are, Liz?" Angie asked, sitting directly in front of me.

My breathing quickened, and a clamminess crawled over my skin.

"I'm hiding under the bed in my room." I pulled up the old familiar image. The wooden floor pressed against my cheek, and I pushed the dust bunnies away with my small hands so they didn't touch me.

"You must be small to fit underneath your bed. How old are you?"

"Young. Four or five."

"What's happening inside?"

"I'm upset. Scared. I don't know how to fix things." It was so easy to go back ... the feeling of being untethered and lost ... the stomachaches.

"Is something broken?"

"Not a thing, it's Momma. She's sad and crying again."

"Why is your mother so sad?"

"Because people hurt her feelings and make her sad."

"What's your mother's name?"

"Marie."

"If a witness were here, she would say that you have a great deal of sympathy for your mother, Marie. But I think little Lizzie feels sad, too, as she hides under her bed. Is that correct?"

I waited to answer, tasting the salty shame dripping down the side of my nose and into my mouth. "Yes."

"Who has hurt your mother Marie's feelings?" Angie said, leaning down to hand me some tissues.

"Lots of people. Daddy makes her cry. He yells at her. But I make Momma cry, too." I squeezed my eyes shut, trying to push away the memories.

"Is that why little Lizzie is hiding under the bed?"

"Yes."

"What is your father's name?"

"Fred."

"How did you make your mother Marie cry?"

"Because when I got mad at her, she told me that I hated her."

"Does little Lizzie hate her mother?"

"I don't think so, but I'm not sure anymore. If I do, I don't want to hate her." I choked down a suppressed sob. "My job is to make her happy. She had a hard life."

"Sometimes, little people think they are responsible for fixing big people's problems. Did your mother think other people hated her?"

"Her stepfather must have hated her. He left her at the orphanage."

"Was Marie an orphan, then?"

"Yes, after her mother died and her stepfather didn't want her anymore. He took Momma and her older sisters and brother to the orphanage. It's hard not to be wanted."

"Does little Lizzie understand how Marie feels when her stepfather doesn't want her?"

I nodded and caught my breath. "It's hard to be a throw-away child."

"Can you bring Marie into the room, Liz?"

I scanned the five available faces before me. "How about Jesse?"

Jesse nodded, repeated Angie's prompt, and said, "I will role-play Lizzie's ideal mother, Marie."

Angie asked, "Where should we place your mother?"

"Over here by me," I said, patting the floor. Jesse sat on her knees next to me on the floor.

"How can we help your mother?"

"I want her to be happy."

"Can we give Marie an ideal mother who didn't die and a stepfather who would never have sent Marie to an orphanage? Then she could have a happier childhood."

"Yes, I want that for her." Doe-eyed Catherine accepted the role of Marie's ideal mother, and tall Kristin took on the part of Marie's stepfather.

Following Angie's prompts, Catherine and Kristin verbalized the roles they had accepted as Marie's ideal parents.

"Can little Lizzie move over to make room for her mother Marie's ideal parents?"

I moved away to make room for Catherine and Kristin to sit on either side of Jesse. Angie suggested that Catherine and Kristin each put a hand on Jesse's shoulder, symbolizing their support.

"How do you feel seeing Marie getting the support she needs from her parents."

"Relieved. It is nice to have help; I wasn't very good at making Momma happy."

"It's a lot of responsibility for little Lizzie to keep her mother happy. Would it help Marie to have a husband who didn't lose his temper or yell at her? Someone who can protect her?"

"I think so."

"Let's give Marie an ideal husband who has a mellow temperament and is kind to her."

I looked for a prop for my father, Fred. I went to the bookshelf and pulled down a book. I opened the book and placed it in front of Jesse, role-playing my mother.

"Might it be better for a person to play the role of Fred?"

"I don't know. Maybe. Okay."

Jenny assumed the role of an idealized husband, saying, "I don't yell at my wife Marie, and I will protect her."

I scooted back further to make room for Marie's ideal husband to sit near my mother, Marie.

"What are you feeling towards your father Fred right now."

"I'm angry with him."

At that point, all I could think of was Ned, and I hid my face in my hands. "But I want a father who protects me, too, and I want a mother who doesn't think I hate her." A high-pitched sound carried my words into the room as my pain squeezed out between them.

"What's happening inside right now? Where are you, Liz?"

"I'm with Ned. It's all mixed up. I was Ned's little girl except that I'm big ... all grown up."

"Let's come back into this room with little Lizzie, with her ideal mother, Marie's ideal parents, and husband."

I looked away from Angie's face, forcing myself back to the imaginary scene.

"Little Lizzie does not have to carry the burden of her mother's happiness." Angie paused and repeated herself. Finally, she said, "Can you take that in, Liz? You are not responsible for your mother's happiness. You do not need to carry that guilt and shame any longer."

INITIALLY, I HAD TRIED to discount Jon's terrifying suggestion that I tell the kids the truth about Ned and me as part of making amends to him. And, well, he wasn't part of my life anymore. The key to his house, still in my possession, hardly constituted a relationship beyond a symbolic one.

But the seeds Jon had planted took root as I pulled back the covers on my shame and guilt of my years with Ned. Living a lie had crippled my most valued relationships, those with my children. I had to address the deceit permeating the years when my four youngest children and I had lived under the same roof with Ned. I asked God to bring good out of evil and that the good of my confession and apology would overcome any potential harm.

Angie had cautioned, "If you feel led to tell your children, you mustn't rob them of their good childhood memories. Your birth father was a big part of their life." She had helped formulate the phrase "inappropriate coupling" to describe the incestuous relationship with my birth father.

Leah had learned the truth only weeks after I'd told Jon. My confession to my thirty-year-old daughter had been more like lancing a boil in my soul rather than a well-thought-out admission of guilt and apology. I'd been an emotional disaster sniffing about for comfort and unconditional love like a wounded puppy in the throes of missing Jon desperately. The memory of that phone conversation, an unfortunate example of me as the broken child and Leah as the loving parent, still made me cringe.

Telling Leah had remained a lesson in how not to tell the other kids. I needed to be much further down the road to healing, where I could speak without crying or shrieking under the heavy thumb of grief and remorse.

Leah had been furious with Ned but not me. Her reaction had reflected the prevalent model of incest between a father and his daughter. But when the daughter was a complicit adult, the picture grew more complicated. There seemed to be no model for that.

"Ned's no more guilty than I am," I had said.

"Well, Mom, how would you feel if I told you that same thing about Charlie Davis?" she had asked over the phone.

"I'd be upset, just like you."

"Exactly. That's my point, Mom."

But lightening a portion of my guilt by shifting more blame onto Ned felt wrong. The pieces began to fall into place after Angie Bell placed Greenberg's 1993 journal article, *Post-adoption reunion—are we entering uncharted territory?* into my hands. She had read this article only weeks before we first met when I'd collapsed in her office.

Greenberg's research helped me place my feelings for Ned into a larger framework of human experience. Of the forty reported post-adoption reunions between adults, 100% had universally reported an irresistible sense of falling in love and intense erotic feelings. The author had hypothesized that without the inhibition that nurturing kinship imprints, the brain interpreted the desire for and experience of immediate intimacy between the reunited adults as sexual. Ned and I fell into the case of the three couples that had reported engaging in sexualized behavior.

From the Pesso-Boyden group work and ongoing sessions with Angie, I learned about my attachment disorder, which had impaired the bonding between my adoptive parents and my husbands. I had a heaping helping of shame about that, too. I compensated by trying to make people happy. When Ned came into my life, I was a perfect storm.

My case with Ned was not only extreme, but due to the length of our relationship, we had entangled members of our families under its dark shadow. Like all sin, it is never just personal; it always impacts others. But understanding the motives of my sins did not lessen my culpability nor make reparation for their harm any less which fell squarely upon my shoulders.

It was time to tell my four youngest children, who still worshiped the only grandfather they'd ever known. I prayed for God's grace to help my family get through the unveiling.

MAY 2005

I DROVE UP TO Los Angeles to meet with Jonah and Hannah separately. Jonah had been cooped up in his office all Saturday morning, so he met me outside the Mathematical Sciences Building. We sat companionably on the ledge of a nearby cement planter, shaded by the lacy fronds of a jacaranda tree still clutching its purple trumpets. As he filled me in on the progress of his dissertation, I thought how my handsome accomplished son was the genetic optimization of Leo and me.

My eldest son was the most cerebral and easy-going of all my children. Perhaps for that reason, and the progress I'd made in therapy, a calm descended upon me as I told Jonah my story and apologized.

"I can see that," he said as if reanalyzing a swath of his life under a new mathematical transform, mapping it into a different but parallel vector space. He processed the new information without any imputation of guilt. His only apparent concern was for my well-being and happiness. That concern extended to his grandfather as well. At the end of our hour talk, Jonah and I exchanged hugs, and he thanked me for telling him.

"I still love you, Mom, and Grandpa Ned, too. What you told me changes nothing."

Hannah and I had dinner together later the same day. Afterward, I'd invited her up to my hotel room, saying, "I want to talk to you about something in a place where we won't be disturbed." Hannah's gift of empathy worried me; I feared she might hold back her emotions or questions for fear of hurting my feelings. On the other hand, Hannah often stuck her finger in her ears, even at twenty-two, when she didn't like the conversation. I hoped she'd hear me out. But Hannah had a surprise for me.

"Mom, I already knew."

"What do you mean?"

"I found all the love letters you wrote to Grandpa Ned before he moved in with us in Kennewick."

"How could that be? I sent the letters to him in Hawaii."

"Right, but the *WordPerfect* files were still on the hard disk of the old computer downstairs in the Big House that we used to write our school papers in high school. I can't say if anybody else read them, but I did. Every single one."

I'd forgotten all about those files, breadcrumbs leading to the open window that peered into my affair with my birth father.

"I'm so sorry that you have borne the burden of my secret all this time. And apologize that I waited this long to talk to you about this. Can you ever forgive me?"

"It's okay, Mom. I didn't hold it against you or Grandpa Ned. I love you both and wouldn't trade those years of living with him for anything."

"I understand, but my relationship with your grandfather was wrong. Terribly wrong."

Perhaps the greatest damage of those years with Ned was that her unconditional love for her grandfather and mother had normalized an intrinsically disordered relationship. Never mind the obvious collateral damage, that I had failed to model the Christian life for my children and instead had thrown them under the dark cloud of my sin. Hardly the gift a mother should bequeath to her children.

JUNE 2005

THE THREE OF US sat in the waiting room at Dalton's Counseling Center. Already in town for Noah's high school graduation, I'd effortlessly persuaded Abby to attend our session with Angie Bell. She was curious about and applauded the changes she'd observed in me over the last months: a vibrant Christian faith, attendance at Mass, and my nursing home ministry.

However, Noah had been a tough sell. Like me, he had an aversion to new social situations, and the idea of attending a therapy session with his mother seemed, well, as he'd said, "Too dang weird."

"It's nothing about you, Noah. There's something I need to get off my chest, and I want my therapist there to support me," I'd said.

Abby and Noah were very close, so I wanted to talk to them when they were together. Angie would keep things at the appropriate level of detail and diffuse any issues that I feared might arise.

Eventually, Noah had agreed to meet. Abby likely had something to do with his change of heart because here he sat alongside the two of us. "Thanks for coming with me," I whispered, taking in his untamed curly mane and anxious-looking green eyes. I lightly cupped his hands to quiet the sound of his cracking knuckles.

Telling Noah was worrisome. At least Abby had dated and had a boyfriend or two. But Noah seemed younger than his eighteen years, and although interested in girls, he was far too introverted and shy to put interest into action. So much of what went on in that brain and heart of his was a mystery to me.

I glanced over at Abby, my bookworm, wholly absorbed in her novel, Francine River's *Redeeming Love.* As if sensing the warmth of my gaze, she turned to me with tears in her eyes, saying. "Mom, you have to read this book. It's so good." My youngest daughter's Christian faith was a testimony to God's grace to work perfectly through imperfect circumstances.

Moments later, Angie opened the door into the waiting room. "Sorry to keep the three of you waiting. I'm ready for you now. Please, come in."

I followed the kids into Angie's cozy office and made introductions. Abby and Noah settled onto opposite ends of the sofa while Angie claimed her usual wingback chair. I repositioned the side chair closer to the kids and angled it to avoid missing any visual cues from Angie's or the kids' faces.

Angie said a short opening prayer, asking the Holy Spirit for wisdom and guidance, to which Abby and I said, "Amen," and Noah gave a nearly imperceptible eye-roll.

At her charming professional best, the kids relaxed as they answered her questions about themselves. She had scheduled ample time for the warm-up. "You can't just bring them in here, cold turkey, and expect them to open up to me. We have to spend time getting to know one another," she had said when I asked her what we would do for a whole hour and a half.

She asked them to share some of their best memories of growing up in the Big House and the San Diego house when Mom and Grandpa Ned still lived together. After she affirmed their memories as precious, she turned her attention to me.

"Liz, why don't you tell Abby and Noah why you asked them to come here today."

I prayed for the right words and the courage to speak them.

"Our years with Grandpa Ned were full of good times, wonderful trips, and beautiful things that I could never have provided for you on my own. But there was another side to those years, a hidden part that was wrong. And for that part, I need to apologize. You see, your grandfather and I shared an inappropriate coupling relationship."

I looked from Abby's eyes to Noah's, attempting to gauge their reaction. Noah remained still as a statue. Abby tilted her head and slightly narrowed her eyes as if digesting what she'd just heard.

"I'm telling you this because I don't want any secrets between us. I am sorry and hope you can forgive me someday." I felt a quiver in my lips, but there it was, out in the open. All the kids knew now. "Let me know if you have any questions, okay?"

"Mom, do you mean like ... physical ... you and Grandpa Ned?"

"Yes."

Abby leaped up from the couch and ran to me. I stood up to meet her and closed my arms around her small form. She held me in a tight bear hug. "I'm so sorry, Mom," she said without a shred of condemnation, pouring a libation of unconditional love onto me.

A minute later, Noah announced defiantly, "I still love Grandpa Ned, no matter what."

"So do I, Noah. But I've asked God to redeem that love, to transform it into a love that's appropriate between a daughter and a father." I waited for the furrows in his brow to soften to continue. "Admitting that a person's choices are wrong or sinful doesn't mean we don't love them. Love never requires that we call wrong right."

All of my children now knew the burden I had carried for so many years. Although they may not understand completely, we could all begin to heal together.

OCTOBER 2005

THE EVENING BEFORE MY fifty-second birthday, my mobile phone rang. Jon's number flashed on the tiny screen. We hadn't spoken since accidentally running into one another on the walking trail on Christmas Eve, a long ten months ago. And now that I attended Mass, I no longer worshiped at Community Fellowship Church. All that remained for us was friendship, although I still wanted more.

"Hello. Jon?" My heart threatened to leap out of my chest.

"Hi, Liz. Yes, it's me." If ears could hear a smile, Jon was smiling. "Do you have plans for your birthday tomorrow night?"

"Other than incrementing one year, nothing at all." I couldn't believe that he had remembered.

"May I take you out for dinner then?"

"I'd love that."

"Great. I'll pick you up at six-thirty."

"Wait ... don't hang up. I bought a place in September. You'll need my new address."

"Congratulations, Liz. It sounds like we have a lot to catch up on."

Twenty-four hours later, Jon and I walked into the bistro side of Champagne. The server invited us to seat ourselves and followed us with menus. Jon chose a table away from the other customers. I'd struggled to keep my expectations in check. "Simply a dinner between two friends with a history of something more," I had told myself.

Jon pulled out the café chair for me and then sat opposite me on the black tufted bench extending along the entire back wall up to the front windows. After ordering, we relaxed into an easy conversation without the threat of being interrupted. He removed his leather coat and laid it next to him.

"You look lovely tonight, Liz. I've missed you terribly."

I'd gone to great lengths to look my best, wearing my favorite dress, a vintage red and black polka swing dress, and black heels. I'd even left work early to pick up some hair dye at the drug store to camouflage the bits of gray that I'd lived with for months.

"I've missed you, too. You look like you are doing well." Jon's gaunt look, now vanquished, was replaced with a healthy-looking vibrancy.

"Prozac has helped tremendously. I've had issues with depression and anxiety my whole life. I may need to stay on it for the rest of my life. Who knows? But I feel great."

"Well, you certainly didn't need me to tip you over the edge. Rather unfair, given that you were the catalyst for me getting the help I needed. My therapist, Angie Bell, has been my angel over the last ..." I counted it out, "... eleven months."

"How would you feel about us meeting together with your therapist to see if she thinks you are ready to begin seeing me again?"

"I think that would be fine, but I need to be upfront with you about something, Jon. I'm not free to date you or anyone else right now."

"Why?"

"I've gone back to the Catholic Church. That's why you haven't seen me at Community Fellowship Church since February. Unless a marriage tribunal grants my marriage to Joe Keller a decree of nullity, I'm still married to him in the eyes of the Catholic Church."

"Hard-core and downright biblical," Jon said, rubbing his chin.

"Yep. And the Catholic Church would consider you still married to your ex-wife unless you received an annulment." I let that sink in for a few moments.

"It would be great to meet together with Angie, Jon. But it's more important that we meet with my parish priest first."

I reached across the table and touched Jon's hand. "I'm still madly in love with you, Jon, but if we are ever going to be together, it has to be right for me. In all ways. I started the annulment process several months ago for my marriage with Joe. There was a lack of proper canonical form in that marriage, as we weren't married by a Catholic priest, and both Joe and I were baptized Catholics. Your first wife was Catholic, and you weren't married by a priest, so I suspect a lack of canonical form also applies to your first marriage. The bottom line is that we can be friends, but only friends until we both have annulments."

"I'm happy to do that for you, Liz. I want us to be together."

"Since I want to understand my Catholic faith better, I started attending class with the group of people at my parish who will come into the Catholic Church this Easter. The priest and the adult faith formation director that lead it are excellent. The adult faith formation director is an ex-Protestant. I think you two would hit it off. If you're interested, I'd love to have you come with me."

"I'm not ruling it out, Liz, but first, let's meet with your pastor to get started on that annulment process for me."

"Oh, and by the way, I did come clean with Pastor Matt, my kids, everyone on Liddy's side of the family. The only hang-up is that Ned has yet to tell his daughters and brother. But without the influence of a Christian counselor in his life, I don't know if that will ever happen."

"I've been praying for Ned lately. Not that I want to, but I feel like God may want me to reach out to him. Would you mind if I met with him?"

"I'd love that."

I entered Ned's contact information into Jon's phone just as the waiter brought our entrees to the table: steaming chicken and mushrooms smothered in gruyere sauce nestled in a puff pastry shell.

Once we finished our meal, Jon said, "I hope you saved room for dessert. We have a two-course dessert." Jon removed something from his coat pocket. He laid a small rectangular-shaped gift on the table near the burning candle. "Here's the first course."

He pushed a wrapped, narrow box towards me. "Happy birthday, Liz."

"Really? Dinner is plenty. You didn't need to buy me a gift."

"But I wanted to." Jon's eyes reflected my anticipation. "Open it."

My fingers tingled with excitement as I untied the purple ribbon and removed the silver wrapping paper. Inside the box lay a delicate gold bracelet with two charms hanging: a heart and a padlock with a tiny key attached. I pursed my lips and blinked away the emotion pooling in my eyes. "Thank you. I love it."

After removing the bracelet from its box, I draped it over my left wrist, fumbling to secure the lobster-claw clasp.

"Here, let me help you with that." Jon came over to my side of the table, repositioned the bracelet, and latched it securely. He then pulled my hand to his lips and tenderly kissed the top of my hand as the two charms dangled from my wrist.

I touched the tiny key suspended from the padlock charm when he released my hand. "You know, Jon, I still have the key to your house."

"Yes, I am quite aware of that. And you still have the key to my heart." He smiled and then winked at me. "Now, how about we walk over to the patisserie side and pick out that second dessert course?"

Chapter 26

Worth The Wait

TRUE TO HIS WORD, Jon reached out to Ned. The two men met at Torrey Ridge Park, a small, secluded park in Carmel Valley overlooking the Del Mar polo fields and the San Dieguito Lagoon. I wasn't there, so what I know of those meetings came secondhand, filtered through Jon's eyes.

According to Jon, they sat at a cement picnic table, word-wrestling their different agendas during that first meeting. He had remained calm, while Ned had become defensive. Ned had wanted back in relationship with me. Jon communicated that I desired that, too, and that as father and daughter, we had a right to a loving relationship. Just not a disordered sexual one.

Jon represented my stipulations to my birth father. I didn't require that Ned apologize to me, but he had to admit to himself and those impacted by our relationship that it had been wrong. And I wanted to send my letters of apology to those last five names on my list.

Ned remained firm in his conviction of no wrongdoing because we had been adults, he had not raised me, and our relationship had been consensual. Hence, he owed no apology to anyone, and culpability or guilt were not applicable.

Jon, however, believed that Ned, as the father and twenty-four years my senior, had abused his natural position of authority and that I had come to him as an adoring adult-child. Jon had explained it to me by analogy, "When God disciplined King David after his affair with Bathsheba, it was primarily for his abuse of power, and secondarily for his adultery."

Ned agreed to a second meeting because he saw Jon as the gatekeeper keeping us apart. My birth father knew that I loved him dearly, and I suspect that he couldn't believe that I would choose on my own to exclude him from my life.

For their second meeting, Jon took copies of the letters of apology that I'd written but never mailed to Ned's side of the family. I'd penned a brief note to Ned stating that my letters would go out in the mail in six months, regardless of his "progress."

After Ned read the first letter, he became distraught. "I can't tell my daughters. My brother, Henri, yes, but not my daughters."

Jon remained firm, "It will be difficult, yes. But with the help of a Christian therapist, you can and will want to come clean."

I understood Ned's fear well. In confessing my sins to those directly impacted, I had allowed myself to be vulnerable in previously unknown ways, opening the door to the possibility of unforgiveness and complete loss of relationship. But without confession, apology, and repentance, the shame of my sins would have held me hostage forever. I wanted that freedom for my birth father, too.

After his third meeting with Jon, Ned began working with a Christian therapist. And in the early spring of 2006, Ned's therapist contacted Angie Bell and requested a meeting with her, Jon, and me.

NED'S THERAPIST INTRODUCED HERSELF as Marlene and thanked everyone for coming. Since her office was in the same complex as Angie's, the five of us gathered in a meeting room down the hall from Angie's office. Jon and I sat on the Lawson-style sofa, and Ned sat stiffly on the matching loveseat opposite us. Angie and Marlene sat on the accent chairs between the couch and loveseat.

A box of tissue, several bottles of water, and a peace plant with its white spoon-shaped lilies sat on an oblong glass-topped cocktail table in the middle of us. Light-drenched artwork, sailboats in harbor encircled by gulls overhead, hung on the beige seagrass wallpaper. Soft lighting from several floor lamps created a warm glow in the room.

A soup of conflicting emotions roiled inside me: anxiety, frustration, hope, concern, and tenderness. I still loved Ned, but this love wanted only the best things for him. But I had no place in his future unless God had redeemed his feelings for me. That thought pierced my heart.

Finally, Ned began to speak. "As Marlene said, Liz, Jon, and Dr. Bell, thank you for agreeing to meet."

I nodded, acknowledging his words as his eyes met mine.

"Especially, I want to thank you, Jon. From the moment you came into Liz's life, I resented you. Perhaps "resented" is too gentle a word. When we started meeting at Seagrove Park, I felt much anger toward you. It has taken me a long time to see things from your perspective because, honestly, to do so left me in a very unpleasant light.

"Through your efforts and Marlene's help, I have realized that you were right." Ned sucked in air before continuing; his raw emotion spilled into the room.

To the group, he said, "From the first time that Liz and I were together ... sexually ... I knew deep down that it was wrong. But I never stopped. I have been in denial all these years."

He then turned to me. "Liz, the adoration, the worship in your eyes for me ... oh my god ... it was like a .... drug." Ned reached for a tissue and blew his nose.

"Thank you for finally breaking it off. To say that I'm sorry doesn't seem sufficient given that I was your father. I apologize for everything. I hope you can forgive me and that someday you will be comfortable relating to me as your father. I pray that one day you can call me Dad."

I wiped my face dry. "Of course, I forgive you. I apologize for being so needy and greedy. I wanted all of your affection. I feel equally responsible and look forward to new memories as father and daughter."

Ned replied, "I have talked with my brother, Henri, and my girls. They all know. You can send your letters now."

At the end of the meeting, I walked over to Ned and embraced him. We wept in each other's arms, hopeful for a new beginning.

My departing words were, "I love you, Dad."

I BROUGHT THE MAIL inside the house and tossed it on the kitchen counter. Two white business envelopes poked out from under a pile of junk mail. I fished them out quickly. One letter was from Uncle Henri, and the other was from the diocesan marriage tribunal office. I held both letters in my trembling hand, debating which to open first. I slid my index finger under the back flap of the envelope from my uncle and read his short, typewritten note.

March 26, 2006

Dear Liz,

Thank you for writing a letter of explanation and expiation about your relationship with Ned. The ability to be candid in honestly discussing this painful experience had to be found in your transformed life.

We understand the feelings you have shared with us. An apology isn't needed, but forgiveness is offered to you even though not required for us. You have found the source of true forgiveness and regeneration.

Thank you for your concern and for encouraging us to support Ned. We love him very much, and we love you, too. Hopefully, the future will bring you both together in a healthy, spiritually cleansed relationship.

Sincerely,

Henri and Mary

I set Henri's note on the counter, filled with gratitude for his kindness. Encountering the person of Christ had left its unmistakable mark on my uncle's magnanimous heart. I contrasted his letter to the phone conversation I'd had with my half-sister Terri two nights ago after she'd received my letter of apology.

She could easily forgive me, but she could not forgive her father. No matter what I said, Terri was resolute and unforgiving. The energy of her impersonal "universe" left her short of mercy and mired in judgment. I didn't expect that I would ever hear from Joni, Sandi, or Vicki, and that was okay. I would continue to pray for them all, especially for Terri.

I hadn't reaped a hundred percent forgiveness from my ex-husbands initially. Joe had forgiven me graciously, while Leo had not. "People don't change," Leo spat out during our conversation with Angie. I had replied, "You are partially right, Leo. People don't change on their own. Only the grace of God can do that."

Picking up the envelope from the tribunal office, I ran my fingers along the edges. Then laying it back down unopened, I walked into my bedroom. After changing out of my work clothes, I knelt beside my bed. I covered my face with the palms of my hands and prayed aloud to the Bridegroom of my Soul.

"Dearest Love, I am your most unworthy bride. You have taken me into your arms and cleansed me. Thank you for never giving up on me, for gathering me into your Heart, for breathing your life back into my soul, and for the river of mercy that continues to wash over me. Regardless of the tribunal's ruling, You, sweet Jesus, are enough for me. Thank You for all the blessings you have showered on me. Jesus, I trust in you."

Walking back into the kitchen, I removed the letter from its envelope with a renewed sense of calm and confidence.

March 24, 2006

Re: Schmidt-Keller 2005-70F

Dear Ms. Schmidt:

After carefully considering the evidence submitted to the Tribunal regarding your marriage to Joseph P. Keller, I write to inform you that the marriage was not valid under the law of the Catholic Church. This finding has no civil effects whatsoever.

The declaration of nullity enabling you to enter marriage in the Catholic Church has been issued and is being held in file. If and when you are being prepared for marriage in the Catholic Church, please notify this office as to the date and place of marriage and the name of the priest who will be officiating at the wedding. We will then mail the decree directly to the priest.

Please contact your advocate, Fr. Timothy O'Malley, if you have any questions or concerns.

With every good wish, I am

Sincerely,

V. Rev James R. McLoughlin, JCL

Judicial Vicar

JOE AND I ENTERED Carmel Valley Middle School's auditorium for Holy Saturday services. The renovations transforming St. William of York into St. Thérèse of Carmel Catholic Church had already closed the old church building for worship before I had joined the parish. I looked forward to moving into the new church building in the fall.

Dressed in our Sunday best, we claimed a pair of folding chairs next to one another upfront. As Jon's sponsor, I had gotten to know the other catechumens and candidates who, like Jon, were entering the Catholic Church that night.

I may have had something to do with Jon's decision to enter into full communion with the Catholic Church. But if so, my influence was a drop in an overflowing bucket of promptings that the Holy Spirit had poured out over him. Jon was most impressed with the Catholic teaching on morality and ethics, particularly with the big green Catechism, which he had read cover to cover before that night.

Jon and the adult Faith Formation director, who had once been Protestant, had formed a deep friendship. Through that friendship, Jon first became acquainted with the Early Church Fathers: Polycarp, Justin Martyr, Clement of Rome, Ignatius of Antioch, and Irenaeus of Lyon. Their writings had affected a paradigm shift in Jon's seminary-trained and intellectually hungry brain.

"The early Christians celebrated Mass, believed in the Real Presence of the Eucharist, the authority of the bishop of Rome, and an objective, not a subjective, interpretation of Scripture," Jon had said, holding up his latest book on the Early Church Fathers months ago.

Jon had not wanted to become Catholic. But as he'd said, "The Early Church Fathers' manuscripts removed all my Protestant objections to Catholicism. Intellectual integrity leaves me no choice."

That night Jon was confirmed and received the Eucharist for the first time–the Body and Blood of Christ. My journey with Jon had started two years and three months ago, but what God's plans were for our lives remained known only to Him. My goal was to have no expectations beyond our friendship.

God had taught me that I did have the ability to temper my passions and wait. Jon had said many times, "Anticipation is better than participation." I was pretty sure I disagreed with Jon's philosophy, but perhaps the road to sainthood was paved with self-denial.

"WE ARE DOING SOMETHING special before your birthday dinner. Dress casually, but bring a light jacket," Jon had said. A whole year had passed since we had last celebrated my birthday at Champagne. Tonight, we would go there to celebrate my fifty-third birthday. He had asked me to leave work early today and be home by five, ready to go.

Parking was already in short supply in downtown Del Mar, so Jon pulled his car into the parking garage across the street from the beach. He led me down railroad tie stairs to the waterfront by the hand. Jon was quieter than usual, yet I sensed the unspoken rumblings of a simmering volcano. We walked away from everyone to a private little cove. Something was up. But what?

He stopped walking and, then facing me, removed a folded envelope from the inside pocket of his jacket. "Happy birthday," he said, handing it to me.

My pulse accelerated when I saw the return address, the Diocese of San Diego. I looked at Jon, barely able to breathe, "Is it what I think it is?"

"Read it and see." His left eyebrow arched in invitation.

Then I saw the postmark on the envelope. "What? You've had this for two weeks and said nothing? You are a stinker!"

I removed the letter, devouring its contents. Overcome with relief and joy, I dropped to my knees and squeezed my eyes shut to contain my tears of joy. The letter and its envelope fell into the fine, gray sand. When I opened my eyes, Jon had knelt in front of me. He took my hands in his and kissed each palm. He removed a black velveteen ring box from his pocket.

"Elizabeth Ann Schmidt, will you marry me? I promise to love and cherish you forever."

"Yes, yes, a million times, yes."

Our kiss held the tenderness of our shared, tangled journey and a deep, burning passion that we had respectfully sacrificed for God and one another.

"Aren't you going to look at the engagement ring?" he asked.

"Only if you insist, I'd rather look at you." And with that, Jon brought his lips to mine once again.

❀❀❀

THE SUN HAD YET to burn off the marine layer as Abby, Hannah, and I hurried from the parking lot to join Jon for the 8 a.m. Saturday Mass. He stood in the paved courtyard just outside the large wrought iron doors leading into St. Thérèse of Carmel Catholic Church. The newly renovated church, with its 57-foot copper dome, golden-brown stucco exterior, and stone archways, formed a breathtaking place of worship.

Jon wore a light grey suit, his tie boasting diagonal stripes in dark charcoal, cream, and peach, chosen to match the pale peach of my simple A-line, mid-calf dress. Abby carried my bridal nosegay, a compact cluster of apricot roses and white carnations. I'd tucked in a few sprigs of purple silk violets here and there. The florist had looked at me like I was crazy when I'd asked for real ones. "Violets? No one cultivates violets anymore. They went out of style after the Second World War!" Oh well, I'd been an outlier from the get-go.

All my children and grandchildren were in town for Thanksgiving, as was Jon's family, so the choice of the day seemed obvious. We had celebrated this Thanksgiving holiday together at Jon's house for the second time, two years after our first celebration.

Jon and I had dealt with all the complications we wanted just to get to the altar. And so, we required no fancy bells and whistles beyond the basics. It was the marriage covenant that mattered for us—a permanent union of our persons in the sight of God—in the presence of our family. Music, flowers, honeymoon, none of that had mattered.

After Father finished saying Mass and most everyone else had left, the rest of our families trickled in. Liddy and Andy sat in the pew behind Leah's clan. Ned, last to arrive, joined Jonah, Noah, and Jon's son across the aisle from Liddy and behind my sister, Jeannie, and Jon's brother, Jackson. Jon's father and his stepmother, who would fly back to Tennessee later that day, sat behind them.

Father motioned our wedding party up to the front. Jackson and Jeannie joined Jon and me at the base of the stairs leading up to the altar. Through the expansive windows behind the altar, the purple-gray undulation of Carmel Mountain formed a dramatic backdrop for the suspended life-size figure of Jesus hanging from a wooden cross behind the altar.

"These two are very eager to begin their married life." The priest's belly jiggled under his white chasuble as he chuckled, glancing at his wristwatch, "8:45, I've never married a couple so early in the morning. I guess these two have waited long enough. Shall we begin then?"

Jon and I smiled knowingly at one another. We had waited in more ways than one.

Father led us in our exchange of vows.

"I, Jon, take you, Liz, for my lawful wife, to have and to hold, from this day forward, for better, for worse, for richer, for poorer, in sickness and in health, until death do us part."

"I, Liz, take you, Jon, for my lawful husband, to have and to hold, from this day forward, for better, for worse, for richer, for poorer, in sickness and in health, until death do us part."

Jon placed the simple gold band on my ring finger, "Liz, receive this ring as a sign of my love and fidelity. In the name of the Father, the Son, and the Holy Spirit."

"Jon, receive this ring as a sign of my love and fidelity. In the name of the Father, and of the Son, and of the Holy Spirit," I said while placing the gold band, matching mine, on Jon's ring finger.

After presenting us as husband and wife, Father offered some advice. "St. Augustine tells us that Christ came to us in the marriage bed of the Cross and that by lying down upon it, He consummated His marriage to us. Jon and Liz, my prayers go forth with you on this joyful day. But when hard times come, as they assuredly will, remember the joy and promises of your wedding day. Your marriage is God's plan to make you holy, and your job is to help one another become saints. Remember the Cross, keep your eyes fixed on the Lord, and he will renew your love daily in good times and bad. God bless you both."

I STOOD ON THE front porch in my wedding dress while Jon placed our wedding gifts just inside the doorway. He insisted on carrying me over the threshold of our home. Yes, it was now to be my home, too. Together, we had transformed it into a place of beauty and hope, chasing out the ghosts of past disappointments. Not so unlike my journey.

Jon scooped me up into his arms, carried me up the rosewood staircase, and into the master bedroom. He kissed my fingertips, one by one, his eyes holding mine. And there, after years of waiting, we sealed our wedding vows in the flesh.

But Jon was wrong about one thing: participation was better than anticipation.

It is Jesus in fact that you seek when you dream of happiness; he is waiting for you when nothing else you find satisfies you; he is the beauty to which you are so attracted; it is he who provokes you with that thirst for fullness that will not let you settle for compromise; it is he who urges you to shed the masks of a false life[.]

~ St. Pope John Paul II
15th World Youth Day
Saturday, 19 August 2000

Acknowledgments

Writing a book feels like giving birth—exhilarating, painful at times, and much work. When an author holds her finished book, she cannot help but marvel at the extraordinary (and often surprising and mysterious) transformation of her embryonic idea that has matured into a fully-fleshed novel. The long process involves many hands and minds, which I acknowledge below. But without you, dear reader, the process lacks its intended end. So, to each reader, I sincerely thank you for your part in this book's intended journey.

My husband, Doug, gets top billing as my labor coach. Not only has he encouraged me to write this book for years, but he has also read every word I wrote—at least once—even those that didn't survive the "delivery." He had the patience of Job as I locked myself away in my writing room for hours on end, day after day, month after month.

Three Southern authors, Leigh, Johnnie, and Kaye, have blessed me greatly. They are the epitome of everything I treasure about Southern women.

My critique partner, Leigh Ebberwein, provided helpful feedback on each chapter in the book. She understood the longings of Lizzie's heart and encouraged me to tell her story.

My two favorite modern-day literary fiction novelists are Johnnie Bernhard and Kaye Park Hinckley. Their brave, gritty novels resonate with a Catholic worldview and have been inspirational in my fledgling writing "career." I profusely thank them for reading my manuscript and providing helpful feedback and encouragement.

Kudos to my cover design artist, Hannah Linder, who took a few seeds and grew a wonderful garden of visual delights. Thanks to my editor, Patrice MacArthur, and my proofreader, Penny Baird, for their meticulous efforts.

And thanks be to the Father, the Son, and the Holy Spirit, the source of life and all that is true, beautiful, and good. A God who loves beyond all reckoning.

About The Author

Denise-Marie Martin's obsessive love affair with books began early in life. At the age of seven, she read and wrote reports on fifty-eight books in one week during a summer reading program. (Yes, one week—not a typo.) This, her first claim to fame, earned her a write-up in the local newspaper.

Many years later, now retired from a career in science, she has penned her debut novel, freeing a story that has rolled around in her head for years.

After living in California and Tennessee, Denise-Marie and her husband retired to the Pacific Northwest. A native Washingtonian, Denise-Marie is a wife, mother, grandmother, and practicing Roman Catholic. Two adorable Ragamuffins cats are her devoted writing companions.

Reading Group Discussion Questions

1. As a newborn, Liz was left in the hospital nursery for almost a week without any mothering. In the book, *The Primal Wound: Understanding the Adopted Child*, Nancy Verrier posits that every adopted child experiences a sense of abandonment in being handed over to strangers after sharing a forty-week journey with its birth mother. Do you think this is true? If so, could this have impacted Liz?

2. In the same book, Ms. Verrier discusses the tremendous guilt an adoptee feels in wanting to be loved by their birth mother. Do you think this was the case for Liz? What do you think is the basis for this guilt?

3. Having healthy boundaries help us to protect ourselves. Which characters had healthy boundaries in the novel and which did not? Can you give examples of situations where certain characters did not exhibit healthy boundaries?

4. Is it a kindness or a weakness that Liz fails to confront Marie when she realizes that information her adoptive mother tells her is false?

5. Liz has an ultra-sensitivity to odors and is very uncomfortable with touching, certainly as a child. Certain facets of her adoptive mother's physicality repel Liz. Does that mean that Liz did not love her mother, Marie?

6. Lizzie grew up hearing Marie tell her that she hated her. What impact might that have on a child? Why do you think Marie reacted that way to Liz when Liz became angry or when Marie was hurting?

8. Why was it so important for Liz to find out the truth about Jeannie's paternity? How did Melanie's disclosure impact Liz?

9. How would you describe the relationship between Jeannie and Liz? Does the relationship progress to a different level by the novel's end?

11. Liz and Ned's relationship was incestuous and taboo. There are support groups now and therapists specializing in helping individuals deal with genetic sexual attraction (GSA). Were you taken by surprise by the sexual relationship between Liz and Ned? What was your reaction?

10. Was it the right thing for Liz to tell her children about the "inappropriate coupling" relationship with her birth father? Did you think the potential for harm was greater than the potential for good?

12. How did you feel about the character Angie Bell? She convinces Liz to join Pesso-Boyden group therapy. Did you think that therapy was helpful to Liz in sorting out her complex feeling toward her mother? Did the therapy group provide Liz with any insight into her relationship with her birth father?

13. Why do you think Liz and her half-sisters never really connected? Did this surprise you?

14. The world has changed dramatically, with open adoption the norm nowadays. Would Liz have benefitted from an open adoption?

15. What did "the dream" symbolize for Liz? Why did it impact her so? How did you feel when you read that scene?

16. Do you think Liz was genuinely remorseful for her sexual relationship with Ned? Or was she just trying to get through her "to do" list?

17. Should Liz have demanded that Ned tell his family about their previous physical relationship as a requirement to continue in her chaste relationship with him? Did your feelings towards Ned change by the end of that last chapter?

18. Did you find Liddy to be a sympathetic character? Why or why not? Did Liddy demonstrate her love for Liz? Do you think Liz loved Liddy?

19. Why do you think Liz was afraid to tell Jon about her relationship with her birth father? Was Jon a character in the story that you liked?

20. Was Jon right to break off his relationship with Liz after she fully disclosed the extent of her relationship with her birth father? If love is "willing the good of the other," did Jon demonstrate his love for Liz?

21. Liz ends up in a recovery group with a group of women struggling with various kinds of addictions. What was the primary value Liz got from participating in that group? Do you think recovery groups have value in general?

22. The Catholic Church grants a decree of nullity (or an annulment) if certain conditions for valid consent (by even one spouse) aren't met *before*

exchanging vows. In this case, the Church states that a sacramental marriage never occurred. Some call this a "Catholic divorce." But does the word "divorce" fit if no marriage occurred in the first place?

23. What do you think the author hoped her readers would take away from this reading experience?

CPSIA information can be obtained
at www.ICGtesting.com
Printed in the USA
JSHW010744060123
35623JS00002B/151